in dog we trust

BETH KENDRICK

BERKLEY
NEW YORK

BERKLEY
An imprint of Penguin Random House LLC
1745 Broadway, New York, New York 10019

Library of Congress Cataloging-in-Publication Data

Names: Kendrick, Beth, author.
Title: In dog we trust / Beth Kendrick.
Description: First Edition. | New York: Berkley, 2019.
Identifiers: LCCN 2018028815 | ISBN 9780399584251 (paperback) |
ISBN 9780399584268 (ebook)
Subjects: | BISAC: FICTION / Contemporary Women. | FICTION / Humorous.
Classification: LCC PS3611.E535 I5 2019 | DDC 813/.6—dc23
LC record available at https://lccn.loc.gov/2018028815

First Edition: January 2019

Printed in the United States of America
1 3 5 7 9 10 8 6 4 2

Cover photographs: Puppies by HTeam / Shutterstock;
Blue Ribbon by Danny E. Hooks / Shutterstock
Cover design by Katie Anderson

Also by Beth Kendrick

Once Upon a Wine

Put a Ring On It

New Uses for Old Boyfriends

Cure for the Common Breakup

The Week Before the Wedding

The Lucky Dog Matchmaking Service

The Bake-Off

Second Time Around

The Pre-nup

Nearlyweds

Fashionably Late

Exes and Ohs

My Favorite Mistake

Praise for Beth Kendrick's Novels

"Kendrick deftly blends exceptionally clever writing, subtly nuanced characters, and a generous dash of romance . . . a flawlessly written story."

—*Chicago Tribune*

"A sharp, sassy, surprisingly emotional story that will make readers laugh out loud from page one and sigh from the heart at the end."

—Roxanne St. Claire, *New York Times* bestselling author of the Barefoot Bay series

"Witty, juicy, and lots of fun."

—Susan Mallery, *New York Times* bestselling author of the Mischief Bay series

"Kendrick's impeccable sense of comic timing and flair for creating unforgettable characters make this effervescent novel a smart bet."

—*Booklist* (starred review)

"Kendrick not only shines in portraying the subtleties of female friendship, but also at rendering the unbreakable bond between man (or woman) and dog."

—*Publishers Weekly*

"A warm, winning story about the complications of sisterhood—and the unexpected rewards."

—Sarah Pekkanen, *New York Times* bestselling coauthor of *The Wife Between Us*

"Packed with humor, wit, and a lot of heart. A charming and exceptionally entertaining story!"

—Jane Porter, *New York Times* bestselling author of *Take a Chance on Me*

"A funny, charming story about the power of female friendship."

—Kim Gruenenfelder, author of *Love the Wine You're With*

"Kendrick manages to cook up a tender, touching, and very funny story." —Ellen Meister, author of *Dorothy Parker Drank Here*

"An engaging, thoroughly enjoyable tale of finding soul mates of the four-legged and two-legged varieties. . . . When you put this book down, you will have a smile on your face and warmth in your heart."

—RT Book Reviews

"A delightful romp with depth." —Heroes and Heartbreakers

"A charming tale about finding the perfect match . . . featuring a lot of laughs, love, and irresistible dogs." —SheKnows Book Lounge

"An astute and charming look at friendship, love, and self-discovery."

—*Kirkus Reviews*

"A smart, funny spin of happily ever after!"

—Beth Harbison, *New York Times* bestselling author of *If I Could Turn Back Time*

For Mark,

love of my life and piece of work

acknowledgments

Thank you to . . .

Becky Hullinger, fearless cattle rancher with flawless fingernails.

Ryan Hoffman, estate attorney extraordinaire, who walked me through the finer points of pet trusts and helped me turn dry legal documents into a hotbed of scandal.

Chandra Years, who turns literary straw into gold.

Danielle Perez, the best editor a writer could ever hope for.

Amy Moore-Benson, the best agent a writer could ever hope for.

Kresley Cole, who has been making my life brighter and my writing better since our fated meeting at the RWA children's table.

Marty Etchart, godsend.

Brianne Butcher, proud mom of the real Carmen.

My family (especially you, Will), who supports me on every step of this journey with grace, love, and humor. I am so, so lucky to have you.

chapter 1

"Why are you running like it's your money or your life?"

Jocelyn Hillier's runner's high plummeted as she answered her cell phone midstride and heard her mother's voice.

"I've got a garage full of dirty laundry with your name on it."

Jocelyn picked up her pace, her sneakers pounding in a steady rhythm against the loose white gravel beneath the heavy gray November sky. "I'll be back in a few minutes."

"We just finished all the Thanksgiving leftovers. How do you have the energy to go for a run?" Her mother sounded incredulous.

"It's refreshing. And I have to work off three days' worth of turkey and mashed potatoes somehow."

"If you need to burn some calories, I have enough laundry here to get you ready for the runway," Rachel promised.

"Be there in a few minutes." Jocelyn lifted her face to catch a few stray drops of cold rain. "Just leave everything and I'll take care of it."

Her mother's tone sharpened. "Where are you right now?"

"Running?"

"Don't play dumb. Running where?"

"Um . . ." Jocelyn slowed to a walk as she tried to catch her breath. "Shoreline Drive."

"Why are you running on Rich Person Road?"

"Why *wouldn't* I run on Rich Person Road?"

"Nothing good ever comes of mixing with the summer people." Rachel clicked her tongue. "How many times do I have to say it?"

"I'm not mixing with anyone. They all packed up and left this morning. Besides, the views are amazing and the road is dirt instead of asphalt. Much better for my knees." Jocelyn rounded a wide bend in the road and noticed a lone pair of seasonal residents still loading up their SUV. An elderly man and middle-aged woman were attempting to coax two black Labs and a chocolate Lab into the vehicle's cargo area with no success. The dogs dodged and darted across the driveway while the humans gave chase to no avail.

She slowed her pace even more as she gazed at the house where the dogs and their owners lived. The vast, sprawling mansion had been constructed two or three years ago and the architect had apparently looked to French chateaus and Tuscan vineyards for his inspiration. The decorative archways, stained glass windows, and curving staircases with marble balustrades looked absurd between the neighboring Cape Cod–style homes covered with cedar shingles and widow's walks. Jocelyn offered a smile and a wave to the man, who responded with a scowl.

"Jocelyn?" Rachel's voice was impatient. "Are you even listening to me?"

"Yes." Jocelyn blew out a breath. "But just to refresh, what did you say?" A rustling in a bush across the road caught her eye, and she nearly twisted her ankle as a muddy-pawed, stocky gray dog emerged from the foliage and trotted toward her.

"Oh my God." Rachel heaved a mighty sigh. "I *said*—"

"Hang on." Jocelyn let her hand drop as she heard the low rumbling of a car approaching. The little gray dog trotted into the middle of the road.

Jocelyn heard barking and shouting behind her and whirled around to see the chocolate Labrador sprinting down the driveway, making a beeline for the gray dog.

The gray dog heard the commotion and froze in the middle of the road, ears pricked up and tail wagging. The Labrador ran faster.

A sporty red convertible vroomed around the bend, kicking up gravel.

"Carmen!" the man called in a booming voice.

"Carmen!" His female companion dashed to the end of the driveway, then stopped and yelled commands from the safety of the lawn. "Come! *Come!*"

Carmen ignored them, preferring instead to initiate a thorough canine meet-and-greet in the middle of the road. The two dogs circled each other, sniffing and snuffling, until all Jocelyn could see was a blur of gray and brown.

The car was fifty yards away.

Jocelyn waved with both hands to catch the driver's attention.

The driver ignored her. The car was forty yards away. Thirty.

Cursing under her breath, Jocelyn dashed directly into the car's path, caught a dog's collar in each hand, and dragged them to safety on the other side of the road.

For a moment, all she could hear was the thud of her heartbeat in her ears, the skidding of tires against gravel, and the panicked screams of the dogs' owners.

"Jocelyn?" Her mother's voice, tinny and distant, drifted out of the cell phone she'd dropped in the road. "Joss?"

The car's driver, a tall, blond man in his late twenties, slammed out of the car. "Are you okay?"

"What the hell?" The scowly old man stormed up to the car. "Watch where you're going. You could have killed someone!"

"I'm sorry." The blond man looked distraught. "This is a new car, I was trying to adjust the seat heater—"

"You nearly ran over my dog!" The old man's face was ruddy with rage.

"And me," Jocelyn added. The old man ignored her. The young man turned to her and continued to apologize.

"Carmen!" The woman pried Jocelyn's hand from the Labrador's collar so she could reclaim the dog. "I told you to come."

The little gray dog surveyed the agitated humans with bewilderment. Jocelyn scooped him up and held him close against her fleece running vest. "Don't worry, little buddy. You'll be okay."

The next few moments were a cacophony of accusation. The old man berated the car driver. The woman berated the Labrador. The car driver retorted that it was obscene to care more about a dog's life than a human being's.

"My dogs are much better people than any of the people I know!" The elderly man harrumphed.

"Carmen is a pedigreed future world champion," the woman added. "How many people can say that?"

Jocelyn rolled her eyes and decided to heed her mother's advice about avoiding Rich Person Road. She gazed down at her scruffy companion. "I think my work is done here."

The car driver stopped arguing with the old man and turned back to her with those soulful blue eyes. "I'm sorry. So sorry. I'll never forgive myself for what almost happened."

"It's fine." Jocelyn was suddenly very aware of the sweat on her forehead and her disheveled ponytail. "I should've worn more visible clothing. All this gray-on-gray is hard to see." The little gray dog whined in protest. "That goes for you, too."

The old man finally looked Jocelyn in the eye. "You saved Carmen."

"Oh, well, I mean . . ." Jocelyn didn't know where to look. "I just did what anybody would have done."

"No. Not everybody would risk their life for my dog." The old man glanced meaningfully at the woman. "Clearly."

"It wasn't just your dog, it was this guy, too." Jocelyn hoisted up the gray mutt. "I'm a sucker for a dog in distress."

The woman glared at her.

"I better get going." Jocelyn shifted the gray dog to one hand and scooped up her phone with the other. "I have to . . ." But she seemed to be physically incapable of telling this trio of one-percenters that she had to hustle on home to wash other people's soiled linens.

"I'll give you a ride," the blond man offered.

Jocelyn took two steps back. "I'll be fine."

"Oh, come on." He smiled, and there were dimples and dazzling white teeth left and right. "I have heated seats."

She found herself smiling back. "So you said."

The old man stepped in between them, all business. "You live around here?" he demanded.

"Yes," Jocelyn said.

"What's your name?" he asked, as though taking a police report.

"Um. Not to be rude, but why do you ask?"

"I've been looking for someone to help care for my dogs. Walk them, play with them, wear them out." He lifted one bushy eyebrow. "Clearly, they're in need of more exercise."

"Hey!" his companion protested. "What about me?"

The old man's glare was withering. "You train them, Lois. You groom them and show them and motivate them to win best in breed. I need someone to take care of them when they're not in the ring. Someone who can love them."

Lois the trainer reacted as if he'd slapped her. "How can you say that? I *do* love them!"

The old man tilted his head toward the scuffs the car's tires had left in the gravel. "Not enough." While Lois continued to sputter protests, he nodded at Jocelyn. "You're hired."

"Yeah, I don't really want to get involved," Jocelyn said.

"Too late." The man fished a business card out of the pocket of his navy blue barn coat. "I'm Peter Allardyce, and these are Carmen, Curtis, and Hester." He pointed out each dog in turn. "Write down your phone number. You'll be hearing from me."

Jocelyn did as she was told, cowed by the authoritarian steel in the old man's voice.

"Okay." The dimpled driver rested his hand gently under Jocelyn's elbow. "Let's get you home safe and sound."

Jocelyn looked at his face and found herself unable to argue. Again. Must be a rich person superpower. "But what about him?" she asked, nodding down at the scruffy gray mutt still in her arms. "I can't take him home with me, and I can't just leave him here."

He smiled again, and Jocelyn realized, *This is what it's like to live in a cologne ad.*

"Does he have a tag on his collar?" he asked.

Jocelyn peered at the tarnished metal buckle on the faded and frayed nylon collar. "No. He doesn't look very well cared for."

"Maybe he ran away," the man suggested.

"Maybe. Or maybe someone dumped him by the side of the road." Jocelyn had witnessed this firsthand. At the end of every summer season, tourists abandoned the pets they'd purchased on a whim when the puppies or kittens became too rambunctious or coordinating air transport proved too costly. Everyone who worked in Black Dog Bay's rental industry had at least one heartbreaking story of a bewildered animal they'd had to re-home when the owners returned to "real life."

The guy looked horrified. "People do that?"

Jocelyn nodded. "Oh yeah."

"Then let's take him to the shelter—"

"We're not taking him to the shelter!"

He held up his palm. "My family just underwrote an animal rescue center out by Bethany Beach. Brand-new, top-of-the-line facilities, veterinary care on call twenty-four-seven. It's really more like a luxury pet resort than a shelter. They can scan him to see if he has a microchip. If he does, we'll contact his owner."

"And if he doesn't?" Jocelyn started to panic. "I can't take him home with me. My mother will—"

"I'll take him home with me until we find him a great home." He took off his spotless suede jacket and wrapped it around the dog. "Smitty here will be spoiled rotten."

Jocelyn quirked an eyebrow. "Smitty?"

The guy patted the little gray dog on the head. "That's his name."

Smitty snuggled into the warmth provided by the jacket.

"How do you know?"

"Look at him. That's a Smitty if ever I've seen one."

Jocelyn laughed as the dog licked her neck. "I guess it is."

"Let's go." The walking cologne ad with the poor driving skills opened the door and ushered her into the warm, walnut-paneled interior of his luxury automobile. "I'm Chris, by the way. Chris Cantor."

Jocelyn feigned total cluelessness, as if she hadn't heard all about the Cantors and their blue-blooded ancestors and social clout. "I'm Jocelyn Hillier."

"Great to meet you, Jocelyn. I've got a lot of making up to do." Chris helped Smitty settle into the backseat, heedless of the muddy paw prints marring the leather upholstery and the suede jacket.

Jocelyn dug a tissue out of her pocket and dabbed at the stains.

"Don't worry about it." Chris put his hand over hers. He left it there.

Jocelyn glanced up at him, her initial rush of attraction replaced by suspicion. Why would a guy like him be flirting with a girl like her? Though she would never admit it to her mother, Rachel was right: the residents of Shoreline Drive didn't cozy up to commoners unless they stood to benefit somehow.

She gazed into those earnest blue eyes. *What do you want from me?*

He squeezed her fingers, then got into the driver's seat. "How long have you lived in Black Dog Bay?"

"Since I was born." She took a breath, then added, "My mom and I run a linen supply service."

He didn't wrinkle his nose or smile condescendingly. He looked genuinely intrigued. "What does that entail?"

"During the summer and holiday weekends like this one, we deliver clean sheets and towels to the rental homes and some of the bed-and-breakfasts. Then, when the guests leave, we pick them up, wash them, and start all over."

"You run the business yourself?"

Jocelyn felt herself relaxing into the supple warmth of the passenger seat. "I do it all. Contracts, bookkeeping, and laundry. Lots and lots of laundry."

He kept looking at her, and his evident interest mixed with something else. Respect.

She reached out and touched his wrist. "Eyes on the road."

He grinned and refocused. "So you're a small-business owner, a stray dog savior, *and* a hottie?"

Jocelyn laughed. "I'm a townie who's not going to fall for some smooth-talking summer boy."

"We'll see about that." His gaze darted back over to her. "What are you doing next weekend?"

"Laundry."

"Great. I love laundry. It's a date."

"No." She shook her head in mock exasperation. "There is no date. I don't get mixed up with guys like you."

"Did you hear that, Smitty?" Chris glanced at the dog in the backseat, who was drooling all over the window. "He's shocked. He can't believe you're so cynical."

"He may have been dumped by the side of the road," she pointed out. "I think he's a little cynical himself."

"You'll see. Stick with me, and you'll see."

Jocelyn brushed back a stray, sweaty hair from her forehead. "See what, exactly?"

He accelerated and the car's engine responded with a low, thick purr. "Friday night. Seven p.m. I'll bring the fabric softener."

chapter 2

Seven months later

"Ooh, show me that one again." Jocelyn leaned in closer against Chris's shoulder.

"The one with the Eiffel Tower?" Chris scrolled back through the series of photos on his phone.

"No, the one of the vineyards."

Chris nodded and kept scrolling. "Okay, but that wasn't actually Paris, that was Loire."

Jocelyn squinted through the bright noon sunlight to study the photo of a pair of wineglasses set against a blurred background of lush green vines. "It looks so beautiful."

"It is." Chris put down his phone and took Jocelyn's hand. "You'll see. You'll love the wine."

"And the chocolate." Jocelyn closed her eyes and smiled. "I've read all about the best chocolatiers in Paris. Maison du Chocolat, Patrick Roger, Hugo et Victor . . ."

"You've already got the chocolate places memorized?"

"I've had them memorized since high school," Jocelyn confided. "I used to spend hours on the Internet, reading about Paris. I knew just where I wanted to shop, eat, and sleep when I finally went."

"Give me a list. Your wish is my command." Chris pulled out his wallet and signaled a passing waitress for the check.

Jocelyn sighed. "I can't believe I'm finally going. I'm so excited to see the Louvre." She knew she'd butchered the pronunciation, but Chris didn't correct her. Instead, he looked into her eyes, warm and indulgent.

"I'm a little nervous about jet lag," she confessed.

"Don't be. They have booze on the plane, and the seats lie flat."

"They do?"

"In business and first class."

Which was, of course, the only part of the plane you flew in when you had an Ivy League building bearing your family name. Jocelyn murmured her thanks as Chris paid for lunch, then forced herself to bring up the topic they'd never touched upon in the weeks since he'd first mentioned going to France.

"So." She nibbled her lower lip. "About paying for the flights and hotel and everything . . ."

"Don't mention it. My treat."

"I can't let you do that."

"My treat," he repeated, his tone firm. He took her hand in his, then frowned down at her fingertips.

"What?" Jocelyn followed his gaze down to her nails, which still bore traces of dried blood from the morning's exertions. "Oh, I helped Bree dig up a septic tank this morning."

"Just the two of you?"

"Yeah, we've done it before. This one wasn't that bad, relatively speaking."

"You should have called me," Chris admonished.

Jocelyn almost laughed. "Honey. I'm not calling you to dig up a septic tank."

He looked affronted. "Why not? You're saying I'm too milquetoast to get my hands dirty?"

His use of the word "milquetoast" pushed her over the edge and she did laugh. "No, but septic tanks aren't really your scene." She tilted her head to indicate his pristine white polo shirt and elegant gold watch.

"Septic tanks aren't anyone's scene," he replied. "Which is why you should have called me. You shouldn't be out there doing all the dirty work by yourself."

"Fair enough; next time I'll text you and you can come out and grab a shovel."

Chris shook his head. "What I'll be grabbing is the number for a plumber. He can dig up the septic tank, and you and I can get brunch."

"What about Bree?" Jocelyn asked.

"She can have brunch with us."

"You make it sound so simple."

"That's because it is." Chris lifted her hand to his lips. "My girl doesn't have to dig up sewage."

"I'm not afraid of a little sewage," Jocelyn assured him.

"And that is why I love you." He stood up, pulled out her chair, and helped her to her feet. "Now I have to go take a conference call, but when can I see you again?"

"Saturday?" she suggested.

"How about tonight?" He brushed her hair back from her cheek. "We could have dinner at the new seafood place in Rehoboth."

He continued to surprise her with his attentiveness, his persistence. For the first few months of their courtship, she'd expected him to disappear. To simply stop calling and texting one day. But he kept showing up, weekend after weekend, and somewhere along the way, she'd let her guard down and let him into her heart.

"Okay, but maybe a late dinner?" she said. "I have to handle a late check-in at seven thirty."

"Pick you up at eight." And there it was—the cologne ad smile in all its glory. Never got old.

Jocelyn beamed, no longer conscious of the slivers of septic tank still lodged under her nails. "Before you go, show it to me one more time."

Chris fired up his phone. "Which one? The Loire?"

"The Eiffel Tower." She pressed her cheek against his as she gazed at the photo and thought, *That would be the perfect place for a proposal.* The thought so stunned her that she stiffened and pulled back.

"What?" Chris squeezed her shoulder. "Everything okay?"

"Of course." She lowered her eyes and cleared her throat. "But I should go. I'm late for work."

"You're late." Mr. Allardyce's voice boomed through the foyer as Jocelyn let herself in the front door of the oceanside French/Tuscan-style mansion. "You should have been here fifteen minutes ago."

"I'm sorry." Jocelyn slipped the key ring back into her pocket with a jingle.

"You should be." Lois, who always had a stinging comment and a snide look for Jocelyn, put on her sunglasses and prepared to make her exit. "They've all had a very demanding training session and they're in desperate need of downtime."

Jocelyn smiled her sweetest smile at the acid-tongued trainer. "Lovely to see you, as always. Good luck at the dog show in Dover next week."

Lois slammed the door in response.

"She's definitely warming up to me," Jocelyn remarked as she strolled into the kitchen. "We're going to be braiding each other's hair and binge-watching *The Crown* soon."

"Everybody's been waiting for you." Mr. Allardyce limped across the smooth travertine tiles, his hand shaking as he leaned on his cane. "Carmen was so upset, she started gnawing on the ottoman."

"Poor Carmen." Jocelyn glanced into the living room to assess the damage. "And poor ottoman."

"Stop flapping your gums and get going," Mr. Allardyce ordered. "I'm not paying you to talk."

"Yes, sir." Jocelyn dropped her handbag on one of the ornately carved oak chairs by the breakfast bar, then hurried to the back of the house to grab the leashes. She could hear the dogs before she even opened the door to the mudroom. The pathetic canine whining intensified as she approached.

Jocelyn flung the door open and braced herself. "Hi, babies!" A whirling dervish of black and brown fur emerged. "Hi, Hester! Hi, Carmen! Hi, Curtis!" She blinked her eyes against the flurry of dog hair drifting through the air and gave each pup a kiss on the head and an ear scratch.

"You guys ready for your run?"

The whining escalated to yipping and woofing as the dogs swarmed around Jocelyn in a mishmash of boxy heads and wagging tails.

As Mr. Allardyce never tired of telling her, he had worked hard to earn his fortune, and he only accepted the very best from himself . . . and from everybody else in his life. He prided himself on surrounding himself with the finest and rarest. Luxury automobiles. Oceanfront property. Purebred dogs of the most prestigious pedigree.

The trio of dogs tumbling over one another in the mudroom were technically Labrador retrievers, but they were so well groomed and athletically conditioned that they barely resembled other Labs Jocelyn saw at the park and the beach. Tall, lean, and long-legged, they were bred to work as field dogs.

Their impressive lineage hadn't bestowed any sense of dignity. Each of the Labs currently slobbering on her had an AKC registered name, a cabinet full of trophies and ribbons, and a case of shampoos, toiletries, and grooming equipment that put a beauty parlor to shame. They had documents proving their parentage and professional photos that were reprinted in glossy magazines. They were high-maintenance, high-priced, high-status members of dog royalty. But right now, all they wanted to do was run.

"I know, you've waited long enough." Jocelyn clipped their leashes on, though this was just a formality. As soon as she took them across the deck and out to the sand, she would let them loose to race across the dunes of the private beach that Mr. Allardyce had fenced off for his prized pooches.

"Don't let them come back until they're worn out," Mr. Allardyce commanded as the dogs towed Jocelyn toward the back door.

"Has that ever happened? Ever?"

"One of these days," the old man said.

"Very optimistic of you," Jocelyn replied. Even Hester, who was pregnant, had an apparently boundless supply of energy.

Jocelyn let the dogs run for a good forty-five minutes before clipping their leashes back on and returning to the house. "They had a blast, as always," she reported to Mr. Allardyce.

"But are they worn out?" He eyed all the perky ears and wagging tails with suspicion.

"'Worn out' is aspirational," she told him.

He was pouring himself an iced tea but didn't offer her any. "Be on time tomorrow."

"Will do." She brightened. "Oh, and I should tell you that I'm probably going to be gone for about a week and a half next month. Let me know if you need me to help find someone else for dog duty when I'm gone."

His bushy gray eyebrows snapped together. "What? Where are you going?"

She couldn't suppress her grin. "Paris."

"With that spoiled millennial who almost murdered my precious Carmen?"

Jocelyn rolled her eyes. "That's the one."

"Why the hell would you want to go to Paris?"

"Uh, let me see." She ticked off her reasons on her fingers. "Pastry, museums, chocolate, romance, the Eiffel Tower . . ."

"Paris is so crowded." He wrinkled his nose. "And everyone speaks French."

"Yes, well, that happens when you go to France."

He slapped his hand down on the tabletop. "I forbid you to go."

Jocelyn blinked. "Excuse me?"

"Hester is going to have puppies any day now, and I'll need someone to be with her around the clock. Someone who knows her and understands her."

"We have plenty of time to find someone else."

"I don't want someone else." This might sound flattering from someone else, but coming from Mr. Allardyce, it was like a threat from a mafia boss. "I want you."

"What about Lois?" Jocelyn suggested. "She's much better qualified than I am to take care of puppies."

"You made the whelping box." He pointed to the towel-lined wooden box in the mudroom.

"By the grace of Pinterest." Jocelyn shook her head. "And Home Depot. I don't think it's up to AKC standards."

"The dogs love you best," Mr. Allardyce insisted.

"That's very kind of you to say, but let's face facts: They love anyone with a pocketful of beef jerky."

The old man set his jaw. "Hester needs you."

This conversation was going nowhere productive, so Jocelyn pointedly glanced at her watch. "Well, I better get going. I've still got some work to do before tonight."

But her curmudgeonly employer wasn't finished. "If I had a daughter like you, I wouldn't let her waste her time with a trust-fund brat in a red convertible he bought with his daddy's money."

Jocelyn grinned. "Aw. So now I'm the daughter you never had?"

"Watch your mouth, young lady." Mr. Allardyce reached into his pocket and pulled out a twenty-dollar bill. "Here. Curtis finally destroyed that stuffed squirrel you got him last month. Buy him another one."

"Please" and "thank you" would be nice. Jocelyn glanced back at the contented dogs and told herself that canine gratitude would have to suffice. "I'll stop by the pet supply store on my way home."

Mr. Allardyce narrowed his gaze. "You going to charge me extra?"

"Nope."

He regarded her with a mixture of suspicion and disbelief. "Why not?"

She shrugged. "It's on my way and it'll only take a few minutes."

"You shouldn't give away your time," he said. "Especially to people you don't like."

"I like the dogs," she said.

Mr. Allardyce was gazing at her in consternation again. "You really do love them, don't you?"

"I must." Jocelyn glanced down at the twenty in her hand. "I'm certainly not in this for the money."

chapter 3

Jocelyn scored the very last stuffed squirrel from the pet supply store at the edge of town, then turned back onto Main Street, driving with extra caution amid the throngs of pedestrians returning from the beach and the boardwalk. She meant to go right home and start on her other job. She meant to be diligent and responsible.

And yet . . . as she spotted the sign for the Naked Finger, Black Dog Bay's estate jewelry store, Jocelyn stopped the car, snagged a parking spot that miraculously opened up (clearly an act of divine intervention), and dashed across the street. A bell chimed as she entered the shop, and a dainty-featured brunette greeted Jocelyn from behind the glass display case.

"Hi there. Welcome to the Naked Finger. I'm Lila." The brunette tapped her pearly pink fingernail on the glass as she tried to place Jocelyn. "You're a local, right? I know I've seen you around at the grocery store and the bank."

"Jocelyn Hillier." Jocelyn offered a handshake, keenly aware of the disparity between Lila's moisturized, manicured fingers and her dermatological disaster of grime and raggedy cuticles. "My mom and I run the linen and towel service for the beach house rentals."

"Oh right." Lila nodded. "You guys supply the napkins and dish towels for the Whinery, right?"

"Yeah. The Better Off Bed-and-Breakfast, too."

Lila smiled. "Nothing like living in breakup central."

Ever since Black Dog Bay had been dubbed "the best place in America to bounce back from your breakup" a few years ago, enterprising local business owners had made every effort to capitalize on the niche tourist market. Charming seaside diners and boutiques had changed their names to the Eat Your Heart Out Bakery, the Jilted Café, and the Rebound Salon to appeal to the "heartbreak tourists" who flocked to the beach along with the regular vacationers. Someone—possibly Hollis, the owner of Black Dog Bay Books—had even made up a legend about an apparition of a black dog that appeared to heartbroken tourists as a harbinger of hope and change.

Jocelyn nodded. "It's about time someone opened a store like this." She surveyed the rows of jettisoned engagement rings, wedding bands, bracelets, watches, pendants, all casualties of heartbreak and betrayal.

A showroom like this should act as a grim reminder that there was no such thing as happily ever after. The cold, hard proof of hundreds of broken promises should wipe the smile off Jocelyn's face.

And yet . . . "So." She sidled closer to the diamond rings, clearing her throat. "I think I'm losing my mind."

"Go on." Lila leaned in for more details.

"Yeah. I, uh . . ." Jocelyn was practically hoarse from all the throat-clearing. "Listen, don't tell anyone, but I, uh . . ."

Lila held her position, her air calm and unhurried. "You can tell me. People tell me things all day, every day."

"Crazy things?"

Lila responded by reaching under the counter and pulling out a crystal jar. She lifted the lid, revealing a cache of individually wrapped chocolates. "Truffle?"

Jocelyn ripped off a foil wrapper and popped the truffle into her mouth. "Mmm."

"Swiss," Lila informed her. "My mother sends them to me from Europe."

Jocelyn eyed the bottom half of the counter speculatively. "What else have you got down there?"

"Nothing too exciting, I'm afraid. Just Windex and Kleenex. The Kleenex is for the criers, but you don't seem to be in a crying mood today."

"Can I try on an engagement ring?" Jocelyn blurted.

"Of course." Lila fanned out her fingers, indicating the array of rings. "Let me know which ones you like."

"I'm not ready to actually buy one," Jocelyn added, her cheeks aflame.

"That's fine. Trying on jewelry is fun."

"I've only been dating my boyfriend for seven months."

"Hmmm." Lila looked Jocelyn up and down, then picked out a ring with a square-cut diamond flanked by tiny side stones. "You might be a princess-cut kind of girl."

"I'm the opposite of a princess." But Jocelyn slipped the ring on and held up her left hand. She couldn't stop staring. The facets of the stone turned the overhead lighting into fiery flashes of white.

"It's lovely," Lila assured her. "Just a hair over a carat, but the cut is excellent, which makes it look a bit bigger."

"Ooh." Jocelyn felt hypnotized. "It's so sparkly."

"Some of that is due to our fancy lighting, but if you want to step outside, you can get an idea of what it looks like in daylight." Lila started for the door.

Jocelyn took off the ring and plunked it back on the glass. "No.

No, no, no. I can't have anyone see me trying on engagement rings. Especially my boyfriend. *Especially* my mom."

Lila nodded agreeably. "Okay."

"You're judging me, aren't you? I would judge me, too."

"No judgment. Who wouldn't want to try on these beauties?" Lila replaced the princess-cut ring in the case and held out an art deco–style band studded with diamonds and sapphires. "Here, give this one a shot."

"I've never had an engagement ring on before." Jocelyn wiggled the band onto her finger. It only fit to the second knuckle, but she could still appreciate the artistry. "It looks so official."

"That's the idea." Lila perused the selection, then handed over a wide platinum band set with a huge oval diamond. "Try this one. Two point four carats."

"I can't." Jocelyn clasped her hands behind her back. "It must cost a fortune. I might scratch it or chip it or look at it wrong." Her eyes widened as she noticed a massive, glittering green gem set amid a halo of tiny white diamonds. "Ooh, that one's gorgeous."

"*This* is the one that costs a fortune." Lila produced a pair of white cotton gloves and slipped them on before holding up the ring for examination. "Genuine Colombian emerald, AGL certified, just over four carats. No heat treatment or enhancement of any kind, not even oil treatment."

"Oil treatment is a thing?" Jocelyn asked.

"It's definitely a thing—ninety-nine percent of emeralds are treated to increase clarity." Lila smiled down at the ring. "But not this one. And the setting is exquisite, too. Platinum, expert benchwork, original from the late 1920s. This is the most expensive piece in the whole store."

"Hence, the gloves?" Jocelyn nodded at Lila's hands.

"Nah, the gloves are because it's cursed."

Jocelyn did a double take to see if Lila was kidding. She wasn't. "Says who?"

"Well, the woman who sold it to me was pretty keyed-up," Lila replied. "When we made the sale, she went out of her way to tell me that this ring was definitely *not* bad luck and would definitely *not* bring financial ruin on any future owners. I hear weirder stuff than that on a daily basis so I didn't give it much thought, but then . . ."

Jocelyn rested both elbows on the glass. "Don't leave me in suspense."

"My mother was in town for a visit when this all happened." Lila glanced from side to side as though she were about to divulge state secrets. "She used to be a model in New York, and she knows all the society gossip. When she saw the name of the seller on the purchase documents, she told me that the seller's great-grandfather lost the family fortune in the Great Depression . . . right after he got married. And then, after the family managed to build some wealth back up, the father lost his shirt when the tech bubble burst in 2000." She gave Jocelyn a pointed look. "Right after he proposed to the seller's stepmother with a family heirloom."

"Maybe that was just a coincidence."

"Maybe. But a few years after her dad got left at the altar, the seller married her husband with the old family heirloom. You'll never guess what business they were both in."

Jocelyn instantly thought of the details of the most recent economic implosion. "Real estate?"

"Ding-ding-ding. He lost everything—including his wife, although from what she told me, he had it coming. The markets weren't the only thing he was shorting, if you get my drift." Lila shook her head. "How did my mother put it? 'The only currency that family has left is social currency, and that's running out fast.'"

Jocelyn regarded the emerald with a mixture of awe and skepticism. "Is that all true?"

"I don't know about the curse, but the parts about the marriages and the finances are verified by Google and the *New York Times.*" Lila straightened up. "There were engagement photos and everything, and it's definitely the same ring. Very distinctive."

"But it's so beautiful. How could it be evil?"

Lila offered up the gem. "Want to try it on?"

Jocelyn snatched her hands off the counter. "No, thank you. I've got enough cash flow problems already."

"Here, try this one instead." Lila replaced the Colombian emerald in its case and pulled out a gold band with an Asscher-cut diamond. "You may not be ready to get engaged, but if your boyfriend happens to wander in here, I'll be able to point him in the right direction."

Jocelyn allowed herself to envision that for a moment: Chris walking into this showroom, announcing he was looking for a ring for his future wife.

"You look happy," Lila observed.

"Let me see the one with the sapphires again," Jocelyn said. Lila obliged. The center stone in the ring looked brilliant, flawless, elegant. Like something a lady would wear, a lady who didn't spend all day digging up septic tanks and collecting bundles of damp, soiled towels. "Ooh, I do like this one. I've never seen anything like it. But I'm sure it's expensive."

"That's his problem," Lila said.

"We're going to Paris," Jocelyn said. "He's taking me to the Louvre."

"So romantic! You guys are going to have a great time!"

"But he's not going to propose. It's way too soon. And besides, his whole family is going to meet us there."

"Even better. You can celebrate your big news with your future in-laws."

Jocelyn indulged in imagining this for a moment, then snapped back to reality. "No, no, no. We're in the phase where he buys me a croissant, not a ring."

"Yes, but when you move to the next phase, you'll know what you want. It's important to know what you want."

"I do. I know what I want." Jocelyn was surprised to hear her voice so steady and clear.

"Well, there you go."

"But what I want and what I have to do are two different things." Jocelyn reluctantly took off the ring. "And right now, what I have to do is go to work."

Lila handed her another truffle for the road. "Come back any time."

"I will." She leveled her gaze at the jeweler. "But, for real, this never happened."

"Never happened," Lila assured her.

chapter 4

"I have a confession." Jocelyn bundled an armful of white towels into the industrial-size washing machine in her garage. "A shameful confession."

"My favorite kind." Bree, Jocelyn's best friend since elementary school, handed her another pile of towels. "Is it about sex?"

"No."

"Drugs?"

"No."

"Partying with multiple members of a rock band all night and waking up in a bathtub full of ice, minus a kidney?"

"No." Jocelyn rolled her eyes. "And for someone who's supposed to be psychic, you're terrible at reading my mind."

"I'm not psychic." Bree made a face.

"That's not what your grandmother says."

"My grandmother's nice and all, but she's a bit delusional. You know this. And, anyway, palm reading is way different than being psychic."

"How so?"

"I don't know the details, because neither one applies to me." Bree shoved a pair of pillowcases into the washer drum with great vigor.

"That's not what your grand—"

"Didn't you have a shameful confession to make?"

"Oh yes. That." Jocelyn couldn't look her friend in the eye. "I had lunch with Chris today."

Bree paused. "Uh-huh."

Jocelyn glanced back over her shoulder. "Do I detect . . . *tone*?"

"All I said was, 'Uh-huh.'"

"Uh-huh." Jocelyn doubled down on the tone. "Anyway, I had lunch with Chris because he's wonderful and considerate and he adores me."

It was clearly costing Bree every ounce of her self-control not to respond with the snarkiest "Uh-huh" of all time, but Jocelyn went on with her tale.

"And while we were at lunch, we talked about Paris again. We're really going, Bree. He bought the plane tickets. We're going to have so much fun. And I know what you're thinking . . ."

"No, you don't. We just established that no one here is psychic."

"Well, I know what you've already said: He's not a full-time resident. He's from a different background. I'm the Molly Ringwald and he's the Andrew McCarthy in the Black Dog Bay version of *Pretty in Pink*."

Bree scrunched up her nose. "It's more like *Maid in Manhattan* and you're J-Lo and he's the rich hotel dude, but okay, close enough."

"I know what you think, and I can't really argue. It's true. All of it is true."

"It's not personal. It's not about Chris," Bree insisted. "He seems really nice. It's just that I don't want you to get hurt."

"I know," Jocelyn said.

"You deserve the best."

"Thank you."

"I'd hate for you to get your heart broken."

"Me, too. And I swear to you, I'm going into this with my eyes wide open. But something about this just feels *right*." Jocelyn leveled her gaze. "I've never had to hide who I am. I told him from the first day we met exactly who I am and where I came from."

"Good."

"He always shows up, Bree. He's been driving down here every weekend to see me since New Year's. That's like a six-hour round-trip."

Bree nodded in acknowledgment. "Just don't rush into anything."

"I won't." Jocelyn couldn't suppress a grin. "Oh, and by the way? I tried on a bunch of engagement rings."

Bree dropped a towel onto the garage floor and covered her mouth with both hands.

"I know. *I know*." It was such a relief to share this sordid secret with her closest friend. "I don't know what came over me. One minute we were eating sandwiches and talking about Paris, the next minute I have a diamond on my finger. Like I was in a fugue state."

Bree lowered her hands long enough to ask, "He went with you? It was his idea?"

"God, no! He can never find out about any of this!"

"Wait, wait, wait. You're trying on wedding rings, in broad daylight, in the middle of Black Dog Bay, and you're hoping he'll never find out about it?" Bree clicked her tongue. "Lady, you are playing a very dangerous game."

"I know." Jocelyn hung her head. "I'm nuts. I'm a stage-five clinger who's ready to buy a ring and a big poufy white dress after like six months of dating."

"You said it, I didn't."

"But I'm not *serious* about it. I was just, you know, looking. Getting the lay of the land."

Bree's eyebrows shot all the way up.

"Fine, I'm a deranged psychopath."

"Thank you."

"But they were so pretty! I've never had a diamond ring on before, and I liked it!" Jocelyn crossed her arms over her chest. "Stop looking at me like I murdered someone."

"I'm not." Bree tried and failed to change her horrified expression.

"You are." Jocelyn glanced down at her hands. "Like I'm drenched in blood."

Bree took a breath, clearly choosing her words carefully. "You know, I heard there's a therapist in town now. Down by the post office. She's taking new clients. I heard."

"I don't need a therapist."

"You said you were taking this slow," Bree pointed out.

"I am. But is it really so awful to hope? What if it works out?"

"What if it doesn't?" Bree asked, her voice flat.

"That's not very supportive."

"Someone has to be the voice of reason," Bree said. "And as usual, it has to be me."

"Chris and I are very compatible," Jocelyn argued. "We come from different backgrounds, but we have the same values. We both love animals."

"He doesn't have any pets," Bree said.

"His family just opened a shelter," Jocelyn retorted. "And we both prioritize family."

"Have you met his parents yet?" Bree challenged. "Has he met your mother?"

"I haven't met his parents yet, but I will. His whole family goes to France every summer, and I'm invited."

Bree looked begrudgingly impressed.

"And of course he hasn't met my mom. You know how she is. It's complicated."

"That's my point. It's not like he'd relocate to Black Dog Bay on a permanent basis, would he?"

Jocelyn nibbled her lower lip. "Well . . ."

"Hold up. Does this mean you'd consider moving to Philadelphia?" Bree's expression lit up.

"I can't. Not right now, obviously. Who would take care of the business?" Jocelyn eyed her friend. "And why do you seem so excited?"

"Because I might be moving to Philadelphia, too." Bree glanced all around the tiny, dusty garage, as if expecting eavesdroppers. "If all goes well."

"What?" Jocelyn's jaw dropped. "Why would you move?"

"Come on." Now it was Bree's turn to get defensive. "We've both been vowing we'd get the hell out of here since high school."

"Yeah, but no one actually *does* it." Jocelyn startled a little as the dryer timer buzzed. "Black Dog Bay is like the Hotel California. Name me one local who successfully made it out of here."

"Um . . ." Bree furrowed her brow. "The mayor's sister?"

"Ingrid Jansen? She's in New York for college. Doesn't count. She's home for the summer; I just saw her last week."

Bree leaned against the washer, deliberating. "That homecoming queen who was on TV?"

"Lila Alders? She's back. She just helped me try on engagement rings downtown."

"Oh! Oh! I know!" Bree smiled triumphantly. "Lila Alders's mother. She moved to Europe."

"For now," Jocelyn said.

"The woman lives across the Atlantic. That counts as relocating."

"Mrs. Alders didn't grow up here." Jocelyn lifted her chin in vindication. "She grew up out of state. But back to you. What's this about Philadelphia?"

"You know how I'm always running my mouth about applying to law school? I finally did it this year. I got my act together really late but they do rolling admissions, so I might still be able to get in for the fall semester. Assuming I can get in at all, which is a big assumption."

Jocelyn refrained from sputtering out questions long enough to remind herself that she was a good friend. A friend who wanted only the best for Bree. And if the best meant moving across state lines . . .

"But there are law schools in Delaware!"

Bree looked determined. "It's tough out there for a law grad these days. The job market's unbelievably tight. It's not enough to graduate from law school anymore—you need to graduate from a top-ten program."

At which point, Jocelyn realized that Bree was probably referring to the university to which Chris's family had donated a building. "As it happens, I might be able to get you a recommendation from an influential donor."

"Oh yeah? How're you going to manage that?"

"I'll ask him while we're drunk on champagne in France."

Bree's eyebrows shot up. "He has some pull?"

Jocelyn explained about the campus library.

"Then I take back everything I just said. Try on diamond rings with wild abandon."

"I can't believe you're actually doing this."

"I have to. I can't keep going like this." Bree shook her head. "Snaking drains and digging up septic systems. Replacing toilets in the middle of the night. I want a real job. A job with benefits and a retirement plan and, God willing, an expense account."

"I get that."

"We're almost thirty, Joss."

"We're twenty-seven," Jocelyn objected. "No need to round up."

"It's time to get our act together. And the timing is perfect—we'll both escape to the big city."

"Yeah." Jocelyn's smile faltered. "Except . . ."

"Your mother."

"Yeah. And the business." Jocelyn sighed. "Oh, and don't forget the dogs."

"Mr. Allardyce's dogs?"

"Yeah, they need me."

Bree shook her head. "No offense, but dog sitters are replaceable."

"That's not what Mr. Allardyce says." Jocelyn recounted that afternoon's post-run conversation. "He forbade me to go to Europe."

"Are you kidding me with this? You saved his dog's life, out of the kindness of your heart."

"It was more of a thoughtless reflex that almost got me killed." Jocelyn brightened. "By Chris. See? We're meant to be."

Bree ignored the little detour to rainbow-and-unicorn land. "That crusty old jackass owes you a debt he can never repay. He should be *sending* you to Europe."

"It's not that simple. I think he sees me as the daughter he never had."

Bree thinned her lips. "Is he even paying you minimum wage?"

"I haven't sat down and figured out the hourly rate, but . . . probably not."

Bree made a noise of disgust low in her throat.

"I feel guilty," Jocelyn admitted. "I know I shouldn't, but I do. Curtis doesn't do well with change, and we're trying to find a good prospect to breed Carmen with, and—"

Bree held up her palm. "I say this with a lot of love: they're just *dogs*. As long as they get food, water, and exercise, they're good to go."

"But Hester is pregnant!"

"Hester is a fancy show dog that probably cost more than my first car." Bree started waving both hands. "You can't knuckle under to the Mr. Allardyces of this world. What has he done to deserve your hard work and loyalty? Has he ever once acted like the *father* you never had?"

"Uh . . ."

"That's how the summer people are. They think that just because we don't live on the private beach, we don't notice how wasteful and entitled they are. They think we're worthless. If you're so important to him and his precious dogs, he should cough up some more cash to keep you around."

"You're pretty fired up about this."

"I'm just getting started." Bree's expression darkened. "We need to value ourselves more. We need to demand that other people value us."

Jocelyn opened the dryer door. "We need to start folding these sheets before the wrinkles set, is what we need to do."

"I mean it." Bree yanked out a pillowcase and waved it like a battle flag. "Our days of settling for the bare minimum are over."

Jocelyn winced against the edge in Bree's words. "Did something happen today?"

"What? No. Something like what?"

"I don't know, but you're being weird."

"No, I'm not." Bree huffed and puffed for a moment, then relented. "Okay, fine. I ran into Dan today." When she saw Jocelyn's confusion, she added, "Dan Hernandez."

"Senior Year Dan?" Jocelyn asked. Bree Heffling and Dan Hernandez had bonded over two things in elementary school—the fact that in any alphabetical-order situation, they were invariably seated together, and the fact that they were the only two children in Black Dog Bay's tiny school who weren't (as Bree put it) as white as the driven snow. In middle school, they bonded over their shared love of playing *FIFA Football* on PlayStation and watching the TV series *Scrubs*. In high school, Bree and Dan found something else to bond over, which were hormones and their mutual attraction. They had a hot, steamy romance during the first half of senior year. They weren't speaking to each other by Valentine's Day. Even Jocelyn had never gotten the details on what went wrong, but every alphabetical-order situation from then until graduation was beyond awkward.

"He's not Senior Year Dan," Bree corrected. "He's Dan Who I Totally Forgot about until I Literally Ran into Him at the Drugstore."

"Oh right. That Dan." Jocelyn studied her friend's expression. "And? How was it?"

"Oh fine. He's back in town for a while." Bree cleared her throat. "Planning his wedding."

"Who's he marrying? Anyone I know?"

"Some girl from Bethany Beach." Bree shrugged. "I didn't recognize the name. Anyway, he just finished medical school."

"I didn't know he went to medical school."

Bree nodded. "I guess all those seasons of *Scrubs* took hold." She looked anywhere and everywhere except at Jocelyn. "He's back for the summer, planning his wedding, being finished with medical school. He looks good."

"Hmm."

"*Really* good."

"Too bad he's engaged."

"It's not like that," Bree insisted. "But . . . you know how you have chemistry with some people? And no matter how long it's been or how far apart, the minute you see them, it just picks up where it left off?"

Jocelyn turned away from the washing machine and focused on her friend, who ducked her head.

"It's chemistry, that's all." Bree was trying to convince herself at this point. "Nothing to see. Just a tall, dark, handsome guy who happens to be a doctor now."

"Are you going to see him again, do you think?" Jocelyn asked.

"Not if I can help it." Bree got back to work. "He had his chance, and he blew it. I wish him nothing but success and happiness."

"And for him to always think of you as the one who got away."

"Obviously." Bree shook out a pillowcase. "Anyway, back to you. When are you going to ask for what you deserve?"

Jocelyn gazed down at the top sheet she was smoothing out. "I guess I could talk to Mr. Allardyce about a raise."

"You can and you will. What's the worst thing that could happen?"

"Well, he could . . ." Jocelyn cleared her throat. "Not like me anymore."

Bree staggered backward in mock dismay. "Oh no."

"Not that he likes me very much now."

"We may not be multimillionaires with giant houses and designer labels plastered all over our bodies, but where would all these pampered summer people be without clean towels and fresh sheets?"

"They'd probably just order new ones off the Internet," Jocelyn said.

"Shipping takes time." Bree's smile was diabolical. "And even the biggest mansion has only so much closet space. Time to take back our power."

chapter 5

"Good news, Mom—we're taking back our power." Jocelyn used her hip to push open the hospital room door so she could carry the vase full of wildflowers with both hands.

"Who's 'we'?" Rachel lifted the remote and turned off the TV, which was blaring an afternoon talk show. She shifted slowly on the mattress, wincing as her back changed positions.

"You okay?" Jocelyn put the vase down on the floor and hurried to her mother's side. "Do you need more pain medicine?"

"I took some an hour ago." Rachel's face was pale and tense. "Still waiting for it to kick in."

"Let's call the nurse." Jocelyn reached for the bedside button, but her mother stopped her with a hand on her forearm.

"I'm fine. Stop fussing. Now, what kind of nonsense is Bree filling your head with while I'm out of commission?"

Jocelyn did a double take. Even through a haze of opioids and discomfort, her mother was sharp as ever. "What have you heard? And how'd you know it was Bree?"

Rachel just watched her daughter and waited.

"She told me I need to start making Mr. Allardyce pay me what I'm worth."

"Hmm. And how much is that?"

Jocelyn didn't have a ready answer. "More than he's paying me now."

"You don't have a dollar figure in mind?" Rachel pressed.

"I'm working on it."

"You can't reach your goal if you don't know what your goal is." Her mother turned her head to look out the window. "Hot outside?"

"Hot and humid." Jocelyn picked up the vase and placed it on the bedside table. "But it might rain tonight, so hopefully that'll cool things down."

"Better bring a raincoat on your big date with the rich boy."

Jocelyn froze.

Her mother was still watching her closely. "I hear about you two. Still kissing and holding hands all over town. Going to fancy restaurants every night."

"First of all, he has a name. It's Chris. He's my boyfriend."

Rachel didn't try to hide her smirk. "Mm-hmm."

"He is!" Jocelyn insisted. "He's very nice. Smart. Considerate. I won't need to bring a raincoat tonight because he'll bring an umbrella and carry it for me."

Her mother sighed and turned back toward the window. "Oh, Joss."

"Mom." Jocelyn hadn't meant to sound so sharp. "Please don't start."

"How many times have I told you—"

"And how many times have *I* told *you* that my life is different than your life?"

"You know what? I think I will ask for more pain meds." Rachel pressed the call button.

"Don't be like that," Jocelyn said.

"Then don't you tell me that you've gone and fallen for Christopher Cantor the damn Third." Rachel's brown eyes blazed. "I raised you better."

Jocelyn forced herself to take a breath before reacting. "We don't need to get into this right now."

"I'd say we do, if you're out gallivanting around with Lord Fancypants while I'm still out of it from surgery."

"That's not fair." Jocelyn's voice was tight. "I've taken care of everything for the last two weeks. All the inventory is where it should be, the laundry is right on schedule, all the customers are happy. Nobody's gallivanting; I'm busting my ass."

"Don't swear," Rachel snapped.

"But you just said . . ." Jocelyn broke off in midprotest when she saw her mother's expression. "Sorry. All I'm saying is, what happened to you isn't going to happen to me. It's a totally different situation. I'm twenty-seven. I know what's up."

"Are you using birth control?" her mother pressed.

"Mom!"

"Are you?"

Jocelyn prayed for the floor to open up and swallow her whole. "Yes."

"Every time?"

"Yes."

"Good."

"Let's change the subject," Jocelyn suggested.

"Fine." Her mother smoothed the crisp white sheet. "But just so you know, I have eyes and ears everywhere."

Before Jocelyn could respond, a nurse bustled into the room. "You called?"

"Yes, I'm in a lot of pain," Rachel reported. "Is there something you guys can give me to tide me over?"

The nurse glanced at the medical chart. "Let me page the doctor."

"When do you think she'll be able to go home?" Jocelyn asked.

"That's up to her surgeon," the nurse replied. "But if all goes well, it could be as early as tomorrow."

"From your lips to God's ears." Rachel shifted uncomfortably again. "I'm ready to get back to real life."

"Going home doesn't mean going back to your normal routine," the nurse warned. "You're going to have some pretty significant restrictions. No strenuous exercise, no heavy lifting, no bending or undue pressure."

"The problem is, I run a linen supply company," Rachel said. "Heavy lifting and undue pressure is my life's work."

The nurse was gearing up for an argument, so Jocelyn intervened. "Luckily, she has me to do the heavy lifting for her. Don't worry, she won't lift a finger until her surgeon clears her."

"Good." The nurse gave them both a stern look. "Because if she injures her back again, she'll be incapacitated for a long time. She may never regain full mobility."

"I'm on it," Jocelyn promised the nurse. Then she turned to her mother. "I have to go get ready for my big date with the guy you hate, but I'll be back tomorrow morning."

"Don't be dramatic." Rachel rolled her eyes. "I don't hate him. I've never even met him."

And, based on the scorn in her mother's voice, Jocelyn wouldn't be making that introduction any time soon.

"And I also have eyes and ears everywhere." She tilted her head toward the nurse. "So take it easy, okay?"

Rachel muttered under her breath.

"Mother-daughter spying works both ways."

"Aw." The nurse smiled as she started dialing the doctor. "It's so nice to see a family getting along."

Jocelyn sat in the driver's seat of her ten-year-old Honda Civic, gazing up at the house where she'd lived since she was born. The tiny, two-story structure was more of a cottage than a house, really. The wooden deck in front had started to sag and the white paint had started to peel. Her grandparents had bought this place decades ago, long before property prices and taxes skyrocketed. Before the recent media campaign designated Black Dog Bay "the best place in America to bounce back from your breakup" and turned this quiet, out-of-the-way beach town into a bustling tourist destination.

The breakup boom had been good for the town; Jocelyn understood that on an intellectual level. Local residents had been able to start new businesses. Resort fees and revenue taxes had been funneled into the public school system and municipal improvement projects under the careful direction of Mayor Jansen. The influx of visitors had brought opportunity and revitalization.

But the downside to living in a popular vacation spot was that the cost of living increased suddenly and exponentially. Housing prices and rents were beyond Jocelyn's means now. She was in her late twenties and still living with her mother while she delivered sheets and towels to the seasonal residents who drove up property values. Until recently, this hadn't bothered her. She'd maintained hope that, with hard work and perseverance, she'd be able to grow the family business enough to afford to buy her own place in the next few years.

Then she started dating Chris. And when she looked at this house through his eyes, she didn't like what she saw. No ocean view, no weekly landscape maintenance, no room to breathe. Her family was close-knit out of sheer financial necessity.

Not that Chris had ever voiced any of that. He'd never seen her house in all these months because she was too embarrassed to let him see it. She knew that was shameful and petty, but it was true. She didn't want to call attention to exactly how far apart their worlds were, though of course he already knew. And he didn't care. *She* cared.

Jocelyn got out of the car, crunched up the gravel driveway in her sandals, and opened the screen door with a rusty squeak.

She put her handbag on the kitchen table and headed upstairs to her bedroom.

The cramped room with the sloped ceiling at the end of the hall had been hers since the day she came home from the hospital as a newborn. In the last few years, she'd made efforts to redecorate and give the space a sophisticated, mature ambiance—dove gray paint on the walls, minimalist black and white photographs in sleek black frames, high-thread-count linens on a queen-size bed—but she would never forget the way these walls had looked as she progressed from little girl to teenager to woman. These walls had been plastered with posters of kittens and horses, followed by magazine pages featuring pop stars and film heartthrobs, followed by Sylvia Plath poems and mass-produced posters of Paris and Rome.

She opened the closet and perused the contents, trying to decide what to wear for dinner tonight. Given the venue, her options were limited: V-neck little black dress or strapless little black dress with silver edging. She'd already worn each of them multiple times with Chris, but she had no other cocktail dresses. Nor did she have the budget to buy more. Nor the time to shop.

She assured herself that men didn't notice things like how often their dates recycled dresses. She would switch up her shoes and jewelry and hairstyle. As Bree often said, *No one's going to notice what you're wearing if you're walking right.*

With a burst of renewed optimism, Jocelyn pulled the black and silver dress from its hanger, turned on the shower, and made a conscious decision to have a good time tonight. She wouldn't worry about the future. She wouldn't try to justify her romantic choices. Just for tonight, she would stop focusing on everything that might go wrong and be happy about everything that was going right.

chapter 6

"You look stunning," Chris murmured into her ear as they entered the beachfront ballroom. Jocelyn knew that tonight's gala was some sort of fund-raiser for the Cantors' animal shelter, but she wasn't certain how it all worked. How did lots of rich people in fancy clothes eating fancy food translate into cold, hard cash for stray dogs and cats?

"Break this down for me," she said to Chris. "You guys hire event planners and florists and caterers, right?"

He nodded.

"And musicians and waitstaff and whoever else. And then people come and have a grand old time." She paused. "And then what? They write checks? Who do they give them to?"

He brushed a bit of lint off the lapel of his black suit jacket. "I'm not sure."

"How does profit and loss work?" Jocelyn pressed. "Do you guys use some of the donation money to reimburse yourselves for the party expenses, or do you write it off as an in-kind donation?"

Chris dropped a kiss on her forehead. "You'd have to ask my father's accountants."

"Do people have to buy tickets? Or spend a certain amount to reserve a table?" Her mind flashed back to the sparkle of the diamond-and-emerald ring. If she was ever going to blend into high society, she'd have to figure out how to run such events.

Chris stared down at her, his eyes wide and slightly panicked.

"What?" She patted her hair, checking for anything out of place.

"Nothing. It's just . . ."

She tilted her head, waiting.

"We don't usually talk about money." His expression turned apologetic. "My sister or my mother handles the details, and my father and I don't ask questions. I should know how it all works, but I don't."

Jocelyn made a mental note to herself: People who had the most money didn't talk about money. How did *that* work?

Chris gave her another kiss. "Come on, let's go inside. I heard a rumor that Smitty's adopters RSVPed yes."

"They did?" Jocelyn hopped for joy, nearly twisting her ankle in her high heels. "I can't wait to meet them. What are they like?"

He shrugged. "I don't know. We'll find out soon enough."

"But haven't you met them?"

He seemed confused by the question. "Not yet. The rescue center employees do all the adoption screenings. I'm just the finance guy."

"But I thought that you kept him with you until you found a good home for him?" she persisted.

"Right." He paused for a beat. "I did. But he stayed at the shelter for a few days while I had to run back to the city. I told you about that, remember?"

She racked her brain. "No."

"I'm sure I mentioned it. In any event, let's go find his lucky owners. I'm sure he's living in the lap of luxury."

Jocelyn tried to shake off her niggling doubts. "Did they bring Smitty? Is he wearing a tiny designer dog bow tie?"

"No." He smiled at her chagrined expression. "If we let them bring a dog, we'd have to let everyone bring their dogs, and those crazy mutts would bogart the whole champagne fountain."

Her mood picked up again. "There's a champagne fountain?"

"Stick with me, baby." He tucked her hand in the crook of his elbow and strode across the dance floor.

Jocelyn held her head high and tried to mimic the casual grace of the socialites surrounding her on all sides. Chris let go of her hand long enough to pluck two glasses of bubbly from a passing server. "Cheers."

"Cheers." She lifted her glass toward his, but didn't clink. She'd read that proper etiquette forbade the actual touching of glasses during a toast. In a book she just happened to be glancing through. While obsessively memorizing Miss Manners and Emily Post every night before bed.

Chris leaned close again, brushing his cheek against hers. "Here's to Paris."

"There you are! I'd nearly given up on you!" A bright, feminine voice interrupted their cozy tête-à-tête.

Chris flagged down a server for an extra glass of champagne as they faced a fine-boned porcelain beauty with high cheekbones and even higher blond hair. "Joss, this is my sister, Fiona."

"Pleased to meet you." Jocelyn offered a handshake. Fiona pulled her in for a hug and a barely-there kiss on both cheeks.

"Goodness, darling, no need to be formal with me." Fiona accepted the champagne flute her brother offered. "I've been dying to meet you. We've heard so much about you."

Jocelyn glanced over at Chris. "You have?"

"Nonstop," Fiona assured her. "It's been Jocelyn this, Jocelyn that." She smiled warmly. "Chris tells us you're quite the businesswoman."

Jocelyn glanced down at her feet and noticed that her big toe was scraped from crawling along a rooftop that morning to retrieve a beach towel that a tenant had left flapping from a weather vane. "I don't know if I'd go that far."

"Don't be shy, go on and brag," Fiona urged. "He said you're an entrepreneur."

Jocelyn felt her face flush.

"She's amazing, runs her own business. She's coming to Paris with us," Chris informed his sister.

"Magnifique!" Fiona raised her glass in celebration. "I adore Paris, don't you?"

"I'm not sure," Jocelyn admitted. "This will be my first time overseas." She watched Fiona's expression closely but didn't detect any trace of disapproval or derision.

"Oh, you're going to love it." Fiona squeezed her hand. "I'll bring you to some of my favorite shops and cafés."

Chris waved to a trio of gray-haired men in tuxedos across the room. "Joss, you should take her up on that. Fiona spent a year at the Sorbonne."

"Wow." Jocelyn's eyes widened. "That's my dream come true. What did you study?"

"Good-looking Frenchmen, mostly." Fiona laughed. "Plus the occasional Italian and German."

Chris put his hands over his ears. "I'm not listening."

"*I'd* love to hear about it," Jocelyn said.

"Let's have lunch this week," Fiona suggested. "We can figure out which art galleries we want to visit."

"Thank you, I would love that." Jocelyn beamed and for a moment, she wondered what kind of bridesmaid's dress a woman like Fiona would want to wear. Something simple but elegant, perfectly cut. "Your gown is amazing."

Fiona glanced down at the cream silk column set off with lustrous golden pearls. "Thanks. I like yours, too."

Jocelyn forced herself to say "thank you" without demurring or trying to explain away her department-store sale-rack score amid a roomful of haute couture.

"I like her." Fiona turned to her brother with a tiny nod. "So will Mom and Dad."

Chris stiffened slightly.

Jocelyn looked from one sibling to the other, trying to determine the source of the underlying tension.

Fiona sidled closer and lowered her voice. "Seems as though it's getting serious between you two?"

Chris stared at the chandelier across the room. "We're just enjoying each day as it comes."

Fiona rolled her eyes. "The soul of discretion as always, I see."

Chris blinked at her, bewildered. "What are you talking about?"

Now Fiona looked confused. "Never mind. May I steal you away for a moment?" She slipped her arm through Jocelyn's and led her away from the crowd. "It's okay, I already heard."

Jocelyn struggled to draw a breath. "Heard what?"

"You were trying on engagement rings at that little shop by the beach."

Damn the small-town rumor mill. Jocelyn didn't know where to look.

She spotted an open door on her right and fled to the outdoor patio. Even at this late hour, the air was humid and stifling. She sagged against the sturdy stone balustrade, struggling to catch her breath and gather her thoughts. She pressed her fingertips, still cool from holding the glass of champagne, against her cheeks.

Fiona followed her out. "I'm sorry. I didn't mean to ambush you. It's really none of my business, but after I heard about the rings, I thought . . ."

Jocelyn found her voice again. "We're just dating, that's all."

Fiona seemed a bit crestfallen to hear this. "You've been dating for quite some time, though?"

"About seven months." Jocelyn finally regained her composure. "Why do you seem so shocked?"

"I suppose I'm not." Fiona sighed, her pearls still gleaming through the darkness.

In that moment, Jocelyn saw herself as the other guests must see her: cheap dress, last year's shoes, drugstore makeup, work-chapped hands.

But Fiona's discomfiture seemed genuine. "You seem lovely, inside and out. So different from Chris's other girlfriends."

Jocelyn cocked her head, unable to quell her curiosity. Chris hadn't mentioned anything about his previous relationships. He was indeed the soul of discretion. A perfect gentleman.

Or so she'd assumed.

"What do you mean?" she asked, wincing in anticipation of the response.

"Well." Fiona adjusted her necklace. "He was forever bringing home these tarted-up, silicone-enhanced Barbie dolls."

Jocelyn glanced down at her non-enhanced bustline. "Really?"

"It was awful." Fiona shuddered at the memory. "We tried, God knows, but you couldn't talk to those girls about *anything*." She paused, then laughed drily. "That's not true; they were quite well versed in fashion and designer logos. But, as my father said, they were purely decorative."

Jocelyn glanced behind her and realized there was no more room to back up. She was sandwiched between the patio railing and the beautiful heiress delivering a rapid-fire round of cold, hard truth.

"Well. As you can imagine, I'm thrilled that Chris finally found someone with some substance. Honestly, you're the woman we've all been waiting for." She seemed nearly teary-eyed with gratitude.

"You have a job, you make your own way, you live in the real world."

"That I do."

Fiona touched Jocelyn's shoulder. "I hope he does marry you. I'll go pick out rings with you myself, if you like."

"That won't be necessary," Jocelyn assured her.

But Fiona wasn't listening. "My parents will be over the moon, believe me. My father went so far as to threaten to cut Chris off if he didn't get his act together."

"Ah." Jocelyn tried to sound as if this weren't all new to her.

"I know how this looks." Fiona gestured to the glittering gala and sequined gowns. "But my family isn't snobby. We know what's important. We have excellent values: hard work, philanthropy, education. We'd be so relieved if Chris settled down with a sweet, sensible, working-class girl."

Jocelyn made a little choking noise.

"Oh God." Fiona clapped her hand to her mouth. "I'm sorry. All this champagne is going to my head. I didn't mean—"

"I need a moment, please." Jocelyn stepped forward, forcing Fiona to step back. "I'll see you inside."

Jocelyn watched the willowy blonde wend her way back into the ballroom, then let her shoulders wilt and her head hang low.

She drew in a deep, slow breath, lifted her head . . . and realized that there had been a witness to everything that had just transpired. Through the darkness, as the clouds shifted and moonlight filtered down, she glimpsed a bright flash of white. A spotless shirt beneath a tailored tuxedo jacket.

Mr. Allardyce stood on the far end of the patio.

They locked gazes for a long moment, and then both looked away. Neither broke the silence. Jocelyn knew that adjusting the bodice of her non-designer black dress and rejoining Chris would be awkward. But remaining out here with the filthy rich man who paid her minimum wage—less than minimum wage, actually—to care for his dogs would be worse.

So she put one high-heel-clad foot in front of the other and strode back in to rejoin the man she'd been stupid enough to fall in love with. The man she might not know at all.

chapter 7

Jocelyn woke up bright and early the next morning to take care of the day's laundry piles before heading over to Mr. Allardyce's house. She wrote a reminder on her phone to pick up more bleach, then got into her car, cranked up the air-conditioning, and drove toward the beach.

The streets were nearly deserted at this hour, save a hard-core jogger or two. The vacationers were sleeping in and the locals were still brewing coffee. She cruised down Main Street and noticed that there was a fresh coat of paint on the Whinery, the town's infamous watering hole. She'd often peeked inside the raucous, feminine bar when she picked up and dropped off their linens, but she'd never sat down for a drink. The place was a tourist trap, and besides, she couldn't justify paying fifteen dollars for a cocktail.

When she turned into Mr. Allardyce's driveway, an unfamiliar SUV was parked in the middle of the cobblestones, blocking her path to the house. She had to pull over, park on the shoulder of the main road, then walk up the long, winding drive.

Beads of sweat had formed on the back of her neck by the time she made it to the front door. A man stood on the welcome mat and she called out to him. "That your car?"

He turned to face her. With his rangy frame, broad shoulders, and thick dark hair, he was probably objectively handsome. Probably. It was hard to tell, what with his frown and obvious annoyance.

Then she noticed the boating shoes. Supple leather uppers, pristine white soles. Another wealthy summer visitor in his fancy footwear, making life difficult for everyone else.

"Yes." He turned his back on her.

"You're blocking the whole driveway."

He didn't reply.

Her patience ran out. "What an old-world gentleman."

His expression flickered. "Who are you?"

"Who are *you*?" She sidestepped around him and rang the doorbell. Inside, she heard barking as the dogs went bananas.

"No one's going to open the door," the stranger informed her.

"That's okay." She fished the house key out of her handbag. "I'll let myself in. Ringing the bell is a courtesy."

His frown deepened as she slid the key into the lock. "Who are you?" he demanded again.

"No one of consequence." Jocelyn eased the door open an inch, only to have it slammed in her face.

She blinked and snatched her hand from the knob.

"Don't open that!" Mr. Allardyce's voice boomed from the other side of the door.

"It's just me," she called. "Jocelyn."

"Go around the side," Mr. Allardyce commanded. "And don't let him in."

Jocelyn glanced over at Boat Shoes. "I'm assuming he means you."

Boat Shoes's jaw twitched. Jocelyn pocketed the key, strolled around to the side door, and unlocked it. Mr. Allardyce met her on the threshold and shut the door behind her as soon as she was in.

"I brought freeze-dried liver, just like we talked about last time," she told the dogs, doling out pats and scratches. To Mr. Allardyce, she said, "Who's the surly stranger?"

He ground his molars together so loudly, Carmen glanced up at him to see what was wrong.

"Should I be calling the cops here? Is this some summer resident feud over, like, who's responsible for trimming the tree on the property line?"

Mr. Allardyce sniffed. "He's just one more person who wants something from me."

Jocelyn grabbed the dog leashes. "So you know him?"

The old man didn't answer.

"Okay, then."

"Everyone wants something from me," Mr. Allardyce said. "And everyone has a reason they feel entitled to it."

"Well, right now, these dogs want a run, and they're going to riot if they don't get it." Jocelyn clipped three leashes onto three collars with practiced precision. "Is that guy still going to be here when I get back?"

"If he is, I'll call the police myself."

"Then I'll assume everything's under control." Jocelyn let the dogs tow her over to the door. She paused and looked at her employer. She wanted to ask how much he'd heard on the patio last night. She wanted to ask for a raise. She wanted to ask why he had so many canine companions but no human family or friends.

"What?" he demanded.

Maybe this wasn't the right time to explain that she, too, wanted something from him and felt entitled to it. "Nothing. We'll be back soon."

"Not too soon," he warned. "They've been cooped up all morning and they need to stretch their legs."

Jocelyn murmured under her breath, "You're welcome."

He narrowed his eyes but didn't respond. So she took the party outside, trying to keep the leashes from tangling as the dogs jostled for position. As she left, she lifted her hand in farewell to Boat Shoes, who was still stationed on the front stoop.

"Nice talking to you." The dogs whined, urging her to pick up the pace. "And FYI, he's about two minutes away from calling the cops."

The stranger stared at the dogs. Jocelyn gave him another jaunty wave and broke into a lope as they hit the sand. "Oh, and I like your shoes!"

"Well? What's the latest?" Jocelyn's mother bundled her pink cotton robe into her duffel bag.

Jocelyn tried to play dumb, even though that never worked with her mother. "The latest on what?"

"Christopher Cantor the Third."

Jocelyn busied herself with checking over the hospital room to make sure they hadn't forgotten to pack anything.

"You two still together?" Rachel pressed.

"Nothing's changed since the last time you harassed me about this." Jocelyn took the bag from her mother and peered out into the hallway. "They have to bring you outside in a wheelchair, right? Legal liability and all that?"

"You went to a black-tie fund-raiser with the man who you're trying on engagement rings for and it was 'fine'?" Rachel scoffed.

Jocelyn's jaw dropped. "How do you do this? Did you install some secret surveillance app on my phone?"

"I told you, I have my ways." Rachel fixed her steely gaze on her daughter. "Start talking."

"There's nothing to report. You've seen one black-tie fund-raiser, you've seen 'em all. My only complaint was, it was a fund-raiser for the animal shelter, and there weren't any animals there. Not so much as a single Shih Tzu."

"Dogs have no place at a cocktail party." Her mother shuddered at the thought.

"Dogs have no place anywhere, according to you," Jocelyn retorted. "I can't believe you never let me have a puppy, ever. You're so mean."

"I'm not mean; I'm a woman who likes clean floors, clean clothes, and being able to leave food on the coffee table for five minutes without it being snatched and eaten. I spend enough time cleaning up after other people's messes as it is." Rachel looked unrepentant. "Also, I'm allergic."

"No, you're not. You just don't like dogs."

Rachel adjusted her cardigan. "When you buy your own house, you can have as many dogs as you want."

Jocelyn made a mental tally of how much she'd need for a down payment and how many years she'd have to work to attain it. "How about just one, Mom? Small. Nonshedding. Non-table-surfing. Maybe a poodle?"

"No."

"Bichon frise?"

Rachel finally cracked a smile. "We've been having this same conversation since you were four years old. The answer will always be no."

"Fair enough. But the answer will always be no when you ask for details about me and Chris."

Rachel nodded. "Probably for the best."

"Oh look, here comes your wheelchair. Ready to go home?"

"Only if we can listen to Duran Duran the whole way without

any complaints from you." Rachel, who still owned every Duran Duran recording on both cassette tape and CD, tended to express her love for them by singing along at the top of her lungs. It made for some very long road trips.

"I make no promises."

Rachel rubbed her eyes. "I can't wait to sleep in my own bed. No one barging in at night to draw my blood or check my pulse or show me off to a bunch of residents."

"Brace yourself." Jocelyn waved as she saw a familiar figure striding down the hall. "It's your other kid."

"Hi, Rachel! So glad I made it in time." Bree swooped into the room alongside the attendant. "I figured you guys could use an extra set of hands."

"Thank you." Rachel beamed. "I think we've got it covered, though." She settled into the wheelchair and rested her feet on the metal rungs. "All I really need you to do is talk some sense into Joss."

The attendant headed for the elevator with Rachel. Bree and Jocelyn fell into step behind him.

"What's going on?" Bree asked Rachel as they all crowded onto the elevator. "Is this about the man in her life? The one I warned her about?"

"We all warned her," Rachel said.

Jocelyn sighed in exasperation. "I told you, I don't need warnings."

"I have talked to her and talked to her," Bree told Rachel, as though describing a wayward kindergartner. "She doesn't listen."

Jocelyn's mother and best friend exchanged world-weary glances. "Where have we gone wrong?"

"We're changing the subject," Jocelyn announced as the doors opened, revealing the hospital's first-floor lobby.

"Fine, but this isn't over." Bree focused her attention on Rachel. "How's your back?"

Rachel shifted her weight. "Getting better every day. The surgeon said everything looks good so far."

"But she has to take it easy," Jocelyn cautioned. "No bending, lifting, or twisting for six weeks. At least."

"That's going a little too far," Rachel said. "I can do some light lifting."

"The surgeon specifically said no," Jocelyn reminded her. "I was there when he said it."

Rachel clasped Bree's hand and appealed to her. "I have to work."

"You can work when your doctors have cleared you to work," Jocelyn said. "Otherwise, you're just going to mess up your spine all over again."

"That sounds painful," Bree remarked. "Not to mention expensive."

Rachel dropped Bree's hand and got grouchy. "The doctors can say whatever they want, but they don't have to worry about paying the mortgage and putting food on the table. If I'm not there to run the business—"

"I'm running it," Jocelyn assured her. "It's going fine. We're on track to make more than we did last summer, as a matter of fact."

"But property taxes are going up, and gasoline, and the energy bills with that old air conditioner . . ."

"Everything's under control," Jocelyn said. "I promise."

"It's true. I can vouch for her." Bree led the way through the lobby and stopped at the sliding glass doors to offer Rachel her arm.

"I don't need your help." Rachel swatted away Bree and the wheelchair attendant. "This whole thing is ridiculous."

Bree jangled her car keys.

"You guys stay here. I'll bring the car around." She jogged off, leaving mother and daughter together.

"I'm not going to stay in bed like a helpless invalid for six weeks." Rachel's tone was threatening.

Jocelyn nodded. "It'll probably be more like eight or ten weeks."

"This isn't funny."

"You're right—your health is serious business, and you need to take your time and recover." Jocelyn closed her eyes against a wave of guilt. "It's bad enough that you've had to work so hard all these years that you need back surgery."

"Don't feel sorry for me." Now Rachel sounded offended. "I never minded working hard."

"Yeah, but if you hadn't had me . . ." Jocelyn didn't finish the thought. If Rachel hadn't had a child, her life would have been so different. She could have traveled, finished college, pursued a career she really loved instead of spending her life doing other people's laundry. But she had made a decision, at age twenty, to devote her life to rearing a daughter. She had given up countless opportunities so she could take care of Jocelyn.

And now it was Jocelyn's turn to take care of her.

As if she could read her daughter's mind, Rachel touched her arm. "I never wanted the high life." She leveled her gaze. "I don't need diamonds and trips to Paris to be happy."

Rather than resuming their earlier squabble, Jocelyn agreed with her mother. "I know. It's like you always said, having more just makes you want more."

"That's right."

"I always think about that when I go to Mr. Allardyce's house. He spent gobs of money to build it and fill it with furniture and art, and for what?" Jocelyn allowed a hint of annoyance to creep into her voice. "His house takes up some of the most beautiful beachfront property in town, and he only lives here two months a year. He spends most of his time in his even bigger mansion in Virginia, and no one else gets to enjoy the beach, and he has to pay for lawn maintenance and utilities and upkeep all year long. It's very selfish. Not to mention environmentally irresponsible."

"Preach it," Rachel said.

"And it doesn't make him happy. He's the sourest sourpuss I've ever met. I've never heard him talk about his family, and he doesn't have any friends. There's Lois, but he pays her to train the dogs and win trophies."

"His own dogs probably don't even like him."

"No, they do." Jocelyn smiled. "That's probably why he has three of them. They're always happy to see him and they never want anything from him, except belly rubs and walks and food."

"And he can't even give them that," Rachel pointed out. "He outsourced the walking and playing to you."

"I'm telling you, if I had money, I wouldn't waste it. I wouldn't buy a giant empty house, hogging all the good views and natural resources for myself."

"You say that, but money changes people."

"Not me," Jocelyn vowed. "Give me an environmental disaster of a beach house and a bunch of cash I didn't earn and I'd give it all away."

chapter 8

The next morning, after transferring the latest load of linens from the washer to the dryer and exacting a promise from her mother that she'd remain on the couch for the duration of the day, Jocelyn stopped by Mr. Allardyce's environmental disaster of a beach house to release the hounds. She rang the doorbell three times before she gave up and let herself in.

"Hello?" she called down the hallway.

Frenzied barking was the only response.

She ventured into the kitchen to find a mug in the sink along with a coffee-stained spoon. After stopping to pet the dogs, who were hurling themselves against the tall safety gate in the den, Jocelyn continued her sweep of the vast house, cringing in anticipation of the moment that she'd hear Mr. Allardyce's voice commanding her to back off and mind her own business.

But that moment never arrived. She checked the office, the living room, the pantry, all five (or was it six?) bathrooms, and even went so far as to crack open the huge, heavy door to the master bedroom. Mr. Allardyce was nowhere to be found.

"Where'd your dad go?" Jocelyn asked the dogs when she returned downstairs.

The dogs responded by galloping over to the water dish in the kitchen and gulping down the contents in a swarm of wagging tails and whines. While Curtis and Hester lapped away at the bottom of the stainless steel bowl, Carmen sat at Jocelyn's feet and stared up at her with the intensity of an FBI interrogator.

"What's wrong?" she asked.

The dog started drooling.

"You ready for your run?"

The stares got more desperate. Hester abandoned the water bowl, padded over to the pantry, and scratched at the door with one paw.

"You didn't have breakfast?" Jocelyn frowned. Mr. Allardyce would never let his prized pups go without a meal—especially pregnant Hester. She pulled out her cell phone and dialed his number. The call went to voice mail.

She decided that even if the dogs had already had breakfast, an extra meal never hurt anybody. The dogs literally jumped for joy while she portioned out the individual servings of kibble, wet food, salmon oil, and powdered vitamin supplements. They stopped leaping and panting only long enough to scarf down the meal—which took approximately seven seconds. Then they crowded back around Jocelyn and started whimpering again.

"Now you want your run." Curtis, ever the class clown, reared back and planted his front paws on her shoulders. She kissed his giant black nose. "You guys are kind of pushy, you know that?"

Carmen responded by snagging the loose end of a leash in her mouth and shaking it. After Jocelyn supervised the barely controlled chaos of three dogs sprinting across the sand and pulling hairpin U-turns to double back, she brought everyone back to the house and tried to call Mr. Allardyce again. Once again, the call went straight to voice mail.

Her next call was to Bree. "Allardyce has gone AWOL, and I think he might have left the dogs without breakfast, which really isn't like him."

"Time to worry?" Bree asked.

"I don't know." Jocelyn couldn't stop thinking about the taciturn stranger in boat shoes who had refused to move from the doorstep the day before. "But there was a guy here yesterday. Irritated, persistent. He kept ringing the doorbell."

"And you're thinking . . . ?"

"I don't know," Jocelyn repeated.

"Do you suspect"—Bree lowered her voice for dramatic effect—"foul play?"

Jocelyn half laughed. "I didn't say that."

"Well then, what are you saying?"

"There was something off about the guy. The whole situation was weird."

"What did he look like?" Bree demanded.

Jocelyn gave her best attempt at a police description, starting with the expensive haircut, including the sculpted physique and crisply pressed casual attire, and ending with the boat shoes.

"Boat shoes?" Now Bree sounded alarmed. "That's, like, serial killer territory."

"Helpful."

"You're welcome."

"What's my move here?" Jocelyn asked. "Calling the police seems kind of extreme, but we do have a missing-person case on our hands. Right?"

"Don't call the police just yet." Bree always knew what to do in a crisis. It was one of the many qualities Jocelyn admired about her. "Let me run a quick recon mission first."

"Recon mission?"

"Yeah. I just met the new owner of the Whinery. Cammie Breyer. Do you know her? She's shacked up with that farmer who grows the world's best strawberries?"

"Yeah, I've met her. I clean her dish towels twice a week. What has she got to do with any of this?"

"Bartenders are the first to know everything. Especially in Black Dog Bay. Give me five minutes."

Three minutes later, Jocelyn's phone rang.

"I have good news and bad news," Bree announced.

"Good news first," Jocelyn replied.

"The good news is Mr. Allardyce isn't missing. He's present and accounted for."

"That is good news."

"Not so fast. I haven't told you the bad news yet."

"No." Rachel's eyes widened as Jocelyn walked through the back door. "No, no, no."

"Wait, Mom. Wait." Jocelyn struggled to untangle the leashes she held in her right hand while she took the key out of the lock with her left hand. "Don't say no just yet."

"Too late." Rachel tossed aside the TV remote, preparing to do battle. "You know the rules. No dogs in the house. Not now, not ever."

"But Mom." Jocelyn took a deep breath and tugged on a leash as Carmen leaped up to snag a leftover toast crust from the counter. "It's just for one night."

"Jocelyn Jane Hillier. That right there is a pack of wild animals and I will not have it."

"They are not wild animals. These are purebred show dogs from championship lines." Jocelyn wished that Carmen and Curtis weren't licking the floor tiles as she extolled their superiority. "They have a whole case full of trophies they've won at dog shows all across the world." Mr. Allardyce had commissioned built-in cabinets with smudge-resistant glass doors and specialty lighting to display his pack's winnings. "They get flown all over the country to breed with other purebreds who are best in show. These aren't regular dogs, okay? They're luxury dogs."

"Then why are they acting like they've never been indoors before?" Rachel cringed as Curtis army-crawled beneath the coffee table and Hester climbed up on the ottoman.

"They're off-duty." Jocelyn snapped her fingers at Hester, who reluctantly lumbered back onto the floor. "They're like little kids—you can't expect them to be on their best behavior all day, every day."

"Do they shed?" Rachel demanded. "Do they poop in the yard? Do they bark?"

Right on cue, Carmen rushed to the window and started barking as a bird landed on the porch railing. Curtis attempted to join her but couldn't wriggle out from under the coffee table. So the giant black Lab galumphed across the floor wearing the table on his back like a giant saddle. Jocelyn managed to wrestle it free just before it fell to the floor.

Rachel shot her daughter a look of vindication. "Mr. Allardyce can call them whatever he wants, but they look like bad-mannered mutts to me."

Jocelyn covered Curtis's sizable ears. "Don't listen, honey. She didn't mean that."

"Oh yes I did." Rachel struggled to get up from the couch.

Jocelyn rested a hand on her mother's shoulder. "The doctor said you're supposed to rest."

"How can I rest with all this chaos?" Rachel scowled as a sprinkling of fur drifted down and settled on the couch upholstery.

A decent point, Jocelyn had to admit. "Mr. Allardyce *died*, Mom."

"What? When?"

"Last night, I think. I don't know all the details. Bree talked to someone at the Whinery, who talked to someone in the post office, who talked to someone sitting in the ER yesterday. I'm trying to figure out exactly what happened, but in the meantime, someone has to take care of these dogs."

Rachel pursed her lips. "Why does that someone have to be you?"

"Well." Jocelyn blinked. "Who else would it be?"

Her mother kept staring at her.

"They know me. I feed them, I walk them, I know everybody's favorite toys and who takes what medication and why. I know all the rules and routines for Hester here, who's going to have puppies any day now, by the way. I love them."

"What about that other lady?" her mother challenged. "The dog trainer?"

"Lois," Jocelyn said. "I'll try to get hold of her, but she's not local. She only comes in once a week or so. And in the meantime, Mr. Allardyce trusts me to take good care of them."

"The man treated you like crap, Joss. You don't owe him anything, living or dead."

"I'm not doing this for him. I'm doing it for them." She nodded to the dogs, who were now chasing one another around the coffee table.

"If you care about them so much, take them back to their house where they have all their food and toys"—Rachel took a moment to cough pointedly—"and room to run, and let them stay there until someone else comes for them."

"Mom," Jocelyn pleaded. "Have a heart."

"I do have a heart. And it's been taken advantage of too many times by selfish men who only care about their own needs while they take advantage of other people." Rachel stared her down.

Jocelyn threw up her hands. "What am I supposed to do with these dogs tonight?"

"Whatever you want, but they can't stay here. If you're too intimidated to overstep some imaginary social boundary with a dead man who never respected you, then you'll have to figure out something else."

"Brutal." Bree shook her head as she and Jocelyn stepped into the country club reception room, which had been draped with somber black bunting for the memorial service. "Your mom really has a way with words." She adjusted the silver pin adorning her black scarf. "Where did the dogs end up?"

"I took them back to Mr. Allardyce's house. I had to—there was nowhere else I could stash three Labrador retrievers."

"Are you staying there, too?"

"No. It's not my house and I'm not sure what happens to it now that Mr. Allardyce died. The last thing I need is to be charged with breaking and entering." Jocelyn took tiny steps on her high-heeled black sandals. She'd bought them on clearance two summers ago, and although they looked cute, they were poorly constructed. She could feel a pair of blisters forming on her heels already. "I've been going over there every few hours to check on them. It's a logistical nightmare."

Bree surveyed the crowd, then nudged Jocelyn and murmured, "Check it out. Three o'clock. Right next to the shrimp at the buffet table."

Jocelyn pretended to be searching the room for someone she knew. When she got to the shrimp station, her eyes widened.

"That's the guy," she whispered to Bree. "The guy with the boat shoes."

"*That's* Boat Shoes?" Bree hustled Jocelyn into a quiet corner. "He's kind of hot."

"Hot is as hot does," Jocelyn informed her. "And the way he was acting was not hot."

"Well, I just heard a juicy rumor about him."

"You did?" Jocelyn frowned. "When?"

"When I was waiting for the ladies' room five minutes ago," Bree said as though this should have been obvious. "Allegedly, he was with Mr. Allardyce when he died. They were having dinner at the Shore Club and they were arguing, and halfway through the appetizer, Mr. Allardyce keeled over."

Jocelyn gasped. "No!"

"That's what I heard," Bree insisted. "The whole powder room is scandalized."

Jocelyn put her hand on her hip. "How is it that I've been in and out of the deceased's house like ten times in the past two days, but everybody else knows more about his personal life than I do? Speaking of which . . ." She checked the time on her cell phone. "I have to go let the dogs out for their run soon. Is it terrible if I slip out of here early?"

Bree brightened as she caught sight of an open bar across the room. "It's not like you're going to offend Mr. Allardyce. But you might as well hang out a while and have a drink on his dime."

Jocelyn glanced around at the crowd, many of whom were seasonal residents. Someone had orchestrated this whole event, from the bowtied bartenders to the vases of white lilies to the tasteful classical music and valet parking outside, in a matter of days.

Bree started toward the bar. "Let's see if they have any good red wines."

"Who do you think is paying for all this?" Jocelyn wondered as Bree peppered the bartender with questions about pinot noirs and cabernets. "Who organized it?"

"The dead dude who had enough money to build a trophy room for his dogs?" Bree ventured.

"He didn't organize his own funeral in advance," Jocelyn said. "Did he? Is that something rich people do?"

Bree flashed a smile as the bartender handed over two glasses of wine. "How would I know what rich people do? You should ask your boyfriend."

"Hmm." Jocelyn averted her gaze and took a sip of wine.

Bree sensed a disturbance in the force and got right up in her face. "What's wrong?"

"Nothing's wrong." It took all of Jocelyn's self-control not to check the time again.

"Confess, before I take a cocktail fork to you." Bree armed herself with a sharp little silver weapon.

Jocelyn, acutely aware that Boat Shoes was still staring at her, sidled back toward the corner. "I told you, it's nothing." She paused. "I hope. I just haven't heard from Chris."

Bree quirked one eyebrow. "How long has it been?"

"Thirty-six hours." Not that she'd been counting or anything.

"Well, what's his deal?" Bree demanded. "Is he working, traveling, tied to the railroad tracks? What?"

"As far as I know, he's in town." Jocelyn took another fortifying sip of wine.

"Does he know that you're wrangling a bunch of dogs in a dead guy's house?"

Jocelyn nodded. "I told him yesterday morning."

"And he didn't cancel his tennis match and run right over to help?" Bree lifted her chin. "I don't like it."

"What exactly was he supposed to do, in your opinion?" Jocelyn couldn't keep a defensive edge out of her voice.

"Provide immediate practical and emotional support," Bree replied without missing a beat. "Hold a few leashes. Pick up some dog poop. Sling some kibble."

Jocelyn had to smile at the idea of Chris picking up dog poop.

"You never should have been in the position where you were fighting with your mom about the dogs staying at your house. Chris should have opened up his palatial estate and welcomed you all with open arms."

"I would never, ever ask him to take in three dogs, one of whom is going to have puppies any day now." She left out the part about Chris offering to make a few calls and put up the dogs in the new animal shelter. No matter how cushy the kennels were, Jocelyn couldn't bring herself to sequester three sensitive dogs who had just lost their owner in an unfamiliar setting with unfamiliar people.

"I didn't say you should ask him," Bree clarified. "He should have offered."

"It's not even his house." Jocelyn stood up a little straighter. "It's his parents' house. His sister is staying there for the summer. There are other people to consider."

Bree must have recognized the expression on her face, because she threw up her hands and said, "Don't get mad at me just because you know I'm right."

Jocelyn forced herself to wait through three slow, deep breaths before replying. "The man is taking me to France. To meet his entire family. The fact that he's not at liberty to offer amnesty to a pack of slobbery, overenthusiastic Labradors is not relevant here."

Bree arranged her mouth in a little moue. "Okay."

"That's right. It is okay." Jocelyn startled a bit as her phone buzzed in her handbag. She opened her purse flap and regarded the phone screen with triumph. "See? He's texting me right now."

Bree muttered something indecipherable.

"What's that?"

Bree cleared her throat. "Taking you to fancy dinners and whisking you off to Paris is nice, but romantic jaunts to Europe are the high points of a relationship. And I don't judge relationships by their high points; I judge them by their low points. And when I look at this guy's behavior—"

"If you'll excuse me, I have to go answer a text." Jocelyn stalked away from her friend, her hand clenched around her phone so tightly it was a wonder the screen didn't shatter. She heard Bree call after her, but she couldn't have a rational conversation right now. She was too angry, too indignant, too hurt.

Probably because she knew Bree was right. She couldn't get Fiona's words out of her mind. *Sensible. Different. Working class.*

My father went so far as to threaten to cut Chris off if he didn't get his act together.

"Excuse me." A stoop-shouldered, gray-haired man with an elegantly knotted navy tie blocked her path to the patio. "Are you Miss Jocelyn Hillier?"

Jocelyn racked her brain, trying to figure out if she'd broken any laws lately. The guy was looking at her as though he were an assistant principal about to give her detention for passing notes during homeroom. "Do I know you?"

"I'm Murray Tumboldt." He reached into the pocket of his dark tailored suit and handed her a business card. "Mr. Allardyce's attorney."

Oh crap. She *had* been breaking laws. Damn those pesky breaking-and-entering ordinances. She put down her wineglass and prepared to play defense attorney to his prosecutor. "I can explain."

A frown line creased Murray's shiny white brow. "Explain what?"

"Explain why I've been . . ." She managed to stop herself in time. The first rule of being a successful criminal was not confessing to your crime the second a lawyer looked at you sideways. "Never mind. You go first."

He regarded her with wariness. "My office is in Rehoboth Beach. Are you available to come in at nine o'clock tomorrow morning?"

She cleared her throat. "Do I have a choice?"

The frown line deepened. "Yes, of course."

"Okay." So he didn't have a warrant or subpoena or whatever. Good to know. "Should I bring my own lawyer?"

He blinked several times in succession. Jocelyn picked up her drink and quaffed deeply while she waited for his answer.

Finally, he said, "Your attorney is welcome to accompany you, should you deem that necessary. But tomorrow is really just a formality. All the paperwork can be sent and reviewed separately."

Jocelyn dabbed the corner of her lips with a tiny cocktail napkin. "I'll keep that in mind."

He kept staring at her. "Do you know what this is about?"

"I sure don't."

"Then why . . . ?" The lawyer shook his head. "Never mind. Let's stay focused on the matter at hand. Tomorrow morning is the official reading of the will."

"Oh." Now Jocelyn frowned. *"Oh."*

"So you'll be there?"

"Sure. Absolutely."

Murray nodded and turned to walk away. Jocelyn stopped him with a hand on his sleeve, which was crafted from the lightest, softest wool she'd ever felt.

"What's going on? Why do I have to go to the reading of the will? I'm just the dog sitter."

"Tomorrow morning," the lawyer repeated. "Nine o'clock."

chapter 9

"The reading of the will! I didn't know that was a real thing that people still did. It's like something out of a soap opera." Jocelyn relayed the details of her encounter with the lawyer to Chris over a candlelit dinner at a restaurant patio with ocean views. "What do you think Murray Tumboldt, Esquire, is going to say tomorrow morning?"

"I'm going to take a wild guess and say he's going to tell you that Mr. Allardyce left you something in his will." Chris smiled fondly at her and offered her a bite of his steak.

Jocelyn shook her head, too agitated to eat at the moment.

"It's all very surreal." She forced herself to pause long enough to nibble at her panko-crusted sole. "I've never been to a law office."

Chris put down his fork, startled. "Never?"

"Nope."

He all but scratched his head in bemusement. "Ever?"

She busied herself rearranging the linen napkin draped across her lap. "My family's not very big on lawyers."

"Why not?"

She'd made the statement knowing she was inviting follow-up questions, and now she had to answer them. Which was what she wanted—it was time he knew exactly what type of girl he was dating. She smoothed back her hair and made eye contact as the candle flame flickered in the warm evening breeze. "My father was a lawyer." She paused, then corrected herself. "*Is* a lawyer."

He lifted his chin, indicating she should go on.

"He's a lobbyist in D.C. Big money, big political aspirations, big family name."

Chris's gaze sharpened, but his expression remained impassive. She couldn't tell what he was thinking. "So now you know my deep, dark secret," she concluded. "I'm the love child of a lobbyist and a laundress."

"Who is he?" Chris asked.

"That's not important." But it was, of course. Her father was so important that she had never uttered his name to anyone except her mother. She'd obsessively Googled growing up—hell, sometimes she still did—but she didn't talk about him. He existed as a grainy image on a computer screen to her. Her brilliant, powerful father, with his beautiful wife and beautiful children and endless connections and clout.

"Do you see him often?"

"Not that often." Exactly once, to be precise. But she knew what his voice sounded like from playing a video clip that had accompanied a *Washington Post* article about corporate regulatory oversight. When she was little, she'd fantasized that he and his family would come to the Delaware beach for a vacation and he'd spot her across a crowded pavilion and recognize her as his flesh and blood. "I probably shouldn't be talking about this."

"I'm glad you are." Chris reached across the table for her hand. "I've been wondering."

"About my father?"

"Your whole family." He looked so steady and accepting. "You still haven't introduced me to your mother."

She glanced down at their intertwined fingers. "Mmm."

"But we can fix that." He leaned in, excited. "How about I take you both to brunch on Sunday?"

She tried to mimic his smile. She failed.

His smile faded. "Joss, what's wrong? You've been acting different since the fund-raiser the other night."

She cleared her throat and rearranged her napkin on her lap. "I have?"

"Yes." He squeezed her hand. "What's going on?"

"I don't know. It's awkward."

He waited until she reestablished eye contact with him. "Tell me."

She intended to warm up to the topic slowly but blurted out, "Are you dating me so your father won't cut you off?"

His face froze. "What?"

Jocelyn's words came out in a rush. "When I talked to your sister, she mentioned . . . she said that I wasn't like anyone else you've dated before. She said your father told you to stop dating busty blondes or else. She said you picked me because if you didn't pick someone like me, you'd be cut off. That's how she put it: 'cut off.'"

Chris sat back, stunned, but he tightened his grip on her hand.

"Well?" she prompted. "What do you have to say about that?"

There was a long, loaded minute while he considered this. Then he said, "It's true."

Now it was Jocelyn's turn to be stunned.

He blew out a breath. "I did used to date, uh, girls about town."

"Very diplomatically put," Jocelyn said.

He shrugged, unapologetic. "They were pretty, they were fun, they were users who wanted money and social connections and didn't give a damn about me or my family. I was stupid, immature. Everything went on much longer than it should have. Then, right before the holidays, my parents sat me down and said it had to stop. They told me I had to find a woman of substance and good character."

"Or they'd turn off the money tap," she clarified.

"As they should. It's their job—and my job—to be responsible financial stewards."

"And you found me." She closed her eyes as the picture snapped into focus. "In the middle of the road."

"Yes." He inclined his head in assent.

"And that's it?" she demanded. "You're not even going to try to sugarcoat it?"

"I'm being honest with you," he countered. "But I'm not going anywhere. I'm staying right here until you hear me out."

"I've heard enough." She pushed back in her chair, but he held on to her.

"That day in the car with you and Smitty, I realized my parents were right."

"Oh please." But she relaxed, watching his expression in the golden glow of candlelight.

"What I was doing before wasn't fair to anyone. It was selfish and stubborn and superficial. And you . . ."

"I know, I know. I'm the scrappy little underdog you can parade around to show how you've matured."

"You're amazing." He ignored the caustic undertone in her voice. "You can dig up septic tanks and look beautiful doing it. I've never been with anyone like you before. I never want to be with anyone else."

"Well." She flipped her hair back. "I do work a septic tank with style."

"Yeah, you do." He picked up her unmoisturized, unmanicured hand and kissed it.

She rolled her eyes. "Now we come to the sugarcoating."

"Every word is true," he vowed. "I'm proud to be with you. I'm proud to introduce you to my family. I'm proud to finally be a man worthy of a woman like you."

She gazed at him, knowing she should walk away. Hearing her mother's warnings in her head. "I wish I could believe all that."

"You will. You'll see. I'll prove it to you." His easy, contagious smile returned. "Starting with brunch this Sunday."

Jocelyn sat back in her chair. "My mom's still recovering from spinal surgery, and she's kind of glued to the couch right now."

"Is there anything I can do to help?"

"No, she'll barely let me help. This surgery really took it out of her, even more than the first time she had to have back surgery."

"I didn't realize she'd had surgery before."

"Yeah. It was so bad, she had to stay off her feet for months. That's why I never finished college."

His expression flickered. "You didn't finish college?"

"I had to take a leave of absence to run the business while she was out of commission. One month turned into six months and we got really busy, and I never made it back to school." She furrowed her brow. "I thought I told you all this."

"No, I definitely would have remembered." He looked so troubled.

"Is that a problem?"

"Of course not. You had to help your mother. Family first."

"I'm planning to start taking classes again during the off-season," Jocelyn added. "They have some online options now."

Chris regarded her for a moment. Then he shrugged and regained his usual sunny demeanor. "Your mother won't have to go anywhere. I'll come over and bring takeout of the famous churro waffles our country club makes."

"Maybe next week."

"Definitely next week. I'll bring some flowers, I'll do the dishes, we'll have a great time."

Jocelyn tried to hold on to her indignation. "You think I'll say yes to anything if you turn up the charm enough, don't you?"

He cupped her cheek in his palm. "I'm hoping. I love hearing you say yes."

And just like that, she was thinking about engagement rings again.

Jocelyn arrived at the law offices at eight forty-five, double-fisting a mocha latte and an iced coffee. She'd been out late with Chris, then had decided to check in on the dogs on her way home. All three of them had acted so clingy and pitiful that she'd ended up staying for hours to watch TV and cuddle with them on the sofa in the living room.

The waiting area of the law office looked like something out of a TV court drama: polished wood and potted plants and supple leather everywhere. Jocelyn gave her name to the assistant seated at a mahogany desk, then perched on the edge of one of the wingback chairs lining the wall.

The office phone rang with a melodious, muted tone, and the assistant got to her feet. "Mr. Tumboldt is ready for you, Miss Hillier."

Jocelyn was ushered into a large conference room with an oval table polished to a gleam and a crystal pitcher of water surrounded by rows of drinking glasses. The room was filled with people wearing black and gray, but the first person Jocelyn noticed was Boat Shoes, who was seated directly across from the chair the assistant pulled out for Jocelyn.

This guy was everywhere. Who *was* he?

He nodded in recognition when he saw her but made no move to rise or speak to her. She reciprocated with an equally brisk nod and sat down. A few chairs down, she spotted Lois Gunther, the dog show handler. All around her, people were murmuring in hushed, urgent tones. She could pick out snippets of conversation:

"They said he died right in his chair at the restaurant. At least he didn't suffer . . ."

". . . would be lovely if he left the bulk of his estate to charity . . ."

"Want to go get coffee after this? There's a new café on Prince Street."

Everyone spoke respectfully, but no one was remarking on what a great guy Mr. Allardyce had been. No one was crying.

Jocelyn busied herself with pouring a glass of water. Due to years of working in the hospitality industry, she felt compelled to offer a glass to her tablemate. "Water?"

Boat Shoes seemed both surprised and suspicious when he realized she was addressing him. He glanced over his shoulder, then adjusted the collar of his white shirt. "No. Thank you."

Jocelyn gazed up at the oil painting above Boat Shoes's head. Boat Shoes focused on the framed diplomas hung behind Jocelyn. Finally, Mr. Tumboldt entered the room, followed by a pair of assistants carrying huge stacks of documents.

"Good morning, all." He took the chair at the head of the table. "Thank you for coming. I understand that many of you had to rearrange your plans to accommodate this meeting and I appreciate that, especially given the short notice."

No one said anything in reply, but they all leaned forward as they waited for the reading to begin.

"Those of you who knew Mr. Allardyce well know that he liked things done a certain way." Mr. Tumboldt smiled a tight little smile. "His way. And it was important to him that you all be physically present for this."

The room was so quiet, Jocelyn could hear the clock ticking on the far wall.

"Very well." The attorney produced a pair of reading glasses from his shirt pocket. "This may take a while, so bear with me. 'I, Peter Allardyce, being of sound mind and body . . .'"

Jocelyn understood not a single word the attorney said for the next five minutes. The legalese was so unrelenting and dense, so jam-packed with "herewiths" and "testators" that it might as well have been ancient Sumerian. She glanced around the table to see if she was the only one not following. Everyone else looked as glassy-eyed and slack-jawed as she felt.

And then Mr. Tumboldt cleared his throat and got to the good stuff. "'I do bequeath my sailboat, the *Portly Porter*, to my groundskeeper, Raymond Young.'"

"Score," hissed a young man.

And the list kept going. As stingy as he had been in life, Mr. Allardyce was equally generous in death, especially to his employees. He left his Bentley to his chauffeur, a large lump sum to his housekeeper, and a piece of undeveloped property to his finance manager. Lois Gunther got three thousand dollars and the collection of dog show trophies.

As the list of assets went on, Boat Shoes became more and more agitated. He shifted in his seat, he drummed his fingers on the tabletop, he tugged at the buttons on his jacket sleeves.

But his name, whatever it was, apparently didn't come up in the will.

At long last, after varying sums had been doled out to various individuals and organizations, the lawyer paused for a moment and gave a tiny but unmistakable sigh. "The bulk of my estate, including all remaining investment accounts, retirement accounts, profits from the sale of my domicile in Virginia and physical property of my domicile in Black Dog Bay, Delaware, I leave in trust to . . ."

Boat Shoes's forehead broke a sweat.

"My three Labrador retrievers, namely, Curtis, Carmen, and Hester Allardyce and any future offspring that they may bear."

The room erupted in gasps and exclamations.

"The dogs? Are you serious?"

"That's so Leona Helmsley!"

"Leona who?"

"Can dogs inherit property? Is that even legal?"

"Order, please." Mr. Tumboldt tapped his pen on the table. "The dogs are to remain at the Black Dog Bay property and are to receive proper care and upkeep courtesy of a trustee and guardian."

Boat Shoes's face had gone from white to red to ashy gray during this pronouncement. Jocelyn rested her palms on the table, stunned. All that money, all the opportunity, all that power . . . and it was going to the *dogs*? Who, while very cute and clever, clearly could not be trusted with a bunch of investment accounts. They couldn't even be trusted not to snatch bread off the kitchen counter.

She tried to process the absurdity of this while the lawyer droned on about the accessibility of liquid assets and fiduciary duties and co-trustees and privilege of property use. Just as she segued into a daydream about what she might do with three thousand dollars and a cabinet full of dog show trophies, she was jerked back to reality by the sound of the lawyer saying her name.

She looked up to find everybody staring at her. Mr. Tumboldt was clearly awaiting some sort of response. Boat Shoes looked as though he were about to pop a vein in his forehead.

She brushed back her hair and folded her hands. "I'm sorry, would you mind repeating that?"

The woman next to her whispered, "You get it all."

"I . . . what now?"

"You're named as the dogs' guardian and co-trustee," the attorney explained. "As the designated custodial guardian for the dogs, you are granted use of the Black Dog Bay property and you have discretion to make reasonable expenditures for maintaining the animals' medical care and domicile."

"I'm a co-trustee?"

"That's correct. The other trustee is Mr. Allardyce's attorney in Virginia. She is in charge of overseeing discretionary decisions about significant financial expenditures and canine lifestyle changes. Together with your co-trustee, you have a fiduciary duty to carry out Mr. Allardyce's wishes. As the custodial guardian, you have a duty to oversee the practical, day-to-day care of the dogs and any descendants they may produce."

"Oh." Jocelyn tried not to get too excited because there was no way this guy was really saying what she thought he was saying. This was legalese, not real life.

"Well?" The attorney's tone sounded a wee bit impatient. "Do you accept?"

Jocelyn's gaze slid sideways. "I guess so."

Boat Shoes finally lost it. "You guess so? *You guess so?*" His heavy chair shot back as he rocketed into a standing position. "This is bullshit!"

All around Jocelyn, voices murmured their assent.

"You're saying that all his money is going to be squandered on a bunch of spoiled show dogs?" Boat Shoes pounded the table. Droplets of water splashed out of the crystal pitcher. "This is ridiculous. It's obscene! It's vindictive!"

"It's what Mr. Allardyce wanted," the attorney informed the room at large. "He was very specific in his wishes."

"I'm going to challenge the will," Boat Shoes vowed. A little muscle was twitching away in his jaw. "It'll never hold up in court."

The collective murmuring intensified into grumbling, which crescendoed into out-and-out derision:

"He's right—this *is* bullshit. I get an old boat full of barnacles and the dogs get millions?"

"Seriously. All those years of putting up with his nonsense and I get five grand?"

"I can't believe I drove all the way out here for this. They could have just mailed me a check that had 'Screw you' written in the memo section."

The attorney rose to his feet and held up his hand to restore order. "I know emotions are running high, but I caution you not to do anything rash." He turned to address Boat Shoes. "And as for you, Liam . . ."

Liam. So Boat Shoes had a name.

"If you'll calm yourself and be patient, I think you'll find that Mr. Allardyce did bequeath you something very meaningful."

Liam sat back down, his eyes dark. "A million dollars' worth of meaningful?"

Mr. Tumboldt picked up the will and cleared his throat. "Yes. You are to receive . . . let's see here . . . the mature ironwood tree on the grounds of his Black Dog Bay property."

Liam's brows snapped together. "What ironwood tree?"

Mr. Tumboldt blinked. "I assumed you were familiar with it."

"I'm not." Liam took out his cell phone and tapped a few buttons. "And 'ironwood' isn't even a specific kind of tree—it's a label used to refer to a whole category of trees."

"There's a lot of trees in his yard," a voice from the other end of the table chimed in. "How is he supposed to know which one?"

"Yeah, does this tree have any type of legal specifier?" Liam demanded.

"No." The lawyer glanced back at his documents. "Mr. Allardyce was very clear on the language he wanted, and that was the level of detail he provided. Against legal advisement, I might add."

Liam stared at the attorney for a long moment, then turned his attentions to Jocelyn. "This is not over." He shoved back the chair again and strode out of the conference room without another word.

After a moment of tense silence, Mr. Tumboldt reached for the water pitcher. "If no one has any further questions, I have preliminary documents I'll need you to sign."

chapter 10

"For real, it was like a riot with imported crystal and framed diplomas on the wall," Jocelyn reported to Bree as she drove home. "Everyone had a million questions and the lawyer kept trying to calm everyone down and no one would talk to me. No one would even look at me."

"But the upshot is, you're Scrooge McDuck rich now?" Bree's voice sounded distant and tinny over the old car's hands-free Bluetooth system.

"I'm not rich, the dogs are." Jocelyn tried to explain the whole guardian/trustee situation, which proved difficult as she didn't completely understand it herself. "They asked me to sign a bunch of papers with my date of birth and social security number. But I asked if I was free to come and go from Mr. Allardyce's house, and they said yes."

"Well, yeah. Because it's your house now."

"But technically, it's not. It's the dogs' house."

"And the dogs' investment funds and the dogs' gold bars stacked from floor to ceiling. I heard you the first time. But since the dogs don't have opposable thumbs, who's going to be in charge of all the credit cards and cash money?"

"They did say something about allowing me to make decisions about property upkeep and discretionary spending," Jocelyn admitted. "Oh, and guess who was there? The hot, bitter guy who was with Mr. Allardyce when he died. His name is Liam, it turns out."

"Ooh, the plot thickens."

"Yeah. He inherited some random tree and he hates me now." Jocelyn braked as a tourist darted out between two parked cars. "Like, blood feud hates me."

"A tree?"

"That's what the will said."

"Is it a magic tree?" Bree asked. "With a treasure chest full of gold buried underneath it?"

"I have no idea, and neither did anybody else who was at the reading of the will."

"Well, who the heck is this guy, anyway, that he thinks Mr. Allardyce owes him anything?"

"That's how it is with money. Everyone thinks they deserve it more than anyone else." Jocelyn nibbled her lower lip. "You know how long I've been wanting to move out of my mom's house, but this is not the way I thought it would happen."

"Moving into Mr. Allardyce's house." Bree sighed in wonderment. "The house that blocks the best views. The house that bogarts water and electricity. The house that jacks up property taxes for people like you and me."

Jocelyn suddenly felt exhausted. "I'm going against everything I ever stood for."

"Boo hoo. Dry your tears with a stack of Benjamins."

"I'll have to hire my own lawyer to review all the paperwork.

Which means I'll have to get the co-trustee to approve of spending the dogs' money on my legal bills. But first, I need a drink." Jocelyn brightened. "What are you doing right now? Want to meet me at the Whinery?"

"Home of the fourteen-dollar Bellini? You know I can't afford the Whinery."

"You don't have to." And with that, Jocelyn made her first executive decision as custodial canine guardian. "Drinks are on the dogs."

"Let's check out the bathrooms." Bree strutted into Mr. Allardyce's foyer like she owned the place. She and Jocelyn had dropped by the Whinery, only to decide that they'd rather check out the new digs than while away the afternoon sipping chardonnay. They'd splurged on a to-go bottle of champagne, which Bree clutched in her fist as though ready to wield it in a bar fight. "No, let's check out the bedrooms first." She paused, deliberating. "No, let's check out the closets."

"We have to fill up the water dishes first." Jocelyn led the way to the mudroom, where the dogs were staging their usual attempt at a prison break. "Oh, thank goodness, Hester didn't go into labor yet." She reached down to stroke the expectant mother's ears. "Don't worry, girl, I'll be by your side from this moment on."

Bree grabbed the stainless steel dog dishes from the floor, turned on the faucet to release a gush of triple-filtered, reverse-osmosis water, and filled them to the brim. "There." Water sloshed onto the mudroom floor as Bree set the dishes down. "Let the grand tour commence. Starting with closets."

"What is your obsession with closets?" Jocelyn headed for the kitchen, where she opened a cabinet door to find stacks of pristine white porcelain plates. "Hmm. Where do you suppose he kept the wineglasses?"

"The good stuff will be in the dining room, not in here," Bree predicted. "And I bet the closets are next-level fabulous. Wealthy people are really into their closets. It's a status thing. Cedar drawers, shoe cabinets, climate control . . . you'll see."

"Climate control?" Jocelyn peered into the dining room where, sure enough, she spied an array of spotless crystal goblets and flutes in a glass-paned breakfront. "In a closet? What does that even mean?"

"I'm not sure, but I know that Hattie Huntington has it at her house." Both women gazed out the window and down the waterline at the massive purple mansion positioned at the far side of the crescent-shaped bay. "Lila Alders told me."

"Lila Alders. She's the one who got me into that mess with trying on engagement rings." Jocelyn extracted two champagne flutes from the breakfront with the care and precision of a CDC lab tech handling a sample of bubonic plague. "Chris's sister heard about it and she . . . you know what? Never mind. That's a story for another time." She carried the glasses back to the kitchen and nodded at the moisture-beaded bottle of champagne. "Care to do the honors?"

"I thought you'd never ask." Bree popped the cork and poured liberal servings into the flutes. "Cheers to the craftiest get-rich-quick scheme ever: dog walking."

They sipped their fine French champagne to the sounds of the dogs lapping up water in the next room.

"God, they're loud," Bree said. "It sounds like an army marching through puddles."

Jocelyn savored the sensation of tiny bubbles on her tongue. "All right, let's go check out the closets. You want to make a bet on the climate controls? Winner buys dinner."

Bree gazed around at the luxury surrounding them on all sides. "No dice. I'd say you can afford to pick up the check. Forever."

"Or as long as the dogs are around. Or their offspring. Or their offspring's offspring." Jocelyn took another swig of her bubbly and led the way up the staircase and down the hall.

Bree stopped in her tracks when they opened the doors to the master bedroom. "If loving this kind of crass, materialistic consumerism is wrong, I don't want to be right."

Jocelyn took in the ocean view from the floor-to-ceiling windows along the far wall. "Wasted on an empty house for ten months out of the year."

"I'm . . . I'm *home*." Bree trailed her fingertips along the white damask duvet draped across the bed. "Feel this. It's like a Hallmark card for my soul. Is it okay if I sleep here tonight?"

"Sure, but you might want to wash the sheets."

"I'll buy new sheets. *You'll* buy me new sheets." Bree drifted into the bathroom while Jocelyn continued to admire the view. A moment later, she heard the water running.

"What are you doing?" She peered into the bathroom to find water pouring into the bathtub and Bree shucking off her shirt.

"Taking a bath. Look at this tub—I bet it's never been used. Sinful." Bree rummaged through the cabinet under the sink. "I wonder if that old sourpuss had any bubble bath?"

"I highly doubt it. Can't you wait to take a bath?"

"No."

"What about the closets?"

"Eh, we'll get to them later. The tub requires my immediate attention." Bree twisted her hair up into a topknot. "And look, there's a TV in the shower. Do me a solid and turn on the Food Network?"

"But the rest of the house," Jocelyn sputtered.

"It'll still be there in an hour or three." Bree tilted her head to indicate the remote placed on the marble countertop. "*Worst Cooks in America* is on in five minutes."

Jocelyn obligingly clicked on the TV and wandered back to the kitchen, where the dogs were busy disemboweling a stuffed hedgehog toy. "Well, guys, it's just you, me, and the bottle of bubbly." She toasted the shredded hedgehog, then topped off her glass.

In the space of four hours, her entire life had changed. Things that she would have sworn were impossible yesterday were suddenly within her reach.

And best of all, she had somebody wonderful to share it with.

She extracted her phone from her bag and was about to call Chris when the doorbell chimed. The dogs lost their collective mind, howling and barking and tripping Jocelyn as she tried to herd them back into the mudroom. While she was closing the door to the kitchen, the bell chimed again.

"Are you going to get that or what?" Bree hollered from upstairs.

Jocelyn started to yell back that it wasn't her house, she didn't live here, but then she remembered. It was her house. She did in fact live here. The front door was now her jurisdiction.

She walked into the foyer, pausing under the massive chandelier that glinted and gleamed in the afternoon sunlight. Through the glass panes on either side of the massive door, she could discern the figure of a tall, broad-shouldered man. Wearing boat shoes.

He rang the doorbell again.

"I'm trying to hear Tyler Florence and Chef Anne up here!" Bree cried.

Jocelyn had no idea what she'd say to this guy, but she also knew that she'd never have any idea what to say to him, so best to get it over with now. She squared her shoulders and opened the door with what she hoped was an air of neutrality. "Oh. It's you."

"You don't seem surprised." Liam stepped closer to the threshold, bristling with energy and frustration.

Years of etiquette lectures from her mother overrode her desire to slam the door in his face. "May I help you with something?"

"Yeah." He took full advantage of her hesitation and sidestepped around her and into the house. "I'm here for my inheritance."

"Ah, yes, the infamous ironwood tree." Jocelyn backed off a bit to regain her personal space. "I have no idea about any of that. You should probably call the lawyers."

Liam veered off to the left.

"Hello? Excuse me?" Jocelyn trailed behind him as he charged into the study. "I don't know which tree Mr. Allardyce intended to bequeath to you, but I'm pretty sure it's *outside* the house."

Liam stopped in the middle of the room, slowly turning to take in the tasteful seascape oil paintings, the heavy antique desk, the masculine plaid drapes and sleek computer.

"So this is where he worked," he muttered.

"Just as a refresher, trees don't grow in home offices. I mean, you're welcome to pick out something else, too, if you want. A little memento." Jocelyn made the offer without thinking it through, but once she'd said it, she felt she'd done the right thing. "Here." She noticed a pair of gold cuff links resting on a shallow silver dish on the desktop. "Would you like to take these?"

The corner of his mouth twisted up in a derisive sneer as he accepted her offering. "That's very generous of you. Are you going to offer me the duck decoys, too?"

"I was just . . ."

"Trying to get rid of me as quickly as possible. I know. That's what happens whenever I show up at this house."

"Well, the good news is, you won't have to show up here anymore," Jocelyn said pointedly.

Liam stopped staring at the walls and turned his focus to her. "Pretty possessive of your new house, aren't you?"

"It's not mine; it's the dogs'."

"But you'll live here. Sleep in his bedroom, enjoy his views, and spend all his money." Liam's frustration had cooled into calculated cynicism.

"I actually haven't decided where I'll sleep."

"You and my father must have been very close." He narrowed his eyes and gave her a thorough once-over.

"Your father." Jocelyn let this sink in for a minute. "Oh."

"Yeah." He kept looking her over.

Even though she was wearing jeans and a baggy T-shirt, Jocelyn felt an urge to shield herself from his gaze. She had so many questions but knew it wasn't her place to ask.

Liam kept staring at her. "What were you, anyway?"

"I . . . what?"

"What were you to my father?"

"The dog walker. Not that it's any of your business."

"What else?" he pressed.

And just like that, she felt cheap and manipulative, as though she had an obligation to explain herself. "I'm not sure what you mean."

"I think you do." He put his hands into his pockets and strolled back through the foyer. "My father was not a generous man. He wasn't into charity, or giving back, or helping his fellow man. He was a mean, stubborn, selfish SOB. If he left you a house and a bunch of money, he thought you deserved them. That you *earned* them." Liam glanced back over his shoulder at her. "Was it worth it?"

Jocelyn strode to the front door and flung it open. "Get out. Now."

He nodded as though she'd confirmed all his suspicions. "I get it. You're willing to take the cash and the house, but you don't want anyone to know what you did to get them."

She pulled out her cell phone. "I'm calling the cops."

"What is the ruckus down here?" Bree padded into the fray wearing a voluminous white plush bathrobe monogrammed in green thread with Mr. Allardyce's initials. Her hair was damp, her feet were bare, but she had the demeanor of a headmistress about to hand out demerits left and right. She positioned herself between Jocelyn and Liam. "Who are you and why is she having to call the cops on you?"

Jocelyn stopped dialing. "That's Boat Shoes."

"Ah, yes." Bree nodded. "From the funeral."

Liam looked bewildered. "Boat Shoes?"

"Shh," Bree ordered. "It's not your turn to talk."

"I'm calling the cops because he accused me of pulling an Anna Nicole Smith and he won't get off my property."

Bree clapped her hand to her mouth. "Ew."

"I know!"

"You?! And Mr. Allardyce?! *Eww.*"

Jocelyn leveled her index finger at Liam. "You're sick."

He seemed intrigued. "Why does this bother you so much?"

"Uh, maybe because you're implying I'm a gold-digging whore with no morals and no money?"

"She runs a successful family business," Bree informed Liam. "She doesn't need to gold-dig."

"This can't be the first time you've heard this." Liam shook his head. "You have to know that this is what everyone's saying."

"No, it's not." Jocelyn gave a scornful laugh.

He stared at her.

"It is not. Is it?" Jocelyn appealed to Bree.

Bree was watching Liam intently. "Who are you, again?"

"I'm the son." Liam sounded defiant.

Bree turned to Jocelyn. "Mr. Allardyce had a son?"

"So he says." Jocelyn shot him a skeptical gaze. "There's no DNA evidence."

Bree nodded and turned back to Liam. "Why have we never heard of you before?"

"My father and I weren't close."

"Then why do you think you have the right to show up and act like all this stuff is your due?"

Liam waited a few beats before answering. "My family history is complicated."

"Why are you always wearing boat shoes?" Jocelyn demanded.

Liam seemed startled by the question. "One of my business associates has a house in this area. He bought a new sailboat and wanted to take me out in it. I didn't want to ruin the deck."

"I see." She nodded brusquely. "And what exactly can we do for you?"

"I came to see for myself what was going on."

"What's going on is none of your business. Be gone."

"Hmm." Bree put her hands on her hips and looked Liam up and down.

"And since you're so interested in what everyone's saying," Jocelyn added, "you should know that everyone's saying that you were with your father when he died."

Liam didn't respond. His body, face, and eyes remained totally unchanged.

"I heard that you guys were having a heated discussion, and he keeled over right there in the restaurant." Jocelyn knew she should shut up, but she was incensed by the implication that she had been sleeping with Mr. Allardyce.

Liam finally nodded. "He went into cardiac arrhythmia. That's what the doctors said."

"Say whatever you want about me, but at least I was here for your father. I didn't traipse into town every five years or whatever just because I needed something."

"You have no idea what my relationship with my father was like."

"Except I kind of do, because he left you nothing in his will. Contrary to what you say, your father was quite generous when he wanted to be. He spared no expense on the things he cared about—like the dogs. But he wouldn't let you set foot in this house, he wouldn't give you anything of value from his estate, he literally died while fighting with you."

"I want what's mine," Liam said, his voice even.

"None of this is yours. Except a tree." Jocelyn gave him a jaunty farewell wave. "Feel free to pick the one you like best from the yard. Then scram."

Liam stepped back outside, then turned around and gave her a warning glance. "We're not done."

"We sure are! Au revoir!"

Bree stepped forward and offered a handshake. "Pleasure meeting you."

Jocelyn frowned. Forced, fake civility was not Bree's usual style.

Seemingly from sheer force of habit, Liam extended his hand. Bree grabbed it, turned it over, and leaned over to study his palm. "Uh-huh . . . uh-huh . . . oh. *Oh.*"

Liam reclaimed his hand, Bree ducked back into the foyer, and Jocelyn slammed the door.

"What was that about?" Jocelyn demanded.

"Nothing. I wanted a quick peek at his palm."

"But you're not a palm reader," Jocelyn mocked.

"Definitely not. This was purely for fun and recreation." Bree cleared her throat and backed toward the stairs. "Anyway. I have to go throw up from the mental image of you and Mr. Allardyce canoodling on a beach towel while the sun rises over the Atlantic."

"Why would you say that? Now I have mental images, too!" Jocelyn pressed her fingers to her temple. "This is horrifying."

"Nightmares for weeks."

"Wait," Jocelyn commanded before her friend could escape. "What did you see? On his palm?"

"Um . . ." Bree turned her gaze upward, pretending to be stumped. "Nothing much."

"Really? Because you seemed interested."

"Don't you worry your pretty little head," Bree said. "If there was anything you needed to know, I'd tell you."

"So you admit you're holding out on me."

"I admit nothing." Bree scampered up the stairs.

As she turned back toward the kitchen, Jocelyn noticed a glint of gold from the marble-topped table in the foyer. Liam had left the cuff links behind. She didn't want him to have any excuse to come back, so she grabbed the cuff links and hightailed it out to the driveway with Carmen on her heels.

"Don't you dare make one of your escape attempts," she warned the dog as they ran out the door. "I might need backup."

chapter 11

"Wait!" Jocelyn yelled as Liam opened the driver's-side door to his SUV. "You forgot these."

When he turned to face her, he looked different. The flat coldness in his eyes had been replaced with fire and anguish. He was jangling his keys. For a moment, she caught a glimpse of a confused, confounded son trying to connect with his father, and she felt a twinge of compassion.

Wordlessly, awkwardly, she offered the cuff links to him. He didn't even glance at them. Instead, he kept gazing at the house.

"I'm not sure what I came for." He finally opened his palm to accept the cuff links. "After all this time, you'd think I'd have figured it out."

She let the silence stretch out between them for a moment. "I'm sorry. I'm sorry for what I said about you and your father."

"It's fine." His expression shifted back into neutral mode.

"No, it's not. I have no idea what went on between you two, and I know firsthand how complicated parent-child relationships can get. I was mad, but I shouldn't have said anything."

He nodded, then turned his attention to Carmen. "Who's this?"

"This is Carmen. She's our resident social butterfly and escape artist. If she could drive, she'd be stealing your car and joyriding right now."

Carmen sidled up to Liam's side, and he scratched her ears.

"She was your father's favorite, I think," Jocelyn confided. "He'd deny having a favorite, but they had a special bond. I think he liked her rebelliousness."

Liam finally cracked a smile. "It's hard to imagine him having a special bond with anyone."

"It's different with dogs."

"That's for sure." He glanced down at the cuff links, then opened the passenger door of the SUV and tossed them into a cup holder. "What happened with your father?"

Jocelyn snapped to attention. "What? Nothing. Why?"

"You said you know firsthand about difficult parent-child relationships."

"Well, our relationship wasn't really 'difficult.' More like 'nonexistent.'" Jocelyn hesitated. This was not something she talked about. She'd told everyone who asked—including Chris—that she'd never met her father. And most of the time, she wished that were the truth. But she recognized the anguish in Liam's eyes. Even though they'd just met, the two of them had a connection. The crappy-father connection. "I met him once. In D.C., where he works. I was twelve. I showed up near his office and followed him inside."

He nodded as though this made perfect sense. "How'd that go?"

"Oh, you know how it goes when your illegitimate kid shows up at your workplace right before a client meeting. The usual." She smiled wryly. Liam smiled back.

"It went better than it should have, actually. I didn't get what I really wanted, but I got his attention." She sighed. "And a little parting gift."

Liam glanced toward the back of the SUV. "Kind of like cuff links?"

"Yeah." Her father had written her a check as fast as he could, the handwriting slanted and scrawled. When she'd accepted it with shaking hands and a trembling lower lip, he'd panicked. Keeping one eye on the clock ticking above the mantel (yes, he had an actual fireplace in the sitting area of his expansive office suite), he'd glanced around the room and yanked a small, abstract, black and white painting off the wall. He'd thrust it into her hands, still refusing to meet her gaze, and said, "Here. Take this. It means a lot to me, and I want you to have it." When she'd asked why, he'd cut her off and said, "I'm sorry, I don't have time for this. This is all I can give you, all right?"

And that had been that. She'd never contacted him, he'd never contacted her, and she'd never cashed the check. She'd kept it in her nightstand drawer for two years, until her mother had found it and insisted on depositing it into Jocelyn's savings account, saying, "It's the least that bastard can do." Rachel didn't understand why Jocelyn had been so fascinated with her father's signature, studying the cursive writing for similarities to her own. She hadn't understood the appeal of the black and white painting, either, stating that *It looks like the inside of my head during a migraine.* Fearful that her mother would throw it out, Jocelyn had stashed the little painting in the back of her closet, where it still remained under piles of high school yearbooks. She didn't really want it anymore, but she couldn't bear to part with it, either. Like so many things related to her father.

"I never told anybody this," she confessed to Liam. She gazed over his shoulder at the tree line across the yard. "It must have been interesting, having Mr. Allardyce as your father."

"I wouldn't really know."

"Why'd he leave you a tree in his will?"

"I have no idea."

"It must suck, seeing some random townie move into your father's house with all his stuff."

Liam inclined his head.

"But I can promise you that I really do love these dogs. They'll be well taken care of and you can come visit them whenever you want."

He regarded her with renewed interest. "You seem nice."

"I am." She smiled up at him.

"But that doesn't change anything." He stepped back and got into the driver's seat of the SUV. "This house is mine by rights, and I intend to take it back."

"And then he drove off with that threat still hanging in the air," Jocelyn reported to Chris that evening. They were sharing takeout and a bottle of wine as part of a Netflix marathon in his bedroom suite's sitting room. "You could practically see the fumes from his tailpipe spelling out *drama*."

"You're sure he's really the guy's son?" Chris asked.

"Not yet. He has zero proof." But she could see a strong resemblance in the jawline and the stubborn set of his shoulders. Liam's eyes were completely different from Mr. Allardyce's, though. Expressive and dark instead of cold and blue.

"What'd he do to get cut out of the will?" Chris asked.

"I don't know. We didn't sit down for a friendly chat about our families." Although she had divulged details to Liam she'd never revealed to anyone else.

"So do you think this guy will—" Chris's question was cut off by his phone buzzing. "Hang on." He put his plate aside, got to his feet, and checked his text messages. "Fiona wants to know if we'd like to meet at the country club later for a drink." He turned the screen toward Jocelyn, amused. "Actually, what she said was, 'I'd love to have drinks with Jocelyn tonight. You can come, too, I guess.'"

"She used the wine emoji and everything," Jocelyn observed.

"She's not usually one for emojis. She likes you."

Jocelyn rolled up the sleeve of her threadbare college sweatshirt. "I thought we were going to stay in tonight. I didn't really dress to go out."

"Okay." Chris typed out a response text. "I'll go by myself. I can drop you off on my way."

Jocelyn froze, trying to figure out what had just happened. He hadn't told her not to worry, that she looked great. He hadn't offered to wait while she went home to change. He hadn't insisted that he stay in with her. He was just going to drop her off on his way to socialize with other people?

Chris settled back into the sofa. "Back to *Frontier*."

"Wait." Jocelyn placed her hand over his as he reached for the remote. "Hang on a second. There's something I need to talk to you about."

His gaze remained glued to the screen. "What's that?"

"It's about Paris." She took a deep breath. "I have good news and bad news."

"Whenever anybody says that, it's always bad news."

She forced a breezy little laugh. "The good news is, well, my financial circumstances have changed. Drastically. As you know."

He looked even more guarded at the mention of money. "Mmm."

"Which means that I can afford to buy my own ticket now." It was amazing how not having to worry about grocery money or rent money or utility money freed up some space in a girl's budget.

"Sweetheart, you know I don't care about that."

"Well, I do. I'd like to pay you back for the plane ticket."

He turned away slightly and poised his thumb over the remote button. "We don't need to talk about this right now."

An icy tendril of dread unfurled in the pit of her stomach. This conversation wasn't going well, but she didn't know how to turn it around. "We do, actually. It's time sensitive." She took a deep breath and tried to remain cheery. "I know we're supposed to go at the end of the month. But, like I said, circumstances have changed. Hester is due any day now."

His expression changed. He looked . . . relieved? "You can't make it for the dates we planned?"

"I really shouldn't leave her alone much after this week. And after she delivers, she'll be recovering and her puppies will need round-the-clock supervision. I've been reading up on puppy care. They need to be weighed twice a day, and kept at a certain room temperature, and constantly checked for signs of distress. And since it's now my official, full-time job to take care of the dogs . . ."

Chris digested this for a moment. "Oh."

"I'm sorry. The timing is terrible, but of course I had no idea when you booked the tickets that I'd be moving into Mr. Allardyce's house and taking over dog duty."

"I know."

"I'd love to postpone the trip until the end of the summer, but I couldn't ask your entire family to . . ." She trailed off when she noticed his expression. More, specifically, his *lack* of expression.

"What?" she prompted.

"Nothing." He patted her hand, but he didn't meet her gaze. "If you can't go, you can't go. No worries."

"You're not mad?" She studied every centimeter of his face for clues.

"Not at all. You have responsibilities. Legal commitments, in fact." He finally cracked a smile. "That's how it goes when you date a successful, independent woman. You can't just go gallivanting off to Europe."

She smiled, too. "Maybe not right this very moment, but we're definitely going. Just the two of us. How does the second half of October sound to you?"

Chris's smile faded.

She tensed up again. "What?"

He put the remote down and spoke very calmly. "I agree that right now is not a good time for us to go to Europe."

"That doesn't sound promising." She set her jaw and took a breath. *Don't panic, don't jump to conclusions, and for God's sake, don't cry.*

He hesitated just long enough that she knew what was coming next.

"But maybe it's for the best. Maybe we should take a break."

She didn't know what to say, where to look.

"I'm sorry, Joss." And he did sound sorry. Sorry but resolute.

"But we . . ." She scrambled to arrange her thoughts. "What happened? Has something changed?"

"No," he assured her, his voice warming. "You're wonderful."

She wanted to ask if he still loved her, but she managed to restrain herself. She couldn't bear to look weak in the eyes of the man who had so much power over her heart.

"Then why?" Her voice broke, and she shut up before she humiliated herself further.

He got to his feet and turned away from her. "I'm glad you got to meet Fiona. I wish you could have met my parents."

Jocelyn's desperation and disbelief started to turn into anger. "But . . . ?"

"But we should take a break." He said this as though it explained everything.

She realized her whole body was shaking. "Where is this coming from? I thought—"

"Let's end this on a positive note," he urged, as though coaxing a child out of a tantrum.

"Then tell me why. I deserve an explanation, at least."

"Here." Chris pulled a small, oblong box out of a dresser drawer. "This is for you."

He handed it to her and glanced down at her sweatshirt. Maybe it was her imagination, but she thought she detected a slight frown as he noted the name of the college emblazoned on the fabric.

She held the box at arm's length. "What is this?"

"Open it."

She regarded the box as though it were a ticking bomb.

"It's something that I saw that made me think of you." He gave her the smile he'd dazzled her with on the day they met. So charming, so confident. "Open it. Please."

So she did. Even though she didn't want to, even though she knew that whatever she would find inside would leave her shattered, she did as he asked. She tried to please him.

She lifted the gold-embossed lid to find a diamond-encrusted tennis bracelet.

"Try it on," he urged.

"What is this for?"

He plucked the sparkling strand off the little bed of velvet and draped it across her wrist. "Here, I'll help you."

Then she understood. This extravagant trinket that had cost him a small fortune he'd never miss was her parting gift. Just like the one her father had given her.

"You're an amazing woman." He gave her a quick kiss on her cheek. "We'll always be friends."

chapter 12

"And then you murdered him, yes?" Bree dropped a load of towels and stood in the middle of a rental cottage living room, arms akimbo. "His body's in the trunk of your car and you need someone to help you dump it in the ocean under cover of night?"

Jocelyn sighed. "No."

"Then you ruined his credit? Dumped red paint on his spiffy white sweater collection? Used the wrong fork at dinner just to watch him squirm?"

"No."

"Then what?" Her face lit up. "Ooh, you're playing the long game, aren't you? Psychological torture! Requires more cunning and patience, but ultimately more satisfying."

"I held my head high and walked out with my dignity intact." Jocelyn knelt down to peer under the couch, where she spotted a cluster of empty soda cans. "And I left the bracelet on the bed."

"Tell me I didn't hear you right."

Jocelyn could feel tiny grains of sand digging into her cheek as she pressed her face into the carpet and snaked her arm into the space between the wall and the sofa. "You heard me."

"He broke up with you with no warning, for no reason, and you let him keep the diamonds? I'm aghast."

"Well, it's not like any other guy has ever thrown a bunch of bling at me on my way out the door." Jocelyn's hand closed around a can, which she pulled out and tossed behind her.

"Me, neither!" Bree raised her voice to be heard as she walked into the bathroom to collect the trash. "But if they did, I would take it, dignity be damned. My rule is: If someone offers you diamonds, always say yes."

"But it didn't mean anything to him." Jocelyn snagged the remaining two cans and placed them with the other recyclables in the bin by the kitchen. "The money he spent on that is a drop in the bucket to him."

"So?"

"And it's not like he spent a lot of time picking it out. He probably went down to the Naked Finger and snagged the first thing that caught his eye."

"Again, I ask: So?"

"So, he didn't break up with me for no reason." Jocelyn plumped the bamboo-patterned throw cushions on the wicker chair overlooking the deck. "There's something else going on here. I just don't know what. Maybe I fulfilled my obligations as the scrappy working-class girl and his dad gave him his inheritance."

"Wait, what?" Bree's eyebrows went all the way up.

"I might have glossed over a few details. I'll tell you later." Jocelyn turned her head away so her friend wouldn't see her eyes. "My mom was right about him. She's always right about men. Do you know how annoying that is?"

"It's his loss," Bree opined. "He adored you. Everyone who saw you guys together could see that."

"I think he adores a lot of people." Jocelyn stripped the sheets off the bed and wriggled the pillows out of their cases. "And many people adore him. The truth is, ever since I hinted about needing a place to stay with the dogs, he's been weird."

Bree opened the sliding glass door so that they could collect the beach towels draped over the deck railing. "Text him right now. Tell him you changed your mind about the bracelet. Then sell it."

"I couldn't enjoy the money; it'd feel tainted."

"Fine, then give it to me."

"The diamonds or the money?"

"Either/or." Bree got serious as they lugged the dirty linens out to the van. "How's your mom doing?"

"She's hanging in there. She's not well enough to lift anything, but well enough to tell me everything I'm doing wrong."

Bree dabbed at her face as a sheen of sweat appeared under the brutal afternoon sun. "Once we throw these in the laundry, want to get an ice-cold sangria at the Whinery?"

"I do, but I can't." Jocelyn tapped her phone. "Got to check on Hester. Behold: I installed an app that lets me monitor the dogs all day through a camera in the mudroom."

"You spy on them all day?" Bree sounded scandalized. "You're like the canine NSA."

"Eyes and ears everywhere. I got the idea from my mom, actually."

"This isn't really about Hester, is it?" Bree asked. "You just want to go and be sad about Chris."

"If I'm going to go cry on the couch, might as well cry on the couch with the dogs. They could use the company. They're pretty sad, too. They keep looking around for Mr. Allardyce and whining. It's heartbreaking."

"I could come over later," Bree offered.

"I don't know," Jocelyn hedged.

"I'll bring ice cream. Cupcakes. A giant bag of barbecue. You name it."

"How about all of the above?" Jocelyn smiled. "Tomorrow night. I need to be alone for a while."

"With three dogs."

"Yeah." Jocelyn gave Bree a quick, one-armed hug. "Thanks, though. I'll text you."

"Text Chris, too!" Bree yelled as Jocelyn got into the driver's seat of the van. "Take what's yours!"

"Bye." Jocelyn closed the door, cranked up the A/C, and headed for home. The place where she would always be welcome, always be loved, always hear the words *I told you so.*

"What's wrong?" Rachel's voice drifted in from the family room as soon as Jocelyn opened the front door.

Damn, she's good. "You can't even see me. How do you know something's wrong?"

"I'm your mother, that's how." The house went silent as the TV clicked off. "Come in here, please."

"Okay, but I can only talk for a second." Jocelyn let the screen door bang closed behind her. "Bree and I cleaned out the rental house on Points Road. I have to get everything in the laundry and then check on the dogs."

Rachel saw right through the piles of linens, along with the excuses. "Oh, honey."

"Everything's fine. I swear."

"You don't look like everything's fine."

"You don't, either." Jocelyn eyed her mother's pale complexion and the bottles of prescription pills on the coffee table. "Are you in pain?"

"Nothing I can't handle," Rachel assured her.

"I can call and have them page your doctor," Jocelyn offered.

"Not necessary." But Rachel looked wan and frail amid her blankets and pillows. "I start physical therapy next week, and then I'll be up and about again."

"Why don't you come over to Allardyce's house with me tonight?"

Rachel grimaced. "Wash your mouth out with soap."

"Seriously, why not? There's plenty of room and the views are amazing. You'd be very comfortable, I promise. And I could help you out. Freshen your water glass, help you wash your hair, paint your toenails if you want . . ."

Rachel's grimace softened into sadness. "You're a good daughter."

This open display of emotion took Jocelyn off-guard. "I try."

"You're a good person, with a good heart," Rachel continued. "You deserve much better than the likes of Christopher Cantor the Third."

Jocelyn rubbed the heel of her hand against her forehead. "It's funny you should mention that."

"I heard that you two broke up."

Jocelyn dropped her hand to her side in amazement. "How . . . ?"

"So it's true?" Rachel pressed.

"*I* barely just found out that we broke up." And then Jocelyn remembered that the Cantor family summer home employed a huge staff. Gardeners, chefs, housekeepers, personal assistants. Seasonal staff with no sense of loyalty to an old-money family who hogged the best stretches of shoreline for themselves.

Seasonal staff who, like Jocelyn and Rachel and Bree, saw everything that transpired behind the façade of pampered perfection. Who emptied the trash and scrubbed away the wine stains after lavish parties. Who literally whisked away the dirty laundry and returned it fresh and pristine. And who got together after their shifts and traded gossip.

"Well, what can I say? You were right and I was wrong." Jocelyn sighed. "You told me so."

"Joss, I wish so much that you were right and I was wrong this time."

"But you weren't. You never are."

"I'm sorry, honey."

"You always expect the worst from men, and you always turn out to be right." Jocelyn shrugged. "I'm the one who never learns."

"I don't expect the worst from all men," Rachel corrected. "Just the spoiled, seasonal men."

"Spoiled, seasonal men." Jocelyn finally cracked a smile. "Sounds like a menu item gone horribly wrong."

"If you want to talk about it, go ahead," her mother offered. "I promise to be supportive. Although I'm due to take my next pain pill in ten minutes, so I might be a little out of it."

"I appreciate that, but there's nothing to talk about."

"Just remember, no matter how much money he has, he doesn't determine your worth," Rachel said.

Jocelyn thought of the diamond bracelet—so valuable yet so worthless at the same time. "I know, I know."

"Yeah, you know it in theory, but I want you to feel it in your bones," Rachel retorted. "And listen, kiddo—I wouldn't know all this if I hadn't been through it myself. I wasted too much time thinking about your father, wishing things could have been different."

Jocelyn held her breath, trying not to break the spell. She'd never heard her mother speak so openly about her father.

"And all that time I was thinking about him, he wasn't thinking about me. He went ahead with what he wanted and never looked back. Never worried about what happened to me—or to you."

Rachel closed her eyes for a moment, and when she opened them, her vulnerability had vanished. "Which reminds me, when you move into Mr. Allardyce's house, you better take that hideous painting with you."

"Will do."

"If you don't, it's going to Goodwill."

"Noted."

"Actually, it's too ugly for Goodwill—it's going to the dump."

"Consider it gone."

"Okay, then." Rachel nodded and sat back. "Good talk."

"Definitely," Jocelyn agreed.

"Pass the pain pills, and do me a favor—next time, date a local boy."

"I'll try."

Rachel lifted her chin. "Don't just try. Go online and make a dating account."

"I'm not ready."

"You don't need to be ready. You need to listen to your mother. In fact, I'm texting Bree right now and asking her to do it for you."

Jocelyn's eyes widened with alarm. "That won't be necessary."

"Too late." Her mother grinned. "It's happening. I feel better already, don't you?"

chapter 13

Jocelyn had been looking forward to the beach house all day. Peace and quiet. Serenity and solitude. A respite from heartache and online dating accounts that were created without her knowledge or consent.

But when she pulled into the driveway, she noticed a familiar black SUV parked by the driveway . . . and a familiar figure standing by the edge of the road.

"Can we do this later?" Jocelyn asked Liam as she got out of her car. "I have had a *day*, and I have a pack of Labs that need my full attention."

"Sorry." He had his hands in his pockets. "I didn't realize you'd be out here."

"Well, I know it's a sore subject, but I kind of live here now."

"I know. I don't want to bother you. You can go in." But he stayed where he was, gazing at the house with evident longing. "I'm just looking."

Jocelyn stood beside him and shaded her eyes with her hand. She tried to imagine what he saw when he looked at the big, new house surrounded by impeccable hedging and freshly raked white gravel.

Note to self: Figure out how to continue lawn service and arrange payment.

"It's pretty impressive," she finally said.

"That was my father," Liam replied. "Always the best."

Jocelyn tried to think of an appropriate conversational segue. "I think he wanted someplace where the dogs could run."

"He was very into his dogs." Liam's voice was flat. "Up to and including leaving them millions of dollars."

"People can get pretty weird about their dogs."

"The inheritance wasn't really about how much he liked his dogs. He did it to make a point."

"What was the point?" Jocelyn was almost afraid to ask.

"'Screw you.'" Liam shrugged. "Which is fine. He doesn't owe me anything. But . . ." He trailed off again, staring at the house.

"What did you want to talk to him about? The day that you showed up on the doorstep and he wouldn't let you in?"

Liam shrugged again. "I had some family business to discuss. I wanted to talk to him in person before I got lawyers involved. I thought I should be direct. Civil. That was a mistake."

"You could come in," Jocelyn heard herself offer. "Take a look around."

He looked at her with a mix of gratitude and incredulity.

"Come on." Jocelyn pulled her keys out of her pocket. "I have to feed the dogs and let them out, but you can give yourself a tour. Just, you know. Do me a favor and don't steal anything."

"You have my word. I realize that doesn't mean anything to you, but you have it."

There was a wistful note in his voice that softened her. "It wouldn't be the end of the world if, like, a stray pen or a commemorative plaque or something *accidentally* fell into your pocket."

"All your pens and plaques are safe," he promised.

"They're not really mine," she reminded him. "They're the dogs'."

"I'm aware."

As they trooped toward the house, Jocelyn felt fatigue settling into her head and her limbs. The physical work today, compounded by the emotional strain of breaking up with Chris and then trying to put on a happy face, finally caught up with her.

She rubbed her eyes as she unlocked the front door. Howls of delight echoed down the high-ceiling halls.

"Duty calls." She left Liam to his explorations and got down to the business of providing food, water, and belly rubs to Curtis and Carmen.

"Hi guys, hi guys, hi guys." She doled out biscuits and vitamins and kisses. "I missed you, too. I know, you're so deprived and alone, here in your five-star abode."

Hester hung back behind the others, her eyes glassy and her breath a bit labored. Jocelyn moved in to give her some special attention. "Hey, girl. How're you doing?"

Hester gazed at her, panted, and thumped her tail against the doorjamb. She turned up her nose at the treat Jocelyn offered.

"Is this it?" Jocelyn asked. "Is it puppy time?"

Hester licked her hand, then retreated to her fleece-lined bed and walked in a little circle before heaving herself down with a sigh.

"Hester?" Jocelyn asked. "You okay?"

Hester had either gone instantly to sleep or was doing a very good job of faking it, snores and all.

"I'm watching you," Jocelyn informed her. "And I've got the vet on speed dial."

As she stepped outside to let Curtis and Carmen run, Jocelyn decided that a quick call to Mr. Allardyce's fancy-pants "concierge veterinarian" was in order. The assistant who answered the phone explained that Dr. Moore was performing emergency surgery but offered to relay information back and forth from the surgical suite. After Jocelyn described Hester's demeanor and behavior, Dr. Moore opined that the best course of action was to "watch and wait."

"What am I watching for?" Jocelyn asked.

"If she starts whining, vomiting, or acting agitated, call us back," the assistant said. "Dogs in labor don't usually take naps. They're too uncomfortable."

"That's kind of what I thought. But I've never been through this before."

"Don't worry," the tech said.

"And she won't go into her whelping box. Should I make her go in the whelping box?"

"No. Let her rest wherever she's most comfortable. Dr. Moore will call you as soon as she's out of surgery."

"Okay. Thanks." Jocelyn assured herself that she was doing everything she should be, but she was still a nervous wreck. What if Hester was already in active labor? What if there was a problem with delivery?

Jocelyn cut the dogs' run short and herded Carmen and Curtis back to the house. "We need to keep an eye on your sister," she informed the disgruntled duo. "You can do an extra mile or two tomorrow, I promise."

On the bright side, she was no longer thinking about Chris.

Hester continued her peaceful slumber when Jocelyn returned, so Jocelyn left her alone and paced the kitchen while waiting for the vet to call her back. In the midst of her worried laps around the granite-topped island, she heard a thump from upstairs and remembered that Liam was still there. She had invited a virtual stranger, a man she knew only from hostile estate dealings, to rummage through the house she'd been living in for a week. *What could possibly go wrong?*

As she started up the stairs, she heard the low rumble of thunder in the distance. The weather forecast called for rain tonight, which would offer a welcome respite from the sweltering heat and humidity.

"Hey," she called when she reached the top step. "Can I get you a soda or a beer or something?"

"No, thanks," Liam called back. She followed his voice to the master bedroom, where she found him standing in the huge walk-in closet, staring at the racks of shoes and carefully pressed golf shirts and chinos.

"Swanky, huh?" Jocelyn leaned her hip against the chest of drawers in the middle of the space. "It's bigger than my bedroom at home."

Liam appeared transfixed by the neatly arranged belts and neckties. He'd never seen the interior of his father's house. Or his father's life. He was trying to piece together neckties and golf shoes to create a cohesive image of a parent he never knew.

"Is that . . . ?" He stepped around Jocelyn, his eyes narrowing.

"What?" she asked. She followed his gaze across a small, very expensive bit of clutter: a bottle of European aftershave, a monogrammed gold money clip, an assortment of coins.

Liam reached out and retrieved a small maroon box tucked in the corner, almost hidden in the shadows from the shelf above. Jocelyn leaned forward as he opened it, holding her breath without knowing why.

He opened the lid and she edged closer to discover what was inside.

"It's lovely," she said when she glimpsed the delicate gold band. The ring looked much too small and dainty to be Mr. Allardyce's. "Who did it belong to?"

"My mother, I think." Liam held the ring up to the light and studied an inscription inside the band. "It looks like her name in here. But that's impossible."

Jocelyn took a step back, giving him a bit of space. Until this moment, it hadn't really registered that the existence of Liam meant that Mr. Allardyce had once had some sort of love life. Mr. Allardyce had been somebody's . . . boyfriend? Husband? One-night stand?

Ew.

She shook the unsavory images out of her mind. "Were they married long?"

"No."

She waited for details, but none were forthcoming. "But he kept her ring all these years?"

"I guess." Liam seemed utterly bewildered.

"Take it," Jocelyn urged. "Take anything you want from here. It's all going to get sold or donated, anyway."

He wasn't even pretending to listen to her. All his attention was trained on that tiny circlet of gold. So Jocelyn left him alone and returned to the kitchen, where she poured herself a glass of pinot noir and sat down next to Hester on the floor.

Curtis and Carmen hurried to join her.

"People are weird," she informed them. "Really weird. As I'm sure you're aware." She sipped her wine and willed her cell phone to ring. Lo and behold, it did ring, and Jocelyn pressed it to her ear. "Thanks so much for calling me back, Dr. Moore."

"Of course." The vet's voice had exactly the soothing, unhurried manner one would expect from a top-paid medical professional. "I apologize for the delay; my current patient is in crisis, but I'll come by and check on Hester myself as soon as we finish up here."

"When will that be?" Jocelyn pressed.

"Maybe an hour. How is she doing?"

Hester, ever the sensitive sweetheart, picked up on Jocelyn's distress and laid her blocky head in Jocelyn's lap in an attempt to comfort her.

"She seems fine." Jocelyn kissed Hester on each ear. "But I'll feel much better once you take a look at her."

"I'll be there as soon as I can," the vet promised. "And if there are any more delays, I'll send my colleague over. You'd be in great hands with Dr. Ruggiero."

The rain started suddenly, a heavy downpour punctuated by flashes of lightning and a thunderclap that had the dogs on their feet and barking. Curtis, in particular, was agitated and howling, so Jocelyn went to the mudroom closet and found the vest with his name embroidered across the back.

"Is he going out in that?" Liam walked into the kitchen.

"Oh, it's not a raincoat, it's a weighted vest," Jocelyn explained. "It helps calm him down during thunderstorms." Right on cue, a deafening thunderclap shook the house. Curtis howled again, but with much less conviction.

"It's not working."

"Yeah, it is," she assured him. "He'd lose his mind without it. This is the equivalent of doggie Xanax."

"He wears it every rainstorm?"

"He'll chew up the ottoman if he doesn't."

Liam glanced down at Hester, who was still panting heavily and trying to worm her way under the foot rung of Jocelyn's chair. "What's wrong with her?"

"She's going to have puppies."

"Right now?"

"Not right now." *I hope.* "But soon."

"You're cutting it close," he stated with authority.

Jocelyn bristled. "Her vet is en route, and if all else fails, I can take her to the emergency vet in Rehoboth."

The next thunderclap rattled the windows. The dogs barked and howled. Jocelyn peered out the window, contemplating the black sky outside the windows. She sat back down on the floor and invited all the dogs into her lap. In seconds, she was engulfed in warm fur and wagging tails.

"I see why he left them to you," Liam said. "If I had dogs, I'd leave them to you, too."

"Do you like dogs?" she asked.

He looked down at the three furry beasts parked on her legs. "If I say 'no,' I'm out in the rain?"

"Obviously."

He smiled. "I do like dogs. Grew up with them."

"Ooh, lucky. I wanted a dog so badly while I was growing up, but my mom wouldn't allow it."

"My mother was a sucker for strays," Liam said. "We always had a few dogs and cats. My favorite was a husky mix named Banjo." Liam's expression softened at the memory. "Poor guy. It was rough being a husky in Florida."

"You're from Florida?" Jocelyn asked. "Which part?"

"Little town called Bexson up by the panhandle. We lived on a ranch in the middle of nowhere."

Jocelyn tried to reconcile her social and financial assumptions about Boat Shoes with rustic ranch life. She failed. "Huh. That must have been interesting."

"Definitely." He grinned, and he was no longer just good-looking in an abstract way.

"What did you grow on your ranch?" she asked. "Or raise? Whatever the right term is."

"Cattle." His smile faded. "But it's not our ranch. My mom and I just worked there."

The rain started coming down in sheets and the wind gusted, to the point that huge splashes of water were hitting the windows sideways. The thunder abated, and the dogs settled down. Jocelyn located a second wineglass and poured some pinot for Liam.

"I didn't know they had ranches in Florida," she said.

"Oh yeah. Big cattle ranches."

"But isn't it, I don't know, kind of swampy in Florida?" Jocelyn had never been to Florida. She'd never been anywhere south of Virginia or west of Illinois. But she made up for her lack of real-world travel experience with excessive binge-watching of the National Geographic Channel and the Travel Channel.

"Cows are tough. Besides, it's not that swampy up in the northern part of the state." Liam smiled again, a real smile. His eyes warmed and if she wasn't very much mistaken, he had a disarming little half dimple in his right cheek. "The landscape there is more like Jurassic Park."

"Really?"

"Palmettos and giant trees as far as the eye can see. Spiders as big as your hand. Gators in the watering holes."

"Your cows could fend off gators?"

"Ranch cows aren't sweet and calm like dairy cows," Liam explained. "They're ornery and unpredictable."

"Gatorproof cows. Only in Florida." Jocelyn shook her head. "So what did you and your mom do out on this ranch?"

"Whatever needed doing." He sat down next to her, and Carmen wriggled out of Jocelyn's lap and into his. "The guy who owned the ranch didn't live there full time. He only came in on the weekends. My mom and I were responsible for the day-to-day stuff. Feeding the cows, making sure the fence posts and barbed wire were in good repair, checking the grass and sending samples in to the university."

"What were the grass samples for?"

"To make sure it was healthy and nutritious. If you're raising cows, you have to have good grass or you're going to spend a ton of money on cattle feed."

She nodded. "So if I ever have any questions about my lawn, you're the guy to talk to?"

"I know more about grass than anyone should."

"Hmm." So he knew a few things about living off the land. So he was a dog lover. So he had a dimple. That didn't mean he wasn't the enemy. "How did your mother know how to run a ranch?"

"My mother could do anything she set her mind to." A note of pride crept into his voice. "She used to work in a museum doing art restoration. When I was little, she was in a car accident and broke two of her fingers. She could never use the brushes and materials the same way, so she found another way to make a living."

Jocelyn noticed he'd glossed right over the details of his parents falling in love, having a baby, and going their separate ways, but she let it slide for now. "She went from fine art to cattle ranching?"

He nodded. "We lived in a glorified camper and used an outhouse until I was twelve. I loved it."

"This should be a movie," Jocelyn marveled. "Is she still doing it?"

"Yeah. She loves the cows and the outdoors."

"What about the gators?"

"Gators are part of life. You have to learn how to deal with them."

"Sage advice." Jocelyn rested her chin on the top of Curtis's head. He responded by licking her chin. "My life story is so boring compared to you. My mom did the single-parent thing, too, but she wasn't a painter or a cattle rancher. She just helped out with my grandparents' business here in Black Dog Bay."

"What's their business?"

"Linen supply and cleaning. We work with the owners of the condos and rental houses. Renters show up on Saturday morning, we drop off clean sheets and towels. Then, at the end of the week, we come back, clean the place up, wash everything, and turn the place over for the next renters."

"I didn't realize people rented towels."

"They're on vacation. They don't want to spend their vacation tracking down the right size sheets and doing laundry. And the property owners don't want to deal with the headache of renters walking off with the towels. So we fill in the gap, send them a bill, and everybody's happy." She grinned. "I know about laundry like you know about grass."

"Impressive."

"I know. I'm also a sand removal expert, carpet-cleaning expert, toilet-fixing expert, and forbidden-cigarette-smoke-smell-removal expert. That's not technically my jurisdiction, but my friend Bree's family owns a rental unit maintenance business, and I help them out sometimes."

He patted Carmen's flank. "And you're the dog expert."

"Not all dogs; just these. I've got to start learning fast, though. They have a show coming up soon in Philadelphia and I have to figure out what the hell I'm doing before then. I've never been to a dog show."

"I thought you were like their second parent?"

"No, I just keep them fed, loved, and exercised. They have a whole glam squad for dog shows: groomers, teeth cleaners, professional handlers. A vet on call twenty-four hours." She frowned, wondering when she was going to hear the crunch of Dr. Moore's tires turning into the driveway. "Allegedly."

He regarded Carmen, who was gnawing on her own paw like it was a chew toy. "How much does all that cost?"

"A lot. Lois Gunther—she was the tall lady with dark hair at the reading of the will—handles all the dog show stuff. I'm just the nanny and the chauffeur."

"With great job perks," Liam stated.

"I have to admit, I've spent years bitching about how these summer houses are wasteful and materialistic and sucking the local economy dry."

He inclined his head. "True on all counts."

"But now that I'm actually living in one . . ." She gazed around at the high ceilings, the warm lighting, the abundance of food and drink and space. "I see the appeal."

"That's usually how it goes when you're rich." Liam's mood soured.

As quickly as he had opened up, he shut down. "Especially when you didn't have to earn it."

Jocelyn stiffened.

"All you had to do is be in the right place at the right time."

Jocelyn nudged Hester and Curtis aside and stood up. "You should go."

He nodded his assent and got to his feet as well.

She tried to maintain an icy dignity as she walked him to the front door. But her resolve cracked halfway across the foyer. "What is *wrong* with you?"

He didn't answer.

"I have no idea what happened between you and your father, but I have been accommodating. I have been sympathetic. I have invited you into Mr.—into *my* home—and invited you to steal cuff links and take your mother's wedding ring."

He opened the front door. A gust of wet, cold wind blasted in, accompanied by tiny hailstones that clattered on the steps.

He had one foot over the threshold, but Jocelyn wasn't finished with her rant. "I showed up day after day and took care of your dad's dogs. I've worked hard for everything I have. I apologize for nothing."

Liam stood tall on the porch, backlit by lightning streaking across the angry dark sky, and seemed almost amused by her tirade.

"I get the dogs, I get the house, you get nothing," she continued. "Deal with it."

The more incensed she became, the calmer he seemed. "Do you need some help with Hester before I go?"

"I can handle my dogs just fine," she assured him.

"Including the one having puppies in your laundry room right now?"

"Hester's not in active labor yet." She thought. She hoped.

"Call your vet again." And with that, he strode into the storm, heedless of the hail pelting down on his head.

She slammed the door, turned the deadbolt, and rushed back to the laundry room, where she found Hester splayed in the corner, panting and wide-eyed in pain.

Jocelyn dialed Dr. Moore, who picked up on the second ring.

"I'm on my way." The vet's voice was barely audible through static. "But . . ."

"But what?! We need you here right now!" Jocelyn described Hester's condition in as much detail as possible.

"Sounds like active labor," the vet replied.

"I know! Where the hell are you?"

"I'm on my way . . ." Dr. Moore's words were engulfed by a burst of static. ". . . the roads are out . . ."

"Are you kidding me?"

". . . take an alternate route . . . might take a while."

Jocelyn hung up, frozen with panic for a moment. Then she forced herself to get moving. Time for Plan B: the twenty-four-hour emergency vet clinic in Rehoboth. She grabbed some clean towels and tried to decide how best to transfer Hester from the laundry room to the back of her car.

When she opened the garage door, Jocelyn realized that Plan B wasn't going to happen. A mixture of hail and rain was pelting down so quickly, she could see water shimmering on the main road beyond the driveway. This was the problem with living down by the shore—the roads flooded much faster than up in town.

Time for Plan C. Just as soon as she came up with Plan C. Hester whimpered on the floor of the garage. Then she went silent. All Jocelyn could think about was the articles she'd read on canine pregnancy. The inherent risks. The surprisingly high possibility of maternal death. The likelihood that at least one puppy would experience distress upon birth. Mr. Allardyce had trusted her with the beings he loved most in the world, and she was failing him.

She knelt to stroke Hester's head. The dog pulled away, straining and yelping.

Jocelyn clenched her keys in her hand and gazed across the lawn. She could see Liam's SUV still parked past the end of the drive. Obviously, he'd given up on trying to drive in this downpour, too.

She didn't like him. She didn't trust him. But she had a dog in distress, and she would do what needed to be done. After draping a towel over her head, Jocelyn ran out into the storm, wincing as the icy edges of hailstones nicked her cheeks.

Liam glanced up and saw her coming but didn't roll down the window. He waited until she knocked on the glass before he deigned to acknowledge her.

Slowly, slowly, the tinted glass slid down. "Yes?" he asked coolly.

"You were right," she forced herself to say. "The dog is having puppies right now."

"Then you better get back in there."

"I know, but . . ." She crossed her arms tightly. "It's not going well."

"You don't really need to do anything. Give her some warm, clean bedding, and leave her alone unless something goes wrong."

"I think something's going wrong. She's yelping, and there's some blood, and . . ." She bid adieu to her pride and implored him with her eyes. "You said you grew up on a ranch, right?"

He was already out of the car and heading down the driveway.

chapter 14

"That was amazing," Jocelyn marveled two hours later. "A little gross, but amazing." Her shirt was drenched with sweat and her adrenaline levels had surged to bungee-jumping levels, but she, Hester, and four tiny puppies had all survived.

"Here." Liam handed her Hester's stainless steel water dish. "She needs to stay hydrated."

The new mama thumped her tail in gratitude. Curled up in a warm towel fresh out of the dryer, Hester was cleaning and feeding her newborns between power naps. The puppies snuggled up to one another on a heating pad next to Hester.

"Good girl." Jocelyn rubbed the dog's shoulder. "Try not to move before Dr. Moore finally gets here and gives you the all clear."

Liam patted Curtis and Carmen, who had been sequestered in the kitchen but were fascinated by the proceedings.

"Thank you for helping," Jocelyn said. "Your father would be grateful."

"I didn't do it for him, I did it for the dogs."

"Even though they bogarted the house you wanted?"

"It's not their fault my father acted like an ass."

"It's not mine, either," Jocelyn pointed out.

He just looked at her.

She gave up trying to reopen that particular topic of conversation and got to her feet. "I better clean myself up before the vet gets here." She glanced out the window, where the weather was still impassable. "I'd invite you to stay over in one of the guest rooms, but, you know. We're sworn enemies."

"You're not my enemy." He seemed surprised by the idea. "You're just the obstacle."

"That's nice."

He shrugged. "It's the truth."

"You can go sleep in your car, then, because this 'obstacle' has things to do."

He left without another word, but not before heating up another towel in the dryer and swapping it out for the one in Hester's bed.

"Good night," he said softly to the dog. He leaned over, gave Hester a gentle kiss on her head, and left Jocelyn wondering (due only to extreme stress and sleep deprivation, obviously) what it might feel like to be on the receiving end of a good night kiss herself.

"It was beyond messed up," Jocelyn reported to Bree the next day as they sat on the front porch of the house Bree shared with her parents and grandmother. "One minute he's a dog midwife, the next minute he's calling me an obstacle."

"Well." Bree paused in the middle of painting her fingernails to shoot a disparaging look. "Rich men are crazy and callous. When will you learn?"

"I don't think he's rich."

"He's an Allardyce," Bree decreed. "He wears *boat shoes*, Joss. That should tell you all you need to know. Speaking of which, what are you going to do with those blue-blooded puppies? I didn't want to mention this earlier, with you under so much stress, but we have a puppy overpopulation in this country. Have you thought about spaying and neutering everybody?"

"It's different with show dogs."

Bree looked unimpressed. "Really."

"Yes! They're ineligible for conformation shows if they're spayed or neutered," Jocelyn explained.

"What are conformation shows?"

"Dog beauty pageants, basically. These are responsibly bred, show-quality puppies. And it's not my choice to make. They already have buyers lined up, plus there's a waiting list."

Bree snorted. "A waiting list. Are these dogs or Birkin bags?"

"The dad is some world-famous champion from Brussels."

"Then how did he and Hester get together?"

"They didn't. She was artificially inseminated. Mr. Allardyce had the sperm FedExed all the way from Europe."

Bree's jaw dropped. "You lie."

Both women stopped talking as a voice from inside the house called, "Girls!"

Bree and Jocelyn jumped to their feet. "Coming, Grandma!" Bree called back.

They hurried into the small, darkened front room, where Bree's paternal grandmother, Veronika, held court in the recliner with the shades drawn against the hot afternoon sun. She was a tiny slip of a woman with wispy hair and skin so papery thin it was nearly translucent, but she ruled with an iron fist. "What nonsense are you two talking about out there?"

Jocelyn glanced at Bree. Bree glanced at Jocelyn.

"Belgian-imported dog sperm," Bree said.

"You have too much time on your hands. Find some chores to do." Veronika glared at her granddaughter, but her gaze softened when she turned her attention to Jocelyn. "How's your mother?"

"Better every day." Jocelyn smiled. "She actually volunteered to come over and puppy-sit while I did the laundry this morning."

"But she hates dogs," Bree pointed out.

"I think she just wanted an excuse to sit on Mr. Allardyce's patio and enjoy the view, but she'll never admit it."

"That's a mother's right." Veronika folded her hands in her lap. She was impeccably turned out in full hair and makeup to watch game shows on basic cable.

"Maybe, but you know what's *not* a mother's right?" Jocelyn glanced at Bree. "Conspiring with my best friend to railroad me into a relationship with a, quote, 'nice local guy.'"

Veronika readjusted her earrings. "Give the local boy a chance."

"Why is no one on my side about this?" Jocelyn demanded. Then she noticed that Bree and her grandmother were exchanging conspiratorial looks between glancing at Jocelyn's hands.

"What?" Jocelyn leaned in. "Is this about what my palm says?" For years, she'd been begging Veronika to tell her fortune, and for years, Veronika had refused, citing platitudes about not mixing personal relationships with business.

"Your palm doesn't say anything," Bree said. "Palm reading is a parlor trick."

Veronika ignored this and addressed Jocelyn. "She's saying that to rile me up. She knows the truth."

Bree was getting more indignant by the moment. "The truth is—"

"The truth is, you're going to put your God-given gift to good use tomorrow afternoon and earn some money. You're booked for a bridal shower."

Bree went from indignant to panicked. "What? No!"

Veronika continued to address Jocelyn. "It's time she started earning her keep."

"I spent all morning snaking a sink at the rental property on Seagull," Bree sputtered. "Last night, I was scrubbing carpet stains until ten p.m. I am busting my ass for the family business."

Veronika pinned her granddaughter with a glare. "That's not the family business I'm talking about."

"I'm not a palm reader. Never have been, never will be. And to say that I am is gross and offensive. It's a stereotype."

"Don't you yell at me about stereotypes." Veronika started to get out of her chair. Bree backed up a few steps. "You're part Hungarian. The part that *I* gave you."

"Don't you guys get tired of having this same fight over and over?" Jocelyn touched Veronika's shoulder to urge her to sit back down.

"You're going to the bridal shower tomorrow, and you're going to read everyone's palm," Veronika informed Bree. "I already told the hostess that I wasn't feeling well and you were filling in."

"You can't make me," Bree stated.

Veronika smirked. "Of course I can." She put her iced tea down with subtle but unmistakable menace.

"Fine." Bree switched tactics with breathtaking speed. "Fine. I'll go to the stupid shower. But I have rules and conditions." She pushed her hair back from her face. "I'm telling everyone that I have no professional training in palmistry and that my readings are for entertainment purposes only."

Veronika reeled in horror. "Don't you dare."

"I have to; otherwise, I'm leaving myself open to legal liability."

"She's going to law school," Jocelyn said proudly.

"She can be a lawyer and still have my gift," Veronika snapped. "Palmistry is not just entertainment. It's a true talent. I got it from my grandmother, who got it from her grandmother."

"Well, the talent skipped my generation. When I look at palms, I don't see anything." Bree held up her own palms, as though offering proof. "I'll just be making stuff up."

Her grandmother narrowed her gaze. "You disappoint me."

"I'm telling the truth, Grandma. *Nothing happens.*"

"Something happened when you saw Liam's palm," Jocelyn pointed out.

Veronika rounded on Jocelyn with great interest. "Who's Liam?"

"The latest shifty rich guy," Bree said. "The other shifty rich guy just broke up with her."

"Oh, him?" Veronika sniffed dismissively. "I knew he'd never last."

"You could have told me that," Jocelyn said. "Saved me some heartache."

"Tell me more about this new shifty rich man," Veronika demanded.

"I barely know him."

"Tell me." Veronika's tone brooked no refusal.

Jocelyn obeyed. "He's the illegitimate son of Mr. Allardyce—actually, he might be legitimate; there was a wedding ring involved at some point—and he didn't get anything in the will, and he keeps showing up at my house."

"He's on the ragged edge," Bree added.

Jocelyn rolled her eyes. "He's not on the ragged edge. He just wants to know who his father was."

"And take your beautiful, gigantic beach house away from you."

"Yeah, that, too."

"Enough." Veronika became impatient with all the details. "What about his palm?"

Jocelyn pointed at Bree. "She had a little episode when she looked at it, but she won't tell me anything."

"I did not have an episode," Bree practically spat. "I had a hunch."

"Aha!" Veronika jabbed her index finger in the air. "It's not a hunch, it's a gift."

"Make her tell me what she saw," Jocelyn implored Veronika.

Bree shook her head. "Grandma, you and I will discuss this later."

"We certainly will. And in the meantime, you need to prepare yourself to read a roomful of palms."

Bree made a face. "What am I even supposed to wear to that? Big gold hoop earrings and a bunch of gypsy scarves on my head?"

"And you accuse me of spreading stereotypes?" Veronika threw up her hands. "Wear what you would normally wear to a bridal shower. And then add one big, unusual accessory. Something to add a little air of mystery and art."

"My accessory is dog hair," Jocelyn decided.

Bree's head jerked around. "You're not coming."

"I'm definitely coming," Jocelyn assured her. "I'm your trusty assistant. I wouldn't miss this for the world."

"No way in—" Bree started, but Veronika intervened.

"You're going, both of you, and you're not going to say one word about 'for entertainment purposes only.'"

"Yay!" Jocelyn rubbed her hands together. "This is going to be great!"

"I hate you," Bree said.

Jocelyn tilted her head. "We'll see how you feel when you need someone to help you replace a leaky toilet next week."

"I'll use you for your toilet-replacement skills, but I'll still hate you," Bree vowed. Jocelyn blew her a kiss.

The theme music for *Jeopardy!* came on, and Veronika banished both of them from her sight. But not before she beckoned Jocelyn closer and murmured in her ear: "The guy that Bree has picked out for you? Go on one date. It will change your life."

"How did you already find a new dating prospect?" Jocelyn demanded as she and Bree headed back to the porch. "My last relationship isn't even cold yet."

"I told your mother I was going to hook you up, and I don't lie to Rachel Hillier. Plus, you might like this guy. He's cute and he has a job instead of a trust fund. He's a catch."

"If this guy is so great, why don't you go out with him?" Jocelyn challenged.

"Because law school. I don't need any romantic distractions right now. I need to keep my eye on the prize: getting the hell out of here."

"This is going to be like a movie," Jocelyn predicted. "The beautiful, mysterious law student who puts herself through school with palm-reading parties."

Bree shook her head. "Palm reading doesn't pay that well. I'd be better off putting myself through school by stripping. Plus, I bet I have more stripping talent than palm-reading talent."

"I will not take that bet." Jocelyn slipped on her sunglasses. "So am I still invited to come to Philadelphia with you?"

"You're always invited to go anywhere with me, but you can't. You live here now, with your dogs and your big fancy beach house. You're not going anywhere. That's why you're going to go out with the guy I found for you."

"I'm going to go out with him because your grandmother told me to. What's his name?"

"Um . . ." Bree glanced away. "It's a family nickname."

"Which is . . . ?"

"Otter."

Jocelyn stopped walking. "No."

"It's just a name! Don't judge."

"Too late."

"Come on. One drink." Bree glanced back toward her grandmother. "You heard the lady: It's going to change your life."

chapter 15

Jocelyn was taking an afternoon power nap with the dogs on a pile of sheets and blankets when she heard the scrape of a key in the lock and the echo of footfalls in the hallway.

She rocketed into a sitting position and surveyed the group of snoring Labs surrounding her on the laundry room floor.

"Hello?" she called out as the footsteps got closer. Curtis opened one eye.

"Hashtag 'worst watchdogs ever.'" Jocelyn got to her feet and shook her head at the somnolent canines. "Have no fear, guys. Don't get up."

For once, they all obeyed.

Jocelyn peered around the corner into the kitchen, where she saw two women in bleach-stained T-shirts and ponytails inspecting a recent scratch in the white apron sink.

She cleared her throat, and they both startled and whirled to face her. One woman was younger than the other, and the older one looked familiar. Jocelyn tried to place the face.

"Hi, I'm Jocelyn." She opened the tall wooden gate separating the laundry area from the kitchen. "I live here now with the dogs. Long story."

"I know." The older woman frowned at her. "I'm Marianne. I'm a friend of your mother's."

"Oh, of course." Jocelyn smote her forehead. "You make that three-berry pie for the Fourth of July party every year, right?"

The woman nodded. "This is my daughter, Abby."

"Hi, Abby. Pleased to meet you." Jocelyn shook hands with the teenager, who refused to make eye contact. She waited for them to explain their presence. They looked at her as if they were waiting for the same. "So what can I do for you?" *And why do you have a key?*

"We're here to clean the house." Marianne's tone sharpened. "We've been coming twice a week for the last three years."

"Ah." Jocelyn cleared her throat. "Well, as you may have heard—"

"No one told us not to come."

"No one told us anything." Abby headed for a storage closet near the pantry and started hauling out cleaning supplies: a vacuum, a bucket, a mop, and bottles of polishes and oils.

Jocelyn considered the staggering logistics of keeping this huge house clean. The dog hair and dust had already started to accumulate. The baseboards went on for miles. The antique furniture needed routine polishing and the windows bore the imprint of a thousand damp dog noses.

She now lived in a house she could not maintain without help. She was perilously close to becoming one of *them*—a pampered princess who lounged around eating bonbons while other people damaged their spines scrubbing her floors and dusting her chandeliers.

"Things are still in transition," she told Abby and Marianne. "You don't have to clean today."

"What?" Marianne frowned. "Why not?"

"We want to." Abby finally jerked her chin up and looked Jocelyn in the eye.

"We need this job," Marianne added. "Abby and I take care of Mr. Allardyce's house and my husband and brother-in-law take care of the yard."

That would explain how the gravel had magically remained raked and the hedges magically remained trimmed.

"I know, but . . . it's a little weird having someone else clean my sink." Jocelyn opened a cabinet and pulled out a pair of drinking glasses. "Can I get you anything? Iced tea? Water?"

"No. We're here to work." Marianne shot a look at her daughter.

Jocelyn tried to explain. "I just don't feel good about making someone else do my dirty work. That's what I do for a living."

"Get over it," Marianne advised. "My car payment is due on Tuesday. Abby, grab the mop and start with the back bathrooms." She turned back to Jocelyn with her jaw set. "We good?"

"How much was Mr. Allardyce paying you?" Jocelyn asked. "If it's anything like what he was paying me, you're due for a raise." She made a mental note to call the estate attorney later and adjust the monthly property maintenance budget accordingly.

The housecleaner regarded her with wariness, then nodded. "Thank you." Without another word, she headed down the hall to help her daughter clean the faucets and tiled shower walls that no one used.

Zero chitchat. Zero pleasantries and lighthearted gossip. Zero acknowledgment that Jocelyn was anyone other than a rich seasonal resident. An employer who must be appeased. Money had made her an outsider in her own community.

Jocelyn listened to the faint sounds of the faucet running and tried to reconcile her guilt and gratitude. And then, in the grand tradition of Black Dog Bay employees, she put her feelings aside and did her job.

"Come on, Hester, look alive. The vet's going to be here any minute."

"Hester's doing great and all the puppies are gaining weight." Dr. Tracey Moore smiled up at Jocelyn as she doled out a treat to Hester.

"Thank goodness," Jocelyn replied. "I have no idea what I'm doing, and I'd never forgive myself if something happened to any of them."

"You're doing great," the vet said. "Try to keep her hydrated to boost her milk supply and let her take some alone time if she wants it. It can get exhausting, having four puppies climbing all over you trying to nurse all day."

"She does look worn out, poor thing." Jocelyn scratched Hester under her collar, which elicited a heavy tail thump against the mudroom floor.

"That's normal at this stage of the game. Just make sure the room stays warm and weigh everybody at least once a day."

"We have weigh-ins every morning and every night." Jocelyn nodded at the postal scale she'd placed on the counter next to the dryer. "I'm a paranoid wreck."

The quartet of squirmy, pink molelike creatures were looking more like actual dogs every day. Two with black fur like Hester's, one with a burgeoning black coat, and one with gray fur who looked like a Weimaraner changeling. The vet had assured her that this was in fact a rare genetic variant, sometimes referred to as a "silver Lab."

"As long as I'm here, would you like me to take a look at Carmen?" Dr. Moore brushed a stray dog hair off her shirt.

"Carmen?" Jocelyn blinked. "Why? She's fine."

"Well, I know Mr. Allardyce wanted to breed her this year, once Hester's puppies were placed in their new homes."

"He did," Jocelyn affirmed. "He said she was the prettiest and the fastest out of all the dogs he'd ever owned. He introduced her to some potential mates a while back, but she didn't get along with any of them. She has very high standards."

The vet looped her stethoscope around her neck. "Mr. Allardyce asked me to coordinate artificial insemination. At least twice, if I recall correctly."

"Ah, yes." Jocelyn nodded. "The frozen dog sperm from Belgium."

"I think it was from England in Carmen's case. It didn't work." The vet got to her feet and petted Carmen and Curtis, who were whining on the other side of the safety gate. "Sometimes the assisted reproduction methods aren't as effective as an old-fashioned, face-to-face meeting."

"I guess we could take a road trip out to New York or Pennsylvania, but—"

"Ireland," the vet interjected. "Mr. Allardyce was going to take her to Ireland."

"What, like *Europe* Ireland? Cross-the-Atlantic-Ocean Ireland?"

Dr. Moore nodded. "Purebred dog breeders do it all the time."

"That seems a bit extreme."

"You have plenty of time to think about it," the vet assured her. "But I know that's what Mr. Allardyce wanted for her."

And Jocelyn was Carmen's guardian. Her job was to take care of her, keep her healthy, bring her to shows, make sure she had a never-ending supply of stuffed squirrels . . . and take her to the Emerald Isle on blind doggie dates. Never a dull moment.

But first, she had to line up a puppy sitter to make sure everybody remained happy and healthy while she accompanied Bree to the palm-reading party. Jocelyn scrolled through her contact list, debating and discarding potential candidates one by one. Mr. Allardyce had been right when he complained it was nearly impossible to find reliable dog care. She begged Dr. Moore to stay for the rest of the day, but the vet could only stay for another hour. That gave her sixty minutes to go pick up the weekly loads of laundry, check on her mother, and return to the beach house.

As soon as she opened the front door to her childhood home, she knew something was wrong. A pot was boiling over on the stove, the TV was on, but Rachel was nowhere to be seen.

"Mom?" Jocelyn hurried to turn off the stove.

"Joss! Thank God you're here!" Rachel's voice drifted down from the staircase. "I left my cell phone on the sofa and I was starting to panic."

Jocelyn found her mother sprawled halfway up the stairs, her legs curled up against her chest. "What happened?" She put her hands under Rachel's arms and helped her mother into a sitting position. "Are you supposed to be climbing stairs?"

"I didn't hurt my back." Rachel bristled. "I think I pulled a muscle in my hip, though."

"Okay, give me a second to think." Jocelyn peered back down at the first floor, trying to figure out the best way to relocate Rachel. "I'll have to carry you down."

"You can't." Rachel's tone was flat. "You'll kill us both."

"Then I'll have to call Bree and she'll help. Best-case scenario, we all make it out of here alive. Worst-case scenario, we all die together."

"I'm so glad I raised you to be an optimist."

Jocelyn produced her cell phone, but before she dialed, she gave her mother a stern look. "You can't go on like this. You're coming to stay with me for a few weeks."

"But—"

"End of discussion." Jocelyn refused to call Bree until Rachel agreed.

"But you live in the house that greed built. *And* you have three dogs."

"Seven, actually. Hester just had puppies." Jocelyn tried to hide her amusement at her mother's dismay. "Relax, they're still basically blind and deaf. They can't do anything except eat and sleep."

Rachel looked horrified. "I don't want to live like that."

"I know, but Mom? We're out of options."

Her mother glowered for a moment, then relented. "Fine. But I'm going to pay you rent."

Jocelyn laughed. "Never going to happen."

"I insist."

"I refuse to take any money from you, now or ever."

"I'll slip it into your wallet when you're not looking," Rachel threatened.

"I'll put it back in your wallet, plus interest," Jocelyn retorted.

"I refuse to be a freeloader."

"You're my mother," Jocelyn pointed out. "You've done everything for me for my entire life. Will you please stop talking crazy and hang out at my house for a few weeks?"

"Fine. But I'll earn my keep somehow."

"Actually." Jocelyn brightened. "There is something I need help with in the immediate future."

chapter 16

"Life is so weird," Jocelyn said to Bree as they approached the front door of the address Veronika had given them.

"I'm aware." Bree was decked out in her rendition of "posh palm reader": little black dress, patent peep-toe pumps, and a huge, multifaceted crystal pendant.

"I'm supposed to scour the earth for a dog that's fast enough, handsome enough, and virile enough to get with Carmen."

"This all sounds very patriarchal," Bree said. "Doesn't she get any say in who she wants to sleep with?"

"Sure. She can refuse to have anything to do with the other dog. She has a long history of doing just that. The vet said I might have to take her all the way to Ireland for the canine version of *The Bachelorette*. She's exhausted all the options in the continental U.S."

"Picky, picky." Bree smiled. "Just like me."

Jocelyn shook her head. "Says the woman who's coercing me into having drinks with a guy named—what was it? Ferret? Muskrat? Meerkat?"

"Otter."

Jocelyn shuddered. "Sounds worse every time you say it. Nice necklace, by the way. Did you find that at Spiritually Gifted R Us?"

"Target clearance section."

"Very nice. Veronika would love it."

"Who do you think picked it out?" Bree set her jaw and rang the doorbell. "All right, let's get this farce over with."

"It's not a farce if you believe in what you're doing," Jocelyn said.

"Yes, well, I don't." Bree pasted on a fake smile as a woman opened the door. The beautiful blonde in a headband and floral sundress looked straight out of a Lilly Pulitzer catalog. "Hi! I'm Bree, the, uh, the palm reader. This is my assistant, Jocelyn."

"Perfect! Come on in." The blonde ushered them in. "I'm Krysten, the bride to be. I can't wait to have my palm read!"

Krysten led them into a living room filled with pink, mint green, and silver decor. Cupcakes and balloons and women in pearls and pastel cardigans abounded. While uniformed caterers passed petit fours and guests sipped pink champagne, Krysten's maid of honor called the room to order and announced, "Girls! We have a special treat today!"

"I don't see any girls here," Bree hissed under her breath. "I see a bunch of grown women."

"Think of the tips and smile," Jocelyn hissed back.

"Shouldn't you be out speed dating with your dog?" Bree shot back.

"Carmen would never get with a guy named Otter. Actual and factual."

The maid of honor continued, climbing atop the coffee table to hush the chattering throngs of women. "We know that Krysten and Daniel are going to have their happily ever after, but I thought that the rest of us might also want to know what the future has in store." She had everyone's attention now.

Especially Bree's. "Daniel? Daniel who?"

"So we invited a real live palm reader," the maid of honor continued. "Where are you, Bree? Wave to the crowd!"

Bree obligingly waved, muttering through clenched teeth.

"Try to look more friendly and less murderous," Jocelyn advised.

"Hi, guys." Bree swiveled her head, making eye contact with every woman in the room. "I know I look familiar to most of you. And I'm sure all of you know my grandmother."

"You're Veronika's granddaughter?" asked a woman in a yellow silk scarf.

"The one and only."

"Did you get the family gift?"

Bree nodded. "So she says."

"Then I'm first in line." The woman tossed aside her pastry and strode across the room. "She's the real deal."

"Are you sure?" A Botoxed redhead tried to wrinkle her forehead. "Her grandmother runs a tourist trap on the boardwalk. I always thought that was just a bunch of hooey."

Bree squared her shoulders. "My grandmother charges fifty dollars for a twenty-minute session, and it's worth every penny."

The redhead laughed airily. "Well, tourists are suckers."

"I'm telling you, it's real," the woman in the yellow scarf insisted. "I went to see Veronika right after I had my third miscarriage, and she told me I was going to have a baby girl in exactly fifteen months."

The Botox enthusiast looked skeptical. "Probably just a lucky guess. Those people just tell you what you want to hear."

Bree was audibly gritting her molars.

"The gender and the birth month might have been a lucky guess," the first woman allowed. "But she told me the name of the on-call doctor that delivered."

"Damn. You can get all that off a few lines in your palm?"

"Check it out." The first woman grinned and held out her hand. "It says Jennifer Schwartz, OB-GYN, right there on my pinkie."

The redhead elbowed her way to the front of the line. "Then you've already had your turn. Let someone else have a chance."

"Yeah, but I had to pay fifty dollars before. This one's free!"

Bree turned to Jocelyn. "Would you please go pour me another gin and tonic? Make it a triple."

"That's what your assistant is for." Jocelyn hastened to make the cocktail, noticing as she did so that the counter was already lined with empty bottles of champagne and vodka. Whoever had bought the booze for this party had seriously underestimated the drinking propensities of the guests.

"I know." A harried-looking bridesmaid was stacking discarded plastic cups and crumpled napkins. "The well's running dry."

"Not to worry; you still have gin." Jocelyn splashed a generous serving into a pink cup. She glanced back at Bree, who was seated on the sofa, peering down at a woman's palm. "This gives her extra psychic powers."

"There'll be more any minute," the bridesmaid promised. "I texted Dan, and he—oh, thank goodness, there he is now."

"I'm not here," intoned a low male voice. "I'm a figment of your imagination."

"What took you so long? I'm dying over here!" The bridesmaid who'd understocked the bar rushed over to assist Senior Year Dan, who was carrying a cardboard box full of bottles.

Across the room, Bree's head snapped up. Jocelyn couldn't blame her—Dan had aged well. Very well. He had grown into his tall, lanky frame, and his formerly frenetic energy had mellowed into infectious enthusiasm. He hadn't shaved that morning, so he had a bit of dark stubble. And bonus: He was toting a case of sparkling wine.

Bree was staring at him in the same way that she had when she was seventeen years old.

"Baby!" Krysten all but pirouetted into his arms. "You're not supposed to be here!"

"She told me to come." He pointed out the abysmal failure of a bartender. "Something about a life-or-death champagne emergency?"

"My hero." Krysten flung herself at him, almost knocking the box to the floor.

The crowd gasped. "Careful!"

Krysten turned to her guests, her smile both smug and sweet. "All this and wine, too. He's a keeper." She fluffed her hair with her left hand, prominently displaying the diamond on her finger.

"You are so lucky," one of her friends said wistfully. "My boyfriend would never show up at a bridal shower."

"Or know how to pick out wine."

"Or look like one of the doctors on *Grey's Anatomy*."

"I know!" Krysten was basking in all the attention. "When he first asked me out, I thought he was too good to be true. I kept thinking he must be a secret serial killer or something."

"Yeah, Dan." The bridesmaid winked. "Do you have a bunch of ex-girlfriends buried in your backyard?"

"That's my cue to leave." He kissed Krysten. "See you later." He took two steps toward the doorway, but froze when he saw Bree.

Dan looked at Bree. Krysten looked at Dan looking at Bree. Bree looked down at the palm in front of her.

"Bree!" Dan sounded delighted. Krysten's eyes darkened. "Great to see you again. I didn't know you knew Krysten?"

"Oh yes." Krysten's voice got syrupy. "My cousins hired her for the afternoon."

"Hi." Bree didn't lift her gaze. "Sounds like you've been busy."

"He just finished medical school," Krysten informed the room, in case there was anyone who needed to hear it for the thirty-eighth time.

"Almost," Dan corrected. "I have one more year of fellowship before they turn me loose on the unsuspecting public."

"What kind of doctor are you?" Jocelyn asked.

"I'm training to be a developmental pediatrician."

Krysten was happy to elaborate. "He takes care of the kids whose parents haven't slept in five years. Kids with autism, ADHD, rare genetic conditions . . ."

"And he's leaving right now." Dan strode out of the room before Krysten broke into song and interpretive dance.

"Bye, baby!" Krysten blew a kiss. Everyone oohed and ahhed.

"Here." Jocelyn handed Bree the gin and tonic.

Bree threw back half the drink in one gulp, then straightened her skirt and adjusted her pendant. "All right, back to business."

"Entertainment purposes only?" Jocelyn murmured.

Bree waved her away. "You know what would make the mood complete?"

"A crystal ball and a Ouija board?"

"A tip jar." Bree clicked her tongue. "Be a lamb and rustle one up, won't you?"

The combination of gin, tonic, and a long-lost ex-boyfriend inspired Bree to unleash her inner palmistry show-off. She traced love lines and life lines with her fingertips. She hummed and exclaimed. She made the kind of vague, positive predictions that placated the bridal brunch crowd:

"You're going to meet a romantic prospect at Krysten's wedding."

"You and your husband are having some trouble communicating. But don't worry; I see you reconnecting on a long airplane flight."

"Buy stock in companies starting with A. You'll thank me later."

"You're going to die peacefully in your sleep when you're almost one hundred."

The more rosy the prognostication, the more generous the gratuity. Jocelyn smiled inwardly as she watched Bree's tip jar fill with five- and ten-dollar bills.

"You'll be a fantastic lawyer," Jocelyn said when she and Bree left the party and walked toward their cars. "You told all those people a bunch of stuff they already knew and got them to pay you for it."

"Plus tip," Bree reminded her.

"Yeah, and it's not what you said, it's how you said it." Jocelyn whistled low. "I'd hate to go ten rounds with you in a courtroom."

"I can't stand this." Bree stopped walking. "I'm a horrible person."

Jocelyn stopped, too. "What do you mean?"

"All those things I said about meeting a romantic prospect, reconnecting with the husband, celebrating your next birthday in a city that starts with *S*?" Bree nibbled her lower lip. "That's all true, but it's not the whole truth. The 'romantic prospect' is going to be a one-night stand who'll never call that woman again. The wife and husband who are going to reconnect over a long plane ride are going to be on their way to her mother-in-law's funeral."

"Oh boy."

"Yeah. She's going to die suddenly."

"How?" Jocelyn couldn't help asking.

"I don't know. I didn't get that much detail, and I didn't want it. But that poor woman thinks she's going to be taking a second honeymoon to Hawaii or something." Bree slouched down as if trying to sink into the sidewalk. "I feel it. I *know* it. God, listen to me. I sound like my grandmother."

"Your grandmother's pretty awesome."

"I've spent the last twenty years talking trash and basically calling her a fraud. And now I'm getting psychic news flashes about people's dead mothers-in-law? No thank you. Do not want."

"Well, look on the bright side—" Jocelyn started.

"There is no bright side." Bree started walking again, so briskly that Jocelyn almost snapped a high heel trying to keep pace with her. "I'm never doing this again. It creeps me out."

"You don't have to do it again." Jocelyn patted her friend's shoulder.

Bree stopped again. "And another thing."

"Oh boy."

"I read Krysten's palm. She's cheating on Dan."

Jocelyn literally bit her tongue for a moment. She tried to proceed with as much tact and caution as possible. "Based on what evidence?"

"I don't need evidence," Bree stated, as though resting her case before a federal court judge. "I felt it. As soon as she opened her palm, it was like a red neon sign flashing: *cheater, cheater, backyard breeder.*" She shrugged. "I couldn't think of anything else that rhymed."

Jocelyn considered this, then asked the obvious question. "I'm not saying you're unfairly biased—"

"I'm not."

"—but given the history you have with Dan, isn't it possible that your emotions are clouding your judgment? Isn't it possible that you just want his fiancée to be cheating on him because you don't want him to get married?"

Bree crossed her arms. "It's possible, but it's not the case here. I know what I know."

Jocelyn nodded. "Let's just say for the sake of argument that she *is* cheating on him."

"She is."

"Who is she cheating with?"

"That I don't know."

"What? I thought you got a big red flashing neon sign!"

"That's not how palm reading works, Joss. It's not like running a background check through the FBI."

"Hmm." Jocelyn fished her car keys out of her purse and resumed walking.

"Well?" Bree sounded about two degrees away from her boiling point. "What are we going to do about this?"

"Nothing." Jocelyn opened the driver's-side door.

"We have to do something."

"What is it you propose that we do? Go track down Dan in the middle of rounds and tell him his fiancée is cheating on him based on his high school sweetheart's hunch?"

"Obviously we're not going to track him down in the middle of rounds. We're not going to tell him anything." Bree paused. "And it's not a hunch, it's a gift."

Jocelyn shook her head. "How the tables have turned."

"We don't have to say anything directly, but we could, I don't know, warn him. Leave an anonymous tip."

"It's none of our business, and we're not getting involved," Jocelyn decreed.

"What if we followed Krysten for a day?"

"What, like tailing her in an unmarked vehicle and staking out her house all night? I've seen this Lifetime movie, and it doesn't end well."

Bree huffed. "If it were you and your fiancé, wouldn't you want to know?"

"If it were me and Otter?" Jocelyn pursed her lips. "I'd want to know if he was cheating on me, sure. But I wouldn't want to know if some bridal shower palm reader had a crush on my man and conveniently decided our relationship was doomed."

"You're completely misrepresenting this case," Bree protested.

"Am I?" Jocelyn got into her car and put on her sunglasses. *"Am I?"*

"Yes. And frankly, I'm offended." Bree did look hurt. "I'm not making stuff up to fit some delusional fantasy."

"I'm sorry." Jocelyn located a roll of Life Savers in the cup holder and gave one to her friend as a peace offering. "Here. I know the orange ones are your favorite."

Bree popped the candy into her mouth but continued to seethe.

"Even if what you sensed is true, it's not our place to do anything. We're not the fidelity police."

"So I just have to sit back and watch a really great man marry some faithless piece of fluff who won't treat him right?"

"I'm sorry to say that yes, you do."

"Palmistry sucks."

"Come on, let's go back to the house," Jocelyn offered. "My mom is puppy-sitting against her will, and she's going to disown me if I don't get back there."

"I want to go to the grocery store and get a whole cake," Bree said. "The fake chocolate kind with the super sweet icing."

"And the bright red roses in the corners?"

Bree nodded. "I need to fill my emotional void with artificial colors and flavors."

"You got it. We'll stop on the way." Jocelyn put the keys in the ignition. "Meet you at the grocery store in five minutes?"

"Why? Why does life work like this?" Bree asked. "Why is it that every time there's a guy you really like, he's already planning a wedding with a preppy blonde who's sleeping with someone else?"

"I believe that Shakespeare asked that very same question in one of his sonnets."

"Whatever." Bree held out her hand for one more Life Saver. "Let's go cuddle the puppies, gorge on cake, then figure out what you're going to wear on your life-changing date with Otter."

chapter 17

"It's about time!" Rachel's voice drifted out from the kitchen as Bree and Jocelyn let themselves in through the front door. "What took you so long?"

"Sorry, sorry." Jocelyn tossed her handbag on the counter and rushed to relieve her mother from dog duty. "You know how bridal showers go."

"I don't, actually." Rachel was seated at the kitchen table with her feet propped up on the chair next to her. "I've never been married, remember?"

"Count your blessings." Bree ripped off her clearance-rack "statement piece" necklace as she trailed in behind Jocelyn. "They're twee, tedious, and interminable."

Rachel put down the can of diet soda she was drinking and glanced at her daughter. "What's wrong with her?"

"Do you remember our senior year when—"

"Nothing's wrong with me that can't be cured with commercial baked goods and a one-way ticket out of this podunk town," Bree finished. "How was dog-sitting?"

"Well." Rachel gazed around at the gleaming marble countertops, fancy bronze fixtures, and cavernous refrigerator filled with treats Jocelyn had picked out especially for her. "We all survived."

Jocelyn proceeded to the mudroom, where Hester was sacked out with all four puppies under the heat lamp Jocelyn had ordered online two days ago. "Where are Carmen and Curtis?"

"You mean the pushiest dogs in the world?" Rachel rolled her eyes. "They wouldn't stop licking me and sniffing me in socially unacceptable places, so I put them in the office."

"Mom! How could you?"

"Have you seen the office?" Rachel scoffed. "It's hardly prison."

Jocelyn hurried to liberate the pushiest dogs in the world. When she returned, Rachel looked at her expectantly. "Bree says you need something cute to wear on your big date."

"Mark my words, I'm going to sign both of you up for Match.com as soon as the puppies are weaned. We'll see how you like it."

"Stop complaining and be grateful you have such caring friends and family." Rachel settled back into her chair, gazing out at the ocean. "You girls go ahead. I'll stay here."

"But you hate it here," Jocelyn pointed out. "You hate dogs. And gigantic mansions. And ocean views."

"Someone has to keep the puppies alive while you play dress-up. Make it snappy."

Jocelyn folded her arms. "What's going on here?"

"Don't ask questions." Bree grabbed the car keys. "Let's get while the getting's good. Rach, do you want anything from the bakery?"

"Almond croissant," Rachel replied.

"We're on it. See you in a bit!"

"You're totally going to snuggle the puppies while we're gone, aren't you?"

"Only George Clooney." Rachel laughed at her daughter's expression. "That's the silver one."

"You named him George Clooney?" Jocelyn started laughing, too.

Rachel shrugged. "It was that or Anderson Cooper."

"Mr. Allardyce is rolling in his grave."

"All the better. Toodle-oo!"

"That looks good," Bree opined when Jocelyn emerged from the dressing room at the Retail Therapy boutique. "Really good."

Jocelyn adjusted the shoulder straps of the teal sundress. "I'm not sure what shoes I'd wear it with, though."

"Try it with those." Bree pointed out a pair of gray strappy sandals adorned with small silver chips of anthracite. "And that bag."

"I'm not buying a new dress, new shoes, and a new bag for one date!" Jocelyn was scandalized.

"Go ahead," Bree urged. "The dogs want you to have it. Carmen told me so."

"I'm the dogs' guardian, not their money-embezzling, hard-partying, no-morals-having stage mother."

"But you could be."

"The stipend is meant for food and grooming and necessary medical care."

"Yeah, and after you've taken care of that, how much is left over every month?" Bree quizzed.

"Um . . ."

"I thought so. Buy the shoes. Buy the bag. Buy it all."

"This isn't about the money, it's about the principle," Jocelyn said. "I'm not going to buy a dress that's not even on sale. Especially for a guy named Otter."

"Every time somebody says it's not about the money . . . it's about the money. Stop being ridiculous and buy the dress." Bree called to the store owner, "She'll take it!"

"I'll ring it up!" the owner called back.

"It's bad luck to buy a new dress for a date, anyway. The more elaborate the preparations, the worse the date goes," Jocelyn predicted.

"Don't be like that. You'll have fun if you go in with the right attitude. I'm telling you, he's a nice guy."

"Mm-hmm. And how did you meet this guy, again?"

"He fixed my brakes. His family owns the auto repair place out by the highway." Bree held up both hands. "I swear to you, he's nice. Cute, too, in a baseball-cap-wearing, good-ol'-boy kind of way. I'd snap him up for myself, but like I said, I'm completely off dating right now."

Jocelyn lifted one eyebrow. "So you're telling me that you'd turn Dan down if he asked you out?"

"He's not single. And don't pretend to have any idea what it's like to be in my situation." Bree busied herself with trying on a cunningly cut leopard print jacket. "I'm like Cassandra from that Greek tragedy. I know exactly what's up, and nobody believes me."

"I believe you," Jocelyn said. "Well, I *want* to believe you."

"You'll see," Bree assured her.

Jocelyn's phone chimed as a text came in. She smiled when she glanced at the screen. "Oh look. It's Otter. He's confirming our date for tomorrow at three."

"How considerate." Bree took off the jacket and perused the rack of sunglasses. "Where are you two going?"

"Picnic on the beach." Jocelyn scanned her messages as a new text arrived. "He says it's fine if I want to bring a dog or two."

"Buy that dress and pick the best-behaved dog," Bree instructed.

Jocelyn grinned. "Tell you what—I'll buy you that jacket as a finder's fee."

"For finding what?"

"A genuinely nice guy." Jocelyn returned the teal dress and shoes to the rack but took the leopard print jacket to the cash register. "I'm actually starting to look forward to this."

chapter 18

"Thank you for inviting Carmen to join us." Jocelyn tucked her skirt under her knees as the breeze picked up along the shoreline. The afternoon had gone from cloudy and still to sunny and windy, and the edges of the white-and-red-checked picnic blanket fluttered against the sand.

"She's a great dog." Stocky and sturdy, with work-hewn hands and an abundance of thick russet hair, Otter McMurray looked every inch the small-town, self-made man. He scratched Carmen's ears. "None of our dogs were ever this well-behaved."

Jocelyn popped a grape into her mouth and crunched down on an errant grain of sand. "What kind of dogs did you have?"

"Growing up, we had a couple of mutts. My favorite, Gus, kind of looked like that one." Otter pointed out a big, reddish brown dog romping with a Frisbee by the boardwalk. "They'd show up in the alley behind my house. Me and my brother would feed them, and a couple of them never left."

Carmen whined softly. Jocelyn tried to figure out what the dog was agitated about but couldn't detect anything out of the ordinary. The perfect weather had brought out crowds of vacationing families who were swimming and digging in the sand. The wooden signs from the town square boutiques contrasted against the clear blue sky, and Jocelyn could smell freshly made kettle corn and saltwater taffy.

Here she was, with a nice man and a nice dog and a nice bottle of pinot gris. Nothing life-changing had happened yet, but the date wasn't over.

Although, if she were going to have any kind of future with this guy, she had to get one thing out of the way. "So." She cleared her throat. "Otter."

He leaned over to top off her paper cup. "Yeah?"

"That's an unusual name."

He laughed. "I know. I'm so used to it by now, I forget how it sounds to other people when they first hear it."

"Is that the name on your birth certificate?"

"No, my parents aren't that mean." He looked a little abashed. "My birth certificate says Orton."

"Orton." She said it aloud, trying it out. "I like it."

"My little brother couldn't say it when he was learning to talk, so he called me Otter. Pretty soon, the whole family started calling me Otter and it stuck."

"Does your brother work in the car business, too?" Jocelyn asked.

"Yeah, he handles the books, the scheduling, the office stuff. He's really good at dealing with the customers. I'm back in the garage, blasting music and up to my elbows in grime and grease. That's why . . ." He broke off in a quick, obviously fake coughing fit. "I don't go out much."

"There's nothing wrong with being an introvert." Jocelyn felt a bit protective toward him. "Especially when you like what you do."

"I've always loved cars. New cars, old cars, European, American . . .

I love driving them, fixing them, the sound the engine makes when you rev it."

Jocelyn tried to imagine a parallel level of passion in her own life, but all she could come up with was the sound of dogs barking and the smell of bacon biscuit breath in her face.

"Even when you were little?"

"Big-time. My mom didn't understand it, but she let me read all the car books I could find in the library. She bought me Viper and Ferrari models for my birthday."

"She must be proud."

"I think she's just glad I'm fixing fast cars instead of driving them. For years, I swore I was going to grow up to be a Formula One driver." He ducked his head before adding, "She hosts family breakfast at her house every Sunday. You should come sometime."

Jocelyn had felt certain that her heart was completely icy and impenetrable after Chris left her, but maybe she'd been wrong. "I'd like that."

"So what about you?" he asked. "Bree said you did something with managing summer rental properties."

"Bree exaggerates." Jocelyn brushed a fly off her knee. "My mom and I run a business that supplies towels and sheets to the renters. You know, so they don't have to spend their last morning here doing laundry."

Otter looked amazed. "People pay money to not do laundry?"

"Three hundred and fifty dollars per household per week," she told him. "I know. I can't imagine paying that much to get out of it, but people do. Most of them don't even ask questions or try to bargain. They just give us their credit card number and tell us their checkout time."

"Wow." Otter adjusted the brim of his baseball cap. "That's not how it is with my customers. Most of the regulars are great, but a lot of the new ones are worried I'm trying to rip them off or add on a bunch of services they don't need."

"Automotive trust issues." She nodded. "I understand all too well."

"It's mostly older guys who collect classic cars or are trying to fix them up. They need parts special-ordered and help putting them in right."

"Sounds much more exciting than doing laundry." Jocelyn popped another cold grape into her mouth. "Although I'm in the middle of a career change, actually." She patted Carmen's head. "I'm a professional dog guardian these days."

He glanced at Carmen, confused. "Like a bodyguard?"

"No, like a nanny-slash-personal-trainer-slash-nutritionist-slash-midwife." She pushed the hair back out of her face as the wind picked up. "I'll give you the bullet-point version. Have you heard of a seasonal resident named Peter Allardyce? Owns that giant gray house?" She pointed across the bay to the Allardyce residence.

Otter shook his head.

"Well, Mr. Allardyce was old, he was stingy, he was very attached to his dogs." Jocelyn provided a summary of events, keeping it as short as possible. ". . . So I'm currently living in that mansion, raising a litter of puppies, trying to get ready for a dog beauty pageant, and searching high and low for a nice fellow for Carmen here to have puppies with." She tugged Carmen's leash as the dog started whining and creeping across the picnic blanket. "Little girl, what is up with you today?"

"But what about the laundry?" Otter asked. "Can your mom handle all of it by herself?"

"She just had back surgery, so she still takes care of the scheduling and customer contact, but she can't do any physical labor. I bring as many towels and sheets as I can to the beach house and throw in load after load all evening. Luckily, Mr. Allardyce has a top-of-the-line washer and dryer."

"I'll bet."

"It's been an interesting summer."

"What about your dad?" Otter asked. "Is he in the area, too?"

Jocelyn had fielded that question so many times she should have been used to it, but she must have tensed a bit, because his expression immediately changed. "Sorry," he said.

"It's fine," she assured him. "It's just that—"

But before she could launch into her standard spiel about why her dad effectively didn't exist, Carmen made a break for it, segueing straight from a prone position to a full sprint toward the boardwalk. And she was *fast*.

"Whoa!" Jocelyn flinched as the leash snapped against her hand. But Carmen was already gone, galloping through sand castles, spraying sand left and right, dodging toddlers with the deftness of an NFL running back. Otter gave chase, calling Carmen's name as he ran. Jocelyn scrambled to her feet and tried to catch up, attempting to stay calm while offering bribes of treats at the top of her lungs. Hot sand burned against the soles of her feet as she ran.

Carmen skidded to a stop next to the reddish brown dog that Otter had pointed out earlier. She went into full canine meet-and-greet mode, sniffing and nosing the other dog all over.

"Sorry." Jocelyn gasped for breath as she snatched up the end of the leash. "I don't know what got into her."

The woman walking the brown dog smiled out from beneath the brim of a wide canvas sun hat. "Oh, that's Friday for you. He's a charmer. Dogs, children, adults—everybody loves him."

Otter seemed quite smitten, himself. "Friday? That's your name, buddy? What a good boy. Good dog."

Friday ignored Otter and sniffed Carmen right back. Carmen was vocalizing her delight with short, sharp yelps.

Jocelyn tilted her head and squinted at Friday. His big, boxy head was disproportionately large for the rest of his frame. "What kind of mix is he, do you think? German shepherd and . . . pit bull? Lab?"

"I have no idea, but I've heard it all," his owner said. "I've thought about doing one of those home DNA kits for dogs, but I'm too cheap to spend that kind of money on dog spit."

"You're not cheap, you're practical," Otter replied, and Jocelyn marveled at how those five simple words intensified her attraction to him. Here was a man who understood the value of money, who had worked hard for every dollar he spent.

Maybe her mother and Bree were right. Maybe what she really needed was a local boy.

Carmen was trying to play chase with her new BFF, and the leashes were tangling around everyone's legs. Jocelyn tipped sideways, bumping shoulders with Otter. He put his hand under her elbow to steady her, and it felt nice. No tingles or swooning or urges to rip his clothes off, but nice. Stable. An excellent start.

Jocelyn gave up on trying to calm Carmen. She handed her business card to Friday's owner. "Here's my e-mail. I'd love to get these two together for a playdate sometime."

The older woman winked. "I'll try to make room in his busy social calendar."

"Any availability you've got, she'll take it." Jocelyn started to disentangle Carmen's leash. "I've never seen her react to another dog this way."

"That dog is a player," Otter remarked as he and Jocelyn strolled toward the parking lot with picnic basket in hand and Carmen trotting along next to them. "Do you think he was born that way, or maybe he read a bunch of books on how to pick up purebreds at the beach?"

"I think it's his confidence that does it." Jocelyn tilted her face up to the warm afternoon sun. "He swaggers around like he just won best in show, and everyone treats him accordingly."

"Where did you park?" Otter asked as they stepped off the sand and onto asphalt.

"Oh, I walked from the other side of the bay." Jocelyn pointed out the Allardyce house again.

"I'll give you a ride back."

"Are you sure? It's a quick walk. Only a mile and a half or so."

"I'm sure." He took her hand for a moment and squeezed it before letting go. Behind them, Carmen sighed the sigh of a disgruntled teenager forced to separate from her boyfriend.

They made their way through the crowded parking lot until they located Otter's painstakingly restored 1960s Chevy pickup truck. He placed the picnic basket in the truck bed and started around the front to open the passenger door.

Jocelyn had to concede, this had been a solid, successful date. No awkward pauses, no social gaffes, no reason at all not to see him again. There might even be a kiss when he dropped her off at her car. Would he initiate? Should she? Would it be weird to have Carmen in the truck with them when they had their first kiss? The kiss that would . . . *change her life*?

"Holy crap." Otter stopped in his tracks on the far side of the truck. "Would you look at that."

Jocelyn peered over the truck bed to see what he was marveling at. About four spaces down, amid the late-model Hondas and Fords, was a sleek, navy blue coupe sparkling in the sunlight. She knew nothing about cars, but this one looked foreign, vintage, and very expensive.

"It's like one of James Bond's cars," she remarked.

"It is." Otter pivoted and started walking toward the car. "It's an Aston Martin DB5. James Bond drove this in *Thunderball* and *Goldfinger*, but his was silver. And it had an ejector seat. And a machine gun."

"Fancy." Jocelyn and Carmen joined Otter in admiring the sporty little car.

"This is one in a million." He sounded almost tearful with awe. "Somebody put a ton of work into restoring this. I'd love to see what's under the hood."

Jocelyn glanced at the license plate. "Florida. Somebody drove a very long way in this."

"Must have been the best road trip ever." Otter leaned in, his face mere inches from the side panels. "Look at this paint job."

Since he was so delighted, she tried to share his enthusiasm. "What's great about it? How can you tell it's a really good paint job?"

He glanced up at her, pleased with her interest—for about half a second. Then his gaze returned to the navy blue beauty. "See how spotless it is? How glossy? If you look at color consistency and the way the light reflects off it . . ."

And with that, he launched into a five-minute monologue about paint viscosity, wax quality, and the importance of the chemical composition of chromework. Jocelyn tried to follow him for the first minute, pretended to be following him for the next two minutes, but gave up entirely by the last two minutes, when Carmen started mouthing her fingers in an unsubtle attempt to spur her to action.

". . . And check out the hood vents!" Otter continued with a docent-level exposition of what appeared to be rectangular slits in the metal.

Jocelyn shifted her weight from foot to foot, looking enviously at the other beachgoers who were getting into their cars and leaving. Carmen paced and whined.

"Yeah, it's something, all right." Jocelyn took a step back toward Otter's truck. "But I guess we should get going."

"Do you mind if we stay a few more minutes?" He looked up at her with earnest blue eyes. "I'd love to talk to the owner. Ask a few questions about the detail work."

"Sure."

"Just a few minutes," he repeated. "If they don't show up, we'll go."

"No worries; we can wait." Jocelyn busied herself with playing with Carmen.

Ten more minutes dragged by, then fifteen, and Otter spoke not another word. He fawned, ogled, and admired while Jocelyn and Carmen engaged in round after round of tug-of-war with an old beach towel.

Finally, as Jocelyn was about to announce that she had to feed the dogs and would see herself home, Otter straightened up. "There he is!"

Jocelyn followed his gaze down the aisle of cars to see Liam in sunglasses and short sleeves, talking to a man she'd never seen. "Him? No, I know that guy, and this isn't his car. He has an SUV."

"The other guy." Otter jerked his chin to indicate the companion. "His keychain has the Aston Martin logo."

"It does?" Jocelyn squinted but couldn't make out anything beyond the glint of silver. "Damn, good eyes."

"When it comes to cars, I'm like a hawk." Otter stretched out his right hand and strode toward the guys. "Hey, is that your car?"

Jocelyn was too far away to hear the reply, but pleasantries and handshakes were exchanged. Then the three men started toward the car. Otter and the stranger were focused entirely on the car. Liam was focused on her.

"Well!" she said as Carmen launched herself into Liam's arms. "This isn't awkward at all."

chapter 19

"Good to see you." Liam gave Carmen a little shoulder rub, which resulted in yelps of joy. "I was going to call you tonight."

Jocelyn glanced over at Otter, who was popping the hood of the car with Liam's companion. Both men disappeared behind the glossy blue metal, exclaiming about horsepower and torque.

"You were?" she asked Liam.

"I've been thinking about you." He took off his sunglasses. The corners of his eyes crinkled when he smiled. "And wondering how the puppies are."

"They're great. The vet's been by every morning to check on them. I was trying to figure out what to name them."

"My father the control freak didn't leave a directive for that in his will?"

"Nope, so my mom did the honors: Pat Benatar, LeBron James, J. K. Rowling, and George Clooney."

Liam laughed. "How's Hester doing?"

Jocelyn was impressed he'd remembered Hester's name but didn't let on. "She's exhausted, but very patient." She tilted her head toward the automotive enthusiasts. "Who's your friend with the car?"

"That's my buddy Paul. He's the one that has the sailboat."

She waited for more details, but none appeared to be forthcoming. "Well, your buddy Paul and that seductive car of his have co-opted my date."

Liam regarded Otter with new interest. "Date, huh? How's it going?"

"It was going great until you and your shiny automotive siren came along." She took a step back and folded her arms. "I feel like I've been jilted mid-slow-dance at junior prom. He's not going to call me."

"He'll call you," Liam stated with total authority.

"You don't know that."

"Yeah, I do." He gave her a look she couldn't quite decipher.

Jocelyn, Carmen, and Liam waited for Paul and Otter to slam the hood and rejoin the rest of the world.

They waited. And waited. And waited.

Jocelyn clapped her hand to her forehead as the guys stopped talking about the engine and moved on to the muffler. "This is never going to end, is it?"

"Do you know how many parts there are to talk about under a car hood?" Liam asked.

Carmen started panting in the heat.

Jocelyn decided that since no one else was showing any social grace, she wasn't obligated to do so, either. She strolled over to the Aston Martin and rapped her knuckles against the hood. "Excuse me? Hi."

Otter's face, flushed with excitement, appeared. "Hi! Isn't this amazing?"

"Life-changing," she said. "But I've got to get back to feed the dogs and check on the puppies."

"Okay, okay, I'll drive you home." His gaze darted back to the automotive innards. "In one second."

"No worries, I'll walk." She tugged Carmen's leash. "Come on, girl."

"No, no, you're not walking, I'll drive you," Otter insisted. But he made no move to disengage from the car.

"It's totally fine, I promise. It's a beautiful day and Carmen wants to see if her new bestie is still by the boardwalk."

"I'll drive her." The way Liam said it was more of a declaration than a suggestion.

"For the last time." Jocelyn set her jaw. "I am walking."

"I can't let another man drive my date home," Otter protested.

Paul jingled his car keys. "Want to take her for a spin?"

Otter looked ready to break into a jig of joy. "Are you *serious*?"

"Come on." Paul opened the driver's-side door. "We'll only be a few minutes. Or, hey, do you guys want to take a turn, too?"

"No," Liam and Jocelyn said in unison.

"Suit yourselves. You don't know what you're missing." And with that, Paul and Otter piled into the little coupe and pulled out of the parking space with a dramatic squeal of tires.

Jocelyn had to laugh as she watched the car vroom toward Main Street. "I think that's the first time I've ever been dumped for an inanimate object."

Liam rested his hand on her back. "He'll call you."

She resisted the urge to lean into his touch. "We're never going to hear from either one of them again. They're driving off into the sunset and they're going to live happily ever after."

"Then we might as well get you home." Liam pointed out his black SUV, which was parked a few cars down.

"No way I'm getting into a car with you." She shook her head. "That's how people end up mysteriously disappeared until a bunch of hikers find the body eight years later in some marshy pine bluff."

He frowned at her. "A marshy pine bluff?"

"That's right. I read true crime. I know how this works."

"Yeah, but it's so detailed."

"You can't even imagine how vivid it is in my mind," she informed him. "I know the color of the hiker's backpack and everything."

"Blue?" he guessed.

"Red. With silver reflector strips."

He stared her down for a minute. "Let's start over. Jocelyn, Carmen, I'd be honored to see you home safely. Emphasis on safely."

"I really—"

"I know you can walk. If that's what you want to do, I'll walk with you."

"And you promise not to murder me in cold blood along the way?"

"Scout's honor."

"Fine, we can drive." She hurried toward the SUV. "I'm roasting."

He opened the driver's-side door and cranked the A/C on full blast, then turned to Carmen. "Does she like to ride in the back or the middle seat?"

"The middle seat, if you let her. Which I usually don't."

Liam opened the door for Carmen. "Make yourself at home."

Carmen turned her soulful eyes up at him. Jocelyn recognized this as the dog's patented "I'm so good, give me all the treats" expression.

"I'll give you dinner as soon as we get home," she told Carmen. "He doesn't have any treats."

As she buckled her seat belt, her phone rang.

"Well, well, well. It's my date." She gave Liam a nod of concession. "As you predicted."

"Told you so."

"You did, indeed." Jocelyn answered the phone with the cheeriest "hello" she could muster.

"Jocelyn?" Otter sounded both muffled and breathless, as though he were racing down an open highway at eighty miles an hour with the windows rolled down. Which he probably was.

"Hi," she said.

"Can you hear me?"

"I can hear you."

"Good, okay, I can hardly hear you. I wanted to make sure you got home okay."

"I'm en route," she assured him. "I'm not going to be a gruesome discovery for a hiker in a marshy pine field eight years from now."

"What?" Otter hollered.

"Nothing." She held the phone a few inches away from her ear. "Thanks for the picnic today. I had a really great time."

"Great! Me, too! Great!" Otter seemed to be in no hurry to hang up.

This was the part of the conversation where someone needed to buck up and ask for a second date, but she'd be damned if she'd do it. Not after she'd been blown off for a British pile of chrome.

"Okay, well . . ." She cleared her throat. "See you around."

"Definitely! We'll get together again soon!" he yelled.

"No, you won't," Liam said into the phone receiver.

"What?" Otter yelled again.

"Never mind," Jocelyn said.

"I've gotta go, but I had to say thank you. I've been talking to Paul, and guess what? He's interested in classic car restoration and storage. We might go into business one of these days!"

"I . . . ," was all Jocelyn could manage to choke out.

"Today was the best! My whole life is about to change!" And with that, Otter clicked off the line and drove straight toward his boyhood dream come true.

"This is an outrage," Jocelyn fumed.

Next to her, Liam was laughing. "I can't believe Paul. He's been talking about finding a business partner for years, but I didn't think he'd ever do it."

"Paul." Jocelyn narrowed her eyes. "Who is that guy, anyway? What is he doing in a town like this driving a car like that?"

"He's a commercial real estate developer who thinks that just because he has enough money to buy classic cars, he's qualified to fix them."

"Ah." She rolled her eyes. "How delightful for him."

"What are you mad about? I just saved you from a lifetime of listening to a guy named Otter yammer about horsepower."

"His name is Orton," she informed him with icy dignity. "And I'm mad because this date was supposed to change my life. Not his. Mine!"

"Says who?" Liam demanded.

"I have it on excellent authority that—wait, stop the car!" Jocelyn clutched her shoulder belt with both hands as she caught sight of a familiar blond figure down the block.

Liam hit the brakes, but not before reaching his hand into the backseat to steady Carmen. "What's up?"

"I'm not sure." Jocelyn lowered her sunglasses to get a better look at Krysten, who was strolling down the street with a man. Except *strolling* wasn't really the right term for what was happening. *Skulking* was more like it.

Liam glanced into his rearview mirror to check the traffic situation behind him. "Should I pull over and park?"

"Maybe." Jocelyn studied the body language of the two people skulking. "Do me a favor, okay? Look at that woman."

"Okay."

"See that guy she's with?"

"The one right next to her? Yes, I do see him."

Jocelyn ignored the heavy overtones of sarcasm. "Does she look like she's with him? You know, *with him* with him?"

"Uh . . ."

"Don't overthink it," she urged. "Just go with your gut. Take your best guess."

The only sound in the car was Carmen's panting as Liam and Jocelyn focused with laser intensity on the twosome in question.

"I have no idea," Liam finally said.

"Unhelpful."

"Who are these people?"

"I don't know who the guy is. That woman, though—she's a person of interest."

"To whom?" he asked drily.

"To Bree. She thinks she's cheating on her fiancé."

Liam put the SUV in gear and edged forward. "She's engaged?"

"I went to her bridal shower myself."

"They do look a little . . ." Liam trailed off.

"Flirty?" Jocelyn supplied. "Cozy? Illicit?"

"Maybe he's her cousin," Liam suggested.

They exchanged dismayed glances as Krysten went up on tiptoe and kissed the man's cheek. Twice. And then his lips.

"I sincerely hope that's not her cousin," Jocelyn said. "Maybe Bree was right."

"They're going in." Liam sounded relieved as Krysten and her mystery companion ducked into a little gray cottage tucked at the end of the street. "We may never know the truth."

"Yes, we will." Jocelyn speed-dialed her best friend. "Pick up, pick up . . . oh good, you're there! Hey, I need you to come meet me right now."

Carmen whined in the backseat.

"Actually, could you please stop and grab some kibble and *then* meet us? We're by the corner of Third and Station. What's that? Who's 'we'? Um, you'll find out in a minute."

chapter 20

"This is a surprise," Bree said to Liam as she climbed into the backseat with a bag full of kibble in one hand and a giant cherry slushy in the other. "Last I saw, you two were sniping and giving each other the side eye."

"I won her over." Liam smiled at Jocelyn.

"Jury's still out," she shot back.

"What happened?" Bree demanded as she doled out handfuls of kibble to Carmen, who wolfed them down as though she'd been on the brink of starvation. "I thought you were on a date."

"Yeah, that didn't work out. Not for me, anyway."

Bree leaned into the front seat to confront Liam. "Did you crash her date?"

"Innocent bystander," he swore.

"My date ran off with his friend," Jocelyn explained. "Although I suspect he's just using him for his car."

"I'm so confused." Bree took a noisy slurp of slushy. "You want to run this whole thing by me again and speak English this time?"

"Maybe later. I called you down here for a very specific purpose." Jocelyn pointed out the tiny cottage where they'd last seen Krysten. "Watch that space."

"What am I watching for?"

Jocelyn summarized the situation. ". . . but we're not sure who the guy is or what's really going on."

"So I was *right*." Bree all but patted herself on the back. "You can apologize for doubting me any time now."

"Wait for the evidence," Jocelyn cautioned. "We can't jump to conclusions. No reason to get irrational."

"We're staking out a random stranger because of a palm-reading prediction," Liam said. "I'd say we passed irrational long ago."

"You're new here, so we won't hold that against you," Bree said. "But here's the real question: If this is a stakeout, shouldn't we have coffee and doughnuts?"

"It was very spontaneous." Jocelyn's stomach growled. "But I wouldn't say no to a doughnut."

"Focus, people." Liam made a chop-chop gesture on the steering wheel.

"I *am* focusing." Jocelyn stared at the cottage. They all did. "There's nothing to see."

"I'm afraid to ask," Liam said. "But if it does turn out that this woman is cheating on her boyfriend, what are you going to do about it?"

"We don't need to worry about that right now," Bree stated. "All we need to worry about is the fact that I was right and Miss Cynic Von Skepticism was wrong."

"We haven't established that yet," Jocelyn cautioned. "Hence, the stakeout."

Carmen woofed from the backseat.

"This is the least stealthy stakeout ever," Liam said.

"At least you're not from around here," Jocelyn said. "Your car isn't recognizable like mine or Bree's."

"Speaking of which, how much longer do you think you'll be in town?" Bree asked, ever so casually.

"I'm not sure," Liam said. "I've got a few things to take care of."

"Oh yeah? Like what kind of things?" Bree pressed.

"Would you stop?" Jocelyn admonished her friend.

"I'm just making small talk on the stakeout," Bree said.

"It's okay." Liam settled back against the tan leather seat. "She can ask."

"Damn right I can."

"I'll be asking the questions here," Jocelyn declared.

"Ask away," Liam said.

"Okay, so first of all, I want to know—"

"Shut up!" Bree cried. "Someone's coming out!"

And indeed, the screen door of the cottage opened. Krysten exited first, followed closely by the mystery man.

"Who is that guy?" Bree wondered.

"I don't know. I've never seen him before," Jocelyn said.

"He's nowhere near as handsome as Dan." Bree put down her drink and pressed her face up against the tinted window. "I bet he's not as smart, either." She had to be bruising her cheek from the pressure against the glass. "Krysten may look good in a pink headband, but she does not deserve a man like Dan. The nerve of her, cheating on him two weeks before their wedding!"

"Hold on." Liam called everybody to order. "We're sure they're cheating?"

The car fell silent again as they craned their necks and strained their eyes and watched the two silhouettes turn the corner and vanish from sight.

"I'm sure," Bree said.

"One hundred percent?" Liam asked.

"Ninety-nine point nine percent," Bree shot back.

"I don't like ninety-nine point nine." Jocelyn nibbled her lower lip. "I mean, they're obviously close, and she did give him a little kiss—you missed that part, Bree—but we'll never know with total certainty."

"We will if we stake out her house tonight," Bree said.

Liam started laughing.

"You know you want to," Bree urged.

"No, I don't," Jocelyn said. "I can think of literally hundreds of things I'd rather do tonight. And the dogs need me. My mom can't puppy-sit forever. Who's going to take care of them if I go to jail on a stalking charge?"

"Whoever the trustees name," Liam said.

"Ooh, someone's bitter," Bree sing-songed.

"Says the woman who's trying to frame the fiancée of her high school boyfriend for infidelity," Jocelyn interjected.

"It's not framing if it's factual," Liam said.

"You know what, Liam? I like you," Bree said.

"Is this what people do in Black Dog Bay?" Liam asked. "Drive around trying to incriminate each other?"

"Yes," Jocelyn confirmed. "We like to call it 'being neighborly.'"

"Stop chitchatting and put this thing in gear!" Bree commanded. "The suspects are getting away!"

Liam did as directed. Carmen hunkered down for a nap in the backseat. Jocelyn dialed her cell phone.

"Hi, Mom. Are you okay to stay with George Clooney and company for a few more hours? Bree's making me go on a stakeout against my will." She hung up with a sigh. "You'd think she'd ask a few follow-up questions, but she doesn't want to know."

"She doesn't need to ask questions," Bree said. "She knows I have excellent judgment."

"That's one way to look at it. Listen, I know we're on a high-stakes mission and all, but can we stop by the drive-through on our way?" Jocelyn asked. "I'm starving."

Bree shook her head. "You would make a terrible detective."

"Whatever. I'm thinking ahead."

"Drive-through it is." Liam got all the way to the intersection before the realization occurred. "But where's the nearest drive-through?"

"I can't believe you wouldn't let us get fries," Jocelyn said to Bree for the third time as they passed a pair of binoculars back and forth. "My stomach can tell the difference between fast food and gas station garbage."

"Detouring all the way to Rehoboth defeats the purpose of a drive-through, which is to save time," Bree retorted. "Don't act like you're too high and mighty for a week-old reheated burrito and bag of chips."

Jocelyn appealed to Liam. "It's your car. You're driving. Why didn't you overrule her?"

Liam's lips twitched as he gazed out onto the dark shadows obscuring Krysten's lawn. "She scares me."

Bree seemed delighted to hear this.

"Besides," he continued. "She's your best friend. If she doesn't like me, I'm screwed."

"He's a smart one," Bree said to Jocelyn. "You should hang on to him."

Jocelyn turned back to the house, which was entirely dark except for the flickering blue light of a television in a back room. "This is like the worst made-for-TV movie ever. Amateur sleuths with a score to settle, a palm reader in denial who's hoping to be reunited with her long-lost love . . ."

"And a dog," Liam added.

"Forget movie of the week, this could be a whole Netflix series." Jocelyn shifted in her seat. "How long do we have to stay out here?"

"As long as it takes to catch her in the act," Bree said.

"We may never catch her in the act," Jocelyn pointed out.

"Ye of little faith." Bree shucked off her jacket and made herself comfortable. "This dog is a seat hog. She's taking up two thirds of the backseat!"

"She's even worse with the bed."

"Well, go ahead and nap if you want," Bree said. "I'm in this for the long haul. I've had two cups of coffee and a will of iron. I'm wide awake 'til dawn."

"Is she out?" Jocelyn whispered forty-five minutes later, glancing into the shadows of the backseat, where Bree and Carmen were draped over one another in a somnolent turf war.

"She's out," Liam confirmed.

"I should have brought blankets and teddy bears." Jocelyn smiled at the naptime tableau. Then she turned her attention back to the house. "What do you think is going on in there?"

"I don't know." He reclined his seatback. "What I do know is that with a little landscaping and some fresh paint, maybe some HVAC renovations, this house would gain about thirty percent in value."

"How do you know that?" she asked. "It's pitch-black out. I can't even see what color the paint is now."

"Look at the neighborhood. Quiet and residential, but it's in a good location, close to the beach and close to downtown. This area's transitioning to a mix of local families and seasonal second homes. If you updated it just the right amount, you could make a decent profit."

"Flip or Flop: Stakeout Edition."

"Maybe this woman is cheating on her fiancé, maybe she's not." Liam shrugged. "But one thing is certain: She could do a lot with her house."

Jocelyn peered through the darkness at the little two-story saltbox. "The day I met Mr. Allardyce, he said something that sticks with me: *My dogs are better people than most people.*"

He inclined his head, listening.

"I thought he was just old and bitter—"

"You thought right."

"—but maybe he had a point. I mean, you'd never catch your dog cheating on you two weeks before your wedding."

"There are so many things wrong with that sentence, I don't know where to start."

"You know what I mean."

"Yeah, I do." They sat in silence for a few more minutes. Jocelyn knew something between them had shifted, but she wasn't sure what or when.

She tucked her hair behind her ear, keenly aware of the silence. "We should probably call it a night."

"Yeah."

"Unless you want to . . ."

He leaned toward her, and she saw the kiss coming. She could have turned her head or pulled away, but she didn't. She met him halfway with a soft slow brush of the lips.

She pulled away first. "We should go."

He started the car, gaze straight ahead and hands on the wheel. The drive back to town was tense and silent.

"What'd I miss?" Bree croaked as Jocelyn nudged her awake once they reached her driveway.

"Nothing. You're home."

Bree opened the side door and blinked at Liam and Jocelyn through the dim overhead light. "I definitely missed something."

"No, you didn't." Jocelyn made a shooing motion with her hands. "Good night."

"Well, what happened with Cheatergate? Do we have incriminating night-vision photos?"

"No."

"Then why did we leave our post?"

Jocelyn got out of the car, walked around to Bree's door, and hauled her friend out into the driveway. "Bye."

This roused Bree's suspicions enough to fully wake her up. "Something scandalous happened between you and Liam, didn't it?"

"I'll call you tomorrow."

"Ooh, this has gotta be good. You won't even look me in the face."

"So long, farewell, *auf Wiedersehen,* good night." Jocelyn strode back to the passenger seat and climbed in without another word. "Drive," she commanded Liam.

"Shouldn't I make sure she gets inside okay?"

They both looked out the windshield at Bree, who was too busy waving and making expressions of exaggerated bewilderment to bother with finding her key and letting herself in the house.

"She'll never go in as long as we're out here," Jocelyn said. "And there's a key hidden under the flowerpot, just in case."

Liam slowly backed out of the driveway, glancing back at Bree one last time to make sure she'd gotten the front door open and the hall light on. They made the rest of the drive to the beach house without speaking. When Liam turned into the long, circular drive, Carmen started whining.

"She knows she's home." As she said this, Jocelyn realized that she, too, felt as though she were coming home. Already. She'd become accustomed to a house full of designer furniture and bespoke linens in a matter of days. Could she really criticize the trust-fund babies who were surrounded by luxury their whole lives for acting a little oblivious and entitled?

"It was a pleasure staking out strangers with you," Liam said. "We'll have to do this again soon."

"Minus the strangers and staking out," Jocelyn said.

He put the car in park, took his hands off the steering wheel, and leaned toward her just an inch or two. "Friday night?"

"Oh." She blinked. "Are you asking me out?"

"Yes. Friday night?"

She leveled her gaze at him. "Nothing personal, but I think that's a terrible idea."

"You're probably right."

"It's going to be nothing but trouble."

He nodded. "Is that a no?"

She paused. "I'll think about it."

He reached for his door handle. "I'll walk you to the door."

"This was quite an adventure," Jocelyn said to Carmen once they were inside. "But there's an important life lesson here: Don't get involved with a guy who wants to litigate your house away from you." She leaned against the doorjamb, indulging in a moment of swoon. "Okay, maybe you can get *physically* involved with him, but not emotionally."

She refilled the water dish, checked on Hester and the puppies, and adjusted Rachel's blanket, which was slipping off the couch. Rachel refused to sleep in the guest room and insisted on the sofa. Jocelyn smiled when she realized her mother had little George Clooney snoozing away on her chest. For a woman who hated dogs, she was awfully buddy-buddy with the silver Lab.

Up in the master suite, alone in the dark, Jocelyn couldn't stop thinking about Liam. Maybe the son Mr. Allardyce never spoke to would end up being the very best part of the old man's legacy. Maybe the money he'd left behind could bring people together instead of driving them apart. Maybe this time, with this man, the pursuit of money wouldn't be the root of all evil. Jocelyn drifted off to sleep, full of longing and hope.

But all too soon, the sun came out . . . along with the process server.

chapter 21

The dogs started barking before the doorbell even rang. This gave Jocelyn time to roll out of bed, peer out the window, and spot the gray sedan in the driveway.

"What now?" she mumbled, pulling on a robe and sliding her feet into flip-flops as the doorbell chimed. She didn't admonish the dogs to quiet down. If someone was going to bother her at this hour with no advance notice, they could deal with a little canine caterwauling.

As she made her way down the stairs, she saw her mother poke her head out of the cocoon of blankets and pillows on the living room sofa.

"Go back to sleep, Mom. I'll handle it."

Rachel muttered something incoherent and settled back into the covers.

"Hello?" Jocelyn opened the door with undisguised impatience.

A balding man in khakis and a forest green polo shirt stood on the welcome mat. "Are you Jocelyn Hillier?"

"Yes." She ran a hand through her tangled hair. "And you are . . . ?"

He thrust a thick brown envelope into her hands. "You've been served."

"Served with what?" she asked, but he didn't answer. He just walked back to his car while she opened the envelope and sifted through the pile of documents.

She read as fast as she could, trying to make sense of all the legalese. She wasn't quite sure what this meant, but she knew who was behind it: Liam's name was, quite literally, writ large on every page.

And so, at the crack of dawn, tamping down panic and brimming with urgent questions, Jocelyn called the closest thing she could to an attorney.

"Look at that." Jocelyn jabbed her finger at the pile of papers. "Look at it!"

"I'm looking, I'm looking." Bree was reading as fast as she could, skimming each page before setting it aside.

"Who the hell does he think he is?"

"Well, from what I gather, he thinks he's Mr. Allardyce's biological son."

"So?"

"So he's saying he has more right to the house than you do."

"What about the dogs?" Jocelyn bit into a cream-filled doughnut.

Bree kept reading. "As far as I can see, there's no mention of the dogs in here."

Jocelyn stopped scarfing down pastry long enough to say, "That callous jackass."

Bree glanced up from the document. "I thought you'd be happy that he wasn't trying to take them from you."

"I am, but he doesn't even pretend to want them! It's all about money and revenge for him."

"Yes, but wouldn't it be worse if he tried to take the dogs just for spite?"

Jocelyn narrowed her eyes to a glare. "Whose side are you on?"

"Yours. Always. I'm just saying . . ." Bree trailed off as she saw Jocelyn's expression darken. "You know what? Never mind. Let's concentrate on his evildoing and keep the dogs out of it."

"Let's." Jocelyn topped off her third mug of high-octane coffee. "He can't do this, can he? I mean, he can't just rewrite the will because he feels like it."

"What's going on in there?" Rachel called from the other room.

"Nothing!" Bree and Jocelyn chorused.

"Uh-huh." Rachel sounded supremely dubious. "I'll deal with you two after I shower. George Clooney just peed on my shirt."

"Here, I'll get him." Jocelyn retrieved the warm little pup from the living room and placed him with his siblings in the mudroom.

Bree settled onto a leather padded stool at the breakfast bar and "accidentally" dropped a piece of her doughnut for Curtis. "Liam's probably banking on the legal precedents set for inheritance law and children. The law frowns on parents cutting their children out of the will entirely. If a will is drafted and doesn't mention children, it can be argued that it was an oversight."

"What, like Mr. Allardyce just *forgot* he had a son? He meant to leave the whole estate to him but it slipped his mind?"

Bree nodded. "If the will doesn't specifically say that a spouse or child is disinherited financially, they can argue it was a mistake or that the deceased was manipulated or tricked."

Jocelyn slumped over the counter as a sickening rush of doubt and dread settled into her stomach. "So he might have a case, then?"

"I honestly couldn't tell you." Bree tapped the legal papers. "That's why I have to go to law school."

They sat in silence for a few moments.

"He can't have this," Jocelyn said, surveying the glorious kitchen spread out before them. "No wonder he was all sweet and seductive last night. He was trying to soften me up so he could sucker punch me."

"Ah, yes." Bree perked up. "I was waiting for you to bring that up. Tell me *allll* about the sweet and seductive."

"We kissed a few times while you were sleeping. No big deal."

"No big deal," Bree repeated. "Then why is your face bright red?"

"Rage," Jocelyn said. "It's bright red with rage."

"Fair enough. But was it any good?"

"As good as it can be before you find out that the guy who's sharing your saliva is a lying, manipulative, low-down, dirty-dealing . . ."

Bree shivered. "Those guys are always the best at making out."

Jocelyn drew herself up into the primmest posture possible. "On some level, I feel sorry for him."

Bree's eyebrow quirked. "You do?"

"Not really. It's more like I want to tie him to the train tracks and laugh evilly while twirling my mustache." Jocelyn paused for another bite of doughnut. "But first I have to take Curtis to the dog show. One crisis at a time."

"I didn't realize you could show them."

"The handler and groomer are meeting us in Philadelphia. I'm just the chauffeur." Jocelyn nibbled the inside of her cheek. "I hope it goes okay. I've been so busy with Hester and the puppies that I've barely spent any one-on-one time with him this week."

"You've had a lot going on. I'm sure he'll be fine."

"We'll practice this morning." Jocelyn glanced one more time at the papers before shoving them into a kitchen drawer. "I can't obsess over these anymore. I have to be productive today, starting with about fourteen loads of laundry."

"I'll help you with that if you'll come help me later." Bree smiled brightly. "Deal?"

"Depends. What do you need help with?"

"Apparently, a bunch of renters had a spaghetti fight on their last night at the cottage on McMillan Road."

Jocelyn winced. "With or without red sauce?"

"With red sauce *and* meatballs."

"Ugh."

"I know." Bree scrunched up her nose. "So, you in?"

"For the girl who brings me crisis doughnuts at eight o'clock in the morning after a stakeout? You know I'm in."

"We finally made it, buddy." Jocelyn reached into the backseat and gave Curtis an ear scratch. "Better late than never."

Curtis, who had been whining and leaving nose prints all over the car windows since they departed Black Dog Bay more than two hours ago, started wagging his mighty tail. Jocelyn could feel the reverberation all the way through the driver's seat.

She texted Lois, the show handler, to announce their arrival and arrange a meeting place. Her phone chimed almost immediately with Lois's response: *FINALLY. Meet me at door 5. Right now.*

"Hmph." Jocelyn gathered up Curtis's leash and a duffel bag full of supplies. "I don't think I care for her tone."

Curtis leaned his full weight against the car door as if this might somehow hasten his exit.

"I'm going as fast as I can." She opened the door and Curtis practically barrel-rolled into the parking lot. "Dude, you need to dial it down before showtime. Pretend you're a professional."

But Curtis wasn't in a "professional" kind of mood. Goofy, charming, exuberant, yes. He pranced through the parking lot, stopping to greet every dog and person within radius of the leash, as though he were campaigning for mayor.

"Save it for after the competition." Jocelyn tugged on the leash. "Your handler is getting antsy."

Sure enough, Lois was pacing and muttering under the placard for door five. Curtis was thrilled to see her. He reared up on his hind legs, planted his front paws on the handler's shoulders, and gave her a shameless, slobbery dog kiss right on the lips.

"Off." Lois redirected him to a sitting position with a single hand signal.

"Sorry we're late." Jocelyn had started sweating from the stress and the pace. "I had to wait for the vet to come check on the puppies, and then Curtis needed like four potty breaks. Next time, I'll cut off his water supply an hour before we leave."

"You're late." Lois appeared to have gotten even more short-tempered and sharp-featured since the reading of Mr. Allardyce's will. "His ring time is in less than an hour, and he still needs to be groomed."

"I'm sorry," Jocelyn repeated. "I brought all his stuff. If there's anything I can do to help . . ."

"You've done enough. Mr. Allardyce would never have allowed this." Lois snatched the duffel bag and charged off with Curtis at her side.

Jocelyn tried to ignore the burn of shame settling into her chest. She distracted herself by admiring the huge variety of dogs: Great Danes and greyhounds, beagles and borzois, collies and Catahoula leopard dogs. The show took place in a huge, open convention center, portioned into individual competition rings with glorified baby gates. At first, all the dogs of each breed looked alike to her untrained eye, but upon closer inspection, she could see differences in the slope of a spine or the width of an ear.

There were a dozen poodles all strutting their stuff in a circle, and a group of collies in the next ring. Two rings over, basenjis marched around the judge with military precision and a palpable sense of competition.

Then there were the Labradors.

In the midst of all this purebred preening and swanning, the Labs were relegated to a corner ring because they simply could not contain their exuberance. Puppies and seniors alike bounced around, trying to befriend one another while their trainers struggled to keep them on task. The judge received countless licks while checking teeth.

Fifty minutes later, Curtis took the ring. His groomer had managed to work miracles, and the slightly scruffy black dog had been transformed into a sleek and regal show specimen. As he trotted into the competition, his eyes were shining, his coat was glossy, and his teeth were pearly white.

Lois, on the other hand, appeared a bit bedraggled. Her hair had started to come loose from the bun at the nape of her neck, and she had drops of what appeared to be drool on her light gray suit jacket. She held the end of the braided leather lead so tightly that her knuckles were white, and Jocelyn shuddered to imagine what shenanigans Curtis had been up to backstage.

The judge made his entrance, a ruddy-faced man in a tweed suit and red bow tie, and the Labs settled down as much as it was possible for Labs to settle down. One by one, the dogs stacked, striking a pose and allowing the judge to inspect their bone structure and musculature. Then each dog took a turn loping to the edge of the ring and back to show off his or her stride.

Curtis focused completely on Lois during their initial stack and stride. Jocelyn let out a sigh of relief, convinced that the class clown had finally decided to get serious. Then Lois pivoted and commanded Curtis to stack again. Curtis looked up at Lois with a playful canine grin, lunged up, planted his front paws on her shoulders, and gave her a "hug."

The crowd erupted into cheers and laughter. Even the judge cracked a smile. This was all Curtis needed to encourage him to do it again.

Delighted with his dead-last finish, Curtis took an unauthorized victory lap to soak up a final round of applause from the audience.

Lois stormed out of the ring and slapped Curtis's lead into Jocelyn's palm. "What have you been doing to this dog?"

"Nothing!"

"That's certainly obvious."

Jocelyn glanced down at Curtis, who all but winked back. "He was just fooling around. He loves attention."

"That's the problem. He was fooling around when he should have been working. Have you been training him at all?"

"We fit it in when we can, but Hester just had her puppies and I've been so busy with work and dealing with the move—"

"You should be running him through basic obedience commands every day."

"But—"

"You should be running them *all* through the basic commands every day."

"Okay, but here's the thing: I'm not a dog trainer."

Lois smirked. "I'm aware. Believe me, I'm aware."

"I've read a few books and watched a few YouTube videos, but I have no idea what a good stack looks like."

"Then figure it out," Lois snapped. "These dogs are your only job now."

Jocelyn's patience finally ran out. "You don't get to tell me what to do. I never did one single training session with Curtis the whole time I worked for Mr. Allardyce. That's not my job. My job is to love them and take them outside and make sure they have a happy, healthy life."

Lois's expression settled into grim lines. "Mr. Allardyce entrusted these dogs to you. Along with a great deal of money."

"Right. So maybe it was more important to him that they be well loved rather than perfectly trained."

"Mr. Allardyce liked to win. I'm Curtis's handler; it's my responsibility to make sure he continues to win." Lois threw up her hands. "I have no idea what Mr. Allardyce was thinking. He wanted champions. He wanted dogs that could carry on a legacy. You can't even get them to a show on time."

Jocelyn blinked. "Are you calling me an unfit parent?"

"Yes, if today is any indication."

Jocelyn turned on her heel. "Let's go, Curtis."

"You can walk away, but this is going to follow you," Lois called after her. "Everybody who's anybody in the dog world saw what happened today. It was a disgrace."

Jocelyn turned back around, spreading her hands in bewilderment. "What's the big deal, really? He had an off day. All dogs have off days."

"He was unprepared and unprofessional. He deserves better than the likes of you."

Jocelyn regarded Curtis, who was gazing up at her with mischief in his sparkling brown eyes. "He looks pretty happy to me."

"You don't know him like I do. I'm his handler." Lois fumed.

"Yeah, well, I'm his owner," Jocelyn retorted.

"You're his *guardian*. Big difference." Lois folded her arms. "An owner can't be replaced. A guardian can."

chapter 22

"Hmm." Murray Tumboldt, Esquire, adjusted his reading glasses and continued to pore over the documents on the polished mahogany desk. "Hmmm." He paused to turn a page. *"Hmmm."*

Jocelyn fidgeted in the tall wingback chair, her anxiety mounting by the moment. "*Hmmm* good or *hmmm* bad?"

The lawyer looked up at her and folded his hands. "What sort of relationship do you have with this man?"

"Liam?" Jocelyn blinked. "Well, I . . . We delivered a litter of puppies together. Had an impromptu stakeout. And we may have kissed once. We were supposed to be going on a date, but obviously that's off now."

His expression remained totally neutral. "Are you on speaking terms with him?"

"Yes. Although I doubt he'd want to hear what I'd have to say right now."

"As an attorney, let me give you some advice about attorneys:

We're expensive. We're argumentative. We tend to drag legal matters out for much longer than you think they should take."

"So . . . you're saying I should settle this with a fistfight behind the Whinery on Saturday night?"

The lawyer didn't smile. "I'm suggesting that you both might be more satisfied with the outcome if you could discuss terms face-to-face."

Jocelyn stopped fidgeting. "Do you think he has a case?"

"In strict accordance with the letter of the law, no, I do not. But if this case were to make it in front of a judge, I can't predict how it would go."

"That's not very reassuring."

"Judges have a lot of discretion when it comes to interpreting and applying legal precedent."

"Then what's the point of even having a will?" Jocelyn demanded. "Why even bother if everyone can challenge everything willy-nilly?" She heard the panic in her voice and tried to quell it. "Why go to the trouble of estate planning when your heirs are just going to have to roll the dice and hope the judge had his coffee that morning?"

The attorney's tone was patronizing. "It's not quite as capricious as that, although there was that one case during my clerkship . . . never mind, another story for another time. At any rate, my advice to parties in situations like this is always to try to work it out amicably first. Amicably and privately."

Jocelyn pounded the desktop. "He's being completely unreasonable!"

"Yes, he is." The lawyer continued to ooze condescension. "And I'm sure he's doing so on the advice of his legal advisers. It gives them room to negotiate."

Jocelyn sat back in the chair, crossed her legs, and stacked her hands one on top of the other. She'd worn a suit (her only suit) to this meeting so she would feel and look like a woman who commanded respect. Yelling and smacking the table wasn't the image she was going for.

"You're saying I should give him something even though he's entitled to nothing," she said crisply.

"I'm saying it's going to cost you dearly in terms of time and money if you don't." The lawyer glanced back down at the papers. "And as far as what he's entitled to, well . . . he *was* Mr. Allardyce's son. His only child, as far as we know."

He didn't say out loud that Jocelyn herself was entitled to nothing by virtue of blood or birth. He didn't have to. She received the message, loud and clear. And frankly, she was sick and tired of all the implications that she was lucky, that she was undeserving, that she had somehow cheated the system. When the going got tough, when Hester was in labor on a dark night full of hail, none of these lawyers or accountants had helped her out.

Only Liam had done that.

"He can't have the dogs," Jocelyn decreed. "Not the dogs and not the beach house. Those are my non-negotiables."

"That's more than reasonable," the lawyer said. "I'd consider offering him a settlement of cash or stock."

"So this is what it's like to be rich." Jocelyn smoothed the polyester of her suit skirt. "Paying people off so they'll go away."

"Happens all the time," the lawyer said.

"Fine. I'll ask him what he wants and get back to you."

"Excellent. Now, there's one other piece of business to discuss." The lawyer took off his glasses and put them aside.

Jocelyn tensed. "What?"

"I received a phone call this morning from an acquaintance of yours."

"Who?"

"Lois Gunther."

Jocelyn crossed and uncrossed her ankles. "Are you serious?"

"I'm afraid so. She expressed some concerns about the welfare of the dogs."

"This is ridiculous. Curtis—he's the big fluffy goofball—was clowning around at a conformation show this weekend."

"She said as much."

"And . . . ? She called you to tattle on me?"

He inclined his head. "I don't think we'll hear from her again—she was angry and annoyed, but not litigious. I think she just wanted you to know that she'd contacted me."

"What does she think you're going to do? Smack my hand with a ruler?"

"She wants to make sure the dogs are well looked after."

"They are. You're welcome to do a welfare check any time." Jocelyn collected the papers from the attorney's desk and prepared to go.

Mr. Tumboldt slid his spectacles back on. "You're leaving?"

"Yep. I don't need this right now. I need a strong drink, a hard-as-nails negotiator that isn't costing me hundreds of dollars per hour, and the human equivalent of a Magic 8-Ball."

"Where are you going to find all that?"

"My laundry room, obviously."

"She actually called your lawyer to complain?" Bree nudged Curtis with her foot until the big galoot got up from the pile of sheets and towels he was napping in. "What a crybaby."

"Lois has been mean-girling me since the day I met her." Jocelyn threw pillowcases into Mr. Allardyce's high-tech dryer as though she were pitching for the major leagues. "I've been nothing but nice to her, and she stabbed me in the back."

"Of course she did." Bree seemed almost amused at Jocelyn's dismay. "You should have expected that."

"But why? I saved Carmen's life." Jocelyn tossed in a dryer sheet and straightened up. "And Mr. Allardyce knew her forever. He liked her. He trusted her to help me with the dogs after he passed."

"But he left all his money to you," Bree pointed out. "What'd he give her?"

Jocelyn tried to remember the details from the reading of the will. "Three grand and some trophies, I think."

"I'd be pissed, too."

"Being pissed is one thing. Starting a custody battle is quite another."

"Eh, I wouldn't worry too much about her," Bree said. "I'd worry about Liam. He's going to be much harder to get rid of."

"Is that a professional legal opinion or a palm reader prediction?"

Bree stuck out her tongue. "Both. And it's worth exactly what you paid for it."

"Well, since you're handing out free advice, what do you suggest I do to get rid of him?"

Bree mulled this over. "That won't preclude me from ever passing the character and fitness requirements of the bar exam?"

"Yes."

"I'd listen to your attorney. Track the guy down and settle this like adults. Make him an offer he can't refuse."

"'Listen to your attorney,'" Jocelyn mimicked. "Ugh. You're already one of them."

"If only that were true." Bree sighed. "I could skip three years of studying and some serious student loan debt."

Jocelyn made a mental note to talk to her co-trustee about setting up a generous scholarship for first-generation law students. She would use it to honor their proud canine legacy: The George Clooney Allardyce Scholarship. Bree must've suspected something, because she shook her head while she measured out detergent.

"Don't even," Bree warned.

"You don't know what I'm thinking," Jocelyn said. "Do you? Stop reading my mind."

"I read hands, not minds, but I know you too well."

No need to press this issue now. There were still months before the semester started. Jocelyn steered the conversation back to the immediate crisis. "How am I supposed to make Liam an offer he can't refuse when I can't even find him? I have no idea where he's staying."

"There's two ways to go about this," Bree said. "Option one: You play sweet and dumb, wait for him to pick you up for your big date, and then tie him to a chair and make him listen."

"I'll take option two, whatever it is."

"Option two is, we run a full recon mission on him right now and show up unannounced at his doorstep. Surprise, you lawsuit-happy jackass!"

Jocelyn nodded. "I like it."

"Me, too." Bree put down the dryer sheets and dusted off her hands. "Go put your hair up and shimmy into your little black dress. We're going fishing for information at the busiest watering hole in Black Dog Bay."

chapter 23

Jocelyn had walked by the front door of the Whinery countless times over the past five years. She'd dropped off clean dish towels and napkins at the back entrance twice per week. The bar had become a haven for "heartbreak tourists." It was pink. It was loud. It was expensive. She never thought she'd actually sit down at the bar, order a drink, and chat up the vacationers.

And yet, here she was, dolled up in high-heeled sandals and a dress, powdered and perfumed and accepting a pink champagne cocktail from the owner and head bartender, a petite ball of energy named Cammie.

As she and Bree clinked glasses, Jocelyn shot a glance of censure at the bubbly. "We're getting soft."

"If we're going soft, we might as well go all the way," was Bree's response. "This is the good stuff. Taste it. Mmmm."

The sparkling wine was effervescent, Jocelyn had to admit. Light and lacy and delicate, this put every other cocktail she'd ever had to shame. "Well, that's just great. Now I'm ruined for all other drinks."

"You're officially a spoiled rich girl, like in that Hall and Oates song. Embrace it," Bree urged.

They glanced around at the late-afternoon crowd, nearly all of whom were well-heeled women from out of town. The Whinery was a stop along the way for most of these people. They wouldn't stay in Black Dog Bay once the weather turned gray and blustery. These women had other lives, other destinations. But the one thing everybody did in a place like this—a breakup bar full of sympathetic strangers—was talk.

Jocelyn propped her elbow on the bar top and leaned in to catch Cammie's attention. "I feel like I should be wearing a trench coat and a fedora, because we're here to do a little PI work."

"You want information?" Cammie grinned. "Let me tell you, you came to the right place. We've got it all: rumors, gossip, scuttlebutt, innuendo."

Bree looked enchanted. "I'm going to come here more often."

"I'm looking for a guy named Liam," Jocelyn started. "Tall, dark, handsome, likes dogs . . ."

"Aren't we *all* looking for a guy like that?" The woman seated on Jocelyn's right sighed wistfully and raised her glass.

"Let me finish. In addition to tall, dark, and handsome, he's also manipulative, money-hungry, and litigious. Very litigious."

The woman lowered her glass. "Ugh. Just like my ex. Never mind."

"He's staying somewhere nearby, but I've called the bed-and-breakfasts and the local hotels, and they deny any knowledge of him." Jocelyn had to raise her voice to be heard over the Adele ballad on the sound system. "I was hoping somebody here might have a hot tip on where to find him."

Cammie didn't ask any questions or offer any opinions. This clearly wasn't her first encounter with a patron on a search-and-destroy mission. She wiped down the shiny metal bar top with a pink dish towel, clocked the new customer that had just pulled up a stool on the far end of the bar, and excused herself. "I'll ask around and get back to you. Give me ten minutes."

"This is the best." Bree started dancing in her chair as an upbeat pop song came on. "Sipping champs while gathering intel. Very *Casablanca*."

"I know. Hopefully, someone will . . ." Jocelyn trailed off as she noticed a couple cozied up together in the corner. She could only see the backs of their heads, backlit by the sun streaming in through the plate glass window, but she knew.

"Joss." Bree snapped her fingers. "Hey. You okay?"

The sweet fizz of champagne turned sour on Jocelyn's tongue.

Bree followed her gaze, confused. "What are we looking at?"

And then he turned around.

"Oh crap." Bree smacked her palm down on the bar. "Two shots of tequila, stat!"

"Shush." Jocelyn pressed her hand over Bree's, but it was too late. They'd been spotted. With an easy grace honed by years of small talk at charity balls and golf tournaments, Christopher Cantor III rose to his feet, offered his hand to his female companion, and headed straight for Jocelyn.

"Kill me," Jocelyn whispered to her best friend. "If you've ever cared about me at all, break your glass and use the shards to slash my jugular."

"If I'm slashing jugulars, it won't be yours," Bree hissed back.

Her heels were too high to make a run for it, so Jocelyn had to stay in her seat, arranging what she hoped was a smile on her face and watching the man she'd hoped to marry rest his hand on the small of another woman's back.

"Jocelyn. Bree. What a pleasant surprise." Chris's smile looked warm and genuine. When neither responded, he continued, "Fun place, huh?"

Bree gave him a look more cutting than any glass shard and turned her back on him. He flinched for a fraction of a second, then focused all his attention on Jocelyn. "You look great. Wearing your favorite dress, I see."

"It's my only dress," she said. "Because, you know. I'm working class and all."

He didn't miss a beat. "This is Alice."

Jocelyn stared at the pale, slender young woman with wavy dark hair tied back with a white ribbon. Alice looked like someone you'd see in the pages of a Saks Fifth Avenue catalog, all silk scarves and porcelain skin. A hundred bucks said that this lady had never once mussed her cuticles by digging up a septic tank.

"We've met." Alice smiled, revealing even white teeth that matched her tasteful pearl earrings. "At the country club a few months ago, remember?"

Jocelyn glanced at Chris, who was suddenly absorbed in reading the cocktail specials listed on the chalkboard above the bar. "No, I'm sorry. I don't." She had met so many well-heeled WASPs with Chris at that club that by this point, they were interchangeable.

"I'm a friend of Fiona's. She and I went to college together."

As the shock started to wear off, Jocelyn realized that beneath the modest linen shift dress, Alice was stacked. Like, surgically enhanced stacked.

"And then I went to grad school with Chris and Fiona's cousin."

Chris beamed with pride. "She's getting her master's in French literature."

And it all made sense. The slow emotional frostbite, the revelation that she'd never finished college, the hit-and-run breakup. Chris had found the woman of his *and* his family's dreams: a Playboy Bunny with family money and an advanced degree.

Alice's smile flickered and she turned to Chris for support. He cleared his throat. "We were just—"

"Bye." Jocelyn sat back down, shoulder to shoulder with Bree. She prayed that he would go away, that he would have the common sense and common decency to get out of here without trying to assuage his conscience or force her to be friends.

And he did. Jocelyn stared straight ahead for two minutes, her hands shaking, until Bree gave the all clear.

"They're gone." Bree wrinkled her nose in disgust. "As they should be. Who takes their new prospect to a breakup bar? I thought he knew basic etiquette."

Jocelyn gulped in air, struggling to contain the shame and sadness flooding through her. "Well. That answers some questions."

"I give them two weeks," Bree said. "Tops."

"They'll be together a lot longer than that," Jocelyn predicted. "He'll take her to Paris and everywhere else. Didn't you hear? She's a friend of Fiona's who's studying French."

"Speaking of Fiona, I thought she was in your corner. Has she reached out to you since the breakup?"

"Radio silence."

Bree exhaled in disgust. "I hope they do stay together forever and make each other miserable."

"I'm so stupid." Jocelyn set her jaw, refusing to cry. "I should have known this was coming."

"You dodged a bullet," Bree said. "Did you really want to spend the whole rest of your life wearing twinsets and nibbling watercress sandwiches with the crusts cut off at country club luncheons?"

"They don't know what they're missing." Jocelyn surprised herself by starting to laugh. "Alice and Fiona are never going to go out with an auto mechanic named Otter. They're never going to see anyone's future from looking at their palm. They're never going to clean up dirty laundry and scrub down the walls after a bunch of tourists have a spaghetti fight."

"And for that, they deserve our pity."

"All right, here's the scoop." Cammie returned, pen and pad in hand. "According to the lady in the red tank top over there, Liam is staying at a private house out by the nature preserve."

"Whose house?" Jocelyn asked.

"I'm not sure; I'm still kind of new in town. But I can give you directions and a detailed description of the property."

"You can?" Jocelyn sat back, a bit startled. "Aren't you worried that I'll, like, lie in wait or vandalize his car or something?"

Cammie crossed her arms and gave Jocelyn an appraising look. "Will you?"

"No. But you don't know that."

"You wash my dish towels every week—I'm willing to give you the benefit of the doubt. Besides, I figure that in a town as small as this one, where everyone talks as much as everyone does, you're going to track the guy down sooner or later, regardless of whether I help you."

"Absolutely." Jocelyn put her champagne flute down.

"Hang on, that reminds me." Bree fished her phone out of her bag. "As long as we're tracking guys down, would you mind if I made the rounds real quick and ask if anyone can ID this perp?"

Jocelyn craned her neck to catch a glimpse of the picture on the phone screen. A blurry image of a masculine stranger came into view. "Oh no. Is that from the other night?"

"Sure is." Bree seemed pleased that she'd had the presence of mind to take photos of Krysten and the mystery man. "Be right back." She slid off her stool and headed for the nearest bevy of boozed-up tourists. "Hi, guys! Can you help a girl out?"

Jocelyn glanced at Cammie. "Aren't you going to ask what that's about?"

"No way. The first rule of owning a bar is, don't ask the question if you don't want to hear the answer."

"Wise." Jocelyn abandoned her champagne with great regret. "I better not finish that; I have to drive out to the nature preserve." She tapped Bree on the shoulder as she started for the door. "I'm going to make Liam an offer he can't refuse."

"Have fun!" Bree made a phone with her thumb and pinkie. "If you need any help hiding the body, you know who to call."

"Good luck ID'ing your perp."

"I don't need luck; I've got networking skills like you wouldn't believe." Bree gave her a look of warning. "Have fun with your arch-enemy. But not too much fun."

chapter 24

Jocelyn located the small stone cottage easily enough. Nestled on the outskirts of the nature preserve, the home offered views of the forest, the meadow, and the edge of the golf course beyond. She could see the golden square of a window illuminated on the far side of the house. It was so peaceful here, with nothing to disturb the silence but the crickets and the rustle of the wind through the grass.

Until now.

She parked her car and loped up the steps to the porch. Her knock began with a few perfunctory raps on the door, then progressed to closed-fist hammering that would befit a SWAT team leader about to break out the battering ram.

"Liam!" *Pound, pound, pound.* "I know you're in there!"

A second window lit up as the hall light came on.

"Open up!" *Bam, bam, bam.* "You can run but you can't hide!"

She heard the click of the lock and a moment later, the front door swung inward to reveal Liam, who wore a gray Florida State T-shirt, maroon boxers, and an expression of evident annoyance.

"What?"

"Put on some pants, 'cause you have company." She barged past him, into the foyer, which was sparsely furnished with a mix of IKEA and World Market wares. Generic watercolor seascapes hung on the wall, and she could detect the faint trace of Windex in the air. Rental houses all looked and smelled the same after a while.

He closed the door behind her. "Would you like a drink?"

"No, I would not. What I would like is for you to pack up your stuff and get the hell out of my town. Oh, but first, give me back the cuff links."

He continued as though she hadn't spoken. "Water? Wine? Beer?"

"The time for social pleasantries has passed." Her high heels clicked on the rough-hewn wooden floor as she paced the perimeter of the foyer.

He nodded, annoyingly agreeable. "Okay, but before we give up on social pleasantries, you look great."

"Cuff links, bruh." She flung out her hand, palm up. "Give 'em here."

"I assume you're referring to my father's cuff links? The ones you insisted I help myself to?"

"Yes."

He shrugged. "You can't have those back. It's too late."

"Guess what? You don't get to decide what's too late and what's not."

His expression was totally impassive. "I already sold them."

This brought her up short. "You *pawned* your dead father's cuff links?"

"Of course not." Liam finally looked disgruntled. "I'd get pennies on the dollar at a pawn shop. I researched their value and consigned them with a reputable estate jeweler in New York. They were solid gold Cartier. Sold like that." He snapped his fingers.

"How did you manage that when you were all up in my business every day here?"

He shrugged. "The Internet and FedEx."

She stared at him. "How could you just . . . sell them?"

"I told you. It was easy."

"There's something seriously wrong with you."

He inclined his head, conceding the point.

She stopped trying to appeal to his sentimental side and got down to business. "What do you want with my house?"

"The dogs' house?" he said pointedly. "I want to gut it, renovate it, and sell it."

"Why?"

"It's a huge lot. Depending on the zoning permit, I might be able to rebuild two smaller houses instead of just one."

"So this is one hundred percent about money?"

"Yes. I have a time-sensitive investment opportunity I want to move on." He looked so detached, so pragmatic, that she believed him. What she didn't believe was that he was telling her the whole story.

"It's your father's house. Currently occupied by the woman you're trying to date."

"I'm aware."

"The dating is never going to happen now, by the way."

"That's too bad. Whatever goes on between us has nothing to do with the house." Her incredulity must have shown on her face, because he continued. "The lawsuit is business. It's nothing personal."

"It's everything personal! It's where I live, where I sleep, where I raise the dogs!" She wanted to shake him. "What happened to the guy who delivered the puppies with me in the middle of the night?"

"I'm still that guy." But his expression shifted slightly. "Again, that was personal. The house is business."

Jocelyn remembered the words of her lawyer and her lawyer-to-be best friend. "Then let's talk business. That's the reason I'm here."

His smile turned cynical. "I was wondering."

"I don't want a long, bitter, expensive legal fight." She matched his detached demeanor. "And neither do you."

"Go on."

"I understand that in your mind, you feel like you have some claim to the house. Just to be clear, you don't, but I understand why you might feel that way."

"Very empathetic of you."

"Here's what I'm proposing: You give up this ridiculous—and ultimately futile, I might add—attempt to get the house, and I'll make it worth your while."

He shook his head. "You don't have enough to make it worth my while."

"A hundred grand." She held her breath. She was taking a risk by coming out with her maximum and final offer, but she sensed that trying to finesse him with a protracted negotiation would be a waste of time.

"No deal." Liam shook his head. "The house is worth way more than that."

"Think of what you'll save in legal fees," she said.

"I am, and it's not going to make up for the value of the house."

"A hundred grand is on the table," she repeated. "Take it or leave it."

"Leave it." He didn't even hesitate.

"You should take it," she advised. "Because you're going to lose that lawsuit."

"You sure about that?"

"Positive."

"Then why are you offering to settle?"

She took a slow, measured breath. "Because, unlike you, I have a heart. I care about things other than money."

"Easy to say when you've got never-ending cash flow and a multimillion-dollar beach house." He turned and walked toward the kitchen. "Come on."

She stood her ground. "Where are you going?"

"I'm getting you a drink and making you some fries." He pulled out a padded stool by the side of the granite-topped kitchen island. "Do you like red or white wine?"

She laughed at his temerity. "I'm not sitting down to share a bottle of wine with you. Let me be clear: I don't clink glasses and eat fries with people who are trying to take my dogs and get me evicted. I don't care how good-looking you are. I don't care if you can cook." She pulled the errant strap of her cocktail dress up on her shoulder.

"Then let's get serious." Liam rounded the granite island with newfound intensity. "You want to make a deal? Let's do it. No threats, no lawyers, no falsified reports to the cops about stolen cuff links."

"Finally." Jocelyn put one hand on her hip. "What's your price?"

He moved in closer, so close she could feel the heat from his skin on her bare arm.

"Don't." She shook off his hand. "You're not going to charm me into giving away my beach house. You're not James Bond."

"If I were James Bond, I wouldn't be charming you; I'd be seducing you."

She lifted her chin. "Well, if you were James Bond, I'd be the deadly sexy double agent, and *I'd* seduce *you* into dropping your claim."

He looked intrigued.

"This whole night was a waste of my time and makeup." She strode to the door and flung it open. "I'll see you in court."

chapter 25

"Here's a hypothetical," Jocelyn said to Bree as they walked the dogs down the shoreline the next afternoon.

Bree winced. "Oh no."

"Let's say that you're my real lawyer."

"I thank God every day that I'm not."

"But let's just imagine that you are. And let's say that I'm fighting a lawsuit brought by a hot but contentious man."

"Uh-huh."

"And let's say that I go over to the hot but contentious man's house to make him a settlement offer. And let's further imagine—"

Bree clapped her hand over her eyes. "Oh *no*."

"That I ended up, um, thinking impure thoughts about him. And there might have been a little bit of accidental touching. Would I be obligated to tell you about it?"

"Yes," Bree answered immediately. "Every gory, graphic detail."

"No, I mean legally. Do I have to tell my lawyer about this kind of conflict of interest?"

"I can't believe this!" Bree started hopping up and down in consternation. "Why would you have impure thoughts about a man who's trying to steal your whole life out from under you?"

"Well. He looks good in boxers, and apparently, he cooks."

"Is he dropping the lawsuit?" Bree demanded.

"Um . . ."

"What the hell, Joss? Don't lose your mind, your heart, your dogs, your house, and your cash flow over a bulge in boxers."

"That's not very nice," Jocelyn muttered.

Bree looked heavenward for divine intervention. "You are forbidden to see him again, do you hear me? I am putting my foot down."

As if punctuating Bree's sentence, Jocelyn's phone dinged.

"Who's texting you?" Bree held out her hand. "Is it him? Hand it over."

"You can't take my phone," Jocelyn countered. "You have no authority."

"Oh yeah? Well then, how about I tell your mother what you just said?"

Jocelyn felt the blood drain from her face.

But Bree wasn't finished. "Or maybe I'll tell my grandmother."

"Don't tell them," Jocelyn begged. "I'm not going to see him again."

"You better not. If you do, I will know. And then the wrath of your mother and my grandmother will rain down." Bree pursed her lips. "And I'm still waiting for your phone."

Carmen chose that moment to bolt, yanking so hard on the leash that her thin leather collar snapped. She dashed toward a nearby cluster of cars parked along the sand. Jocelyn followed the trajectory of the dog's run and knew exactly where she was headed.

A familiar reddish brown dog was clambering out of a Subaru parked by a trio of pine trees.

"Be right back," Jocelyn told Bree as she dashed after Carmen.

"You need to get a better leash for your dog," Friday's owner remarked when Jocelyn caught up with Carmen, who was nuzzling and licking her long-lost love's face.

"It was the collar this time, not the leash." Jocelyn leaned over, trying to catch her breath. "I'll have to get a replacement made from titanium mesh."

"She's quite determined, isn't she?" The older woman, again wearing her sun hat, patted Carmen's head.

"She's a desperado."

Friday's owner seemed pleased by this description. "Well, as long as they're both here together, why not let them play?"

Because this dog is only supposed to associate with upper-crust, aristocratic purebreds and her previous owner would come back from the dead to haunt me if he knew that his pampered little princess was palling around with a roughneck with no papers? "Sure, why not?"

"This is Friday," Jocelyn announced to Bree as the dogs and their human chaperones made their way down the sand dunes. "And this is Friday's owner—what is your actual name?"

"Violet Kilgore." She offered a handshake to Bree. "I've been coming here every summer since I was twenty-two."

"I'm Bree." Bree obliged the handshake after a moment of reluctance. "I've lived here all my life."

"Every year I rent the same house by the point." Violet pointed to the edge of the bay. "You must love living by the beach all year round."

"I live inland," Bree said. "On the other side of town. Most of the locals can't afford an ocean view anymore."

"What about you?" Violet asked Jocelyn. "Do you live nearby?"

"Right there." Jocelyn jerked her thumb in the direction of the Allardyce mansion.

And with that, Violet stopped talking to Bree and addressed herself only to Jocelyn, a phenomenon Jocelyn had come to think of as "The Tunnel Vi$ion Effect": When a new acquaintance found out you had tons of money, other people became invisible.

"How long have you lived here?" Violet asked.

Jocelyn glanced at Bree, who was rolling her eyes. "Oh, not that long."

"And what is it you do for work, dear?"

Jocelyn smiled. "I'm an entrepreneur. Run my own business."

Next to her, Bree perked up. "She's brilliant and so resourceful."

"My goodness." Violet sounded awed. "Are you in tech? The Internet and whatnot?"

"No, I got my start in the lifestyle and hospitality sector," Jocelyn said. "I saw some needs not being met, and I filled the gaps."

"And what about the young man you were with at the beach the other day?" Social boundaries were not something Violet seemed to be very familiar with. "Is he an entrepreneur, too?"

"Oh, him?" Jocelyn scoffed. "No, he's just my kept man."

Violet's brow furrowed. "Pardon?"

"He's a hottie, isn't he? Abs of steel." Jocelyn winked. "And a surprisingly good conversationalist. I gave him a subscription to the *Wall Street Journal* so he could keep up at the breakfast table."

"Oh my." Violet's voice quavered. "If you'll excuse me, I . . . I have to . . ." She drifted away, pretending to fiddle with her cell phone.

Bree started cracking up. "Lifestyle and hospitality. You're the next Martha Stewart."

"It could happen," Jocelyn assured her. "Martha Stewart has dogs. Chow chows, I think."

"Speaking of dogs, look." Bree nodded over at the sandy bluff, where Carmen and Friday were capering. "They're in love. The show dog and the pound puppy. It's very *Lady and the Tramp*."

"Except she's not supposed to fall in love with a mutt. The last romantic prospect she met was European nobility."

"No wonder she's having a summer fling with a bad boy," Bree said. "It's very *Dirty Dancing*."

"This is never going to go anywhere. The relationship is doomed." Jocelyn watched the dogs frolicking. "She's supposed to get knocked up and have a bunch of puppies with another show-quality Lab. That's literally her job. Plus, he's neutered."

Bree clasped her hands to her heart. "It's very *The Sun Also Rises*."

"That's it—we're not friends anymore."

"You should be happy that she found her soul mate," Bree said. "They're obviously meant to be together. Is it the end of the world if she doesn't breed?"

"Listen, I'm already in trouble with Lois for not taking this stuff seriously enough. If I let Carmen waste her fertility on a sterilized shelter mutt, she'll probably kill me with her bare hands."

"Fine, then what about IVF?" Bree asked. "Shell out a few bucks on more frozen dog sperm."

"The vet said if it hasn't worked by now, it's probably never going to work. I need to find another Lab to make her forget about Friday. A Lab with champion lines and virile, nonfrozen sperm." Jocelyn watched the pair of pups, who were literally rolling around in the sand together.

"I've got it." Bree snapped her fingers. "You set up a steamy, no-strings-attached liaison with a good-looking Labrador she'll never see again. Then she and her beloved can raise the puppies together. Like that Heart song from the eighties. She's like Nancy Wilson and—"

Jocelyn held up her palm. "Stop talking."

Bree grudgingly obliged as Violet approached them again.

Violet looked directly—and solely—at Jocelyn and stated, "I've got to run, but I'd love to arrange another time to meet up with the dogs. How does tomorrow morning work for you?"

"That should be fine," Jocelyn said. "Right here? Ten o'clock?"

"Assuming you've finished your shareholder meeting," Bree cautioned.

"I'll wrap that up in plenty of time." Jocelyn beamed. "After all, my dogs are always my priority."

"I completely agree," Violet said. "Friday should get to spend as much time as possible with his new friend before we leave for home."

"And home is where?" Jocelyn asked.

"Just north of Chicago."

"And you're leaving when?"

"Next week." Violet clapped her hands until Friday trotted over, his tongue lolling out of his mouth. "See you soon!"

"Oh no." Jocelyn regarded Carmen with sympathy. "They'll never see each other again. She'll be heartbroken."

"See? It's totally *Dirty Dancing*."

"Yeah, well, nobody puts Carmen in a corner."

chapter 26

After a whirlwind weekend of late-night stakeouts, early-morning dog shows, legal wrangling, and boxer bulges, Jocelyn was ready to get back to real life. Saturday morning was checkout time for most of the local rental properties, which meant she had a metric ton of laundry to pick up and process. Plus a prescription run for her mother, a vet checkup for Hester and the puppies, and a trip to the grocery store. Jocelyn always made the drive to the supermarket in Bethany Beach because the local grocery, a small emporium by the boardwalk, carried fresh, organic, artisan foods at obscenely high prices. No matter how good her cash flow situation was, Jocelyn would never be able to justify spending what used to be an hour's wage on a single jar of jam.

By the time she finished her errands and was leaving the grocery store, it was nearly three o'clock. She was wheeling her shopping cart across the parking lot when a high, feminine voice called her name.

Bride-to-be Krysten waved from the next aisle of cars, hopping up and down to be seen over the row of minivans and coupes. "Jocelyn! Come here!"

Jocelyn cast a wary glance at her groceries, which included fresh fillets of sole and a carton of ice cream, but obliged. She threaded her way through the cars to find Krysten accompanied by Dan and another guy. Specifically, the guy they'd all been spying on the other night.

"You guys, this is one of the girls I've been telling you about." Krysten gestured to Jocelyn as though she were a newly acquired accessory.

"We've met," Dan reminded her.

"Oh right, at the shower," Krysten said.

"And also all the way through school." Jocelyn raised her hand in greeting to Dan. "We both know Bree."

Dan's eyes brightened a bit at the mention of Bree's name. "How's she doing? We didn't get a chance to catch up at the party."

"Well, of course not—she was the entertainment." Krysten giggled.

"She's great," Jocelyn said to Dan. "She's hoping to start law school in a few months."

"Oh yeah? Good for her. Where does she want to go?" he asked.

"Philadelphia." Jocelyn named the school, and Dan perked up even more.

"I'm going to be doing my fellowship at the hospital right near there. We should exchange contact information since we'll be neighbors."

"Bree was the palm reader at my shower," Krysten was telling her other male companion. "And Jocelyn was her assistant. They were amazing—everybody had such a good time. We totally want to hire you guys again. Maybe for my next book club meeting."

Jocelyn turned to face the guy she'd been surveilling. "Hi, I don't think we've met. I'm Jocelyn Hillier."

"Brian." His posture and body language were entirely different than the last time she'd seen him. He kept a measured, almost formal distance between himself and Krysten.

"Are you new in town?" Jocelyn asked. "Or just visiting?"

"I live near Lewes." Brian shifted his weight from foot to foot, looking everywhere but at Krysten. Jocelyn started to wonder if she had the wrong guy. Could this stiff, mild-mannered stick in the mud be the same hand-holding, lip-kissing canoodler she'd witnessed under the cover of darkness?

Jocelyn smiled cheerily. "And how do you know Dan and Krysten?"

Krysten looped one arm through Brian's and the other through Dan's, nearly blinding Jocelyn as her diamond ring gleamed in the sunlight. "Brian is our peer counselor."

Jocelyn nodded. "Oh, like a . . . What is that, exactly?"

"It's part of this thing we're doing through church," Krysten explained. "There's a whole class for couples who are engaged. Communication, conflict, stuff like that."

"Sounds like a good idea."

"And Brian here is the group leader." Krysten beamed. Dan nodded. Jocelyn felt one eyebrow inch upward.

"You're like a relationship counselor?" Jocelyn clarified.

Brian laughed. "I don't have any fancy degrees, but I do my best to help."

"He's too modest," Krysten gushed. "He's so smart and funny. He always has the best advice."

Dan's smile dimmed a few watts. Krysten must have sensed this, because she turned toward her fiancé and rested her hand on his cheek. "And what a great fiancé I've got to work with."

"You two are going to have a bright future together," Brian said a bit too heartily.

Jocelyn took in the arm linking and the gushing and the peer counseling for a minute and tried to imagine what good could possibly come from continuing this conversation. "Okay, well, I've got some frozen stuff I need to get home." She turned her shopping cart around and headed back toward her car.

"Okay, but before you go, I want to set up a time for book club!" Krysten called.

"We'll be in touch. Bye!" Jocelyn opened her trunk and started piling brown bags in. She slammed into her car, cranked up the air conditioner, dialed Bree, and drummed her fingers on the steering wheel as the phone rang and Bree's voice mail came on.

"Breaking news, Bree. The perp is the peer counselor. Call me back!"

When she made it back to the beach house, she had to park under the portico by the side door because there was an unfamiliar sedan blocking one end of the circular driveway.

"Again?" Jocelyn muttered as she cut the engine and started hauling groceries out of the trunk. "What now?"

As she was offering up a prayer that she wasn't about to be embroiled in yet another legal drama, a lilting female voice behind her called, "Let me help you with those."

Jocelyn turned around to see a lithe middle-aged woman in cowboy boots and a pristine white T-shirt striding toward her. She had no idea who this lady was, but the newcomer had a bouncy blond ponytail swinging out the back opening of her baseball cap and the kind of tan that only came from working all day, every day in the sun.

"I've got it," Jocelyn insisted. "I don't need any help."

"Too late." The woman wrestled a pair of bags out of Jocelyn's grip, beaming all the while. "Oh, you've got frozen food in here. Better get that inside before it melts."

"Yes, good point." Jocelyn seized the opportunity to slip inside and lock the doors behind her. "If you'll excuse me . . ."

The woman adjusted her grip, shifting both bags to her left hand so she could offer Jocelyn her right. "Honey, I am being so rude and I apologize. Here you are in a puddle of melting ice cream and I haven't even introduced myself."

"No worries." Jocelyn tried to grab all the remaining bags at once so she wouldn't have to come out here again. "I'll just be—"

"I'm Nora Sheridan." The woman paused as if waiting for Jocelyn to make some sort of acknowledgment. "You must be Jocelyn. Liam's told me so much about you."

Jocelyn almost dropped a bag of fresh peaches on the brick pavers. "You know Liam?"

Nora laughed, full and throaty. "You could say that. I'm his mother."

Jocelyn took another look at Nora, trying to reconcile the woman's warm, friendly vitality with Liam's guarded reserve. How could those two be from the same family? Her confusion must have shown on her face, because Nora laughed again. "I know, I look much too young to have a son his age."

"How often do you two talk?" Jocelyn asked.

"Not very often, these days. He spends most of his time ducking my calls and pretending he doesn't get my texts." Nora threw up one sun-weathered hand, which Jocelyn noticed was tipped with long, tapered, freshly manicured nails. "So I gave up on calling and decided to show up in person."

"You live nearby?"

"No, I do not. I just made the trip from Florida." Nora headed for the side door, still carrying the grocery bags. "Four hours in a plane and three more in a car just so I can try to talk sense into him." She leaned closer, confiding, "You might not know this yet, but he can be extremely stubborn."

"You don't say." Jocelyn unlocked the door and found herself inviting this stranger in cowboy boots into her home.

"Oh, you have dogs." Nora leaned over to pet the canine greeting committee. "These must be the famous Allardyce Labs."

"They're not famous for their manners." Jocelyn winced as Curtis licked Nora full on the face while Carmen tried to snatch the loaf of bread she'd just unpacked. "You've heard of Mr. Allardyce's Labs?"

Nora straightened up, her tone cooling. "I know everything there is to know about Mr. Allardyce."

Oh right. Since you were married to him and all. Jocelyn smote herself on the forehead. "Sorry, I wasn't thinking." If she couldn't imagine Nora and Liam in the same family, she *really* couldn't imagine Nora and Mr. Allardyce together.

"It's fine." Nora waved this away. "All that's in the past, thank God."

Jocelyn stashed the ice cream in the freezer and forced herself to ask the obvious question. "Are you here to file another lawsuit?"

"What? Good lord, no. I'm not the lawsuit type."

Jocelyn sagged against the counter in relief. "The world needs more people like you."

"No, I'm here to make Liam see reason. And if I can't, I'm hoping you can."

"You're going to have to be more specific," Jocelyn said. "What, exactly, would you like me to make him see reason about?"

"Hang on." Nora pulled out her cell phone and pulled up her contact list. She pressed the phone to her ear and held up her index finger while it rang.

Then her face lit up. "Oh, hello, dear. I'm so glad you finally picked up. Guess where I am?" She winked at Jocelyn.

"No . . . no . . . you're getting colder, dear . . . ice cold." Nora waited another few moments, then announced, "I'm standing in your father's old house with your new girlfriend." Nora's eyes widened. "No, I'm not kidding. She's a very gracious hostess, even though she had no idea who I am." Nora maintained the sweet, lilting tone, but there was an undernote of pure steel. "She has no idea why I'm here, does she?"

And with that, Nora ended the call and turned off her phone with evident satisfaction. "He'll be right over."

chapter 27

"Has he told you why he's doing all this?" Nora handed Jocelyn a glass of freshly squeezed, freshly spiked lemonade. "Anything about his family?"

"Not really." Jocelyn took a sip. The lemonade was refreshing, delicious, and strong enough to take the edge off what was becoming an increasingly weird day. "He's not big on giving long, newsy speeches about his motivations."

"That's my fault." Nora sounded proud. "When he was growing up, I always told him what my mother told me: Never complain, never explain."

"He definitely took it to heart."

"He took it too far this time, I think." Nora sat down on the stool next to Jocelyn's. "He's doing this for me. He thinks . . . Well, I guess he thinks he can use his father's house to give me my home back."

"He's not going to make this into a home," Jocelyn informed her.

"He's planning on gutting it, remodeling, and selling to the highest bidder."

"Oh, not this house. I'm talking about the ranch."

"The ranch?" Jocelyn glanced down at the well-worn cowboy boots that were such a stark contrast to the manicure and mascara. "Yeah, he mentioned that he grew up roaming the land with the cattle."

"Loved every minute of it."

"And you took care of the cows?"

"I did everything." Nora smiled. "Fixed the fence posts, dug out the water holes, branded the calves, kept the coyotes away."

"I can't even imagine," Jocelyn marveled. "How did you come to work at a cattle ranch in Florida, of all places?"

"Well, that's the thing." Nora's smile turned wistful. "I didn't always work as a farmhand at that ranch. Once upon a time, I owned it."

Jocelyn took another sip of lemonade. "What happened?"

"I married Peter Allardyce, that's what happened." Nora's smile faded entirely. "He could be very convincing when he wanted to be. A silver-tongued charmer."

Jocelyn tried to envision Mr. Allardyce as a silver-tongued charmer and failed miserably.

"I was very young," Nora said. "Just turned nineteen, and I thought I knew everything."

"What was he like?" Jocelyn had to know. "When he was younger?"

"Strong. Confident. Always knew what he wanted." Nora rolled her eyes. "And he wanted me. It was a whirlwind courtship, filled with drama. My parents warned me to stay away from him, so of course I ran off with him to Reno in the middle of the night after six weeks."

"Wow. That sounds . . ." Jocelyn tried to think of an appropriate adjective.

"Stupid? Reckless? Ten pounds of trouble in a one-pound bag? It was." The ice in Nora's glass clinked as she added an extra splash of vodka. "My parents always said he married me for my money, but I don't think that was it. Don't get me wrong—that man was tight with a dollar, but he did love me, I think. In the beginning." She sighed. "Then I came into the bulk of my trust. That's when things really went to hell."

"Money changes everything."

"It certainly changed me. I had gotten married so young . . . I went a little wild. He left me, but before he did, he convinced me to sell the ranch and give him the profits as a divorce settlement."

Jocelyn frowned. "Why would you do that?"

Nora cleared her throat. "When you're twenty, you have some misguided notions about love being more important than money." She clearly wasn't going to divulge any more details, so Jocelyn moved on.

"How old was Liam when you two separated?"

"He wasn't born yet. I was in my second trimester, I think."

"Mom?" Liam's voice boomed through the foyer and down the hall. "Jocelyn?"

"We're in here," Nora called back. "And you're too late—I already told her all of our deep, dark family secrets."

Liam strode into the kitchen looking both alarmed and annoyed. He surveyed the scene, taking in the pitcher and the vodka bottle and the ice cream that had somehow made its way out of the carton and into two dessert bowls in front of Jocelyn and Nora. "What the hell?"

"Hello to you, too, honey." Nora got up to give him a hug.

"Try knocking," Jocelyn advised. "This isn't your house."

Liam narrowed his eyes. "Yet."

"Oh my lord, would you stop with that?" Nora swatted him on the shoulder. "Leave this poor girl and her dogs alone."

Jocelyn nodded. "Listen to your mother."

"What are you doing here?" Liam demanded.

"What does it look like?" Nora released him from the bear hug and stood with her hands on her hips. "Drinking lemonade and waiting for you to come to your senses." She glanced at Jocelyn. "He's like a mule."

Jocelyn sipped and smiled, thoroughly enjoying the show.

"This isn't funny," Liam told her.

"I beg to differ." Jocelyn held up the pitcher. "Care for some lemonade? Your mother made it."

He shoved his hands in his pockets and glowered. "No."

"It's got booze in it."

"Yeah, okay." He opened the cabinet Jocelyn indicated and pulled out a glass.

"How many times have we been over this?" Nora exhorted. "This isn't worth it. Not the house, not the money. Nothing about your father is worth all this fighting and heartache."

"This isn't about him," Liam stated. "It's about you."

"And I am telling you to let this go," Nora said. "I don't need my child to fight my battles for me."

Liam paused to pet Curtis, who had sidled up next to him. "Couldn't you have told me this over the phone, Mom?"

"I could've if you would've returned any of my messages." Nora spooned up a bit of ice cream. "But since you wouldn't, I had to take time off work and come up here myself to talk sense into you." She rubbed her temples. "Why is this place so far away from an airport?"

"How's it going on the ranch?" Liam asked.

"Everything's fine." Nora shrugged. "I'm holding my own. The guy who owns the next ranch over isn't too pleased about a woman running the whole operation herself, but he'll have to get used to it."

Jocelyn leaned in. "How do you know he's not pleased?"

"Because last week when I was driving in from the main road, he stopped me at the gate and said, 'We don't like women ranchers.'"

"That seems pretty clear."

"And then, a couple of nights ago, I found a hatchet in one of my fence posts."

Liam all but spit out his lemonade. "What?"

"Relax, he's not going to do anything." Nora twirled a lock of her shiny, shampoo-commercial-worthy hair. "All those old grizzled guys are a bunch of bluster." She laughed. "Besides, that's why I keep a Smith and Wesson on the dash of my truck."

Jocelyn was starting to see where Liam got his grit and determination.

"You're kind of a badass," Jocelyn told Nora.

"You can take the 'kind of' out of that sentence." Nora placed one hand on Liam's arm. "I can take care of myself. Now. We can all move past this and enjoy a home-cooked dinner as soon as you promise me you'll stop meddling in your father's affairs."

"No." Liam remained resolute.

Nora blew out an exasperated breath. "Are you really going to make me fight with you in your dead father's kitchen? In front of your girlfriend?"

Liam took a moment, clearly contemplating the large number of problematic points in that question, and decided to blow right past it. "We can go fight somewhere else."

"I'm not his girlfriend," Jocelyn piped up.

"Of course, sweetie." Nora was too busy staring down her son to glance Jocelyn's way.

"I'm not going to give this up." Liam set his jaw. "I'm sorry if that upsets you."

"I don't need to steal someone else's property to get mine back." Nora turned off the sweetness and light entirely. "This house isn't mine and it isn't yours. We've got no claim to it."

"He bought it with money he took from you," Liam said. "How much did he get out of you before he left? Ballpark figure?"

"He got what I was willing to give him," Nora said in reply. "I didn't do what I should have done to protect myself. People tried to tell me, but I didn't want to hear it. It's my own fault I lost the ranch."

"He sold it without your permission," Liam countered.

"Which he was only able to do because I let him talk me into putting him on the deed." Nora shook her head at Jocelyn.

"How much did he pay in child support over the years?" Liam demanded.

"He would have paid if I'd asked him to."

"You shouldn't have to ask! It was his responsibility!" Liam said.

Jocelyn found herself nodding along with him. She'd had similar conversations with her own mother many times over the years.

"I'm your mother. You're *my* responsibility. As I said, I can take care of myself." Nora softened her tone. "I love the ranch. You know I do. And if there was any good way for me to get it back, I'd do it in a heartbeat."

"There is." Liam crossed his arms. "It's up for sale. This is your chance."

"The owner died six months ago," Nora explained to Jocelyn. "His children have no intention of dealing with the cattle, so they're ready to sell. But I'd have to make a reasonable offer, preferably in cash."

"Which you can only do if I sell this house," Liam said.

"Which you can only do if you boot out this young lady and these innocent dogs." Nora sank down on her stool again, staring out the huge picture window at the ocean. "I don't want to get my home back by displacing somebody else from theirs."

In the silence that followed, they could hear the heavy panting of dogs anticipating dinnertime.

"Can't you see that?" Nora asked Liam. "If you do what you're wanting to, you're no better than him."

"You have more right to his money than anybody else," Liam countered. "You have a moral right and a legal right."

"Taking her house out from under her is not my moral right." Nora nodded at Jocelyn.

Jocelyn was imagining how it must feel to be wildly in love with someone who would ruin you. To take the ultimate leap of faith and go crashing to the ground. To spend decades working as an employee on the ranch that was your birthright, that had been entrusted to you by the generations before for the generations to come.

"If someone else buys the ranch, you're going to have to move," Liam pointed out.

Nora's gaze slid sideways. "I've moved before."

"And where will you work?" he challenged. "What's your retirement plan going to be?"

"Peter might have run off with all my money, but he could never take away my social currency." Nora lifted her chin and for a moment, Jocelyn glimpsed the regal poise of the debutante she'd been decades ago. "I can make a few calls and get a new job next week if I want. One where I won't have people leaving hatchets in my desk."

"A job doing what?" Liam pressed.

Nora addressed Jocelyn. "See? Do you see how he is?"

Jocelyn nodded.

"Obstinate and ornery as the day is long. And he's always been exactly like this."

"It's probably an asset in the real estate world," Jocelyn remarked.

"Yes, but we're not doing a real estate deal." Nora's bright smile returned. "That's the whole point."

"You can talk about me like I'm not here all night, but you can't tell me I'm wrong on this." Liam picked up his glass. "Even if you don't care about keeping the ranch, I do. It belongs in our family."

"I'm sorry," Jocelyn told Nora. "About the house. I had no idea."

"Well, of course you didn't." Nora glared at her son. "It isn't your problem."

"Yes, but it does seem unfair that Mr. All—Peter screwed you over when he was alive and he's screwing you over again now that he's dead."

"He had his reasons for leaving me," Nora said. "It wasn't right of him to do what he did, but the heartbreak went both ways."

Liam looked as though this was all news to him. "The financial hardship only went one way."

Jocelyn thought about the evening when she and Mr. Allardyce had regarded each other across the terrace of the cocktail party. She could have sworn she'd glimpsed empathy in his eyes, if not kindness. But maybe she'd been mistaken.

"Well." She swigged the last of her lemonade and slid off her stool. "It seems like you two have a lot to catch up on. I'm going to walk the dogs and give you some time to chat." At the mere mention of the *W* word, the Labs went ballistic.

Nora clapped her hand to her heart, scandalized. "You're going to leave Liam and me alone? In your house? Knowing that he's scheming to take it away from you and not knowing anything about me at all? Darling, you're far too trusting."

Jocelyn waded her way through the churning pool of overexcited dogs to open the mudroom closet and pull out the leashes. "Him, I don't trust. You seem cool."

"I am, but you have no way to be sure of that." Nora sighed and murmured something about kids these days.

"Hey," Liam objected. "I'm trustworthy. I have been one hundred percent up front about wanting to take your house since the moment I met you."

Jocelyn clipped on Curtis's and Carmen's leashes, casting a regretful glance at Hester, who was trapped in her whelping box amid the quartet of nursing puppies. "Sorry, girl. I promise I'll take you on a nice slow stroll later."

"You want company?" Liam got to his feet.

"Nope. I need some fresh air and some time by myself." She pointed to her eyes, then to Hester's. "Keep an eye on 'em."

Hester panted in response.

"Good dog." Jocelyn led the pack out the side exit, her mind reeling. Liam had a mother. Who looked and dressed like a former Miss Texas and wasn't afraid to take matters into her own hands.

And if Nora's version of events was true, if Mr. Allardyce had coerced a wealthy young heiress out of her family's legacy . . . then Nora did have some claim to the house. More so than anyone else. Jocelyn had to respect Liam for trying to do right by his mother. He wasn't just a selfish, entitled brat.

That made it a lot harder to be enraged at him.

"But somehow, I'll manage," Jocelyn vowed as she broke into a jog. The dogs tried to shift right into a sprint, tugging on their leashes like Santa's reindeer.

"Easy," Jocelyn cautioned them. "I'm not letting you off-leash today. Especially not you, Carmen."

After nearly forty-five minutes of running, Jocelyn's mood improved and her mind cleared. She headed back toward the beach house with renewed energy and optimism, confident that whatever little plot twist life threw at her next, she was ready. She was smart, she was capable, and she had legal possession of this house and its contents. She was in control here.

As she started up the sloping dune toward the back patio, the dogs strained at the leashes, whining and yelping.

"What's up, guys?" Jocelyn asked. "Aren't you tired out yet? I am."

As soon as she slid open the back door, she identified the source of their consternation. Eighties pop music was blasting from the kitchen, glasses were clinking, pots and pans were clattering, and . . . was that Bree's voice?

"What are you doing here?" Jocelyn demanded when she dashed

into the kitchen to find her best friend, Liam, and Nora chopping vegetables and sautéing chicken.

"You can't just call me and yell 'peer counselor' and not expect some follow-up." Bree popped a cube of tomato into her mouth. "I called you like fifty times."

"I didn't have my phone with me." Jocelyn retrieved it from her purse and started to untether the dogs. She shot a sidelong glance at Bree, who was glancing sidelong at Liam. "Don't bond with him."

"I'm not," Bree promised. "I'm bonding with Nora here. I'm about ready to buy a big shiny belt buckle and move out to the ranch."

"You really should come down," Nora yelled over the sizzle from the sauté pan. "Both of you. Come in the spring, during calf season."

Liam appeared at Jocelyn's elbow, smelling of black pepper and paprika. "Can I talk to you for a minute?"

"Not so fast," Bree said. "You want to talk to her? Take a number, pal, there's a line." She raised her eyebrow at Jocelyn. "Peer counselor. Start talking."

"Peer counselor?" Liam glanced at Jocelyn for clarification.

"Yeah, that's who the bride we've been surveilling is two-timing her fiancé with." Bree moved her knife in a circle, indicating they should move this story along. "Right?"

"I ran into them in the grocery store parking lot," Jocelyn said. She summarized the introductions and the awkward tension. "I mean, I can't swear under oath that there's something shady going on, but it didn't look good."

"It didn't look good when they were kissing outside her house, either." Bree's eyes darkened. "How can she do this to Dan? She has no idea how lucky she is."

"Who's Dan, again?" Nora was gamely trying to keep up with the story.

"A brilliant, handsome doctor who takes care of sick children." Bree clicked her tongue.

Jocelyn turned to Nora. "Bree's a little bit in love with Dan."

"I'm picking up on that. How long has the bride-to-be been together with the brilliant, handsome doctor?" Nora wanted to know. "When's the wedding? And why do they have a peer counselor?"

While Bree explained the backstory to Nora, Liam pulled Jocelyn aside. "Let's talk."

chapter 28

Jocelyn followed Liam into the formal dining room, where they each pulled out a heavy hardwood chair at the oval table. Everything in here was polished and Windexed to a glossy sheen, from the windows to the European porcelain to the tabletop. Jocelyn felt like she was sitting down in the Palace of Versailles for a treaty meeting.

"Fajitas are getting cold," she told him.

"You heard those two—they're not going to eat dinner anytime soon."

"I wasn't expecting Bree to drop by," Jocelyn said.

"I wasn't expecting my mother to drop by, either."

"But they did." Jocelyn spread out her hands. "And you did. Now what?"

"We have a lot to talk about." His dark eyes flashed.

"I don't. No offense, but you're a plague on my life." She took a moment, then added, "Actually, you can go ahead and take offense."

"I'm not the enemy, Jocelyn." He lifted his chin to indicate his mother. "I don't want to take anything from you. I want to give back what was always hers."

"Motivation doesn't matter." Jocelyn shrugged one shoulder. "Outcome matters. And your desired outcome is kicking me and the dogs out of our rightful home."

He regarded her for a moment before opening his mouth again. "I told you, it's not p—"

"If you say it's not personal, I'll throw you out the back door and into the ocean."

"Fine. It *is* personal, and it's not right." He held her gaze while he admitted this. "But the ranch is up for sale and I don't have enough cash to cover the whole down payment right now. Bids are due at the end of the month."

Jocelyn looked around at the crystal and antiques and imported marble. "Believe it or not, I understand what you're doing. I'd do the same thing for my mom."

He waited for her to finish the thought.

"But my mom is staying here, too. She took the shuttle to Dover for two days of orthopedic appointments, but she'll be back. As much as you want to keep the ranch for your mom, I want to keep this place for mine. There is no moral high ground here." She pushed her chair back from the table. "There's only what's written in the will. Nothing personal."

"Joss." His gaze softened. "I don't want to take you to court."

"Awww." She pretended to swoon. "Flatterer."

"There are other ways to resolve this," Liam said. "If we work together."

"Working together." She scoffed. "What could go wrong?"

"Hear me out," he urged. "The reason I focused on this house is it's worth a lot of money. The mortgage is paid off and the land is well situated. But I don't actually want to live here."

She nodded, waiting for him to continue.

"You want to keep living here and I want enough liquid assets to buy the ranch." He leaned back in his chair as though surveying a room full of potential investors. "Both of us can have what we want."

Jocelyn rested her chin on her hand. "You want me to take out an equity loan?"

"Short-term," he said.

"But why would I do that?" she asked. "I hate your guts."

He didn't even blink. "Yeah, but you like money at least as much as you hate me, right?"

"Eh."

"We'd go through the bank and sign all the legal documents. I'll pay you back every penny, plus interest."

She mulled this over. "That seems reasonable, assuming the co-trustee will cooperate."

"Who's the co-trustee?" Liam produced his phone, ready to Google.

"Some high-powered lawyer in Virginia. I can't remember her name offhand."

"She'll probably approve if you tell her you're in favor. It ultimately benefits the estate, especially if the interest rate is better than what you'd get from a commercial lender."

Jocelyn was shocked to realize that she was actually considering this. For Nora's sake, not for Liam's, obviously. But still. "Why didn't you just ask me about this in the first place?"

He finally shifted his gaze down to the table. "It's possible I was a little angry."

"With me?"

"With my father. Even though he's dead." Liam sounded more uncomfortable—and more honest—than she'd ever heard him. "Especially because he's dead."

"That, I understand." Jocelyn reached out to rest her fingers on his wrist.

He nodded. Neither one of them wanted to keep going with this topic.

Jocelyn pulled her hand away. "Look at us, pretending to be adults."

He reached out and recaptured her hand. "My father got one thing right, at least. You deserve to live here. No one else could care for the dogs like you do."

She slid her fingers to the inside of his wrist. "Are you sure you don't want to try to seduce me out of it one more time?"

He leaned forward. "We can work together on that, too."

Her body reacted as though she'd just downed two shots of vodka. "Oh yeah?"

"Yeah." He pulled away, shoved his chair back, and stood up. "Get your purse. We're going out."

She shoved her chair back, too. "Moonlit stroll with the dogs? Romantic stakeout for two?"

He laughed. "I was thinking more like dinner and drinks."

"It's the least you can do, considering you had me served with legal papers at the crack of dawn."

He yelled toward the kitchen, "Hey, guys? Go ahead and eat without us."

The chatter and clatter in the kitchen hushed for a moment, and Jocelyn knew that Bree was whispering to Nora about the state of affairs between Liam and herself. Then, after a minute or two, the sounds of dishes being placed on a marble counter commenced. "Will do!" Bree called. "Have fun, you crazy kids."

"Don't worry," Jocelyn ducked her head to hide a grin. "We will."

Three hours later, Jocelyn and Liam returned to the beach house with a rough draft of a lending agreement and a doggie bag full of leftovers that would literally go to the dogs.

They opened the front door as Bree was preparing to leave. She paused, one arm into her hoodie, and gave them both a good once-over, noting the take-out bag, fistful of papers, and starry eyes. "I see dinner was a success."

"I'm going to be rich," Jocelyn informed her. "Richer than I already am."

"I'm going to be a rancher," Liam added. "Again."

"*I'm* going home to bed." Bree didn't bother trying to cover her yawn. "Liam, your mother is a hell-raiser. I like it."

He looked around the dark, quiet rooms. "Where is she?"

"Sleeping. We partied hard until eight, and then she hit the wall. She was falling asleep at the kitchen table. I put her in one of the guest rooms." Bree turned to Jocelyn. "The one with the green quilt and all the pictures of conch shells."

"I can drive her to my house," Liam offered.

"No, no, it's fine." Jocelyn waved this away. "Let her sleep. We've got plenty of room. Bree, you're welcome to stay, too, if you like."

"Nah, I'm heading home." Bree slid on the other sleeve of her sweatshirt.

"You can take your pick of rooms," Jocelyn offered. "I know how you like the one with the blue toile."

"Tempting, but I'll pass. I've got to go unclog a garbage disposal first thing in the morning. I want my own coffeemaker and my own crappy play clothes in the morning." She explained to Liam, "When I say 'play clothes,' I mean 'work clothes.'"

"Call me if you need help," Jocelyn said. "I love a good garbage disposal unclogging."

"*We* love a good garbage disposal unclogging," Liam corrected.

"'We.'" Bree smirked. "Look at you two. Offering to unclog a disposal together. When did you stop wanting to murder each other for real estate purposes?"

"Stop it." Jocelyn shook her head. "No one wants to murder anyone."

"Yeah, we were both just hoping the other one would get abducted by aliens."

Bree scrunched her nose in disgust. "Get a room."

Jocelyn held the doggie bag up high as Curtis scented steak and came running. "Did you and Nora come up with a plan for dealing with Krysten, Dan, and the peer counselor?"

"We discussed it," Bree replied. "At length. The problem is, there's no good way to explain all this to Dan without incriminating myself."

"Really." Jocelyn quirked a brow. "Why's that, do you suppose?"

Bree ignored her and told Liam, "The best option we've got right now is an anonymous letter, but that lacks credibility."

"You could stay out of it," Liam suggested.

"Staying out of it isn't really my style." Bree fished her car keys out of her pocket. "I'll keep you posted." She opened the door and stepped out into the humid night air. "And I might call you in the morning, depending on how horrific the disposal turns out to be."

"Cool. The only thing I've got scheduled is an appointment with a family who's been promised one of Hester's puppies," Jocelyn said. "They're a big deal in the Labrador world. They get the pick of the litter."

"Have fun. And just FYI, we left half a bottle of wine in the kitchen. I have no idea what kind it is, but I took it from Mr. Allardyce's stash from the cellar. The man might have been stingy with his employees, but he was willing to splurge on the vino. It's red, it's French, and it goes down smooth like silk." With that, Bree disappeared into the night.

"With a sales pitch like that, I guess we should taste it." Jocelyn led the way to the kitchen, which was immaculately clean. All the pots, dishes, flatware, and glassware had been washed, wiped, and put away. The only trace of the earlier meal was the faint smell of spices. "This is what happens when Bree comes over for dinner.

When your job is cleaning up after other people's messes, you tend to be rabidly neat in your own house."

"My mom is the same." Liam uncorked the bottle of Bordeaux on the counter. "Everything in its place, all the time."

"She seems pretty amazing," Jocelyn said.

"I can wake her up and drive her back to my place," Liam offered again. "It's no trouble."

"Let her sleep." Jocelyn pulled out two wineglasses. "She's exhausted from traveling. You should stay over, too."

"Done," he said before she'd even finished the sentence.

She noted the speculative gleam in his eyes and clarified, "In a guest room. I don't sleep with people I'm doing business with."

He grinned, his eyes still gleaming. "Then I guess we'll both have something to look forward to when we wrap up this deal."

chapter 29

Jocelyn awakened early the next morning to the smell of freshly brewed coffee. Even over the hum of the ceiling fan, she could hear the soothing sound of the surf pounding on the shore. She eased out of bed, careful not to disturb any of the slumbering guest room occupants, and headed downstairs in her bare feet.

The first floor of the house was quiet—too quiet. Where was all the barking and whining? Where was the customary breakfast riot? She quickened her pace as she approached the kitchen, which turned out to be empty. All the dogs were MIA, even Hester and her puppies.

With a mounting sense of alarm, Jocelyn checked the laundry room, the mudroom, the living room and dining room—all empty. She grabbed her cell phone, debating. Should she call 911? And if she did, what was the appropriate answer to "What's your emergency, ma'am?"

An intruder made off with a whole pack of giant, slobbering Labs that would willingly go with anyone with a biscuit in their pocket. Right after he brewed coffee.

While her fingers were still hovering above the screen in indecision, she heard Curtis's deep, booming bark through the triple-paned window. She raced out to the deck and followed the canine noises to the pine bluff by the edge of the beach.

Nora had set up an artist's colony for one in the sand. Somehow, she'd managed to rustle up a sketchbook and pastels, plus two sawhorses and a large plywood board to rest everything on. She wore an elegantly draped pink robe and her white baseball cap. The dogs were strewn about at her feet in various states of relaxation. Curtis and Carmen were sitting and Hester was sprawled on a sand dune with her puppies.

"Good morning!" Nora waved when she saw Jocelyn. "Isn't it beautiful out here?"

Jocelyn squinted in the piercing morning sunlight. "It's . . . early."

"I hope I didn't wake you." Nora frowned in concentration as she selected a dark blue pastel. "I tried to be quiet, but this crew makes it hard to be stealthy."

"No, you were quiet," Jocelyn assured her. "I almost had a heart attack when I got down there and everyone was gone. But then I figured a hardened dog-napper probably wouldn't make coffee."

"I made orange juice, too. Squeezed it fresh from the oranges in the bowl. It's in the glass pitcher in the fridge."

"You've already done more than I'm going to do all day," Jocelyn marveled.

"I'm an early riser. Can't help it—all those years of getting up with the sun on the ranch." Nora gazed into the distance and smiled.

"You love the ranch," Jocelyn said. It was more an observation than a question.

"Yes." Nora returned her focus to her artwork. "I don't need to own it, but I'd hate to leave."

"I don't think you'll have to. Liam and I got to talking last night, and I think—well, I hope—we've found a way for me to keep the house *and* you to get the ranch back."

"Is that what you two were doing last night?" Nora's tone was teasing. "Talking?"

"For now." Jocelyn tilted her head, examining Nora's seascape-in-progress. "You really have talent."

Nora glanced up, her expression almost rebuking. "You're too kind. I dabble."

"Liam said you studied art."

"It's true." Nora laughed. "I spent my summers studying the masters in Paris, London, New York . . . and look where it's gotten me."

"There are lots of art fairs out here in the summer," Jocelyn said. "Have you ever considered selling your pieces?"

"Lord, no. No one would pay for this, and I wouldn't dream of asking them to." Nora put down the blue pastel.

"I'd pay for it."

"Then, darling, you can have it. I'll mail it to you when I'm finished." Nora's eyes sparkled beneath the brim of her white cap. "I like the poetic justice of it—one of my drawings hanging in Peter's house. He'd hate that."

"From what I've heard, he didn't have any reason to hate you," Jocelyn said. "He took your money and your family land and then left you and Liam to fend for yourselves. What'd you ever do to him?"

"It's never that simple." The mischievous sparkle in Nora's eyes dimmed. "I did plenty."

Jocelyn leaned in. Carmen pricked up her ears. "Like what?"

"I was very young when I got married." Nora cleared her throat. "Too young, in retrospect. But I wanted to feel important, and here was this confident, older man who swept me off my feet.

"It was infatuation, not love. At least on my part. Peter did love me. No matter how much anyone wants to rewrite history, I know he loved me once upon a time. That made everything harder in the end." Nora paused. "He wasn't one for grand gestures or romantic displays."

"Oh, I'm aware."

"But the day we got back from our honeymoon, he planted a tree in our yard. A big, sturdy sapling. He carved our initials in a heart and said he'd love me as long as that tree lived."

"That . . ." Jocelyn struggled for words. "Doesn't seem like him."

"It was his one and only grand gesture."

"What went wrong?"

"I did." Nora lowered her gaze. "I fell in love with someone else, a boy I'd known since high school. He came back after college, showed a little interest in me, and I lost my head . . . and my heart. It was platonic for a long time, but it was still wrong. They have a term for it these days—an emotional affair."

Jocelyn could feel the shame and remorse emanating from the other woman.

"I told Peter that I wanted to leave, that I'd given my heart to someone else."

"What'd he say?"

Nora lifted her gaze, her expression pensive. "You know that expression, your money or your life?"

"Yes. Yes, I do."

"Well, he wasn't going to let me go without making me pay. He wanted to hurt me the way I'd hurt him. So in the end, I let him have my family land in the divorce. He got a lot of the family money, too. I thought I was getting the better deal. I thought love was worth more than money. The day I left him, I took off my wedding ring and threw it at him. We were standing outside. It bounced right off that sapling he planted and it's probably still in the dirt where it landed."

Jocelyn waited to hear the end of the story. Now was not the time to interrupt Nora with the news that Mr. Allardyce had squirreled that wedding ring away.

Nora smiled ruefully. "When the other man found out I wasn't rich anymore, he didn't want me. Then I found out I was pregnant with Peter's child and he *really* didn't want me."

Jocelyn's eyes widened. "Are you sure Liam's father is . . ."

"Oh, he's Peter's son, no doubt about that. I did a DNA test after Liam was born. I sent the results to Peter, but he never responded." Nora cringed at the memories. "The day I told him I was pregnant, he looked at me with such contempt. I gave him my money and my family land, but it wasn't enough. He could never forgive me for falling out of love with him."

"He never wanted to see Liam grow up?"

"He knew where we were." Nora sounded harder now. "It's not as though we ever left home, really. After Peter sold the ranch, I went back and started working there. It was the only home I knew." She smiled wryly. "And when Peter left, he ripped up the sapling with our initials. Left a giant hole in the ground for all to see."

Jocelyn sat up straighter as a thought occurred. "What do you think he did with the tree?"

"Chopped it up for kindling, I'm sure." Nora sighed. "Now I see that I was wrong letting him punish Liam as part of punishing me. I should have fought harder for Liam's sake. I should have *made* Peter be a father, whether he wanted to or not."

"You can't make anyone be a father if they don't want to," Jocelyn said with total authority.

Hester got to her feet and whined in greeting as footfalls crunched on the sand-dusted deck. Jocelyn turned around to see Liam approaching, bleary-eyed and barefoot in jeans and the rumpled T-shirt he'd slept in. He held a mug of coffee in each hand, one of which he gave to Jocelyn.

"Morning."

"Look who's finally awake!" Nora teased. "You've gone soft, living in the city."

"It's six fifteen," Liam pointed out.

"Practically lunch hour on the ranch."

"Check it." Jocelyn pointed to Nora's artwork. "She's really good."

"She's exaggerating, but I'll take it." Nora obliged as Curtis pushed his whole face into her lap for an ear scratch. "You should bring her down to the ranch soon."

"I'd love to see it," Jocelyn enthused. "I've heard so much about it, I'm all invested now. Literally."

Liam looked a bit uneasy. "You two sure are getting along."

"She got up and made coffee and fresh OJ for everyone. And she took the dogs out," Jocelyn said. "What's not to love?"

"She let me stay the night and drink her vodka even though she thought I might try to steal her house away," Nora said. "And she has all these adorable puppies."

Liam backed up a few steps. "I'm going back to bed."

"You'd think he'd be happy we're getting along," Jocelyn said to Nora.

"You'd think."

Jocelyn nibbled her lip for a moment, considering the implications of the words she was about to voice. "So this tree, with the initials. Do you happen to remember what it looked like?"

Nora shrugged. "Just a regular tree. Trunk, bark, leaves. The usual."

"Was it an ironwood tree, by any chance?"

"You know, now that you mention it, that does sound familiar." Nora tilted her head, puzzled. "Why do you ask?"

"Did Liam happen to mention what his father left him in the will?"

"He said he got nothing. Repeatedly."

"Yeah, well, as with so many things about your ex-husband, there may be more to the story." Jocelyn got to her feet and invited Nora to do the same. "Humor me. Let's take a little stroll around the grounds. Tell me if any of these trees ring a bell."

"I'm happy to oblige, sugar, but I don't think I'll be any help." Nora put down her art supplies.

They started right where they stood in the patch of shade on the back patio. "Nope, nope, no." Nora pointed out and dismissed trees with rapid-fire rapidity. "Jocelyn, I have to tell you that if you need an expert opinion on a fourteenth-century Tuscan altarpiece, I'm your girl, but I know nada about trees."

"Keep going." Jocelyn led Nora toward the side of the house.

They didn't have to go far. Nora froze midstride and stared up at a huge, twisted tree that overlooked the window of the master bedroom. "Oh my goodness."

Jocelyn felt a little frisson of triumph. "Is that it?"

"It can't be." But Nora stepped forward, her eyes welling, and traced a scarred, warped, barely recognizable heart carved into the tree's trunk. A heart that had literally been broken by the ravages of time and weather, but a heart that remained nonetheless, after all these years.

And beneath the weathered, warped old heart was a fresh carving, two letters still white and sharp against the coarse bark: *L. S.*

Nora was silent for a moment, resting her fingertips on the gnarled edges left from the pocketknife. Then she whispered, "Liam Sheridan."

"Mr. Allardyce must have added that," Jocelyn said. "Right before he passed." He knew Liam was his son. This was his ultimate acknowledgment of family—contrary and ornery and utterly dysfunctional. But still . . .

Nora turned and yelled. "Liam! *Liam!*"

He strode out the back door, his expression alarmed at the urgency in his mother's voice. His pace slowed as he saw Jocelyn.

"What is it?" he asked.

Jocelyn reached up to cup his cheek, then stepped away to let mother and son have a moment of privacy. "It's your inheritance."

chapter 30

The breakfast dishes were still soaking in the kitchen sink when Polly and Roger Derridge arrived to begin the process of picking their new puppy. Liam had helped to bathe Hester, and Jocelyn had done everything she could to prepare for the famed breeders who were essentially royalty in the Labrador world. Mr. Allardyce had been smug and self-satisfied about brokering this deal with the Derridges, crowing that it would vault his dogs to the next level of prestige and showmanship.

But Hester had apparently missed the memo re: prestige and showmanship, and she insisted on rolling in freshly raked sand the moment she escaped from her shampooing. After a second rinse, she galloped into the laundry room and frolicked in a pile of soiled, staticky sheets.

"At least you're feeling good enough to be naughty," Jocelyn told Hester as the doorbell chimed. "Do me a favor and pretend to be obedient for twenty minutes. Please? There's a leftover pancake in it for you."

Jocelyn opened the door expecting to greet the perfectly put-together couple in matching plaid sweaters pictured on the Derridges' kennel website. But without Photoshop and expert lighting, Polly and Roger Derridge looked like unpretentious, everyday dog lovers. And bonus, they were already covered in dog hair so Jocelyn didn't have to apologize for the tornado of post-bath shedding they were about to step into.

She apologized, anyway. "Welcome! Come on in! Sorry in advance about the shedding."

Roger offered a hearty handshake, and then Polly engulfed Jocelyn in a hug. "It's so good to finally meet you in person!" Polly gushed. "Peter bragged about you so much, I feel as though I already know you."

"He did?" Jocelyn hadn't meant to sound so incredulous.

"Oh yes, he went on and on about you. He said you were so good to the dogs. Always went the extra mile to make sure they were happy and healthy."

"Oh." Jocelyn blinked. "Well."

"It's no wonder he chose you as their guardian." Roger's voice boomed through the foyer. Down the hall, Curtis and Carmen went nuts. "He was lucky to find you."

"Don't we know it," Polly lamented. "We're always on the road for shows, and we worry about the dogs we have to leave at home."

"In fact," Roger added, "if you're ever looking for another employer . . ."

"No business talk today," Polly admonished her husband. "We're here for the puppies."

"Sorry, sorry. Lead the way."

Jocelyn obliged, opening the door to Mr. Allardyce's office, where she had sequestered Hester and the four puppies. Hester managed to detach herself from her brood long enough to get to her feet and give a proper, polite greeting to their visitors.

"Good girl." Jocelyn stroked the dog's head. "She's such a good mama, too."

"I'm sure. Hester was always the sweetest and prettiest of Peter's kennel." Polly cooed into Hester's face. Hester reveled in the attention.

"Are these all of them?" Roger sounded disappointed as he inspected the quartet of pups.

"Yes. I'm no dog expert, but the vet said it was a small litter," Jocelyn said.

"Very small." Roger stood back, studying the wriggling little fur balls.

"Well, dear, what do you think?" Polly winked at Jocelyn. "He takes this very seriously."

"Puppy selection is serious business," Roger replied. "If we're going to devote our time and money to a dog—not to mention the Derridge name—he or she needs to be worthy."

Jocelyn smiled, thinking he was kidding. But he wasn't kidding.

"Hmm." He walked a few steps to the right. *"Hmmm."* And now a few steps to the left.

"What are you—?"

"Shh." Polly put a dramatic finger to her lips. "This is the most important part of the whole process."

Jocelyn couldn't think of anything appropriate to say, and she wasn't allowed to speak, anyway, so she watched and waited.

Roger hunkered down on his knees and picked up the puppies one at a time. He checked their teeth, their paws, the inside of their ears, and then he rubbed them as if kneading little balls of bread dough.

Little George Clooney he put aside after mere moments. "This one needs to be neutered as soon as possible."

"Why?" Jocelyn asked. "He's adorable. Everyone loves him."

"He's a silver Lab." Polly spoke these words as though she were going to follow them up with *and he should be drowned in the river.*

"What's wrong with silver Labs?" Jocelyn asked.

"They're not breed standard," Polly declared.

"They're an aberration," Roger agreed. He thrust poor George at Jocelyn without another glance.

Pat Benatar was also quickly eliminated from competition. "Her topline is faulty." Roger pointed out a dip in the tiny dog's spine.

"How can you even tell?" Jocelyn asked. "She can barely stand up."

"Shh!" Polly hissed.

The third puppy, J. K. Rowling, a peppy little girl who was slightly bigger and more rotund than her siblings, merited a more thorough inspection. "Good bones, good musculature." Roger stopped kneading long enough to place the puppy on the rug.

"Aw." Polly melted. "She's precious."

"I suppose." But Roger seemed reluctant. "But I worry about her bite. Looks like it could be the beginning of a wry bite."

"What's a wry bite?" Jocelyn asked.

"It's when one side of the jaw is longer than the other," Polly explained in hushed tones. "The teeth won't be in proper alignment."

"It's the worst possible structural flaw a dog can have," Roger concluded with great authority.

"But her baby teeth haven't even come in all the way."

"Her saving grace," Roger stated. "Let's have a look at number four, here."

"Number four has a name," Jocelyn said as Roger eyed the final puppy, the sleepy, snuggly little boy. "It's LeBron."

"No." Roger dismissed LeBron without even picking him up. "Look at that tail."

Jocelyn looked. All she saw was a brown bit of fluff. "What's wrong with it?"

"It's kinked. He won't last two minutes in the show ring."

"He'll make some family a lovely pet, I'm sure." Polly's tone was consoling.

"Yes." Jocelyn's voice was crisp. "He will."

"Don't be offended, my dear. They can't all be champions." Roger all but patted her head in condescension. "And there's only these four? Are you sure?"

"Uh, yes." Jocelyn crossed her arms. "I delivered them myself."

Polly looked startled. "You did? Why?"

Before Jocelyn could reply, Roger was snapping his fingers in her face and demanding a blanket and a quiet room in which to continue his vetting process for J. K. "I need to get her away from her mother and her litter and all this chaos."

Jocelyn glanced around at the freshly vacuumed handwoven rug, antique furniture, and damask drapes. "Yes, of course. It's a wonder you can hear yourself think."

Oblivious to her sarcasm, he picked up the puppy like a football and prompted, "Blanket, please?"

"What do you need a blanket for?" Jocelyn asked.

"An IQ test," Roger said. "I can't have any dumb dogs in my kennel."

"But Labs are dumb," Jocelyn protested. "That's their thing! That's why everyone loves them!"

"Correction: *Most* Labs are dumb." Roger exchanged a look of supreme superciliousness with his wife. "Not Derridge Labs. Derridge Labs are the valedictorians of the retriever world. And we keep them that way by weeding out the underperformers."

"Which is about ninety percent of the puppies we see," Polly said.

"So you're saying if she doesn't pass your Mensa blanket test, you're not interested?" Jocelyn asked.

"We'll keep her under consideration, but the final purchase will be contingent upon her bite development." Roger was already holding the puppy as though she were his possession. "We can't waste our time and resources on anything less than the best."

Jocelyn looked at the tiny, exuberant little dog. "She's a great dog."

"She is a great dog," Polly soothed. "But we have to be sure that she's perfect. A sweet disposition isn't enough to make it in the big leagues."

"You should be flattered," Roger said. "The fact that we're even keeping her under consideration will raise the prices for your next litter."

Hester whined as she watched her baby wriggling in the arms of a stranger.

Jocelyn reached out and reclaimed her puppy. "Well, you don't have to keep her under consideration."

"Yes, we do." Roger held out his hands, waiting for Jocelyn to come to her senses. "She's the best of the lot."

"The lot is off-limits," Jocelyn decreed. "You can't have her. You can't have any of them."

Hester's tail thumped against the rug.

"Excuse me?" Polly's sweetness-and-light routine vanished. "We certainly can have her. We have a contract in place."

"My recent experiences in the legal world have taught me that contracts can always be contested," Jocelyn said. "And if you'll give me a second . . ." She rifled through the files in Mr. Allardyce's desk drawer. "Here we go. Your rights to this puppy are contingent upon you paying a deposit fee."

"Which we did," Polly informed her. "I still have the canceled check in my accounts."

"Yes, but read on." Jocelyn slapped the contract down on the desktop. "According to this clause right here, I can void the terms of this agreement if I pay you back your deposit. And I just so happen to have my checkbook burning a hole in my pocket."

The Derridges both gaped at her.

"You can't do this!" Polly exclaimed.

"And yet I'm doing it." Jocelyn started writing the check.

"This is ridiculous," Roger said. "And I'm not taking a personal check from a woman who goes back on her word like this."

Jocelyn put down the pen. "Fine. I'll give you a cashier's check. Expect it from FedEx tomorrow."

"You're making a big mistake," Polly warned her as Jocelyn escorted them to the front door. "The biggest mistake of your life."

"Don't exaggerate." Jocelyn had to laugh. "I make bigger mistakes than this on a daily basis."

Jocelyn was reassuring Hester that her puppies would not be going to live with the Miss Hannigans of the dog show world when her cell phone rang. She didn't recognize the number, so she let it go to voice mail.

It rang and rang and rang some more. She relented and answered, "Hello?"

A shrill, loud feminine voice sliced into her eardrum. "What just happened?"

"Um, who is this?" Jocelyn frowned and pulled the phone away from her head.

"It's Lois Gunther. Your dog handler."

Jocelyn frowned. "How did you get through? I thought I blocked your number after you called my lawyer to complain about me."

Lois ignored this and launched into a tirade. "How could you turn away the Derridges?"

"It was easy," Jocelyn said. "They were talking smack about J. K. Rowling."

"Once again, you have no idea what you're doing." Lois stopped haranguing and started hissing. "The Derridges know everything and everybody in the Labrador world, and Mr. Allardyce promised them the pick of the litter!"

"I know, but I didn't like them, and I don't think Hester did, either." Jocelyn sat down in the comfy leather chair and spun around, propping her feet on the desk. "So I went with my gut."

"You can't go with your gut. You have to go with the contract."

"The contract says that I can rescind the offer as long as I return their deposit. Which I will. We don't have a problem here."

"We certainly do. Polly and Roger are dear friends of mine."

"They were going to make Hester's baby girl do an IQ test! Did they tell you that? Your 'dear friends' are elitist snobs."

"That's why they're the best. They demand the highest standards of the breed. Anyone else would be honored to sell them a puppy."

"Well." Jocelyn shrugged. "Good to know."

There was a short pause while Lois gnashed her teeth. "That's all you're going to say?"

"Yep."

"You cannot do this. You cannot just take over the Allardyce Labrador legacy and—"

"I can do whatever I want. They're my dogs."

"Not for long."

"Yeah, yeah." Jocelyn wished she had a glass of scotch and a cigar. There was something about this office that made her feel like Don Draper. "Are you going to call my lawyer again?"

Lois responded by hanging up.

"Don't worry." Jocelyn addressed Hester as she swung her feet back onto the floor. "I would never hand over your precious babies to such coldhearted cutthroats."

Hester, who was simultaneously nursing three out of four puppies, looked harassed but grateful.

Jocelyn knelt down to kiss the tip of Hester's nose. "But, just between you and me, I'm not sure *any* of you guys could pass the Derridge IQ test."

Hester gave her a big, goofy dog smile and a slobbery lick on the cheek.

"I know, I know, you think you can get by on your good looks and your charm. Well, as long as I'm in charge, you can. Don't you worry about a thing."

chapter 31

While Jocelyn spent the morning fending off the Derridges, giving Curtis a refresher course in how to stack without giving his handler a bear hug, and taking Carmen for a playdate (emphasis on "date") with her beloved boyfriend Friday, Liam started putting together a formal loan proposal. Nora, despite her insistence that she was going to get out of everyone's way in a matter of minutes, stayed on at the Allardyce house and did, well, basically everything.

"You weeded the front garden?" Jocelyn marveled upon returning from the beach with Carmen. "You didn't have to do that."

"Only took a minute." Nora, who was elbow deep in soapy water at the sink, barely glanced up. "I just got the big ones."

"We have a landscaper who comes once a week." Jocelyn was scandalized. "And a housekeeper who comes twice a week. Stop doing the dishes. You're my guest."

"I showed up unannounced at your doorstep. That's not exactly a guest."

That's when Jocelyn noticed the smell of freshly baked chocolatey goodness. "Did you make brownies, too?"

"Coming out of the oven in five minutes." Nora redoubled her efforts to scrub the mixing bowl. "My grandmother's recipe."

"And why is the vacuum out?" Jocelyn demanded.

"Stop fussing," Nora said. "I'm just cleaning up the dog hair before I start lunch."

When Liam entered the room, Jocelyn said, "Tell your mom to chill."

"Ranch life doesn't allow for chill." Liam lifted his head and sniffed the air. "Is that brownies?"

"Your great-grandmother's recipe, apparently. How's the paperwork coming along?"

"So far, so good. I think we can get the initial documents finalized by next week. I'll make an appointment to talk to your attorney and the co-trustee in the next few days."

"*We* will make an appointment," Jocelyn said. "Curtis included."

Liam smiled at the fluffy jester of a dog. "Curtis is a good negotiator?"

"Look at that face. Who could say no?"

"I see your point."

"Besides, it's his money, really."

"Then I better keep giving him treats." Liam fished yet another biscuit from his pocket. Curtis raced to his side.

"Don't give him any more of those. He's got to be slim and trim for the dog show next month." Jocelyn sighed. "Or maybe not. I think his best-in-show days might be behind him." She filled Liam in on the Derridge drama.

"You did the right thing," Liam said.

"I don't know," she admitted. "It felt right at the time, but now . . . What if I've made a huge mistake?"

"You haven't." He took her hand.

"What if we're blacklisted forever?"

"Who cares?" He pulled her toward him.

Jocelyn startled as the dryer buzzer sounded. "Those are the sheets. I'd better get them out and folded before the wrinkles set. My mom will be here to pick these up any minute."

"It'll be great to meet her," Liam said.

Jocelyn froze, nearly tripping him in the hallway. "Oh, I don't know if today is a good day for official introductions. She's pretty busy and, um . . ." *And she wants me to date a nice local boy with a steady job and a stable family instead of a fast-talking, house-flipping love child of the richest, stingiest old man Black Dog Bay has ever seen.*

"No big deal." Liam remained totally relaxed. "She can have a brownie. Just a few minutes."

"She's not a huge fan of the dogs, either," Jocelyn hedged. "Except George Clooney."

"Jocelyn." Liam placed both hands on her shoulders and turned her around to face him. "Are you worried about what she'll think of me or what I'll think of her?"

"Neither." Jocelyn cast her gaze downward. "Both. It's just that she has some preconceived ideas about guys who show up for tourist season, and I don't want you to take it personally."

"I'm not here for tourist season. I'm here for going-fifty-rounds-with-my-dead-father's-estate season."

"Yes, well, I'm not sure she's going to make that distinction." Jocelyn turned her focus to the ceiling. "My last boyfriend—"

"Was clearly dumber than Curtis." Liam glanced back at the dog. "Sorry, buddy, but it's true."

"Be that as it may . . ."

The doorbell chimed.

"Don't worry." Liam pivoted and headed for the door. "It'll be great."

Amid Jocelyn's protests, he opened the door and offered a handshake. "Hi, I'm Liam Sheridan."

"Oh," was Rachel's reply. Jocelyn cringed inwardly.

"Here, let me take that from you." Liam helped himself to the empty laundry basket Rachel held in her arms. "Come on in. Would you like a brownie?"

"Jocelyn?" Rachel called. "Are you in here?"

"Yes, Mom." Jocelyn rushed into the foyer. "I'm here. And you really should have a brownie."

Rachel sidestepped around Liam, eyeing him as though he might pull out a shiv at any moment. "I didn't know you had company."

"Things have gotten a little crazy over the last twenty-four hours." Jocelyn gave her mother a hug and a kiss. "How are you feeling?"

"I'm fine." Rachel shook her off. "You don't have to treat me like some kind of invalid." She looked at the way Liam was looking at her daughter and narrowed her eyes. "I thought you were going out with that nice local boy Bree found for you."

"I tried. Didn't take."

Liam pretended not to hear Rachel's pointed remark. "Would you like some lemonade, Ms. Hillier? Or water?"

Rachel nudged Jocelyn's ribs and whispered. "What is going on? Isn't this the guy who's trying to take your house away?"

"Well, actually, it's a funny story," Jocelyn started. But Rachel wasn't listening anymore. She'd spotted Nora in the kitchen.

"I don't believe we've met." Icicles dripped from every syllable.

"You must be Jocelyn's mother." Nora tossed her dish towel on the counter. "You're the spitting image!" She rounded the counter and went in for a hug.

Rachel was having none of it. "Yes. I'm Rachel Hillier." She offered a stiff, formal handshake.

"I'm Liam's mom," Nora explained. "It's such a pleasure to meet you. Jocelyn's told me all about you. She's very proud of you."

Rachel's gaze darted back to her daughter. "Really?"

"Of course, Mom."

"You should be proud of her, too." Nora swept back her blond hair. "She's a force to be reckoned with."

Rachel tilted her head, assessing Nora. "You're very comfortable in this house. How did you know Mr. Allardyce?"

"Mother." Jocelyn gave her a look.

But Nora just laughed. "If I'm going to unpack that whole suitcase of scandal, you'd better sit down with a brownie and a glass of milk."

Liam pulled out a chair.

"No, thank you." Rachel backed out of the kitchen. "I have to go."

"Mom." Jocelyn followed her back to the foyer. "What's wrong with you?"

"Nothing's wrong with me." Her mother sounded furious. "What's wrong with *you*?"

Jocelyn frowned. "Is this a trick question?"

"I told you that money would change you." Rachel's words were angry but her tone and expression were exhausted. "I told you that it changes the way you treat other people and the way they treat you, and here we are."

Jocelyn glanced around. "Doing laundry and eating brownies?"

"Rubbing elbows with rich people."

"Mom."

"Let me finish. I know you think I'm still bitter and angry with your father, and who knows, maybe I am, but there's a reason I always told you to avoid the Shoreline Drive crowd. They're not like us, Joss. They think about people in terms of money and opportunities. If you lost all this tomorrow"—she opened her arms to encompass the house and its contents—"you'd never hear from them again. I know it's hard to hear, but it's true. Think about how easily your father walked away from us. How easily your boyfriend left."

Suddenly, Jocelyn felt exhausted, too. "Can we not drag my father into this? Please?"

"It's all about money. Image. *Things*." Rachel's eyes welled. "I know I have not always been a great mother. I spent your whole childhood being tired and busy and cranky."

"Mom—"

Rachel held up her hand. "Let me finish. I was not perfect, I am not perfect, but at least I tried. I showed up every day." She dabbed at her eyes with the sleeve of her threadbare T-shirt. "And I know you'd rather have grown up with some pretty blond princess who made brownies every day, but you got me instead."

"And I'm so glad." Jocelyn hugged her. "I would never want another mom."

"You're in here playing house with her!" Rachel's voice was almost inaudible. "Have you looked at her fingernails? That woman does not do laundry for a living."

Jocelyn grinned at the irony of this. "You're right about that."

"That's the kind of woman who would be your stepmother, if your father had ever bothered to introduce you to his family."

"Which he didn't," Jocelyn finished for her. "And you know what? That's okay. We've got each other. The two of us against the world, Mom."

Rachel looked more drained and tired than Jocelyn had ever seen her, as if the worry and strain and doubt of the last twenty-seven years were slamming into her all at once. "I could have done better."

"Wrong." Jocelyn stepped back and spun around under the chandelier. "I'm living proof of your excellent parenting."

Rachel relaxed just a bit. "Are you sure?"

"Yes. The only thing that could have improved my childhood was having a dog."

"Speaking of which, where's George?"

"Right where you left him, ready for you to continue to spoil him rotten."

Rachel smiled. "That is my right as his grandmother."

"Come in for ten minutes and snuggle your grandpuppy and have a brownie," Jocelyn pleaded. She tilted her head back toward the kitchen. "If it makes you feel better, those two don't have Shoreline Drive money."

"Are you sure?" Rachel furrowed her brow. "Blondie definitely has the old-money look about her."

"Her name is Nora," Jocelyn said. "And she did grow up wealthy, but now she's basically broke."

"What happened?" her mother whispered.

Jocelyn couldn't betray Nora's confidence. "Long story short, Mr. Allardyce happened. Liam and I both have the same deal with our dads."

Rachel softened. "Why didn't you tell me that before?"

"I would have, but you were too busy assuming the worst."

Jocelyn put an arm around her mother's shoulder and ushered her back to the kitchen. "We're back and we're famished."

Liam pulled out the chair again and this time, Rachel sat down.

"Have you met the puppies yet?" Liam asked.

"I not only met them, I named them." Rachel rattled off the puppies' names. The puppies responded by yipping from their whelping box. "It was either that or John Taylor, Simon LeBon, Nick Rhodes, and Roger Taylor."

"Duran Duran!" Nora served up a huge brownie on a fine china plate. "I love it."

Rachel regarded Nora with renewed interest. "You like Duran Duran?"

"I *love* Duran Duran." Nora clasped her hands, a middle-aged fangirl with a big brass belt buckle. "And what about Andy Taylor?"

"Next litter," Rachel said.

"Don't forget Andy Wickett and Stephen Duffy."

And with that, two soul mates found each other. While Nora and Rachel chatted about the music video for "Rio," Jocelyn cut herself a tiny sliver of brownie, tasted it, and then cut a bigger piece.

"This is delicious," she told Liam through a mouthful of crumbs.

"I know. These were the highlight of my childhood."

"You want one?"

"I'll wait until you three finish and see if there's any left," he said.

Rachel pulled out her phone and started blasting "A View to a Kill."

"We should leave now, before karaoke starts," Liam advised.

"I kind of like this one," Jocelyn admitted.

Liam looked at her for a moment, then said, "It's no 'New Moon on Monday.'"

As if on cue, Curtis started to howl. Carmen joined in, followed by Hester.

"Canine karaoke." Liam stepped back from the island. "Let's go. I'll grab the sheets and we'll take them wherever you need to go."

"Oh, you don't want to do that," Jocelyn said. "We had some midweek checkouts. I have to spend the next four hours putting sheets, blankets, and pillowcases on a bunch of mattresses with stains that don't bear thinking about."

"It'll only take two hours if I help you."

Jocelyn turned to him. "Really?"

"Sure. Why not?"

"I don't know." She'd never had a romantic prospect offer to help make beds with her. And she'd certainly never asked. "It's not very glamorous."

"I'm not a glamorous guy," he said. "And I bet putting on pillowcases is way better than deworming a calf or tracking down gators in the watering hole."

"Haven't lost a finger yet." Jocelyn brightened. "Plus, I bet you've seen some horrific stuff flipping houses."

"The carpet situations alone would give you nightmares."

They headed out together, laden with lavender-scented sheets, as the sing-along segued to "Union of the Snake."

As she climbed into the passenger seat of Liam's car, Jocelyn's phone buzzed.

"Hey, Bree. What's up?"

"What are you doing right now?" Bree sounded tense.

Jocelyn frowned with concern. "Hanging out with Liam."

"Can you ditch him and meet me? I'm at a bar in Lewes called Davy's Dive."

"Right now?"

"Yeah." Bree cleared her throat. "I wouldn't ask if it wasn't important."

"Okay, I'm leaving in two minutes. What's going on?"

"I'll tell you when you get here. Come alone, and hurry up."

chapter 32

"Thanks for meeting me here and not asking any questions."

"No problem." Jocelyn glanced around at the bar, which featured straw wrappers and bottle caps strewn about the sticky floor tiles, and drink specials with names like "Sand in the Crack." "Can I ask questions now?"

"In a second. I have good news and bad news." Bree patted the barstool next to her. "Which do you want first?"

"Good news." Jocelyn sat down and glanced at the menu.

"The good news is, I've decided what to do about Dan, Krysten, and the peer counselor." Bree cradled a mug of coffee with both hands. "I was up all night, tossing and turning and weighing my options."

"And?"

"Bottom line: There are lots of cowardly ways to tell Dan what's going on." Bree paused to slug back the rest of the coffee. "I mean, we've all seen this play out on TV, right? I could leave a note in his mailbox. I could threaten Krysten to tell him or I will."

"But you're not going to do that?"

"No." Bree put down the empty mug and sighed. "Because, when I actually look at my behavior here, I'm not proud of myself. I've crossed a few lines."

"I did, too," Jocelyn admitted.

Bree lifted her chin in determination. "Dan deserves better than what he's getting from Krysten, but he also deserves better than what he's getting from me. He deserves honesty, transparency, and accountability."

Jocelyn blinked. "Well. That's very mature of you."

"I'm trying." Bree glanced longingly at the array of liquor bottles lined up behind the cash register. "A shot of Bailey's would make this easier, but I need my wits about me. Dan will be here any minute."

"Dan's meeting you here?"

"Yeah, I called him and told him I needed to talk to him about something."

"Why here?" Jocelyn pressed. "Why not someplace that meets health code standards? Was this your secret rendezvous spot in high school or something?"

"No, I've never been here before. That's the point. We have no memories here and I won't be back, so it's not like I'm tainting a coffee shop I visit regularly."

"Good thinking."

"Yeah. I noticed this place yesterday when I was driving through town, and I thought, there's a good place for the truth to come out." Bree indicated the booth on the other side of the bar. "Can you go sit over there before he shows up?"

"You invited me here to make me sit somewhere else?" Jocelyn glanced at the booth's worn and torn upholstery. "That's not very friendly."

"I need you here for moral support. Since Dan's probably going to hate me and all, I thought it'd be nice if you could help scrape me off the floor afterwards." Bree caught the bartender's eye. "Hi! We'll have two more cups of coffee, please."

"Maybe it won't be as bad as you think," Jocelyn said. "Maybe he'll be grateful you told him. Maybe he'll realize that he's loved you all along."

"That also only happens in Hollywood. But I have to do this." Bree set her jaw. "Even though I really, really, really don't want to."

"Let me do it," Jocelyn urged. "I'll say it was me who hunted Krysten down. I'll tell him I acted alone."

Bree peered at her with supreme skepticism. "What would your motivation for all that be?"

"Uh . . ."

"Exactly. Everyone involved in this whole steaming sewer pipe of a mess has lied and evaded enough. There is truth to be told, and I'm telling it." Bree checked her phone. "He'll be here any minute."

"I'll be over here." Jocelyn pointed to the booth across the bar. "Question: What if he notices me?"

"Here." Bree picked up a discarded newspaper from a nearby stool. "Read this. Hold it so it covers your face."

"Stealthy."

"Oh wait." Bree snatched back the newspaper. "Before you go, what's happening with Liam?"

"We had a long talk with Nora about the lawsuit and why he was filing it, and I think we've worked out an arrangement that lets everyone get what they want."

"What? So you're not archenemies who can't help succumbing to the passion between you?"

"Nah. We're business partners who are going to succumb to the passion between us with no qualms whatsoever."

Bree stuck out her tongue. "Boring." She made shooing motions as she spotted Dan through the bar's front window. "Go, go, go!"

Jocelyn went, sequestering herself in the booth and shielding herself with the sports section. She heard, rather than saw, Dan sit down at the bar with Bree, and strained her ears to pick up every word above the low, mournful twang emanating from the jukebox.

Bree had never been one for idle chitchat and today was no different.

"Dan," Bree said as soon as his back pockets hit the vinyl seat, "let me ask you something. Have you ever watched a Lifetime movie?"

Dan laughed. "Hello to you, too. What's going on?"

"Anything else to drink, hon?"

Jocelyn startled as a waitress peered over the top edge of her newspaper. "Just some more coffee, please."

The waitress glanced at the seat Jocelyn had just vacated, but didn't remark on her relocation. "You want me to bring you a new cup?"

"Yes, please."

By the time the waitress departed, coffee carafe in hand, Bree was getting to the good stuff:

"What would you say if I had a premonition that day I read palms at Krysten's shower?"

Dan didn't hesitate. "I'd believe you."

This threw Bree off. "You would?"

"Sure. Remember that time in high school when you told me that Mr. Turner was going to have a heart attack in the middle of the final exam? And then he did?"

"Could've been a lucky guess."

"You've always had something special," he said. "Everybody could see it but you."

There was a long pause. Jocelyn shifted, crinkling the newsprint, wishing she could whirl around and check out Bree's face.

Finally, Bree replied, "Yeah, about that. I have to tell you something."

"Okay." Dan made a big show of bracing himself . . . just as the door to the bar swung inward. Krysten and Brian strolled in, holding hands.

Dan's eyes widened. Bree froze. Jocelyn's phone rang, blaring a merry digital tune. She seized the phone behind her flimsy paper shield and answered in a whisper. "Hi, Mom, I'm right in the middle of something. Can I call you back?"

"No need." Her mother's voice sounded distant and tinny. There was a distinct rushing sound on her end of the line, like wind through open car windows. "I just wanted to let you know we're leaving for a few days."

"Leaving for where?" Jocelyn asked. "And who's we?"

"Nora and I." Rachel stated this as though it were the most obvious conclusion in the world. "We're taking a road trip."

"Is this a joke?"

"No. She mentioned that there's a great Duran Duran cover band at a casino in Connecticut, and one thing led to another, and next thing you know, we jumped in my car."

"Hi, Joss!" Nora's voice chimed in from afar.

Jocelyn hunched down in the booth, trying to hold her phone and the newspaper simultaneously. "You're just up and going to Connecticut? What about your back? What about your hip?"

"Don't make me sound so old," Rachel admonished. "I'll be fine. Nora's doing all the driving. I'm the DJ."

"Did you even pack?" Jocelyn asked.

"Who's the mom here, you or me?" Rachel shot back.

"When are you coming back?"

"When we're done." Rachel sounded exhilarated.

Jocelyn digested this for a moment. "You're going to call me from jail tonight, aren't you?"

"Don't worry, we'll call Liam instead." Both moms cracked up.

Jocelyn had no idea what else to say except: "Thanks for letting me know. Have a good time."

"Oh, we will." And in a flurry of laughter and life, Rachel clicked off. If it hadn't been for Caller ID, Jocelyn wouldn't have recognized her own mother. Rachel didn't do anything reckless or spontaneous. She didn't talk to strangers, and she certainly didn't road-trip with them on a whim.

Until now, apparently.

Meanwhile, things were heating up at the bar.

"What are you doing here?" Krysten was demanding, her voice shrill.

"I asked you first," Dan shot back.

Brian was nowhere to be seen.

"I don't know what you're accusing me of, but it's not what it looks like," Krysten said. "I can explain."

Jocelyn waited for Dan's response, the newsprint crinkling as she clutched the paper in suspense.

But all she could discern of his response was a low, dark-toned murmur. She wanted to turn around to read the body language but didn't dare. And then, with his ball cap low on his brow and ramrod posture, Dan strode out of the bar. He didn't look back or make eye contact with anyone. He left with his fists jammed into his pockets and his head held high. Krysten trailed after him, still protesting her innocence.

Jocelyn threw down the paper, shoved out of her booth, and slid back onto the barstool next to Bree. "What was *that*?"

Bree's expression was shell-shocked. "I don't know."

"Tell me everything. I only heard the beginning because my mom called and I thought there might be an emergency." She waved all this away. "Start talking."

"You pretty much saw all you needed to see. The only big thing you missed was Brian fleeing the scene like a criminal caught in the act."

"Dan looked so hurt," Jocelyn said.

"Yeah, but he didn't look surprised, did he?" Bree drained the last dregs of her second cup of coffee.

"Hmm. I guess not."

"He said a few things . . . I don't think that this is the first time Krysten's done this."

"Then why would he propose to her?" Jocelyn asked.

"We didn't have time to get into a long, detailed psychoanalysis," Bree said drily.

Jocelyn thought about the people in her life who she'd desperately hoped wouldn't let her down . . . right before they let her down. "Poor guy."

"What are the odds, though?" Bree smoothed out the creases in a paper napkin. "I mean, I picked this place at random. How is it possible that Krysten and Brian showed up at the exact time Dan and I did?"

"Gee. Maybe we should ask your grandmother for some insight on that."

"I feel awful." Bree dropped her forehead into her hands. "It's like I had this burden of truth, and I shifted it from me to Dan, and now he has to lug it around."

"But it's still the truth," Jocelyn said. "What else could you have done?"

"So many things." Bree closed her eyes. "But this is for the best. The prospect of having to admit to Dan's face that I surveilled his cheating fiancée in a black SUV is enough to get me to leave this town forever. The shame has set me free. Philadelphia, here I come."

Jocelyn decided that this was not the right time to remind Bree that Dan was moving to Philadelphia, too.

"Well, what's done is done." Jocelyn tossed a twenty-dollar bill down on the table. "Let's get out of here. Want to go to the Jilted Café and get some coffee that doesn't taste like mop water?"

"No, thanks. I have to go curl up in the fetal position for the next few days."

"Come over to my place," Jocelyn offered. "Go fetal in style."

"No. Solitary confinement is the only way."

"You can have it," Jocelyn promised. "The blue toile bedroom is all yours. You can close the door and no one will bother you. Just text me every time you want me to leave some food outside your door."

"I can't." But Bree lacked conviction.

Jocelyn upped the ante. "Text me every time you want me to leave a bottle of booze outside your door."

"All right, all right. But it'll have to be booze I don't like. I'm doing penance."

"Then look forward to your peach schnapps."

"Peach schnapps." Bree recoiled. "Hang on—it's not like I *murdered* someone."

They gathered their bags and stepped out of the darkened bar and into the sunny, sea-breeze-scented afternoon. Bree's spirits lifted for a moment—and then panic took over.

"Come on." She took Jocelyn's hand and dragged her toward the car. "Move it along."

"What?" Jocelyn glanced around in confusion, then realized that Dan and Krysten were seated right across the street on a wooden bench. They were in the midst of what could be tactfully described as a "heated discussion." Hands were waving, tears were flowing, voices were raised.

They both stopped arguing long enough to stare directly at Bree. Jocelyn clicked the button on her key fob to unlock the car, and they dove inside.

Bree hunched down in her seat. "Drive."

Jocelyn jammed the key into the ignition and revved the engine.

"Drive more subtly."

"I'm trying." Jocelyn pulled out of the parking lot and didn't glance back.

"Ugh." Bree sounded as though she was going to be sick at any moment. "That was . . ."

"Yeah."

"I feel . . ."

"Yeah."

Bree pressed her fingers to her temples. "I'm never, ever going to do anything like this again."

"Me, neither," Jocelyn agreed.

"I don't know how I'm going to face him again," Bree said. "Or her. Or anyone."

"It won't always be this awkward, I swear."

"You don't know that."

"Yes, I do. You did the right thing. It sucks right now, but it'll be okay. Everything will work out in the end."

Bree scoffed. "I wish I could believe you."

"You can. Life is about to get so much better." Jocelyn's sunny optimism dimmed when she turned into her driveway and an unfamiliar man materialized next to her car.

He established eye contact and knocked on the window.

"Gun it," Bree ordered. "Run him over if necessary."

But Jocelyn had already lowered her window a few inches. "What?"

"Are you Jocelyn Hillier?"

Jocelyn knew exactly what would be coming in the aftermath of the question. But she also knew there was no point in trying to escape. "That's me." She lowered the window farther and held out her hand.

There was a dry slapping sound as the envelope hit her palm.

"You've been served."

chapter 33

"Dear lord, what now?" Bree took a swig of peach schnapps straight from the bottle and offered it to Jocelyn, who managed a tiny sip before gagging.

"I can't believe this." Jocelyn's rage mounted with every sentence she read. "That conniving, two-faced traitor."

"You'll have to be more specific."

"Lois Gunther. The dog handler." Jocelyn's chest tightened. "She's actually doing it. She's suing for custody of the dogs."

"Dog custody? Is that even a thing?"

"Her lawyer seems to think so."

"On what grounds?" Bree demanded. "You're the best dog owner I know."

"Lois disagrees." Jocelyn kept reading through the complaint. "Oh, this is interesting. She doesn't just want the dogs. She wants the full benefit of being the dogs' guardian."

Bree gasped. "She's coming for your beach house!"

"Looks like it. She wants the house, the stipend, all the entitlements." Jocelyn put the papers aside. "This is a money grab."

"Call your lawyer," Bree advised. "Now."

"I had no idea being rich was so much work." Jocelyn picked up the phone. "I thought it'd be all bonbons and spa days. Turns out, it's nothing but phone calls and lawsuits."

Bree coughed and put aside the schnapps. "Start dialing, moneybags."

"I'll dial, but this is a triage situation. Before I call the lawyer, I have to call Liam."

"I'm freaking out." Jocelyn met Liam at the front door of his rental house with a copy of the legal documents.

"Don't freak out." He leaned in for a kiss. "Why do you smell like peach schnapps?"

"Bree and I were punishing ourselves earlier today."

"You must have done something really bad."

Jocelyn summarized the fiasco at Davy's Dive. "As you can imagine, Dan didn't take it very well. He and Krysten had a huge fight. And then I got served with this." She handed him the papers.

He skimmed the first two pages of the complaint. "Come in and you'll get served with lasagna."

Jocelyn stepped over the threshold and sniffed the air, which was redolent with garlic and oregano. "Is that what smells amazing?"

"Yeah." He led the way to the kitchen. "It's almost ready."

Jocelyn made herself at home on a kitchen stool at the island. Liam opened the oven, pulled out a pan steaming with heat, and plated a piece of lasagna for her.

"This is a much better coping skill than peach schnapps." Jocelyn's mouth watered at the sight of melty cheese and red sauce amid layers of noodles. "This is possibly the sexiest thing you could do without taking your clothes off."

He handed her a fork and a napkin. "Want to watch me chop up an onion?"

"Oh yeah, baby. Nice and slow."

He grinned. "I've got knife skills that will blow your mind."

Jocelyn knew she'd burn her mouth, but couldn't resist taking a taste. "Oh my God."

"You like it?"

She forked up another bite, scorched tongue be damned. "Did you make the sauce yourself?"

"Of course." He looked offended. "Do I look like the kind of man who would use jarred tomato sauce?"

While she ate, Liam got serious about reading the documents from Lois's attorney. His smile twisted into a frown, which deepened with every page he turned.

"This is bad," he said.

"I know. I can't believe she has the gall. Bree thinks this has nothing to do with the dogs and everything to do with the money and lifestyle that comes with them."

"I agree with her."

"So my freaking out is warranted, yes?"

"No." His tone was calm and reassuring. "This case is going to cost her a ton of money in legal fees, and there's a good chance she's going to lose. She might drop the whole thing after a few months of testing the waters."

"Okay." Jocelyn put down her fork. "Then why does your face look like that?"

"Because this lawsuit is going to temporarily freeze all your access to the trust accounts."

"Meaning we can't get the equity loan for the ranch."

"You can ask your lawyer about it, but it's very unlikely you'll have the latitude to make that kind of financial transaction while the estate is being disputed."

Jocelyn hadn't even considered this possibility in her outrage.

"Don't worry. I'll figure out something else before the end of the month." He sounded so confident, but they both knew he was out of time. If there were any other options, he would have pursued them already.

"I'll help you," Jocelyn vowed.

Liam's whole body stiffened. "You don't need to do anything. I've already taken advantage of you."

She stood up and put her arms around him. "You haven't taken advantage of me."

"I asked you to take money out of your home and give it to me."

"You asked me to help arrange for a loan to help your mother, which you are going to pay back. That's not taking advantage." Jocelyn tried to figure out when this conversation had stopped being about Lois's lawsuit and started being about her and Liam's relationship.

"I should be able to handle this without help," he insisted.

"You helped me," she pointed out. "With the puppies and the dogs. Before you even knew me."

"That was different," he said.

"In what way?"

"*I* was helping *you*."

"We're partners," Jocelyn decreed. "Business partners and personal partners. And lasagna partners. We work together. Make your peace with that." She patted the stool next to her. "And make yourself comfortable. Let's figure out how to rip this woman apart. Legally speaking, of course."

chapter 34

"This whole thing is ridiculous, right?" Jocelyn waited a beat for Murray Tumboldt, Esquire, to confirm that this whole thing was, in fact, ridiculous. But he just stared at her, silent and poker-faced in his suit and tie.

His inertia exacerbated her restlessness. She started to pace the perimeter of the rug surrounding the desk. "Who gets to decide this, anyway? Are we going to have to go to canine family court?"

"The co-trustee has ultimate decision-making power," the attorney replied. "You'll make our case, the opposition will make theirs, the trustee will do her best to consider the wishes and intentions of Mr. Allardyce and act accordingly."

"So I'll finally get to meet this woman?"

"Yes. And the woman has a name: Frances Jarvinen."

Jocelyn frowned. "Why does that name sound familiar?"

"Perhaps because we've discussed Ms. Jarvinen's role in your life at great length?"

"Let me ask you something. We're all supposed to consider Mr. Allardyce and his wishes, but what about the dogs?" Jocelyn demanded. "Who considers them?"

"Ms. Jarvinen will take into account the affection and intentions Mr. Allardyce had for the dogs. If she believes, for whatever reason, that Lois would better meet the standards of care Mr. Allardyce stipulated for the dogs, she might side with her. But I doubt that would happen. Mr. Allardyce named you, and he did so for a reason." The attorney looked so detached, she wanted to smack him.

Jocelyn planted her high heels in the thick pile of the rug. "May I ask you a personal question?"

His eyes darted downward, but he didn't say no.

"Do you have a dog?"

He adjusted his glasses on the bridge of his nose. "No."

"A cat?" she persisted.

"No."

"A ferret, a turtle, a parrot, a fish? Anything?"

He shook his head. "I'm not what you would call an animal lover."

"Well, I am. I'm an official crazy dog lady. You know people who treat their pets like their kids? That's me." Jocelyn ticked her neuroses off on her fingers. "I dress them up for Halloween. I let them share the last bite of my ice cream cone. I have birthday parties for them, with special low-sugar oatmeal cake."

The attorney glanced at his watch.

She didn't care. She was on a roll, and her dogs were paying his hourly rate. "I keep hearing about the trustee and all her power and Mr. Allardyce, who, I hate to be the one to point out, is dead. Why are we still so concerned about him? The only people I'm concerned about are the dogs. And I'm guessing this trustee has never even met them."

The attorney finally broke down and used a facial expression—

one of great skepticism and superiority. "And I suppose that the fact that Ms. Gunther is attempting to wrestle away your home and discretionary funds has nothing to do with your outrage?"

"Well, obviously I'm pissed about that, too." Jocelyn balled her fist. "I was on the verge of sealing a lucrative deal with a real estate investor that was going to benefit the trust. And of course I like living in the Delaware version of *Million Dollar Listing*. But mostly, I'm mad because that traitor thinks she would be a better dog mom than me. Spoiler alert: She wouldn't."

"Be that as it may." The attorney's leather chair creaked as he leaned forward. "If this is really about the dogs' welfare, there's a simple solution. Just give her a puppy and perhaps one of the adults."

Jocelyn stepped back, stunned. "What?!"

"You're allowed to do as you see fit with those puppies. If it's truly the dogs Ms. Gunther wants, that should placate her."

"I don't want to placate her; I want to annihilate her." Jocelyn dug her fingernails into her palm. "She can't have so much as a single tuft of hair."

"Offer her one puppy," the lawyer suggested. "That should make clear whether she's after the canines or the cash."

"Even if she agreed to that deal, she'd pass the puppy right along to the Derridges. I'm not using Hester's babies as bargaining chips."

"Think it over carefully before you decide. Either you use a bargaining chip wisely now, or risk gambling away the whole estate."

"I'll take my chances." Jocelyn still couldn't believe the advice she was hearing. "My dogs are not for sale. Neither is my integrity."

"Oh my dear." The lawyer laughed, genuinely amused. He pulled out a crisp linen handkerchief and dabbed the corner of his eyes. "Everything is for sale. Everything. It's merely a matter of naming the right price."

chapter 35

Late that afternoon, Jocelyn took Carmen for a playdate with Friday. As if she could sense where they were headed, Carmen spent the car ride whining with impatience and smearing the windows with slobber.

Jocelyn had to smile, even though she dreaded the task of cleaning the car windows. "Look at you, literally drooling over a guy. Hasn't anyone ever talked to you about playing hard to get?"

No one had, obviously. Carmen pulled at the leash and pranced in place at the pre-arranged meeting spot on the sand. She didn't pretend, she didn't act cool. She reveled in her joy and anticipation, and it made Jocelyn love her even more.

Jocelyn tried in vain to distract Carmen with a tennis ball and a Frisbee, but the besotted chocolate Lab stood watch on the top of the dune, her eyes trained on the parking lot below. A few minutes later, a weathered gold Subaru turned in from the main road and Carmen decompensated, barking and thrashing and snapping at the air in delight.

"Playing easy to get," Jocelyn mused. "You may be on to something."

Friday jumped out of the hatchback as soon as Violet opened the door. He sprinted toward Carmen as fast as his sturdy legs could carry him. Jocelyn stepped out of the way as he approached, fearful that if he sideswiped her by accident, it would be the equivalent of being tackled by a linebacker.

"Lovely day," Violet commented as she trailed behind her dog, leash in hand. "I'll certainly miss this weather when I go back home."

Jocelyn watched the two dogs chase and pounce on each other. "You still have some time left, right?"

"Just a few days. We leave on Friday." Friday glanced over at the sound of his name, then resumed frolicking.

Jocelyn's heart ached for Carmen. "What a shame. They have such a good time together."

"Yes, they do." Violet put on her omnipresent sun hat and adjusted the brim. "They're quite a pair."

"Can't you stay an extra week or two?" Jocelyn coaxed.

"We'd love to, but the house I'm renting is already booked solid for the rest of the season. Besides, I'm afraid we're needed back in our real lives."

"Carmen will be devastated." Jocelyn turned to the older woman. "Are you sure there's nothing I can say to persuade you to stay just a bit longer?"

"Well." Violet cleared her throat delicately. "You could make me an offer."

Jocelyn raised one eyebrow, confused. "Excuse me?"

Violet glanced at Friday, then back at Jocelyn. "Make me an offer."

Jocelyn was sure she was misunderstanding. "For what?"

Violet held her gaze. "I asked about you, after our last meeting. People here love to talk."

"That's an understatement."

"I heard about what happened, how you got the dogs."

"Yes, well . . ."

"You love them, you treat them well, you give them a good life." Violet's tone had shifted to breezy nonchalance. Jocelyn tried to adjust accordingly.

"I try my best."

"I'd love for Friday and Carmen to be able to stay together. I know you'd take excellent care of him." Violet lifted her hand, offering Jocelyn his leash.

Jocelyn accepted, almost as a reflex, still trying to figure out exactly what was transpiring here. "But wouldn't you miss him?"

"I'll miss him terribly." The old woman rested her hand on her heart as her eyes welled with tears. "But he loves it here. He loves Carmen. Think what a gift you'll be giving her."

Jocelyn stared down at the braided leather leash in her hand. "So you want me to . . . take him? Forever?"

"I can drop off his dish and his bed tonight." Violet's gaze sharpened. "Of course you understand what it means to me to leave him here." She cleared her throat. "What it will *cost* me."

"Uh-huh."

"Emotionally."

"Uh-huh." Jocelyn wished for the millionth time that she had a Rich Benefactress Decoder Ring. "Would it help if I offered a little adoption fee? You know, like when you adopt a dog from a rescue group?"

"It would." Violet beamed.

Jocelyn inhaled slowly, buying some time to think. "What did you have in mind?"

"Nothing extravagant," Violet assured her. "Just enough to distract me while I grieve his loss."

Jocelyn mulled over her options, up to and including leaving without another word. But then she looked at Carmen and Friday, so happy together. So unaware that they were about to be parted. So oblivious to the fact that Friday's owner was willing to put a dollar amount on his companionship and devotion.

Well, if she's selling, I'm buying.

Jocelyn's doubt and empathy seeped out, only to be replaced by something colder but stronger: Power.

She adjusted her sunglasses and asked Violet to name her price. "Will you take a check?"

"Absolutely." Violet beamed. "A check will be fine."

Bree was waiting on the steps of the beach house with a book and a bag of freshly picked cherries. She frowned when she saw Jocelyn pile out of the car along with Carmen and Friday.

"Why do you look like you look?"

Jocelyn slung her purse over her shoulder. "I just bought Carmen's boyfriend on the black market."

"Rich people problems." Bree held out her hand for Carmen's leash.

"I was minding my own business at the doggie playdate." Jocelyn tried to explain how events had transpired, even though she didn't completely understand it herself. "I guess we have a new member of the family."

Bree grinned as she looked over Friday's blocky pit bull head, German shepherd coat, hound nose, and Lab tail. "You think Lois is going to include him in her lawsuit, too?"

"Lois wouldn't be caught dead with him."

"I don't know. This dog's got charisma." Bree fished a cherry out of the bag. "Rags to riches, buddy. You're living the American dream."

"I'm glad you're here." Jocelyn unlocked the front door and stepped out of the way so Carmen could race in and introduce the newest member of the pack. "I have to handle all the laundry myself today. My mom's in Connecticut. At a casino." Jocelyn recounted the phone conversation. "I don't even know who she is anymore."

"So your mom and Liam's mom are bonding," Bree mused. "That could be really, really good or really, really bad."

"You know what's comforting?" Jocelyn helped herself to a cherry as they entered the house. "No matter how crazy life gets or who shows up out of the blue, some things never change. And one of those things is laundry." She opened the mudroom door and doled out treats to Curtis and Hester. "Tonight could be the flesh-eating zombie apocalypse and there would still be clothes to wash."

"And some very stubborn stains, I'd imagine." Bree refilled the dogs' water dish.

"I'm not going to worry about my mom and Liam's mom. You're not going to worry about Krysten and Dan. We're just going to bleach some stains, clean out the lint trap, and carry on as usual. And we're taking a mental vacation from the lawyers." Jocelyn's phone rang. Her heart sank when she saw the contact name on the screen. "Or maybe not."

"It's the lawyer?"

"It's him," Jocelyn confirmed. "And if *he's* calling *me*, it's something big." She clicked the button to pick up. "Hello?"

"Did Mr. Allardyce ever say anything to you about Lois Gunther before he died?" the lawyer demanded, skipping all introductions and pleasantries.

"Um . . . in what capacity?" Jocelyn asked.

"Any capacity," the lawyer said. "Did he ever mention her in any exchange he had with you, written or oral?"

"Well, sure. She was the dogs' handler."

"Did he speak highly of her?"

"Yeah, he said she was the best. Why? What's up?"

For the first time since she'd met him, Murray Tumboldt, Esquire was at a loss for words. All she heard on the other end of the connection was a heavy sigh.

"What?" she pressed.

"I just got off the phone with Ms. Jarvinen, your co-trustee."

"Ah yes, the infamous Ms. Jarvinen."

"The infamous Ms. Jarvinen just got off the phone with Ms. Gunther's attorney. Apparently, they have e-mails."

"Like what kind of e-mails?"

"E-mails from Mr. Allardyce praising Ms. Gunther's performance and indicating that he would like her to take care of his dogs if anything were to happen to him."

Jocelyn's expression must have been alarming, because Bree started hovering and trying to overhear the other side of the conversation.

"When was this?" Jocelyn demanded.

"Four years ago."

"That was before I even met him."

"Yes, but apparently, he sent the e-mails to Ms. Gunther shortly before he went into the hospital for surgery."

"For what?"

"I'm not privy to that information, but Ms. Gunther's attorney assured Ms. Jarvinen that they can provide documentation confirming the hospital stay and the fact that he entrusted the dogs to her care while he was admitted."

"Okay, but that was still four years ago," Jocelyn pointed out. "If he really wanted her to be the custodial guardian of the dogs, he would've named her in the will instead of me."

"Apparently, he *did* name her as the custodial guardian in an earlier version of the will."

Jocelyn mouthed this information to Bree, who mouthed back: "I can't read lips."

"But he changed his mind," Jocelyn said to the lawyer. "So she's SOL."

"Yes, well, Ms. Gunther's opinion differs. She is alleging that Mr. Allardyce always intended for her to act as the dogs' custodial guardian."

"Then why did he change the will?"

"I believe her team intends to argue that he was mentally incompetent at the signing of the new will."

"Are you kidding me? This is like a damn soap opera."

Bree held out her hand and wriggled her fingers. "Give me the phone."

"Anyone who ever had any contact with that guy could tell you he was sharp as a tack and mean as a snake until the very end," Jocelyn said. "He wasn't just mentally competent, he was a mastermind."

Bree was still gesturing madly. "Give me the phone."

"Be that as it may." Mr. Tumboldt cleared his throat. "You need to prepare yourself for a long and potentially messy custody battle."

"Messy?" Jocelyn put her hand on her hip. "What does 'messy' mean?"

Bree physically wrestled the phone out of her hand. "Hello? Yes, hi, this is Jocelyn's in-house legal counsel. What's that? Yeah, I know, but I'll be representing Ms. Hillier for the remainder of this conversation. Listen, counselor, let's get to the bottom line. What does this woman want and what's it gonna cost us to get her to go away?"

Jocelyn watched in fascination as Bree grabbed a pen and started scribbling on a series of Post-its. "Uh-huh . . . uh-huh . . . uh-huh. And is there any precedent for this kind of maneuvering? Got it. And what's the worst-case scenario? Okay. I'll relay that to my client and we'll get back to you as soon as possible. Thanks! Bye."

Bree hung up the phone and addressed Jocelyn, all business. "I'm going to ask you a question and I need you to be brutally, totally honest. Both with me and with yourself."

Jocelyn braced herself. "Shoot."

"How attached are you to these dogs?"

"Very."

"Be more specific."

"You can't quantify love," Jocelyn protested.

"In a court of law, you can and you must. Let me ask you this," Bree said. "Would you be willing to part with one or two of them?"

"Well, two or three of the puppies will go to new families, obviously. But no, the adults all need to stay together. We're a family."

"So you wouldn't be willing to throw one over to Lois? Just to shut her up?"

"No!"

"Would you be willing to pay her to shut up?"

"How much are we talking?" Jocelyn asked.

"I have no idea. But you better start thinking about how much is too much."

chapter 36

"Read it for yourself." Jocelyn handed over the printed e-mail she held in her hands. She and Liam had arranged an emergency legal summit at the Jilted Café in downtown Black Dog Bay. "This is unbelievable. She's saying that your father always meant for her to take care of the dogs. She's accusing me of swooping in at the last second and, like, hoodwinking a senile old man." She drummed her fingers on the table. "Which, now that I think about it, is pretty much what you accused me of the first time I met you."

Liam cleared his throat. "And again, I am sorry for that."

"Yes, well, we'll revisit that later. Right now, we have to figure out how to fight this. She's got nothing but a four-year-old e-mail and a vendetta. That's not going to hold up in court."

"Are you sure?" Liam looked skeptical.

"She's not taking my dogs. I'll do whatever I need to do to stop her." Jocelyn held her fork up. "The good thing about the trust is that, at the end of the day, I can outspend her."

"Sorry, hang on one second." Liam pulled out his phone as a text came in. "It's Paul. I told him I'd meet with him when we finished up here." He replied to the text.

"Is Paul the one who derailed my date with his fancy European car?"

"That's the one."

"Don't look so smug. It wasn't going to work out between me and Otter, anyway."

"Yeah, because I would have stolen you away from him." Liam put his phone away. "Want some more coffee?"

"No thanks, I'm good." Jocelyn finished the last few drops in the mug. "If I have any more caffeine they'll have to peel me off the ceiling."

"No word from my mom in twenty-four hours," Liam said. "Have you heard from yours?"

"Yeah, she said they're on their way back, and they have a surprise for us. I tried to get more details, but she wasn't talking."

Liam covered his eyes with his hand. "It's probably matching tattoos, the way they're going."

"They're having a good time. It's way overdue. My mom has worked nonstop for the last twenty years."

"Mine, too."

"And I don't know about your mom, but mine doesn't have a lot of girlfriends. So let them go to Connecticut and have their fun. They're grown women. How much trouble could they really get into?" Dozens of possibilities immediately sprang to mind. "Don't answer that."

They discussed Lois's e-mail and the legal implications for a few more minutes until Paul walked in. The keychain for his fancy European sports car jingled in his hand.

"Hey!" His face lit up when he spotted Jocelyn. "It's the lovely lady who introduced me to my new business partner."

"The one and only. How's that whole venture going, by the way?"

"Fantastic. We've picked out a location and started spreading the word in the car-collecting circles. We've got our first two months booked out already, and we haven't even opened the doors yet!"

"Good for you." Jocelyn was delighted on behalf of her erstwhile date. "Sounds like a perfect match. You're a lucky guy."

"Yeah, he's a real find, that Otter." Paul took a seat next to Liam. "It's nice to have a new opportunity on the horizon. I've had it with real estate."

Liam looked surprised. "Yeah?"

"It's not worth the hassle these days, what with all the lawsuits."

Jocelyn leaned forward. "You have lawsuits, too?"

"Six of them going right now."

Liam shifted in his seat. "I thought you were at four."

"The seller's insurance company and the inspector got involved, and then a couple of the subpoenaed witnesses lied on the stand, so now we're up to six."

"But how?" Jocelyn felt like a camper listening to the scariest ghost story at the campfire.

Paul exhaled with exasperation. "I bought a house that I knew better than to buy. My gut told me no, but it was such a good deal that I went ahead. Turns out it had black mold, the sellers knew and didn't disclose. I say I have proof, they say I don't, and here we are. Lawsuits flying left and right."

"Yeah, but *six*?" Liam looked as horrified as Jocelyn felt.

"They multiply like cockroaches in the dark, man."

"Suddenly, our one little lawsuit doesn't sound that bad," Jocelyn said.

Paul regarded her with great pity. "You've got one, eh?"

"Yeah. Liam dropped his, and another one came out of nowhere."

"Like cockroaches." Paul smiled grimly. "I'm telling you."

"How much are you spending on legal fees?" Liam asked.

"I'm hemorrhaging money," Paul replied. "But it's not just the money, it's the time and the energy. Every waking moment is taken up with phone calls and depositions and subpoenas. Lawsuits are my full-time job now." He pointed at Jocelyn. "My advice to you is to get out now. Settle. Concede. Fake your own death. Do whatever you have to do to, but get out."

"But it's totally without grounds," Jocelyn protested.

"Doesn't matter. The time and expense it's going to take to prove that in court is unimaginable. You think you can imagine it right now, but trust me, you can't."

Jocelyn closed her eyes and tried to envision battling six Liams and Loises at once.

"If there's one thing I can tell you for sure about the legal system, it's that they don't care about common sense. It's all about who has what in writing."

Jocelyn's eyes snapped open and she glanced at the e-mail Mr. Allardyce had sent to Lois. "Hmmm."

"You still have the power to stop at one lawsuit. Don't be like me." Paul took off his hat and started kneading the brim. "Talking about this gets me so worked up I need a cruller."

"Try the bear claws," Jocelyn advised. "They're really good here."

"And remember," Liam advised, "you've always got the vintage car business."

"Yeah, until somebody's brakes fail two months after we install them and they decide to sue us." Paul slumped in his chair.

"Don't worry about that," Jocelyn said. "Otter does excellent work."

Liam gave her a side eye. "How do you know?"

"I have it on high authority." Jocelyn remembered Bree's ringing endorsement. "Why? Are you jealous?"

He sipped his coffee. "I don't need to be jealous."

"Look at you two." Paul's voice was tinged with both despair and disgust. "So happy. So hopeful. You know what's going to ruin this beautiful life you're sharing?"

"Lawsuits?" Liam and Jocelyn said in unison.

He nodded. "Mark my words."

Jocelyn braced her forearms on the tabletop and leaned toward him. "I'm picking up what you're putting down here. But it's not that simple. How would you go about putting a stop to a lawsuit before it starts?"

"I'd arrange a sit-down with the other party."

"Sounds mafia," Liam said.

"I'd meet them wherever they felt comfortable," Paul said. "Their favorite coffee shop, dive bar, tattoo parlor. Wherever they could let their guard down. Attorney's offices are not warm, reassuring environments."

"No kidding," Jocelyn muttered.

"And then I'd ask what they wanted, explain what I wanted, and get them to hammer out an agreement right then and there."

"But that's the hard part," Jocelyn objected. "*How* would you get them to agree to come to an agreement?"

"If you'd asked me that question six lawsuits ago, I wouldn't have an answer for you." Paul straightened up as the server approached. He ordered a bear claw, which seemed to cheer him up. "But now that I've been to court a zillion times and read a kajillion books on psychology and litigation, I can tell you: What you do is say to the other person, 'We need to work this out today.' And when they ask why, you say, 'Because we need to work it out today.'"

Liam and Jocelyn exchanged a look. "But that doesn't answer their question."

"It does. It's not a good answer, but it's an answer, and that's all that ninety-five percent of people need to come to the table."

"Hmm," was all Jocelyn said.

"Just try it." Paul lifted his palm as though preparing to testify under oath. "Call bullshit on me now, thank me later."

Jocelyn looked back at Liam, who shrugged. "Worth a shot."

Paul's eyes lit up as the server approached with the bear claw. "I'll bet you a lobster dinner that it'll work on your lawsuit opponent. *If* you can get them alone in a place they feel at home."

"You're on." Liam extended his hand so Paul could shake it.

"I can already taste my lobster." Paul ripped into his pastry. "With lemon butter dipping sauce. I'll spare no expense."

"I wouldn't tie your lobster bib on just yet," Liam said. "We'd have to figure out where this woman—what's her name again?"

"Lois," Jocelyn supplied.

"Where she feels comfortable and goes on a regular basis." He looked horrified. "Oh God, we're going to have to go surveilling again, aren't we?"

Paul stopped chewing his bear claw. "You're going to have to do what, now?"

"No need," Jocelyn said. "I know exactly where we're going."

chapter 37

"I've never seen so many dogs in one place," Liam marveled as he and Jocelyn entered the huge convention center, which had been turned into a dog show. "And they're all so well-behaved."

"That's because Curtis isn't here," Jocelyn said. She led Liam through the booths selling beds and bones and organic dog treats. "Let's see, we have to find show ring nine."

"Hold up." Liam placed his hand on her arm as they passed a booth with two employees handing out brochures on procuring and storing frozen dog sperm. "That's a real thing?"

"It's a multimillion-dollar business," Jocelyn replied. "Remind me to tell you about Carmen sometime."

"I have so many questions, but I'm scared to find out the answers."

"Grab a pamphlet and let's go," Jocelyn ordered. "Time is of the essence."

Liam bypassed the table without taking a pamphlet. "I'm better off living in ignorance."

They located ring nine just as the judge arrived to evaluate a group of gorgeous cocker spaniels, all of them groomed to perfection. Lois was handling a small tricolor spaniel with soulful eyes and silky curls on his ears.

"How do you get out of these shows without getting a new dog each time?" Liam asked.

"Well, they cost thousands or even tens of thousands of dollars apiece, so that helps."

Lois put her dog through his paces with practiced expertise. They trotted around the ring and posed like models on the catwalk.

"The dog looks like he's having a good time." Liam sounded surprised.

"He is. Most of them really enjoy it. They know they're the center of attention, and they love it. The best ones, like Carmen, are super competitive. They're in it to win it every time."

"But Carmen's so nice," Liam said.

"Not in the ring. In the ring, she's a backstabbing, throat-slitting, side-eyeing diva who will accept nothing less than best in breed."

"She's the one who's in love with a mutt from the pound, right?"

"Yep."

Liam nodded. "Makes sense."

They watched Lois do what she did best, and politely applauded along with the crowd when Lois's charge was pronounced best in breed. When the officials announced that the spaniels had to clear out to make way for some black and tan coonhounds, Jocelyn turned to the man who had sworn to be her partner and protector in avoiding frivolous litigation.

"Ready?"

"Ready." He took her hand and together they stepped forward. But before they could make their presence known, Lois was swarmed with congratulatory owners and handlers who gushed over the spaniel and exclaimed about Lois's finesse. Lois beamed and feigned modesty.

"I'm getting a contact high just looking at her," Jocelyn said.

"This was a great idea," Liam said. "Look at her—this is her comfort zone. Nothing we say or do will threaten her right now."

"Well, then, let's go close this deal." Jocelyn waved to catch Lois's attention and tried to look surprised. "Lois! Hi! Fancy meeting you here!"

Lois, understandably, was suspicious. Her smile vanished as Liam and Jocelyn approached.

"Here." She handed the cocker spaniel's leash to its owner. "I'll catch up with you in a minute." She stood her ground as Jocelyn approached. "What are you doing here?"

"Honing my dog-training skills, same as you," Jocelyn said.

"I'm getting paid to win," Lois pointed out. "My skills are already honed, thank you very much."

Jocelyn took her hand out of Liam's and presented him to the dour older lady. "Lois, this is Liam."

"How are you?" Liam turned his charm up to eleven. "I've heard great things."

"Oh really? Have you heard that I'm going to be rescuing Mr. Allardyce's poor dogs from your girlfriend?"

Liam's eyebrows shot up and he took a breath to reply. Jocelyn jumped in with, "I'm so glad you brought that up. I've been wanting to talk to you."

"I bet you have." Lois smirked. "But I have nothing to say. Everything goes through my attorney and Fran—sorry, I mean, Ms. Jarvinen."

Jocelyn narrowed her eyes. "How do you know Ms. Jarvinen?"

Lois's smile was laced with satisfaction as she said, "Fran came to all of Curtis and Hester's shows in Virginia. She's seen my love for the dogs firsthand."

That was when Jocelyn figured out why Frances Jarvinen

sounded so familiar. She'd heard the name when Mr. Allardyce was forcing her to sit through a minute-by-minute account of his dogs' latest victory. Frances Jarvinen was lined up right next to Mr. Allardyce and Lois Gunther in several of the best-in-show photos.

"Hang on a second." Jocelyn excused herself to the ladies' room, where she scoured Lois Gunther's social media accounts as quickly as she could. While there was nothing relevant posted since Mr. Allardyce's death, she managed to find several photos of Frances and Lois palling around at dog shows and discussing where they should all go for a celebratory dinner afterward.

Jocelyn turned her face heavenward and addressed Mr. Allardyce's spirit. "I should have known you wouldn't let me live in peace that easily."

Jocelyn strode back to Lois and Liam with trembling hands that she hoped to compensate for with full-body bravado.

"Talk to my attorney," Lois was saying to Liam. She turned her back as she saw Jocelyn approach.

"Lois." Jocelyn's words came out as a demand, not a request. "It's imperative that we reach an agreement today."

Lois glanced back over her shoulder. "Why?"

Jocelyn's gaze flickered over to Liam for a nanosecond. "Because we need to reach an agreement today." She held up her arm, indicating that Lois should have a seat on a nearby bench.

Incredibly, Lois obliged, even as she protested. *Score one for Paul.*

"I don't see why I need to say anything to you. My attorney says our case is very strong. Mr. Allardyce clearly chose me to be the dogs' guardian." Lois narrowed her eyes. "You know, *before* he lost his mental faculties."

"Let me ask you something," Liam said. "Have you ever been involved in a lawsuit before?"

Lois blinked. "No. Not that it's any business of yours."

"I see." Liam crossed his arms.

"That's right—I don't have a history of suing people left and right. So whatever shoddy defense you were planning on building won't work."

Jocelyn slid right into the role of good cop to Liam's bad cop. "No one's planning on accusing you of anything. What Liam's trying to say is, lawsuits are kind of like cockroaches. If you see one, you can be sure there's more."

Lois sniffed. "I haven't the faintest idea what you're talking about."

"You filed this lawsuit, but it's not going to stop there. We're going to counterfile," Liam said coolly. "We'll subpoena everybody Mr. Allardyce ever met. His doctors, his accountant, his estate planners, his veterinarians."

"Bring it on," Lois challenged.

"And sadly, even though we don't want to, we're going to have to bring in lots of people that you know. People from the show circuit, your accountants and estate planners."

"People who might have reason to believe that my co-trustee—sorry, I mean *Fran*—might be unfairly biased in your favor. Since the two of you are having dinner all over Facebook." Jocelyn nodded somberly at Liam. "It'll be a mess."

"Some of these people are going to be very upset to be dragged into a suit," Liam said. "Doctors and lawyers and accountants can't divulge the kind of information we'll ask for without a court order. Some of them will fight back and countersue."

"Start with one lawsuit," Jocelyn added, "next thing you know, you've got six."

Lois forced out a scornful laugh. "Nobody has six lawsuits."

Liam chuckled right back. "Spoken like someone who's never had a single deposition."

Lois kept blustering, but the righteousness had vanished. "You're trying to scare me."

"We're trying to work with you." Jocelyn waved to the owner of a passing Dalmatian. "Which is why we need to reach an agreement today."

"Fine." Lois shrugged. "Turn the dogs over to me and we're done. Problem solved."

Jocelyn settled back against the wall and prepared for a protracted negotiation. "I can't do that."

"Why not?"

"Because they're my dogs. Legally, emotionally, and practically, I'm part of the pack now."

For the first time, Lois looked genuinely hurt. "No, you're not. Not like I am."

"I delivered Hester's babies." Jocelyn leaned over to kiss Liam's cheek. "And he helped."

"You don't care about any of that," Lois insisted. "You just want that big house and the money."

Translation: YOU just want the big house and the money.

"On the topic of money," Liam said. "Let's say we did have to take a quick peek at the state of your finances, just to rule out debt and greed as a possible source of motivation."

Lois visibly stiffened. That was when Jocelyn knew for sure—this had nothing at all to do with the dogs.

She focused on what mattered. "Listen, Lois, I love those dogs. I really do. I would fight for years to keep them." She waited until she caught Lois's gaze. "I would spend every penny of the estate fighting to hang on to them. I mean it. Every. Last. Penny."

Lois scowled at the concrete floor.

"But I can understand why you want them," Jocelyn added. "Why you think you deserve them. I mean, Mr. Allardyce *did* really like you."

"Yes." Lois's anger had dampened. "He did."

"I try my best, but I'm not a perfect dog mom."

"That's right." Lois looked vindicated. "You're not."

"What would it take for you to give me a chance with the dogs?"

"There's nothing you could possibly do to persuade me," Lois said, but she lacked conviction. Jocelyn recognized the tone; it was the same tone Friday's owner had used when she wanted Jocelyn to make her an offer.

"I know you care about the dogs more than any other details of the estate." *Such as beachfront property and millions of dollars.* "But I'd be happy to make some concession. A show of good faith."

Lois leaned in. "Like what?"

Jocelyn played dumb. "Like . . . oh, I don't know. Maybe you could take the dogs one weekend a month."

Lois took her time responding to this. "That's not going to work for me."

Jocelyn cupped her hand to Liam's ear and pretended to initiate a dramatic whispering debate. After a few moments, she straightened up. "Every other weekend, but that's my final offer. Take it or leave it."

"Leave it," Lois said.

Liam leveled his gaze at her. "What do you think would be a reasonable solution?"

"Other than getting full custody of the dogs, which I'm probably going to get anyway?"

"You're not getting full custody." Jocelyn rolled her eyes.

"Other than that, yes," Liam said.

"Well." Lois put on an unintentionally hilarious display of soulful pondering, complete with stroking her chin and furrowing her brow. "Maybe you could try to prove to me that you really love them. That it's not just about the money to you."

Jocelyn was all wide-eyed innocence. "And how would I do that?"

"Let me think."

Jocelyn nudged Liam. "Okay. Take your time."

She and Liam admired the parade of purebreds passing them by.

"I don't know if you knew this," Lois finally said, "but I don't own my home. Real estate prices are crazy in Fairfax County. I've rented for decades."

"You don't say."

"I've been in the same house for the last seven years," Lois continued. "But my lease is up at the end of next month, and my landlord won't renew it. He wants to sell, and I can't afford the down payment."

"Isn't that a shame." Jocelyn braced herself for a big buildup, but Lois got right to the point.

"I want to live in your beach house for a year. Maybe two."

Jocelyn didn't know what she'd been expecting, but it wasn't that. "Like, um, like a roommate situation?"

"No, like you move out and I move in." Lois cleared her throat. "You could take the dogs with you, but only if we reach an agreement today."

"So you want me to rent out the house to you?"

"No, I want you to let me live there."

"Rent-free?" Jocelyn pressed.

"I'm letting you keep the dogs," Lois said. "You said that was all you care about."

"And *you* said that was all *you* cared about," Jocelyn reminded her.

"I'm willing to compromise if you are."

Jocelyn paused for a moment, weighing her words. "Let me see if I have this straight. You want me to move out of the beach house, take the dogs with me, and all of us will go live somewhere else while you live rent-free in Mr. Allardyce's house, for at least a year? Is that right?"

"And I get the stipend," Lois added.

Jocelyn's jaw dropped. "What?!"

"I heard there's a monetary stipend that goes with the house."

"It goes with the dogs," Jocelyn corrected.

"Well, I need the stipend. You should have no problem giving it up for a year if you truly care about the dogs more than money." Lois shot her a look of challenge.

Jocelyn turned to Liam. "This is crazycakes, is it not?"

"It's only for a year." Lois had the decency to look a bit embarrassed. "It would be the surest way to prove your devotion to the dogs."

"No deal." Liam got to his feet. "We're done."

Jocelyn stood up next to him, but Lois wasn't going to let them leave so easily. She crossed her legs and crossed her arms and looked them right in the eye.

"That's my offer, take it or leave it."

"Leave it," Liam and Jocelyn chorused.

"Then I'll see you in court. And I'll bring my e-mails. And you can talk to whomever you want—they'll all tell you the same thing. Mr. Allardyce loved me. The dogs love me. I'm the one who should be caring for them."

"And yet you're trying to trade them away for money and a lavish lifestyle."

Lois got even tenser. "It's a sacrifice I'm willing to make."

"I thought you were better than this," Jocelyn said.

Lois's smile sharpened. "You know I'm right about going to court. I have a good case and lots of documentation. If I didn't, you wouldn't be here right now." She stood up and walked away.

Jocelyn turned to Liam. "So this is what it's come to. My money or my dogs."

"We'll fight it," he vowed.

"But we might lose. Even Mr. Tumboldt admits we might lose. And then I'll have no money, no house, *and* no dogs."

"Keep the dogs," Liam advised. "Do whatever you have to do to keep them. Even if you end up having to give her what she wants . . . it's only a year." No qualifiers, no judgment, no urging her to be practical and financially prudent.

That was when she realized she could love him.

"What?" he demanded when he saw her expression change.

"Nothing." She forced herself to stay on topic. "I lived my whole life without beach houses and stipends, and I was happy. I have my family, my friends, my dogs. And now I have you. That's all I need." She faltered. "But if I give Lois what she wants, we lose your family's ranch."

He squared his shoulders. "I told you, I'll find another way."

"Your mother deserves to have it back. So do you."

"I don't want it if it means you have to give up your dogs."

She looked at him for a moment, and then they both started laughing. "I can't believe this is a real conversation we're having in real life. Beach house blackmail, dog custody battles . . . Who does this?"

"We do." He pulled her close while a pair of Old English sheepdogs looked on. "In the immortal words of the Notorious B.I.G.: Mo' money, mo' problems."

chapter 38

"You're *sure* that if I move out of the beach house for a year and let someone else move in, I can't still get an equity loan?" Jocelyn pressed.

"Yes." Mr. Tumboldt looked impassive as always in his office full of dark wood and seascapes.

"You're positive?"

"You can keep asking, but the answer will remain the same. If you hope to secure any sort of equity loan, your commitment to the house and its upkeep will have to be strongly established."

"And that's coming from the bank?" Jocelyn pressed.

"It's coming from everyone involved in Mr. Allardyce's estate, up to and including myself." The lawyer glanced at his computer screen as a new e-mail arrived.

"No offense, but you guys ruin everything."

"On that note, it's not at all clear to me that you'll be allowed to cede the house to someone else, even for a year."

"Why not? Can't you see that I'm only doing it to avoid a huge legal battle that will spend down the trust assets?"

"A trustee's primary objective is to ensure the well-being of the dogs. You'd have to convince Ms. Jarvinen that any relocation you undertook would be in the dogs' best interests." The attorney looked skeptical. "And I don't see how moving from a spacious house on the shore to a tiny house with a tiny yard in the middle of town qualifies."

"What if I have reason to believe that Ms. Jarvinen has a preexisting relationship with Lois Gunther?"

Mr. Tumboldt gave her his full attention. "What sort of relationship?"

"They used to go to dog shows together with Mr. Allardyce. They're Facebook friends. They're conspiring against me." Jocelyn sat back and waited for the fire and brimstone to commence.

Mr. Tumboldt seemed unfazed. "Facebook friends?"

"Yes! She's going to favor Lois in any legal ruling, obviously."

"That's not obvious to me at all." Mr. Tumboldt didn't quite suppress a patronizing smile. "In order to overrule Ms. Jarvinen's authority, you'd have to go to court—"

"Another lawsuit." Jocelyn moaned. "Like cockroaches."

"—and request that another co-trustee be appointed in her stead. And there's no predicting how the new co-trustee would view any of this situation."

"But at least the new trustee would be impartial."

"You'd have to prove that Ms. Jarvinen is unfit and, even assuming that you succeeded on that point, it would take considerable time to appoint her replacement. Time during which all major business dealings and non-essential expenditures would be frozen."

"So this equity loan is never going to happen, no matter what," Jocelyn deduced.

"Correct."

Jocelyn stared at the attorney. He stared right back.

"You're saying the devil I know is better than the devil I don't."

"I'm not attempting to sway you one way or the other." He stated it loudly and clearly, as if going on record in a deposition. "But no matter what you do, you're going to have to build a strong case for your actions and the dogs' welfare."

"That's fine," Jocelyn said. "I'm very persuasive."

"Persuasion won't suffice. We're talking about lawyers, remember? They'll need evidence."

"Like what?" Jocelyn didn't try to hide her frustration. "Are we going to put Carmen and Curtis on the stand and have them testify under oath?"

The lawyer ignored her sarcasm. "Document what you've done for the dogs and why. Collect attestations from the vet and the groomers and anyone else who can affirm you've provided excellent care. Write a statement expressing what the dogs mean to you and why you're the ideal caregiver."

"Like an essay?" Jocelyn had to laugh. "Like in high school?"

"You have to build a strong evidentiary case. Otherwise, we're facing a legal battle with the dog handler and I'm not at all confident in the outcome."

Jocelyn got to her feet and dusted off her hands. "Well then, I better get to building."

"It's total nonsense." Jocelyn carried piles of jeans and shoes out of the spacious closet and piled them in the middle of the bedroom. After the most recent conversation with the lawyer, she'd decided not to get too comfortable in the swanky master suite. "Lois is basically blackmailing me out of this house, and instead of helping me, the lawyers act like they're doing me a favor letting me plead my case. And the co-trustee, who's supposed to be impartial, is brunch buddies with Lois."

"Outrageous," Nora agreed as she started folding the clothes and piling them into a suitcase. She and Rachel had returned from their road trip sunburned, exhausted, bedraggled, and brimming with a renewed zest for life and eighties music.

"I can't believe they're making you write an essay," Rachel called from the bathroom, where she was gathering up shampoo bottles.

"I'll write it." Liam arrived with cold bottles of water for all. "You have better things to do than explain to Lois's Facebook friend why you love your own dogs."

Jocelyn headed back into the closet for another armful of clothes. "It's a pointless, degrading assignment. That's why they're making me do it. They're putting me in my place."

As she reached down to scoop up a pair of black boots, her fingers brushed a cold metal edge. The frame of the picture her father had given her. All these years and she still had it buried in the back of the closet, unable to look at it but unable to get rid of it. Now she'd have to haul it to yet another closet, where it would remain in darkness—almost but not quite forgotten. The last tether of hope to a family life that had never existed.

"Avert your eyes, Mom." Jocelyn held the picture against her chest, faced inward so as not to trigger her mother any more than necessary.

Rachel made a gagging noise and turned back toward the bathroom. "That thing again?"

"What is it?" Nora asked.

"The ugliest picture in the world," Rachel said. "Should have dumped it at Goodwill long ago."

"My father gave it to me." Jocelyn sounded as though she were apologizing. "It's a long story. I don't know why I hang on to it."

"Let's see it," Nora urged.

"Seriously, it's bad." Jocelyn turned to Liam. "The dogs could do better."

She waited for someone to ask why she still had it if she thought it was so objectionable. But nobody did. One thing that everyone in this room understood was the need to hang on too long and too tightly to things that should have been cut loose years ago.

"It's bad," she repeated, slowly turning the frame over.

Nora's jaw dropped when she saw the splotches of black, green, and white. "Is that an Echbar?"

"A what?"

"Mikolas Echbar." Nora looked as though she might drop to her knees and genuflect. "He's a famous Basque painter."

Jocelyn squinted down at the blotchy signature on the bottom right corner of the canvas. If she used her imagination, the first letter could be construed as an *E*. Maybe. "Never heard of him."

"We studied him in college. He spent his whole life in poverty, getting raked over the coals by art critics. His work wasn't properly appreciated until twenty years after his death. He was way ahead of his time." Nora held out her hands. "May I?"

"Help yourself." Jocelyn passed it over.

"My God." Nora stared at the canvas. "Is this a reproduction?"

"I don't know."

"It looks real." Nora's voice had faded to a whisper. "But it can't be. Can it?"

Rachel leaned against the doorjamb. "I don't see what's so impressive about it. A three-year-old could paint that."

"You're wrong." Nora's tone was thick with emotion.

Rachel regarded her with a mix of awe and horror. "Are you crying?"

"Yes." Nora traced the surface of the paint with one finger. "It's beautiful. So moving."

"It's a bunch of smears and dots." Jocelyn looked to Liam. "Do you see what she's talking about?"

He was still packing the suitcase. "I have no opinion."

"Helpful."

"I'm packing. That's helpful."

Nora raised her gaze to Jocelyn. "Where did you get this?"

"Long story short, my father gave it to me when I was a kid so I'd get the hell out of his office before his secretary started asking questions."

"You've had it in a closet for all these years?"

"Yes." Rachel rolled her eyes. "And I've been begging her to donate it to the thrift store the whole time."

"I told you, I'll donate it when I'm good and ready and not a moment before."

Nora clutched the frame protectively. "You'll do no such thing."

Jocelyn pointed to her mother. "Tell that to her."

"This belongs in a gallery," Nora stated. "A museum."

Rachel scoffed. "Are you kidding me? No museum is going to hang that out in public."

"Not only will they hang it, they'll pay dearly for it."

At the mention of money, Jocelyn's ears pricked up. "Are you sure?"

Nora nodded.

"How sure are you?"

"If this is a genuine Echbar, it could be worth hundreds of thousands, maybe a million." Nora pulled out her phone. "If I have your permission, I'd love to take a picture of it and send it to a few contacts. Some of my old classmates work for auction houses now."

"Knock yourself out," Jocelyn said.

Liam rested his hand on her arm. "You don't want to sell it."

"I don't?"

He lowered his voice. "It's the only thing you have from your father."

"Speaking of which . . ." Jocelyn looked over toward the window, which offered a partial view of the infamous ironwood tree. "What do you want to do about that?"

"The tree?" Liam's tone was light, but his eyes were solemn. "Leave it alone. It's not like it's going anywhere."

"Yeah, but, you know. It's the only thing you have from your father."

Nora adjusted her position on the floor, clearly eavesdropping and trying to make it look like she wasn't.

"It's old, it's huge, the roots probably go on for miles," Liam pointed out. "I don't think we have a lot of options."

"But your father wanted you to have it."

"I think he just wanted me to know about it." Liam glanced down at his mother. "A tip of the hat from beyond the grave." He adopted the same casual tone that Jocelyn did when discussing her own father. "He wouldn't acknowledge his paternity to my face, but he did it on a tree. It doesn't do me any good. It's not worth anything."

"The value is emotional," Nora stage-whispered. "The tree is a symbol. It's bringing us together."

"There you have it," Liam told Jocelyn. "It's a symbol. Nothing more, nothing less."

"Well, this painting is a symbol, too. A symbol I've been hauling around and hiding for twenty years." She harkened back to the words of the lawyer. "Besides, everything is for sale. Everything. It's merely a matter of naming the right price."

"Except the dogs," Liam said.

Jocelyn gazed out the window at the ocean and the endless blue sky stretching over the horizon. She thought about her father, the shame and desperation on his face when he'd thrust the painting into her hands and shooed her out of his life for good. Then she turned to the woman who had lost her birthright and her independence to another man who valued money and pride above love.

"Nora, assuming this is the real deal, how soon do you think we could put it up for auction?"

"As soon as we get it authenticated and appraised." Nora was still gazing down at the artwork as though it were a beautiful newborn baby. "There are scientific tests they can run now, with pigment analysis and materials dating."

"And how long does that take?"

"I'm not sure." Nora finally raised her gaze. "But the sooner I look into it, the sooner we can get the process started."

Rachel emitted the ***humph***iest of ***humphs***. "All this fuss over that piece of garbage?"

Liam was still at Jocelyn's side. "You don't have to make any decisions now. You can take your time and think it over."

"I've never been more sure of anything. This is my legacy, and I know exactly what to do with it." Jocelyn nodded at the phone in Nora's hand. "Make the call."

chapter 39

Once that first phone call was dialed, the painting changed. What had been a shameful remnant of a broken family transformed into a mystery to be solved and a fortune to be made. What had been mocked and hidden away was brought to light in an intoxicating blend of intrigue and excitement. Nora bundled up the canvas and hand-delivered it to a curator in Washington, D.C., who retained a team of experts to examine it. In the space of a week, answers started to emerge.

"It's a genuine Echbar, all right," Nora trilled into the phone. "But that's not all. It's a *lost* Echbar. He called it *Racing Dogs*. There have been rumors about this painting in the art community for years, but no one could ever substantiate them."

"Racing Dogs." Rachel, who was listening in on speakerphone, shook her head. "In what world are there any pictures of dogs in that mess? This Echbar guy must have done a lot of drugs."

But Jocelyn was delighted. "So it was all about dogs all this time.

You know, I can kind of see it." She pulled up the digital photo of the painting on her computer screen. "See that part, Mom?" She outlined a silhouette in the corner of the canvas. "See? A big black dog. There's his legs and there's his tail."

"It looks like a blob," Rachel retorted.

"The real question is, how did your father get it?" Liam asked.

"He bought it," Nora replied. "From a private collector in Paris." There was the sound of flipping pages on her end of the line. "There's no available ownership history before that, but he bought it before he got married. The painting was his sole and separate property. What he did with it was his decision alone. And he gave it to you, Joss," Nora said. "To keep, to sell, to do whatever you want with. It's yours."

"Sell it," Jocelyn commanded.

"Don't be hasty," Nora cautioned. "You might—"

"I won't. I've made my decision. Sell it as soon as possible and pray for a bidding war."

"There'll definitely be a bidding war," Nora said. "This is a rare find."

Next to Jocelyn, Rachel looked a bit alarmed. "What do you want all that money for, anyway? We've been over this—money doesn't do you any good."

"I don't want the money." A victorious smile played on her lips. "I want the freedom."

chapter 40

One month later

Jocelyn left a hefty cash tip for the cleaning team on the marble-topped table on her way out. Her arms and back ached from the exertions of the last few days, but the soreness brought a sense of satisfaction. She had been effectively maneuvered out of her home for a year, but she hadn't left a mess for anybody else to clean up. She'd taken out the trash and recycling. She'd packed and stored everything she could.

The backyard, however, was another story. But at least she'd arranged for fresh sand and cedar chips to be spread across the area.

Before she opened her car door, she texted Bree:

Echbar $$$ burning a hole in my pocket. Meet me at the Naked Finger in 10 mins.

Twelve minutes later, Bree opened the door to the jewelry boutique with a flourish. "What're we buying? A diamond tiara? Ruby slippers?"

"I don't have *that* kind of discretionary income." Jocelyn had reinvested the bulk of the profits from the sale of the painting immediately . . . after setting some aside for Bree's law school tuition. She hadn't mentioned this to Bree, of course, because she'd been so busy prepping for the move that she didn't have the energy to withstand the argument she knew Bree would give her. "But my mom's birthday is coming up, and I thought it would be nice to buy her some pearl earrings. She's always wanted them."

"If I ever have children, I hope they're just like you."

Bree threw up her hand to block Jocelyn from entering the showroom. "Oh crap."

Jocelyn spotted Chris immediately. He had his back turned to them, but she recognized the expensive haircut and the suntanned forearm with the gold watch. He was chatting with Lila, who was offering up various pricey baubles.

"He's probably buying a diamond bracelet for his next ex-girlfriend," Jocelyn muttered.

"He doesn't have to, since you left yours at his house," Bree muttered back. "Like a fool."

Ever the gentleman, Chris was devoting his full attention to Lila. He didn't notice Jocelyn or Bree as they pretended to peruse the display cases near the door. Lila clocked them, though, and a note of sympathy crept into her voice as she extolled the virtues of a stickpin topped with a Burmese ruby. Clearly, she'd heard about what had happened between Chris and Jocelyn.

"That's nice, but I want something really special," Chris said. "My parents finally gave me the bulk of my trust, and I want to mark the occasion. Here." He dug into his pocket and produced a thick gold money clip. "This was my grandfather's. There used to be an onyx right here, but it fell out." He pointed out an oblong divot in the metal. "I want to replace it with something amazing. What's the very best you've got?"

Lila made eye contact with Jocelyn and cleared her throat. "I just got this Colombian emerald. Incredibly rare, incredibly clear and well-cut." She donned the white gloves and extracted it from the case. "My bench worker could take it out of the ring and set it into the money clip."

"What're the gloves for?" Bree muttered.

Jocelyn recalled what Lila had said about the emerald: *The woman who sold it went out of her way to tell me that this ring was definitely* not *bad luck and would definitely* not *bring financial ruin on any future owners.*

"I'll tell you later," Jocelyn muttered back.

"Let me take a closer look." Chris reached out and took the ring from Lila, turning it over and over in his bare hands. When he held it up to the light, he finally noticed Jocelyn. His complexion went ashen and he took a step toward her, his free hand outstretched. "Joss. Hi. I—"

Bree took this as her cue to bust into the conversation. "Christopher Cantor, as I live and breathe! Fancy meeting you here." She regarded the emerald for a moment, opened her mouth, and then closed it again.

Chris looked concerned. "What?"

Bree's smile was forty-nine percent sweet, fifty-one percent sinister. "Ooh, it's just so stunning. There's something really unusual about it."

Bree looked at Jocelyn, then Lila. None of the women said anything, but they all knew.

Chris perked up. "Fancy, huh? It lets people know I've arrived."

Jocelyn glanced at the cursed gem, then up at the man who had broken her heart because she wasn't in the right tax bracket and hadn't gone to the right school. "It sets off your eyes."

He looked almost shy as he regarded her, so eager for her forgiveness. "Yeah?"

"Oh yeah." She nodded. "You should snap it up."

"It's one of a kind," Bree added.

"It's a bit pricey," Lila cautioned.

He puffed out his chest. "I can afford it."

"Let me write up the terms of sale and get a time estimate from my bench jeweler." Lila walked across the room to grab her phone.

"Nice seeing you," Jocelyn told Chris, turning back to examine the earring selection.

"You, too." He clutched his antique money clip. "I'm glad we can be friends."

"Enjoy that money clip," Bree said. "I hope it brings you all the riches you deserve."

After Chris left, whistling and mentally counting his trust fund, Jocelyn selected a pair of top-quality akoya studs with Lila's expert guidance.

"Rachel's going to love those," Bree said.

"Want me to wrap them?" Lila offered.

"No time." Jocelyn turned to Bree. "I've got to run. I'm meeting a forklift in fifteen minutes."

"A forklift? What for?"

Jocelyn glanced down at the stubborn trace of dirt that remained under one fingernail. "A symbol."

chapter 41

"It really does look like Jurassic Park." Jocelyn shaded her eyes with her hand and gazed out over the ranch's landscape. Rolling green pastures gave way to scraggly palmetto bushes, which turned into dense, prehistoric-looking forests.

"Told you." Liam slung his arm around her. "What do you think of your new investment?"

"I'm expecting a pack of velociraptors to come racing out at any second." Jocelyn tightened her grip on Carmen's and Friday's leashes and did a quick head count to ensure that the other dogs were safe and secure.

"Wait 'til you see the beetles," Nora teased. "They put velociraptors to shame."

Jocelyn looked up at Liam. "That's it. We're buying a house in town. We can commute in the morning."

"That's going to be a long commute," Liam said.

"What is this?" Rachel wrestled a knobby yellow globe off a nearby tree branch.

"That's a mutant lemon." Nora, resplendent as always in a pale pink shirt, a white sun hat, and a fresh French manicure, plucked another fruit off the tree. "They're delicious in cocktails."

"There's the dog run." Liam pointed out the newly constructed wood-and-wire compound complete with shading, a water trough, and ample room to run. "They'll be safe in there while we're busy with the cows."

As if they could understand him, the dogs swarmed toward the play area. Jocelyn unlatched the gate and let them pile in to explore.

"They'll love it here," she murmured, and knew that it was true. In Black Dog Bay, they'd had sand and seagulls, but here they had meadows and trees, fresh air and fields that stretched out as far as the eye could see. "I should take a photo and send it to Ms. Jarvinen and Mr. Tumboldt. 'Thanks for letting me move the dogs to paradise.'"

"Maybe the puppies will grow up to be herders." Nora smiled as she watched George Clooney and Pat Benatar tumbling around next to Hester.

"Speaking of herding, where are all the cows?" Rachel asked. "I thought this was a cattle ranch."

"We have—sorry, *Jocelyn* has over a hundred acres, so they have lots of room to roam," Nora explained.

"*We* have over a hundred acres," Jocelyn corrected. "I'm not doing this by myself."

"Fair enough." Nora turned back to Rachel. "They're not like dairy cows—they're skittish around new people. We'll get in the Polaris and go track them down later." She nodded at the sturdy all-terrain vehicle parked next to the clapboard ranch house.

"You drive that thing around?" Jocelyn asked Liam.

"*You* drive that thing around," Liam told her.

Jocelyn imagined herself behind the wheel of what was essentially a jacked-up Jeep and wondered if perhaps this whole whirlwind transition—selling the Echbar, ceding the beach house temporarily to

Lois, buying a cattle ranch sight unseen, moving down to Florida with her pack of dogs to work alongside a man she'd known for only a few months—might have been a wee bit hasty.

Liam was studying her expression. "What?"

"Nothing." She took a breath. "Everything."

"We'll go find the cows as soon as Bree gets here," Nora told Rachel.

"Where is Bree, anyway?" Rachel asked. "I thought she was right behind us."

"She was following the flatbed, but she pulled over right before we left civilization," Jocelyn said. "She texted me and said she wanted to use her cell before she lost service."

"The Wi-Fi situation here is not great," Liam admitted.

"But who needs Wi-Fi when you've got mutant lemons?" Jocelyn said.

Nora glanced over at the dog run, then at her watch. "When does the arborist get here? I thought he said two thirty."

"I'm sure he's on his way." Rachel tossed the enormous lemon up in the air and caught it on the way down. Her anxiety and type A ways had vanished the moment they crossed the state line between Delaware and Maryland. She'd only called her new employee once today to make sure that the towels and linens of Black Dog Bay had been washed and folded without her direct supervision. Even though Rachel would be returning to Delaware in a few days, Jocelyn vowed to coerce her mother into visiting the ranch at least every other month.

"We need to get this thing into the ground as soon as possible. All this upheaval's not good for the roots." Nora gazed up at the massive ironwood tree in the huge wooden crate. It had taken four days of branch trimming, root pruning, trench digging, hessian wrapping, and forklifting onto an extra-wide flatbed truck to prepare the tree for the sixteen-hour drive to Florida. "They said it can suffer shock."

Rachel waved this away. "It survived the move from here to Delaware and all that saltwater in the soil for all those years. It'll last a few hours longer."

"I'm going to water the soil again, just to keep it hydrated." Nora moved toward the garden hose, but Liam stepped in.

"You're going to drown it. Let it be."

Nora stood down but she wasn't happy about it. "I'll feel a lot better after it's been in the ground for a few weeks."

Jocelyn studied the huge hole in the soil that had been dug in preparation for the replanting. Then she stared at the tree, marveling at the gnarled branches and thick foliage that seemed impervious to any natural or man-made disasters. "This thing is going to outlive us all."

"Want to go check out the house?" Liam said. "They should be almost done with the remodel."

Jocelyn glanced at the structure which, though sturdy and in good repair, looked as though it had been built by the Marlboro Man fifty years ago. "Please tell me it has indoor plumbing."

"Don't be so spoiled," Rachel chided. She apologized to Nora. "I didn't raise her to be such a princess."

"I'm a princess because I want a toilet that flushes?"

Rachel looked mortified. "Lucks into a little money and thinks she's too good for an outhouse."

Nora laughed. "Yes, there's plumbing. Even the trailers where the seasonal ranch hands live have plumbing. Air-conditioning and flat-screen TVs, too."

Jocelyn quirked a brow at her mother. "Are you going to call the ranch hands spoiled, too?"

But Rachel had segued to juicier territory. "These ranch hands." She looked at Nora. "Are any of them single?"

Liam urged Jocelyn toward the house. "Let's go check out the inside."

"What, you don't want to hear our moms rate the employees on a scale of one to beefcake?"

"I've got enough psychological scars already, thanks." Liam held her hand as they stepped up to the porch, which was slightly uneven as the long, hand-hewn boards had swelled and settled in the heat and humidity. A newly hung screen door opened up to reveal a simple, clean, serviceable living space. Lots of light, lots of rustic furniture, everything you needed and nothing you didn't.

Jocelyn stood in the sunlight, inhaling the scents of grass and sawdust and freshly turned earth. "And to think, we could still be living in a gigantic house full of luxuries by the ocean."

"We barely escaped."

"Poor Lois. She doesn't know what she's missing." Jocelyn went up on tiptoe to kiss him. He brushed her hair aside and kissed his way along her shoulder to the strap of her simple blue sundress. A dress she'd worn twice already this week and might have to wear again, depending on how quickly she could locate the rest of her wardrobe packed away in the pile of boxes on the porch.

"You're beautiful," he murmured.

"Even though I'm wearing this same dress on repeat?"

"I love this dress," he swore. "I hope you wear this dress every day. The only thing I like better than you in this dress is you out of this dress."

"This is crazy, you know." She wrapped both arms around him and held on tightly.

"Which part?"

"All of it. I mean . . . what if I don't like ranch life? What if we start fighting over stupid stuff like whose turn it is to clean up the dog corral?" She tried to figure out the exact nature of her worries. "What if, you know, it just doesn't work out?"

He pulled away far enough to hold her face in his hands. "What if it does?"

She'd heard that before. But never from him, never this way.

A car horn blared in the distance. "That's Bree."

"We better go open the gate." Liam started for the door.

"I'll go." Jocelyn gestured to the stovetop. "If you want to start lunch, I won't try to stop you."

"I'm on it."

While Liam returned to the car to collect the groceries they'd bought before leaving town, Jocelyn let Carmen out of the corral and prepared to jog the half mile to unlatch the metal gate that allowed access to the ranch from the main road.

She looked down at her feisty, furry companion, who gazed back with complete adoration. "Okay, girl. You want to run? Let's run." They both sprinted full speed under the blue sky.

Bree was waiting in her car, radio and air-conditioning cranked up to eleven. "Why are you running like it's your money or your life?" she demanded when Jocelyn and Carmen piled in.

"It's a long way! This place is huge," Jocelyn told her. "Huge and open and wild. Like nothing I've ever seen. What took you so long? Did you get lost?"

"No." Bree adjusted her sunglasses and turned the radio down. "I stopped to take a call."

"Do you have anything more to say about that?"

"Well. It was Dan."

"Innnteresting." Jocelyn pulled her hair back off her neck. "What did Dan have to say?"

Bree put the car in gear and started driving down the unpaved, bumpy road. "He didn't get married."

"I figured."

"He said he'll be in Philadelphia for the next few years, doing that fancy fellowship."

"I heard."

"He wanted to know if I'm still planning to move to Philly." Bree stopped the car and pulled a folded piece of stationery out of her handbag. "Which I am."

Jocelyn unfolded the paper, which was embossed with a university logo. She skimmed the first sentence: *We are delighted to inform you that you have been accepted . . .*

"Bree!" She tossed the letter aside and engulfed her friend in a hug. "This is fantastic!" Then she noticed the date on the letter. "You got this weeks ago. Why didn't you tell me?"

"I've been trying to decide what to do," Bree mumbled against Jocelyn's shoulder. "Get off. You're suffocating me."

"Sentimental as always." Jocelyn sat back. "And of course you're going. What's to decide?"

"It's a big change." Bree gripped the steering wheel with both hands, even though the car wasn't moving. "Relocating, going back to school, I won't know anybody in Philadelphia . . ."

"You'll know Dan."

Bree waved this away. "He's not ready to date."

"So don't date him. You can still hang out. Bide your time. Be friends."

"And then, the second he is ready to date, pounce on him?"

"Exactly."

Bree released her death grip on the wheel but kept her hands at the ten and two o'clock position. "My grandmother says I have to go."

"She's right. Between me and Veronika, your fate is sealed. Make your peace with it," Jocelyn advised. "Besides, you've been talking about this for years. You worked so hard to get here. Remember all that prep we did for the LSAT?"

"I get these weird flashes and feelings about what's going to happen to other people. I don't even want to, but I can't help it. But for my own future, I get nothing. It's not fair."

Carmen hung her head over Jocelyn's left shoulder and joined the conversation, drooling and panting all the while.

"It's all just so much, so fast." Bree let go of the wheel and turned up her palms. "After all these years of sameness, everything's changing like that." She snapped her fingers. "You're becoming a crazy dog lady and falling in love and buying an actual cattle ranch in the middle of nowhere—"

"The good news is, there's indoor plumbing."

"—and I'm supposed to read a bunch of law books and go to eight a.m. lectures with a bunch of twenty-two-year-old whippersnappers and it's going to take three whole years of my life."

Jocelyn nodded and let Bree talk.

"What if I hate it?" Bree's voice was soft and scared. "What if I can't do it? What if I give it everything I have and it doesn't work out?"

Jocelyn put her hand in Bree's. "What if it does?"

Carmen licked them both.

Bree put the car in gear and started down the grassy road full of potholes and orange wildflowers. "Then I guess we'll just have to live crazily ever after."

"Yeah." Jocelyn basked in the sunlight. "Isn't it great?"

When they finally arrived at the ranch house, they found Rachel, Nora, and Liam gathered beneath the boughs of the ironwood tree, pouring out tiny splashes of Mr. Allardyce's carefully aged, ridiculously overpriced brandy into red Solo cups.

"Welcome!" Rachel handed servings to Bree and Jocelyn. "We were just about to toast."

"Here's to new beginnings," Nora said.

"To continued success," Rachel chimed in.

"To love." Bree smiled at Liam and Jocelyn.

"To the dogs," Liam said.

Jocelyn closed her eyes as she stepped out of the bright glare of the sun and into the cool sanctuary of shade. This tree had been rooted here before and would root here again, offering protection and shelter to the place that meant the most to Liam and both of his parents. The place she intended to make her home, granted to her all these years later by the father who would never be family.

She opened her eyes and regarded the loyal companions, both human and canine, who gathered by her side as she forged her future. "To our pack."

READERS GUIDE
in dog
we trust
BETH KENDRICK
READERS GUIDE

QUESTIONS FOR DISCUSSION

1. Mr. Allardyce says, "My dogs are much better people than any of the people I know," and he puts his money where his mouth is. Chris's family also devotes a lot of time and resources to raising money for animal charities. Do you think there is any moral conflict in devoting so much money and effort to animal welfare as opposed to focusing on humanitarian causes?

2. When Chris breaks up with Jocelyn he offers her an expensive "parting gift." Do you think she should have accepted the bracelet?

3. Mr. Allardyce and his acquaintances from the dog show world place a premium on preserving breed standards (both aesthetic and behavioral). In your opinion, what responsibilities do owners of purebred dogs have to adhering to historical breed standards and to providing their purebred dogs with access to the activities for which they were bred (e.g., herding opportunities for border collies)?

4. Lila, Jocelyn, and Bree stand by while Chris purchases an emerald that is allegedly cursed. If you could bestow a curse on a piece of jewelry, what would the curse be and who would you give it to? What if you could bestow a blessing on a piece of jewelry?

5. On multiple occasions throughout this novel, characters have to decide what matters most to them: "Your money or your life?" How do you see this dilemma playing out in your own life and your own choices?

6. Given what Nora tells Jocelyn about the circumstances of her courtship, marriage, and divorce with Mr. Allardyce, to what extent did she "deserve" what she got? Did Nora's disclosure change your perception of Mr. Allardyce at all?

7. Was it right or wrong of Friday's owner to effectively sell him to Jocelyn? Was Jocelyn right or wrong to agree to the sale?

8. What would you like to see happen to Bree as she embarks on the next step of her journey?

9. After she becomes the de facto beneficiary of Mr. Allardyce's estate, Jocelyn experiences immediate differences in the way she is treated and perceived by others. How do you think your social, familial, and/or romantic relationships might be affected if you unexpectedly inherited tens of millions of dollars?

Photo by Anna Peña

Beth Kendrick is the author of thirteen women's fiction novels, including *Once Upon a Wine*, *Put a Ring On It*, *New Uses for Old Boyfriends*, *Cure for the Common Breakup*, *The Week Before the Wedding*, and *Nearlyweds*, which was turned into a Hallmark Channel original movie. Although she lives in Arizona, she loves to vacation at the Delaware beaches, where she brakes for turtles, eats boardwalk fries, and wishes that the Whinery really existed.

CONNECT ONLINE

bethkendrick.com
facebook.com/bethkendrickbooks
twitter.com/bkendrickbooks